SNOOPY™

FIRST BEAGLE IN SPACE

Other *Peanuts* Kids' Collections

Snoopy: Cowabunga!

Charlie Brown and Friends

Charlie Brown: Pow!

Woodstock: Master of Disguise

Snoopy: Contact!

Snoopy: Party Animal

Charlie Brown: Here We Go Again

Snoopy to the Rescue

Snoopy: What's Wrong with Dog Lips?

I'm Not Your Sweet Babboo!

Snoopy: Boogie Down!

Lucy: Speak Out!

Charlie Brown: All Tied Up

SNOOPY™

FIRST BEAGLE IN SPACE

A PEANUTS™ Collection

CHARLES M. SCHULZ

Andrews McMeel
PUBLISHING®

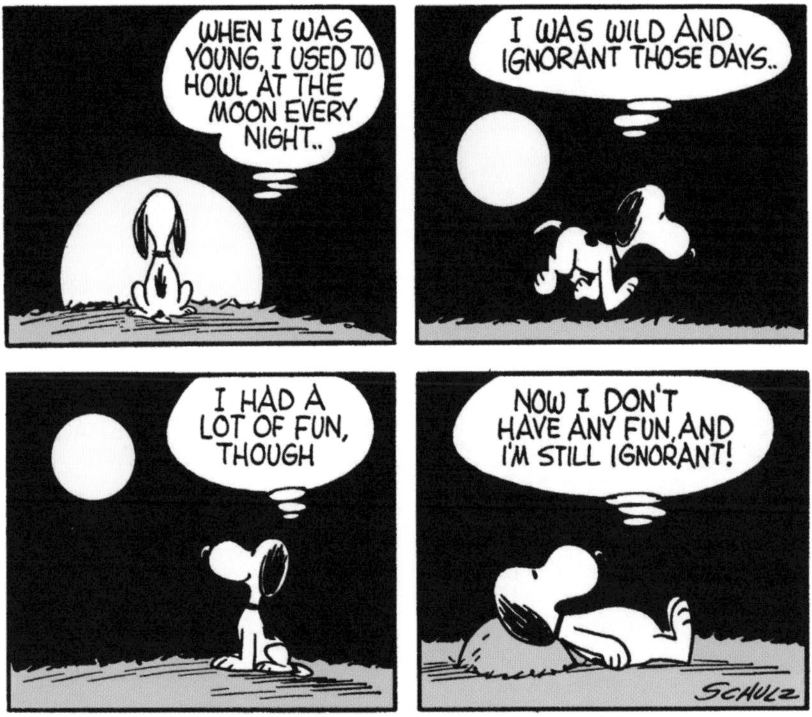
WHEN I WAS YOUNG, I USED TO HOWL AT THE MOON EVERY NIGHT..
I WAS WILD AND IGNORANT THOSE DAYS..
I HAD A LOT OF FUN, THOUGH
NOW I DON'T HAVE ANY FUN, AND I'M STILL IGNORANT!
SCHULZ

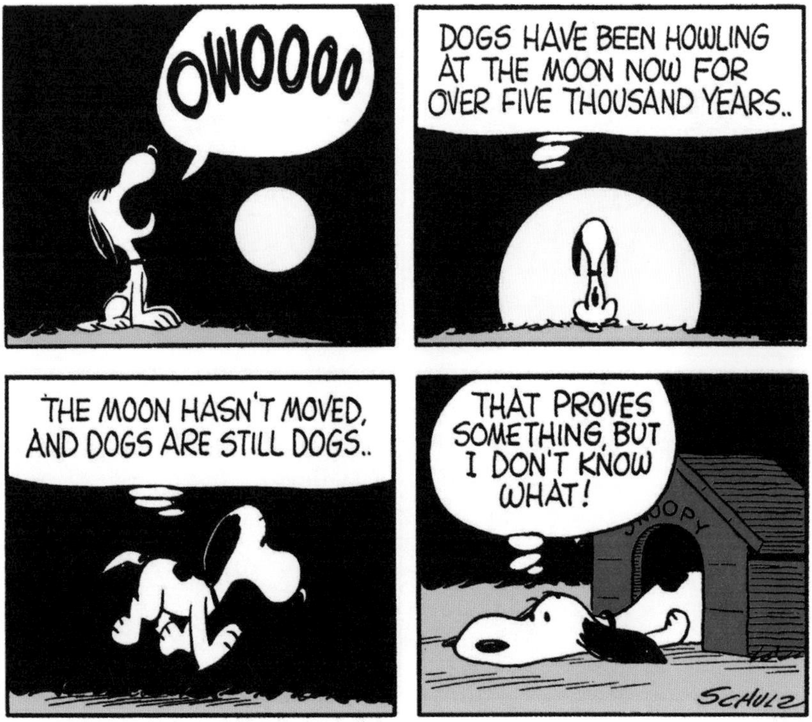
OWOOOO
DOGS HAVE BEEN HOWLING AT THE MOON NOW FOR OVER FIVE THOUSAND YEARS..
THE MOON HASN'T MOVED, AND DOGS ARE STILL DOGS..
THAT PROVES SOMETHING, BUT I DON'T KNOW WHAT!
SCHULZ

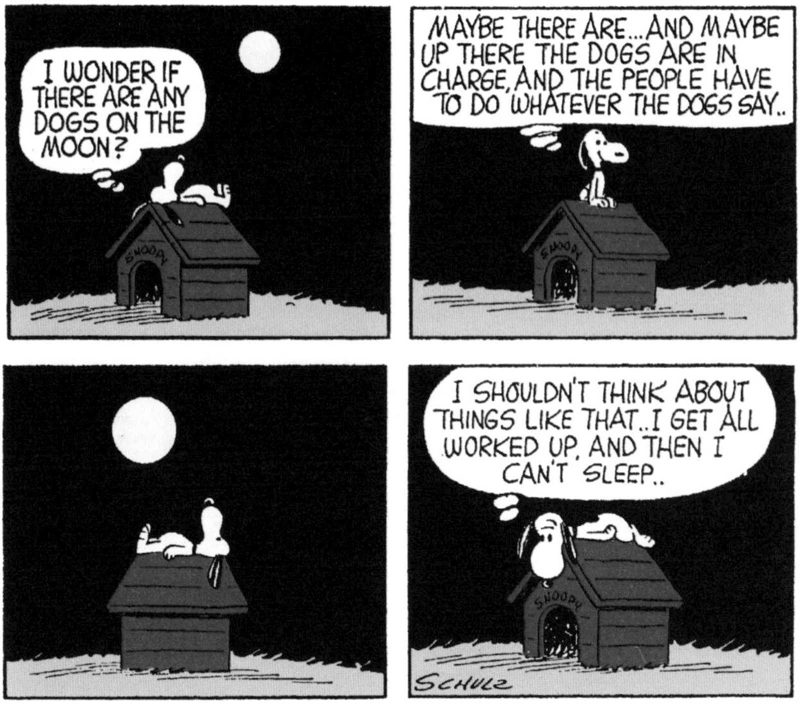
I WONDER IF THERE ARE ANY DOGS ON THE MOON?
MAYBE THERE ARE...AND MAYBE UP THERE THE DOGS ARE IN CHARGE, AND THE PEOPLE HAVE TO DO WHATEVER THE DOGS SAY..
I SHOULDN'T THINK ABOUT THINGS LIKE THAT..I GET ALL WORKED UP, AND THEN I CAN'T SLEEP..
SCHULZ

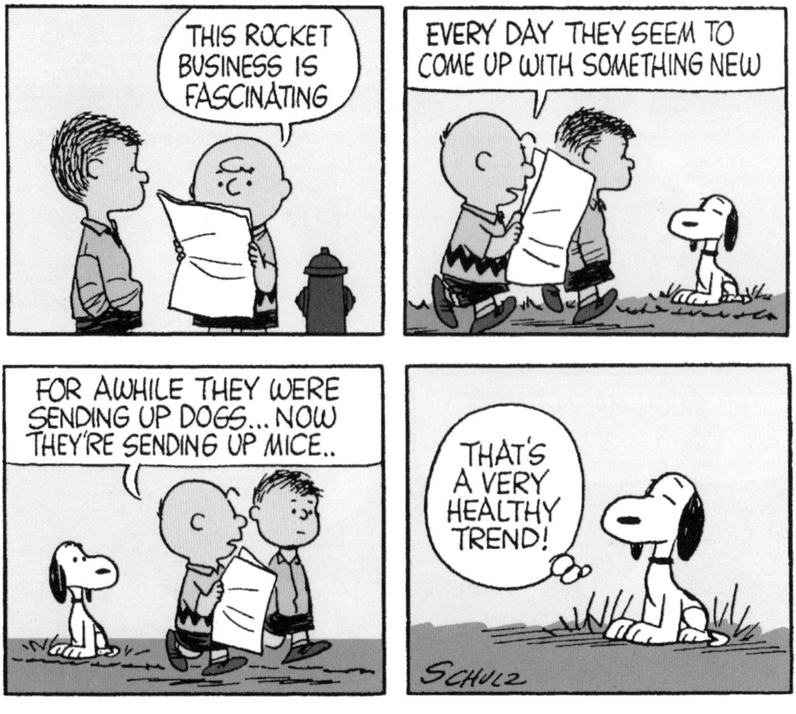
THIS ROCKET BUSINESS IS FASCINATING
EVERY DAY THEY SEEM TO COME UP WITH SOMETHING NEW
FOR AWHILE THEY WERE SENDING UP DOGS... NOW THEY'RE SENDING UP MICE..
THAT'S A VERY HEALTHY TREND!
SCHULZ

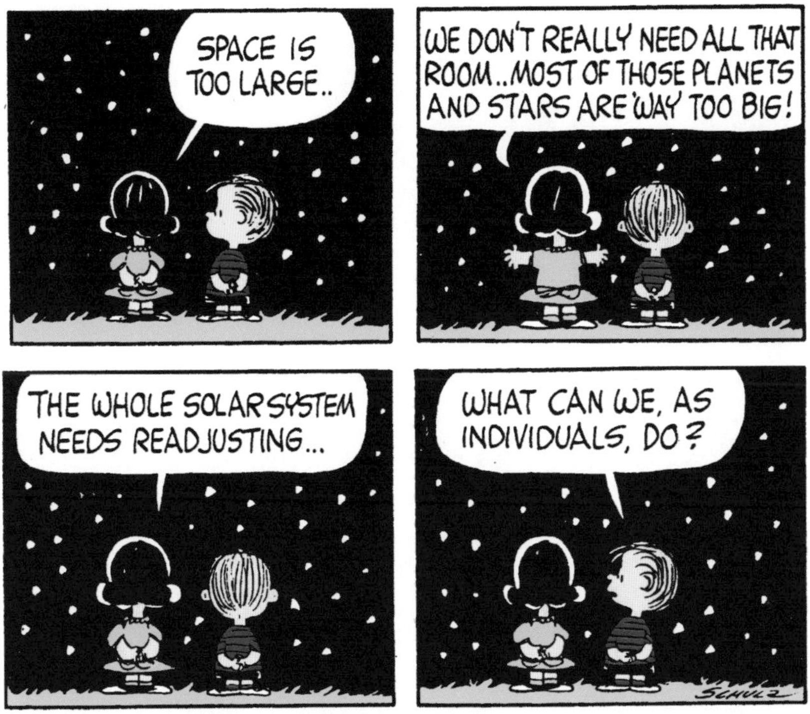
SPACE IS TOO LARGE..
WE DON'T REALLY NEED ALL THAT ROOM..MOST OF THOSE PLANETS AND STARS ARE 'WAY TOO BIG!
THE WHOLE SOLAR SYSTEM NEEDS READJUSTING...
WHAT CAN WE, AS INDIVIDUALS, DO?
SCHULZ

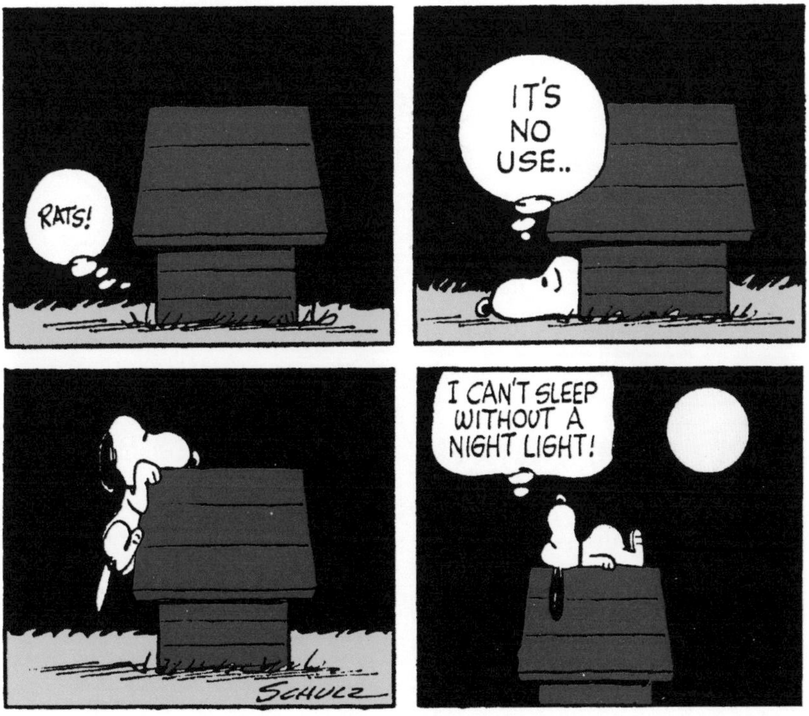
RATS!
IT'S NO USE..
SCHULZ
I CAN'T SLEEP WITHOUT A NIGHT LIGHT!

BEAUTIFUL, ISN'T IT?
YES, BUT SOMETHING SEEMS STRANGE...
"WHEN THE EARTH WAS YOUNG AND THE MOON WAS FIRST FORMED, THE MOON WAS ONLY ABOUT 15,000 MILES FROM THE EARTH."

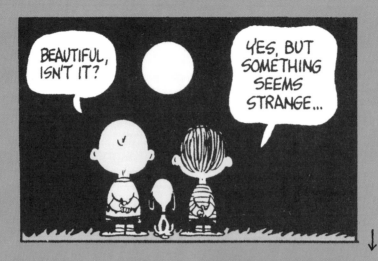

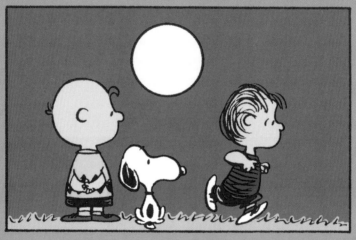

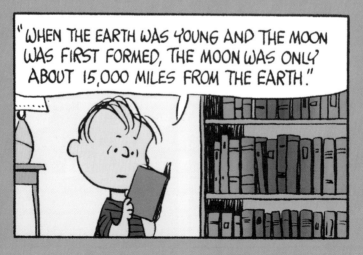

"OVER A PERIOD OF MILLIONS OF YEARS THE MOON HAS BEEN MOVING AWAY FROM THE EARTH AT A RATE OF ABOUT FIVE FEET EVERY ONE HUNDRED YEARS."
I THOUGHT IT LOOKED A LITTLE FARTHER AWAY THAN BEFORE..

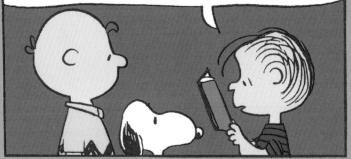

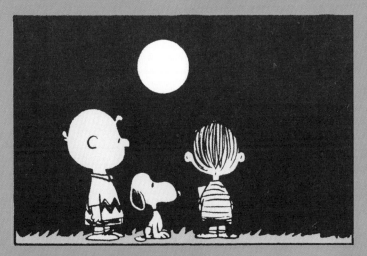

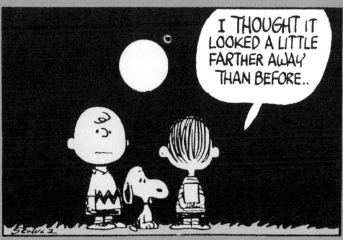

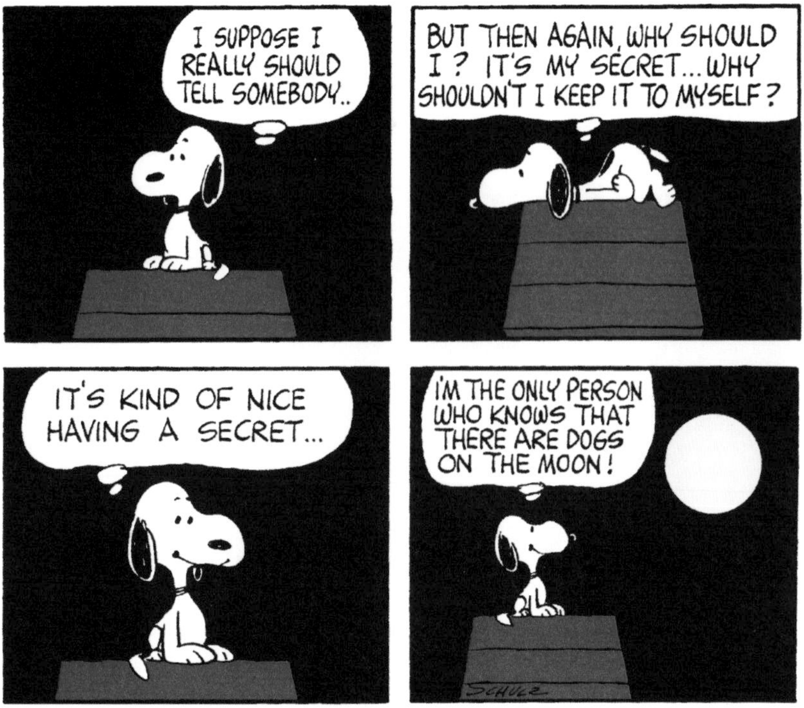
I SUPPOSE I REALLY SHOULD TELL SOMEBODY..
BUT THEN AGAIN, WHY SHOULD I ? IT'S MY SECRET... WHY SHOULDN'T I KEEP IT TO MYSELF ?
IT'S KIND OF NICE HAVING A SECRET...
I'M THE ONLY PERSON WHO KNOWS THAT THERE ARE DOGS ON THE MOON !
SCHULZ

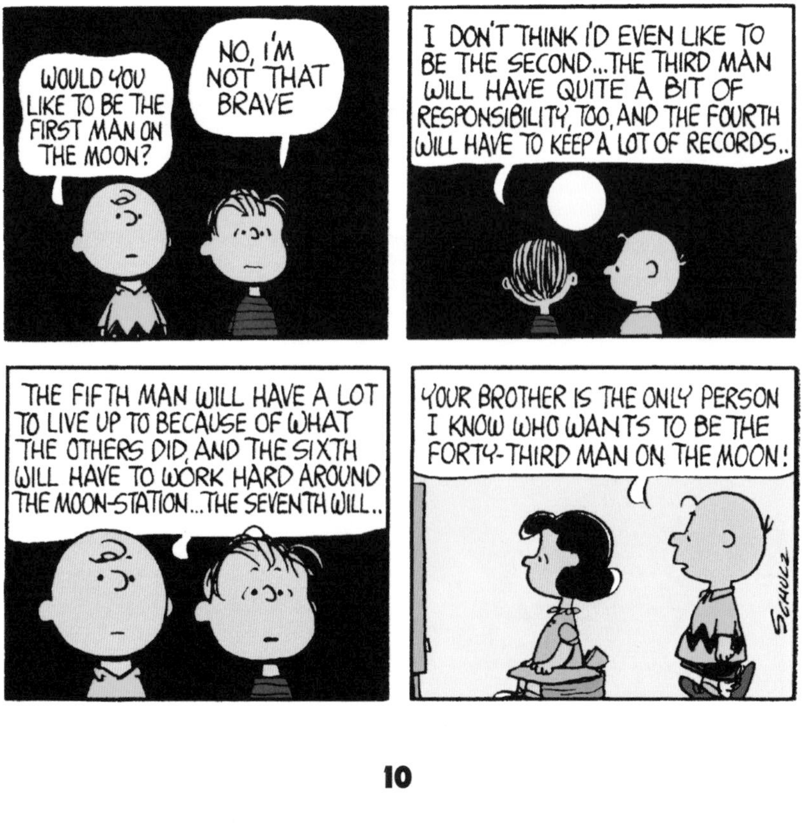
WOULD YOU LIKE TO BE THE FIRST MAN ON THE MOON?
NO, I'M NOT THAT BRAVE
I DON'T THINK I'D EVEN LIKE TO BE THE SECOND...THE THIRD MAN WILL HAVE QUITE A BIT OF RESPONSIBILITY, TOO, AND THE FOURTH WILL HAVE TO KEEP A LOT OF RECORDS..
THE FIFTH MAN WILL HAVE A LOT TO LIVE UP TO BECAUSE OF WHAT THE OTHERS DID, AND THE SIXTH WILL HAVE TO WORK HARD AROUND THE MOON-STATION...THE SEVENTH WILL..
YOUR BROTHER IS THE ONLY PERSON I KNOW WHO WANTS TO BE THE FORTY-THIRD MAN ON THE MOON !
SCHULZ

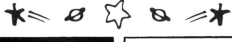

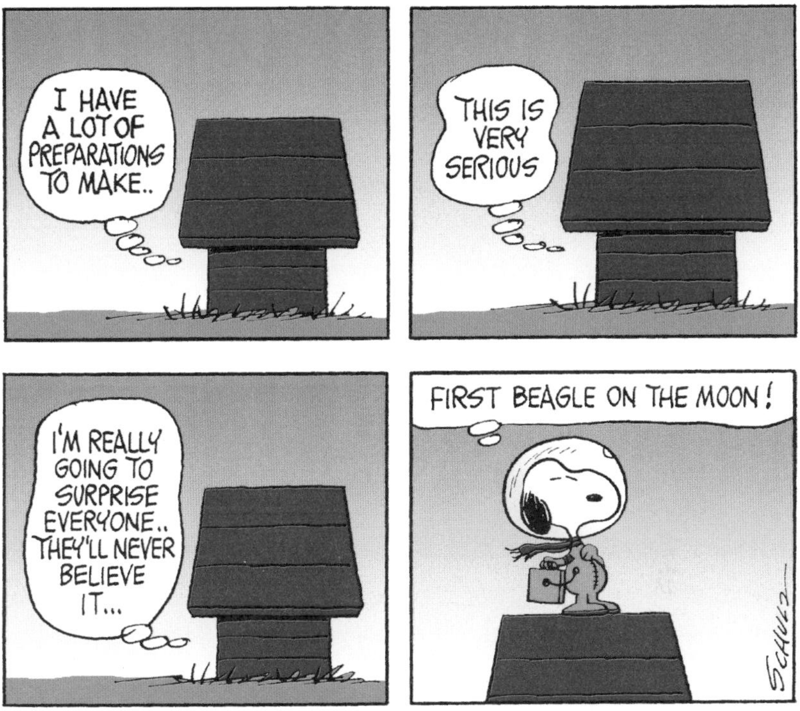
I HAVE A LOT OF PREPARATIONS TO MAKE..
THIS IS VERY SERIOUS
I'M REALLY GOING TO SURPRISE EVERYONE.. THEY'LL NEVER BELIEVE IT...
FIRST BEAGLE ON THE MOON!
SCHULZ

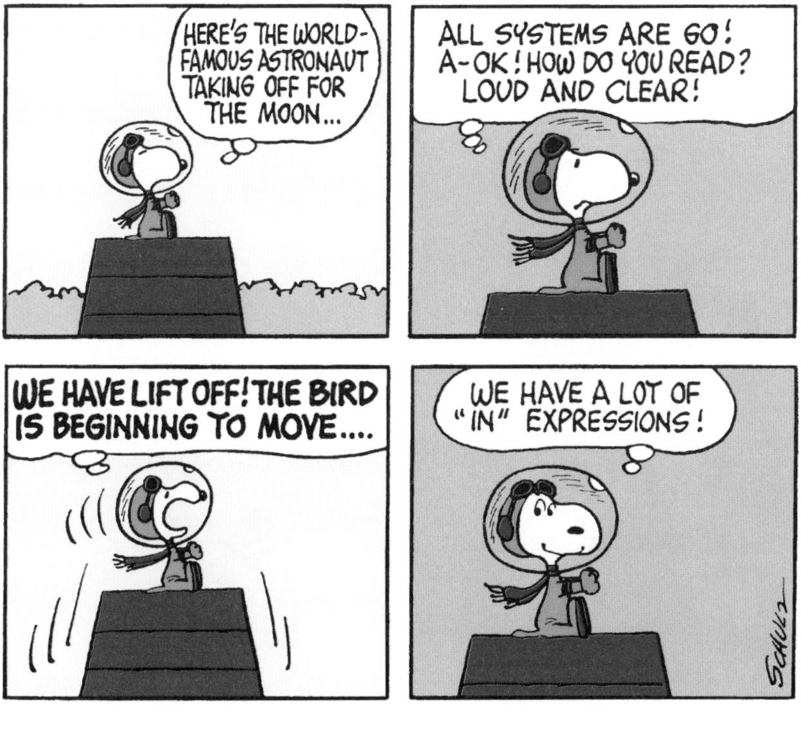
HERE'S THE WORLD-FAMOUS ASTRONAUT TAKING OFF FOR THE MOON...
ALL SYSTEMS ARE GO! A-OK! HOW DO YOU READ? LOUD AND CLEAR!
WE HAVE LIFT OFF! THE BIRD IS BEGINNING TO MOVE....
WE HAVE A LOT OF "IN" EXPRESSIONS!
SCHULZ

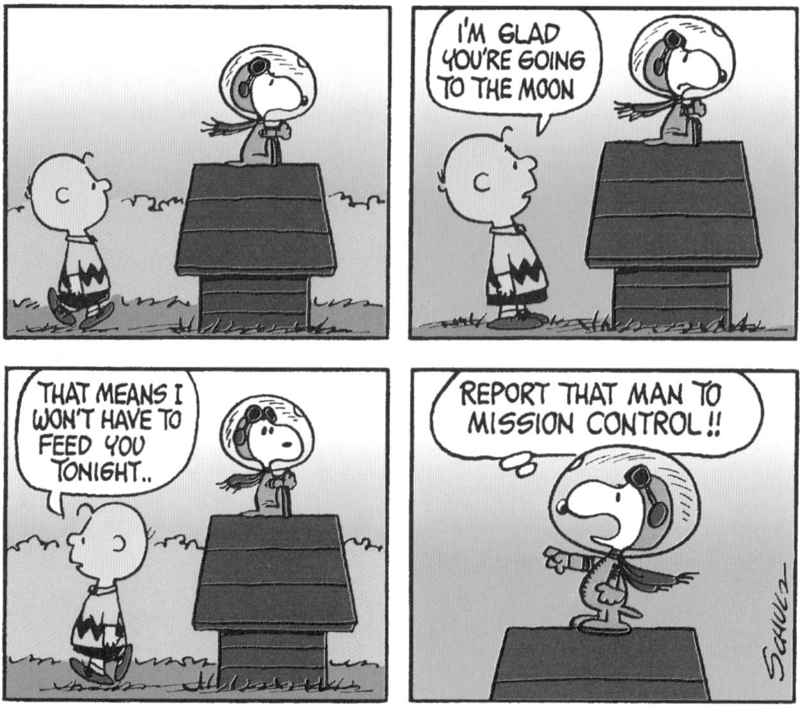
I'M GLAD YOU'RE GOING TO THE MOON
THAT MEANS I WON'T HAVE TO FEED YOU TONIGHT..
REPORT THAT MAN TO MISSION CONTROL!!

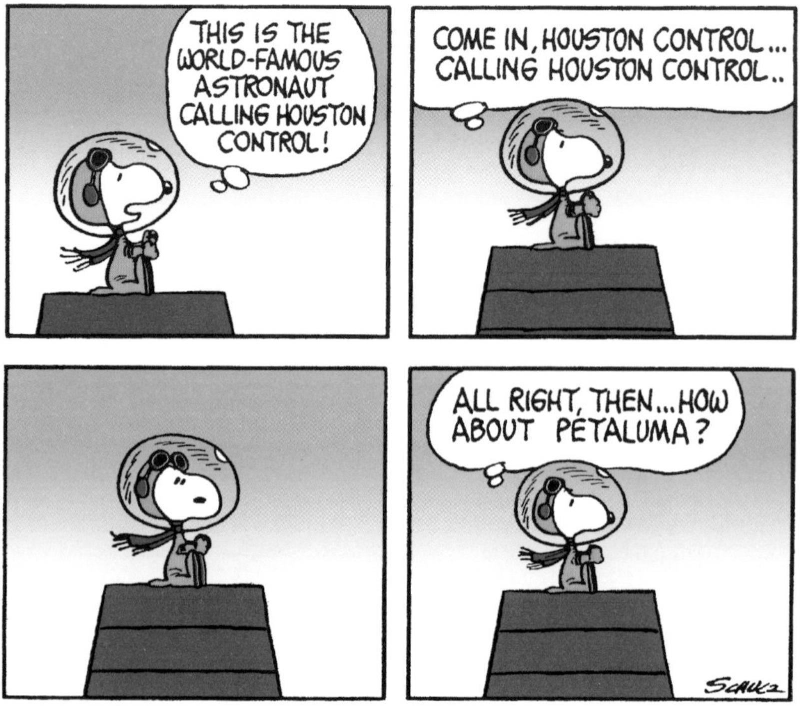
THIS IS THE WORLD-FAMOUS ASTRONAUT CALLING HOUSTON CONTROL!
COME IN, HOUSTON CONTROL... CALLING HOUSTON CONTROL..
ALL RIGHT, THEN...HOW ABOUT PETALUMA?

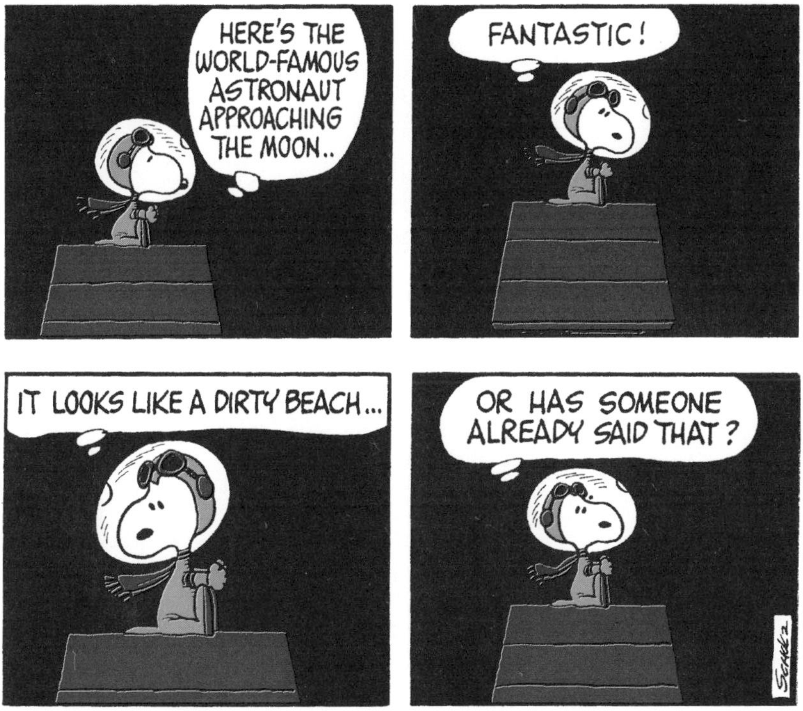
HERE'S THE WORLD-FAMOUS ASTRONAUT APPROACHING THE MOON..
FANTASTIC!
IT LOOKS LIKE A DIRTY BEACH...
OR HAS SOMEONE ALREADY SAID THAT?

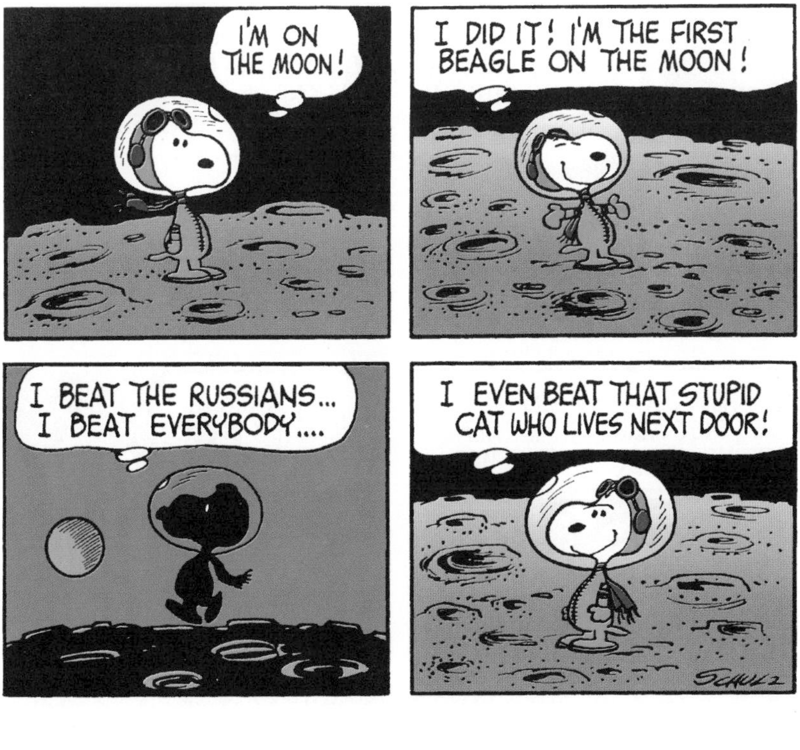
I'M ON THE MOON!
I DID IT! I'M THE FIRST BEAGLE ON THE MOON!
I BEAT THE RUSSIANS... I BEAT EVERYBODY....
I EVEN BEAT THAT STUPID CAT WHO LIVES NEXT DOOR!

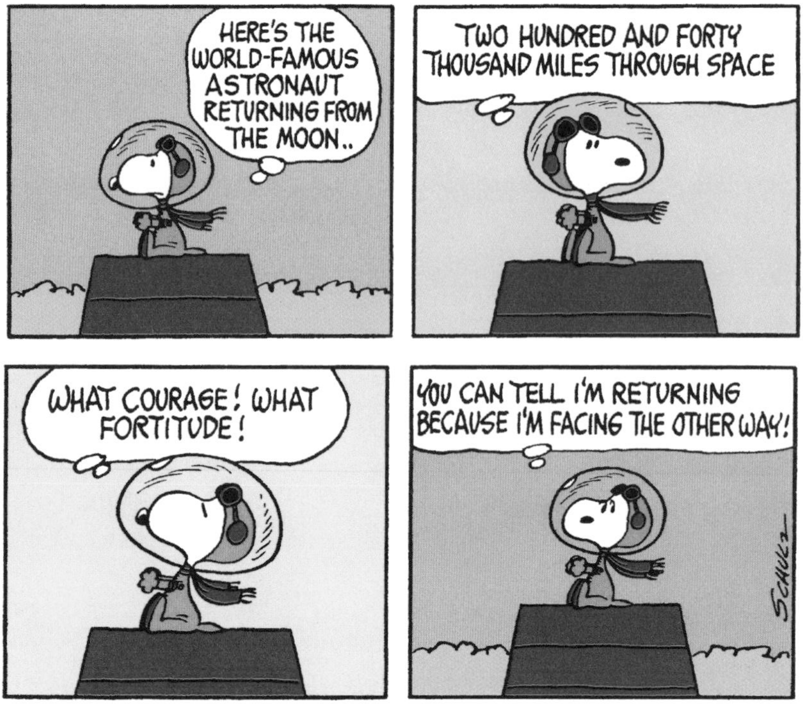
HERE'S THE WORLD-FAMOUS ASTRONAUT RETURNING FROM THE MOON..
TWO HUNDRED AND FORTY THOUSAND MILES THROUGH SPACE
WHAT COURAGE! WHAT FORTITUDE!
YOU CAN TELL I'M RETURNING BECAUSE I'M FACING THE OTHER WAY!
SCHULZ

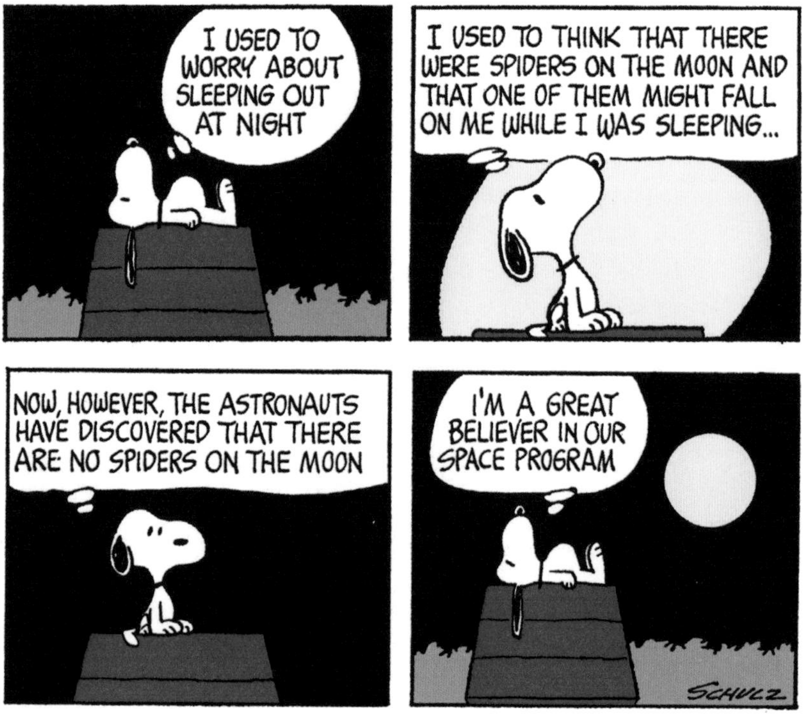
I USED TO WORRY ABOUT SLEEPING OUT AT NIGHT
I USED TO THINK THAT THERE WERE SPIDERS ON THE MOON AND THAT ONE OF THEM MIGHT FALL ON ME WHILE I WAS SLEEPING...
NOW, HOWEVER, THE ASTRONAUTS HAVE DISCOVERED THAT THERE ARE NO SPIDERS ON THE MOON
I'M A GREAT BELIEVER IN OUR SPACE PROGRAM
SCHULZ

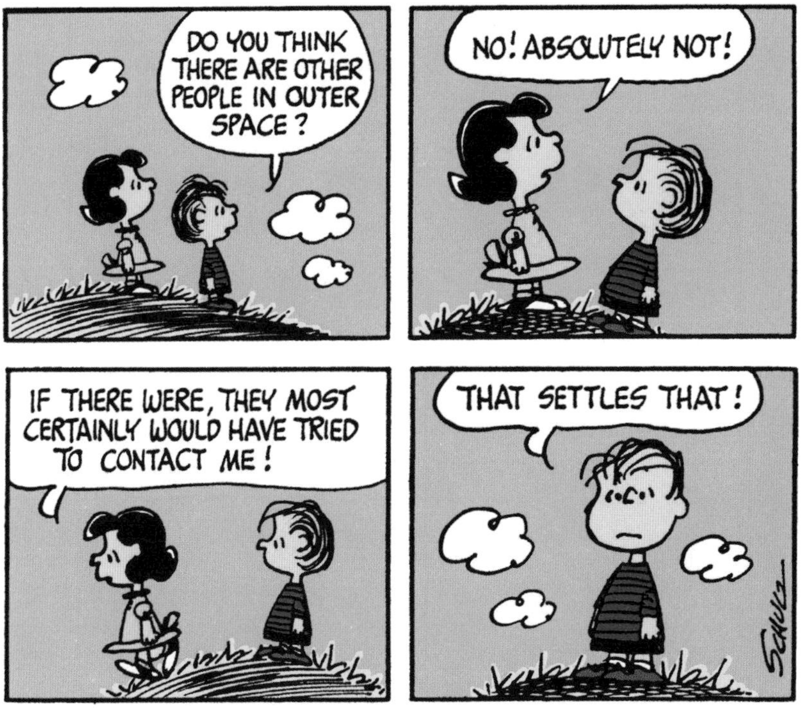
DO YOU THINK THERE ARE OTHER PEOPLE IN OUTER SPACE?
NO! ABSOLUTELY NOT!
IF THERE WERE, THEY MOST CERTAINLY WOULD HAVE TRIED TO CONTACT ME!
THAT SETTLES THAT!
SCHULZ

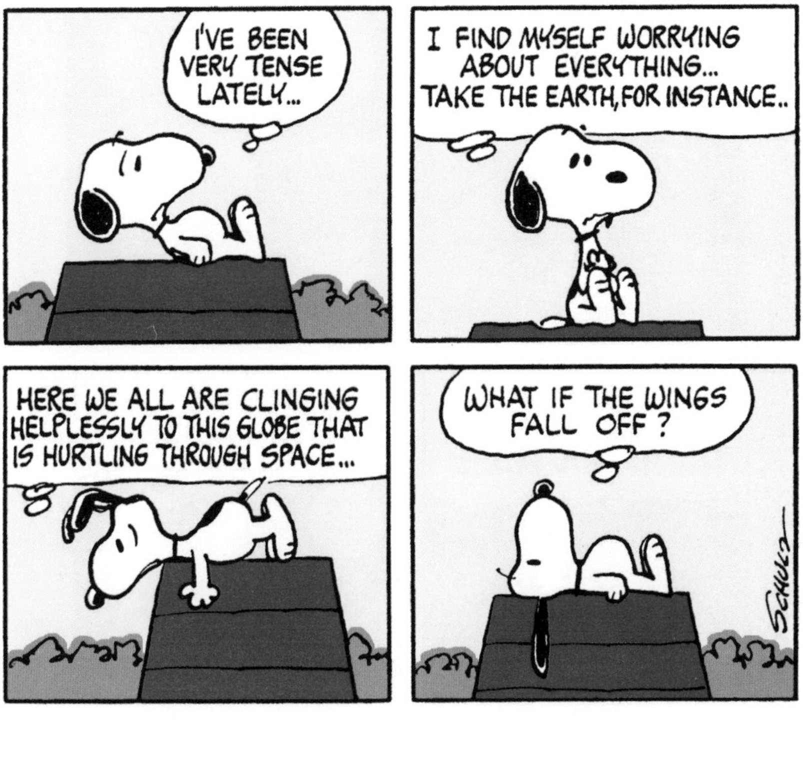
I'VE BEEN VERY TENSE LATELY...
I FIND MYSELF WORRYING ABOUT EVERYTHING... TAKE THE EARTH, FOR INSTANCE..
HERE WE ALL ARE CLINGING HELPLESSLY TO THIS GLOBE THAT IS HURTLING THROUGH SPACE...
WHAT IF THE WINGS FALL OFF?
SCHULZ

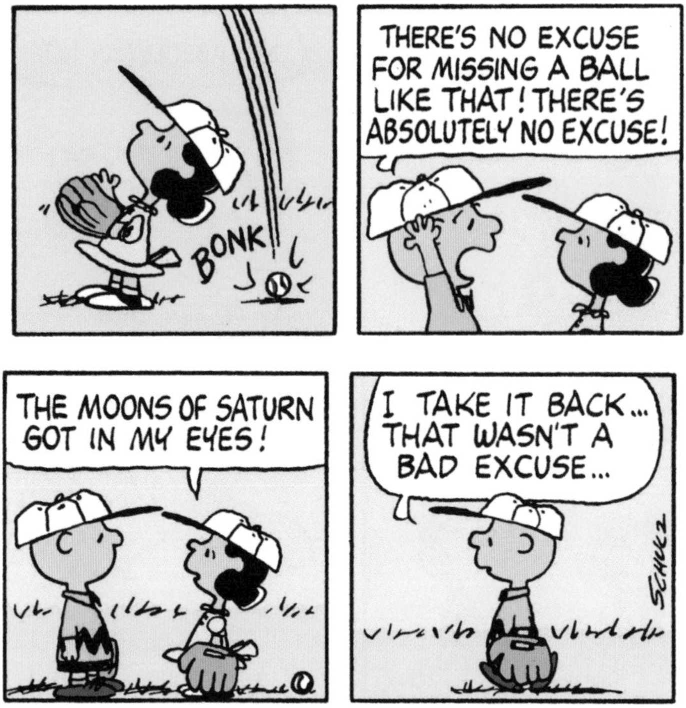
BONK
THERE'S NO EXCUSE FOR MISSING A BALL LIKE THAT! THERE'S ABSOLUTELY NO EXCUSE!
THE MOONS OF SATURN GOT IN MY EYES!
I TAKE IT BACK... THAT WASN'T A BAD EXCUSE...

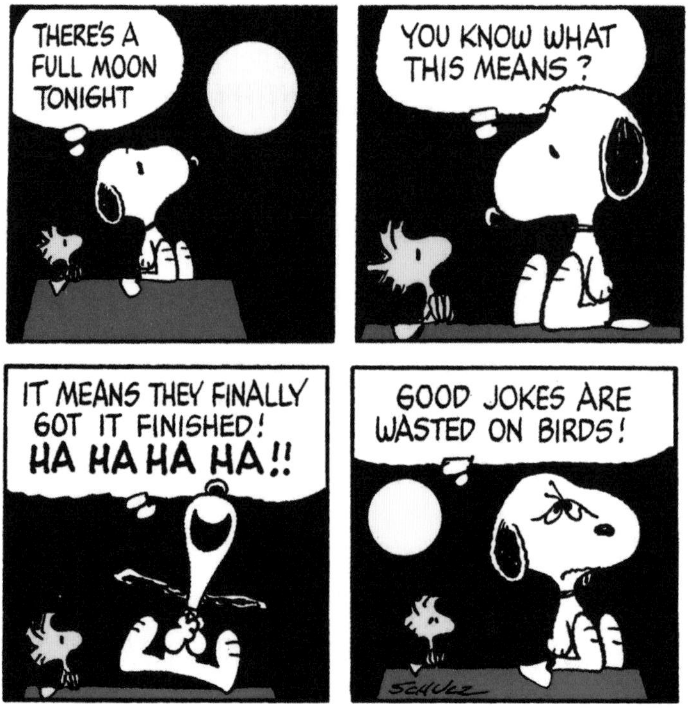
THERE'S A FULL MOON TONIGHT
YOU KNOW WHAT THIS MEANS?
IT MEANS THEY FINALLY GOT IT FINISHED! HA HA HA HA!!
GOOD JOKES ARE WASTED ON BIRDS!

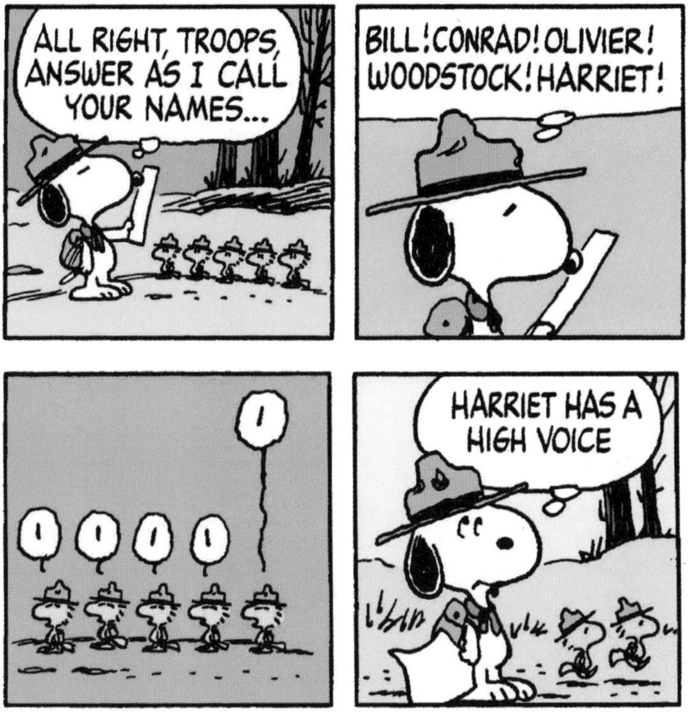
ALL RIGHT, TROOPS, ANSWER AS I CALL YOUR NAMES...
BILL! CONRAD! OLIVIER! WOODSTOCK! HARRIET!
HARRIET HAS A HIGH VOICE

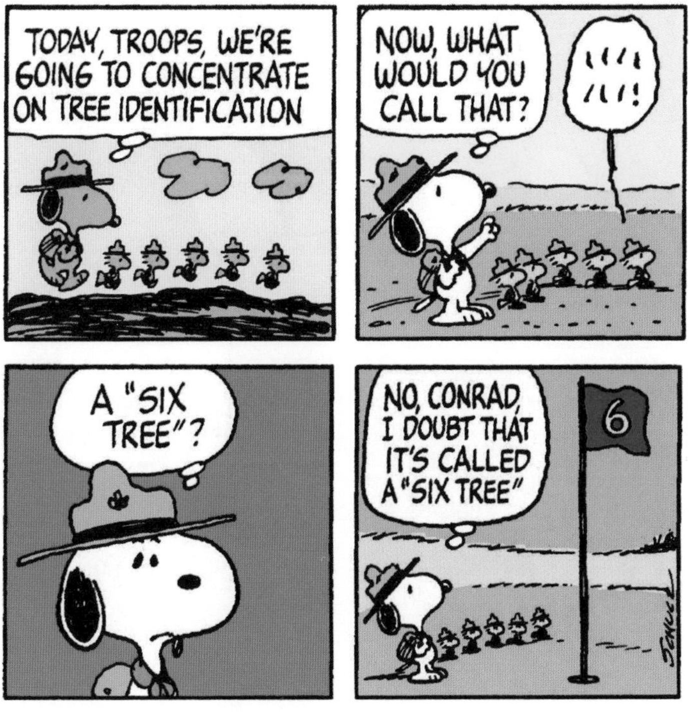
TODAY, TROOPS, WE'RE GOING TO CONCENTRATE ON TREE IDENTIFICATION
NOW, WHAT WOULD YOU CALL THAT?
A "SIX TREE"?
NO, CONRAD, I DOUBT THAT IT'S CALLED A "SIX TREE"
6

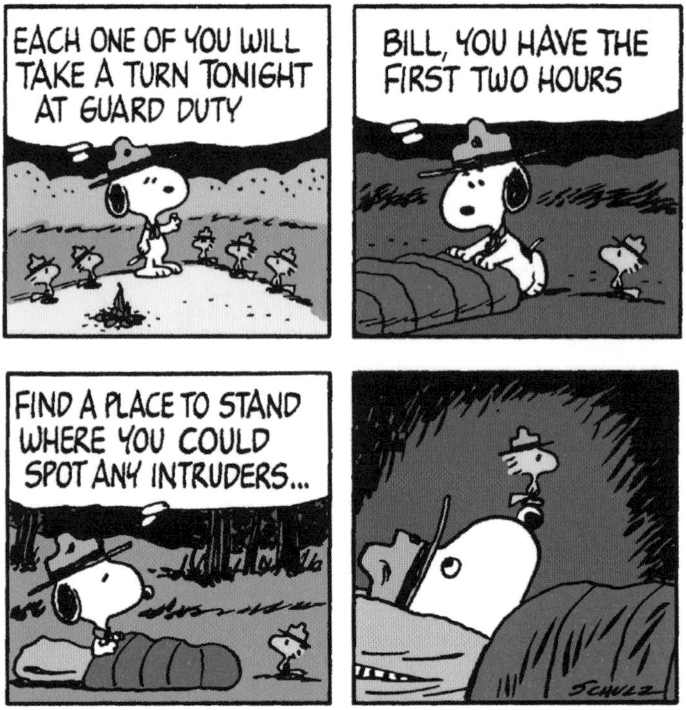
EACH ONE OF YOU WILL TAKE A TURN TONIGHT AT GUARD DUTY
BILL, YOU HAVE THE FIRST TWO HOURS
FIND A PLACE TO STAND WHERE YOU COULD SPOT ANY INTRUDERS...
SCHULZ

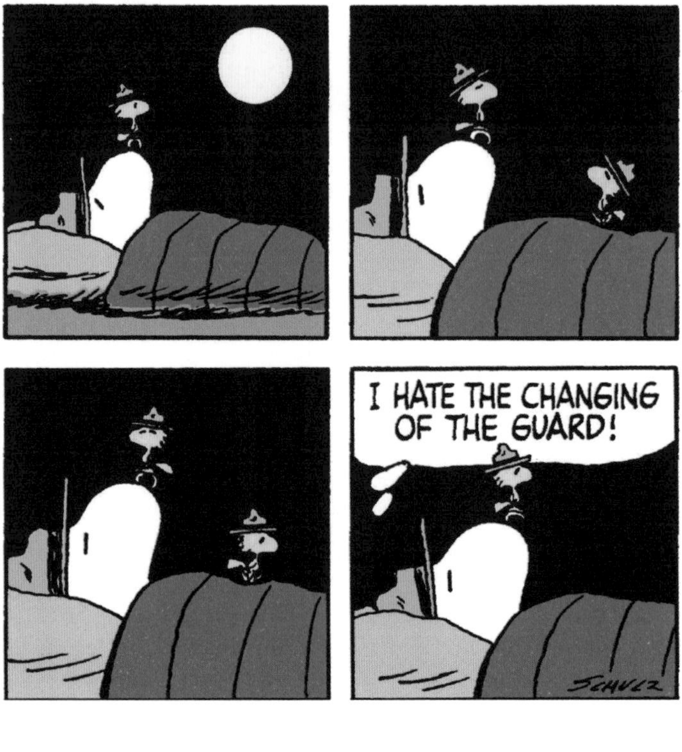
I HATE THE CHANGING OF THE GUARD!
SCHULZ

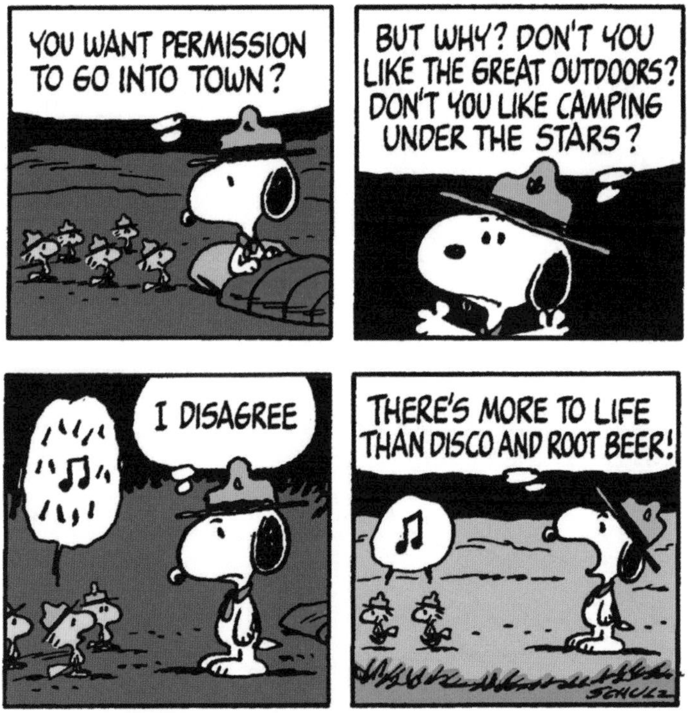
YOU WANT PERMISSION TO GO INTO TOWN?
BUT WHY? DON'T YOU LIKE THE GREAT OUTDOORS? DON'T YOU LIKE CAMPING UNDER THE STARS?
I DISAGREE
THERE'S MORE TO LIFE THAN DISCO AND ROOT BEER!
SCHULZ

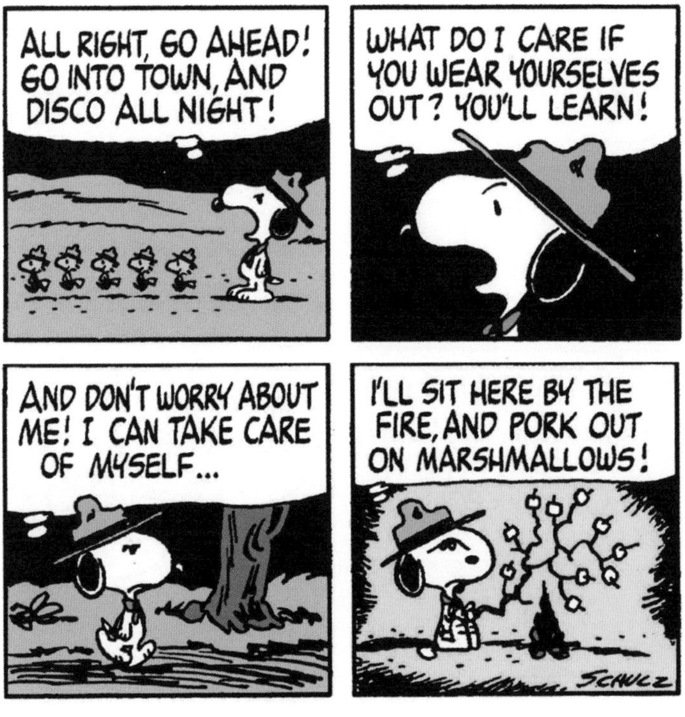
ALL RIGHT, GO AHEAD! GO INTO TOWN, AND DISCO ALL NIGHT!
WHAT DO I CARE IF YOU WEAR YOURSELVES OUT? YOU'LL LEARN!
AND DON'T WORRY ABOUT ME! I CAN TAKE CARE OF MYSELF...
I'LL SIT HERE BY THE FIRE, AND PORK OUT ON MARSHMALLOWS!
SCHULZ

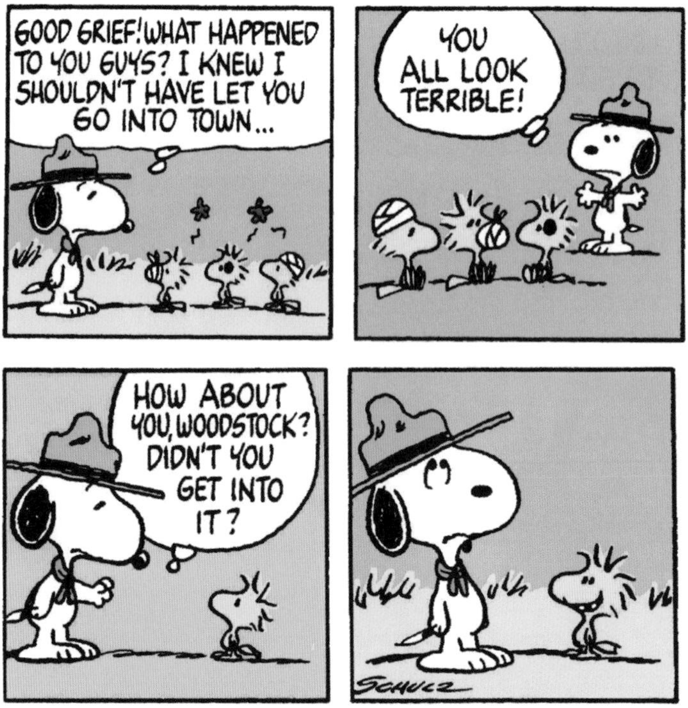
GOOD GRIEF! WHAT HAPPENED TO YOU GUYS? I KNEW I SHOULDN'T HAVE LET YOU GO INTO TOWN...
YOU ALL LOOK TERRIBLE!
HOW ABOUT YOU, WOODSTOCK? DIDN'T YOU GET INTO IT?
SCHULZ

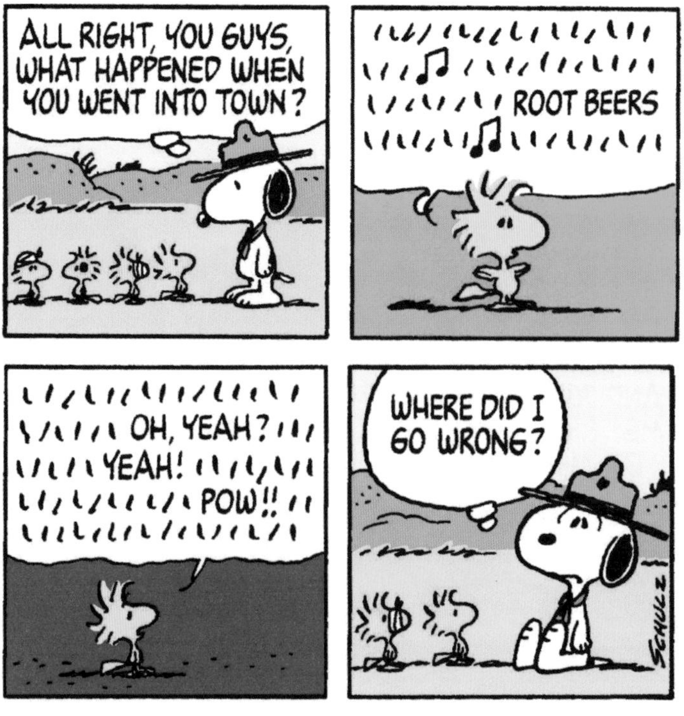
ALL RIGHT, YOU GUYS, WHAT HAPPENED WHEN YOU WENT INTO TOWN?
ROOT BEERS
OH, YEAH?
YEAH!
POW!!
WHERE DID I GO WRONG?
SCHULZ

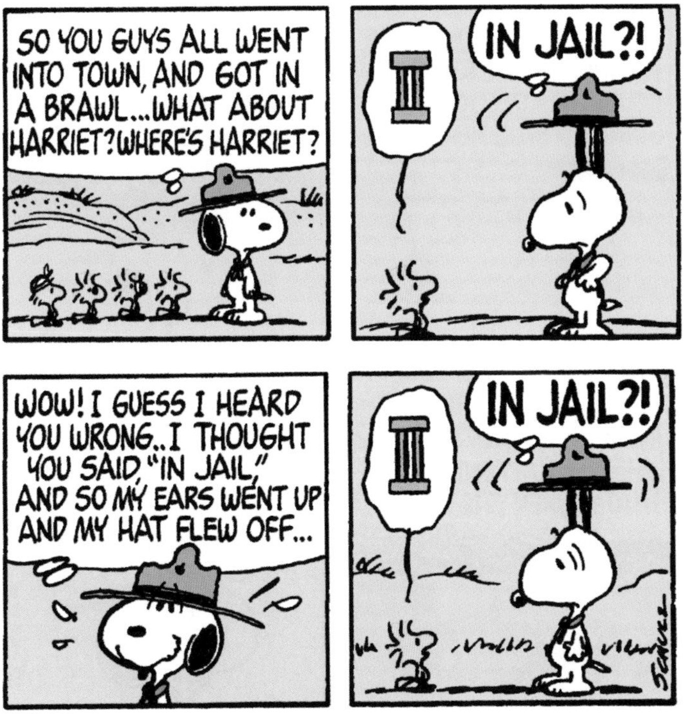
SO YOU GUYS ALL WENT INTO TOWN, AND GOT IN A BRAWL...WHAT ABOUT HARRIET? WHERE'S HARRIET?
IN JAIL?!
WOW! I GUESS I HEARD YOU WRONG..I THOUGHT YOU SAID "IN JAIL," AND SO MY EARS WENT UP AND MY HAT FLEW OFF...
IN JAIL?!
SCHULZ

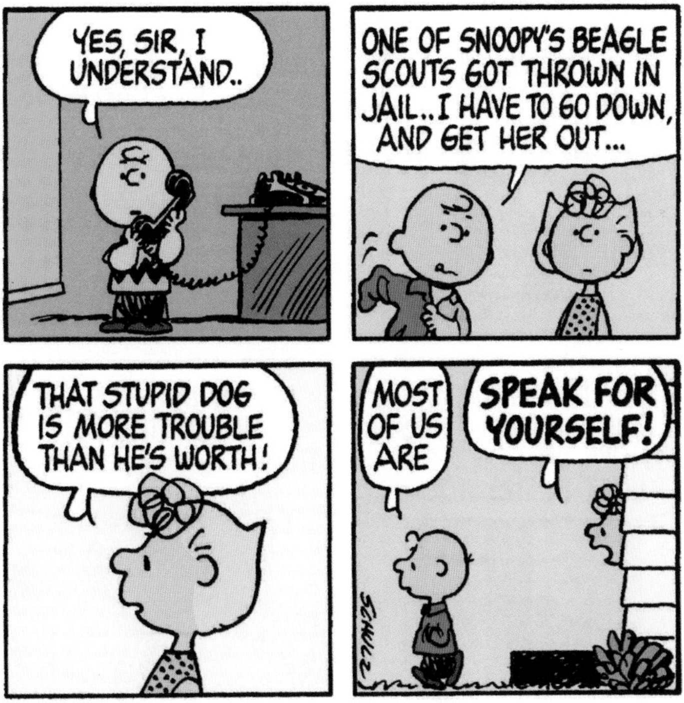
YES, SIR, I UNDERSTAND..
ONE OF SNOOPY'S BEAGLE SCOUTS GOT THROWN IN JAIL..I HAVE TO GO DOWN, AND GET HER OUT...
THAT STUPID DOG IS MORE TROUBLE THAN HE'S WORTH!
MOST OF US ARE
SPEAK FOR YOURSELF!
SCHULZ

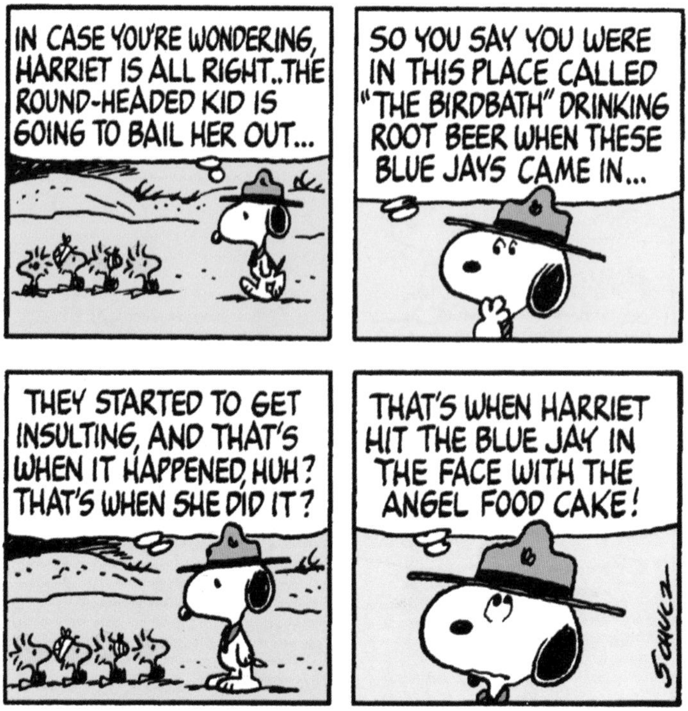
IN CASE YOU'RE WONDERING, HARRIET IS ALL RIGHT..THE ROUND-HEADED KID IS GOING TO BAIL HER OUT...
SO YOU SAY YOU WERE IN THIS PLACE CALLED "THE BIRDBATH" DRINKING ROOT BEER WHEN THESE BLUE JAYS CAME IN...
THEY STARTED TO GET INSULTING, AND THAT'S WHEN IT HAPPENED, HUH? THAT'S WHEN SHE DID IT?
THAT'S WHEN HARRIET HIT THE BLUE JAY IN THE FACE WITH THE ANGEL FOOD CAKE!
SCHULZ

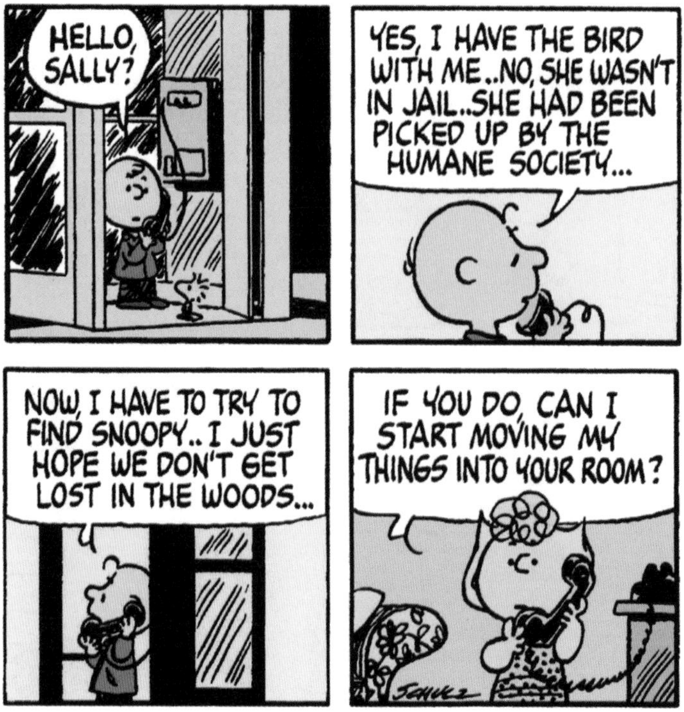
HELLO, SALLY?
YES, I HAVE THE BIRD WITH ME..NO, SHE WASN'T IN JAIL..SHE HAD BEEN PICKED UP BY THE HUMANE SOCIETY...
NOW, I HAVE TO TRY TO FIND SNOOPY..I JUST HOPE WE DON'T GET LOST IN THE WOODS...
IF YOU DO, CAN I START MOVING MY THINGS INTO YOUR ROOM?
SCHULZ

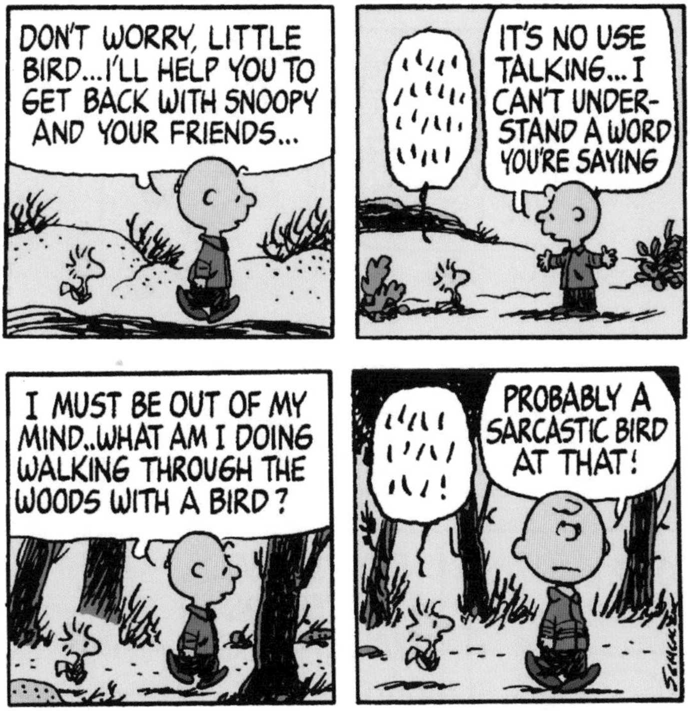
DON'T WORRY, LITTLE BIRD...I'LL HELP YOU TO GET BACK WITH SNOOPY AND YOUR FRIENDS...
IT'S NO USE TALKING...I CAN'T UNDER-STAND A WORD YOU'RE SAYING
I MUST BE OUT OF MY MIND..WHAT AM I DOING WALKING THROUGH THE WOODS WITH A BIRD?
PROBABLY A SARCASTIC BIRD AT THAT!

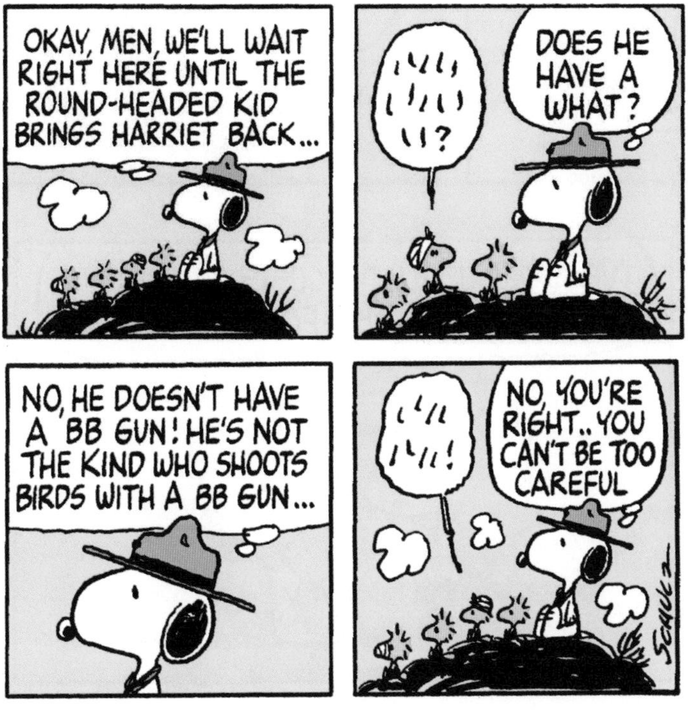
OKAY, MEN, WE'LL WAIT RIGHT HERE UNTIL THE ROUND-HEADED KID BRINGS HARRIET BACK...
DOES HE HAVE A WHAT?
NO, HE DOESN'T HAVE A BB GUN! HE'S NOT THE KIND WHO SHOOTS BIRDS WITH A BB GUN...
NO, YOU'RE RIGHT..YOU CAN'T BE TOO CAREFUL

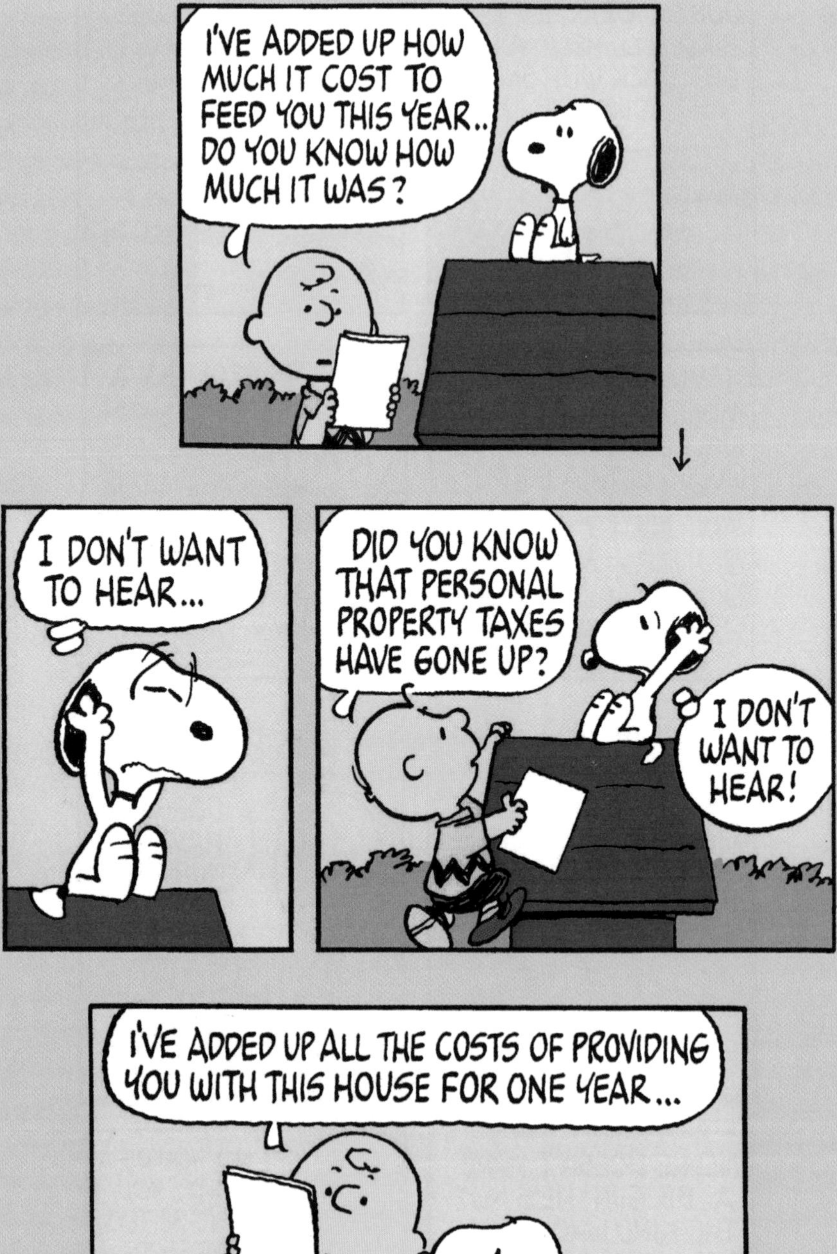
I'VE ADDED UP HOW MUCH IT COST TO FEED YOU THIS YEAR.. DO YOU KNOW HOW MUCH IT WAS?
I DON'T WANT TO HEAR...
DID YOU KNOW THAT PERSONAL PROPERTY TAXES HAVE GONE UP?
I DON'T WANT TO HEAR!
I'VE ADDED UP ALL THE COSTS OF PROVIDING YOU WITH THIS HOUSE FOR ONE YEAR...

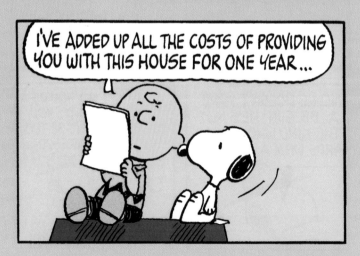

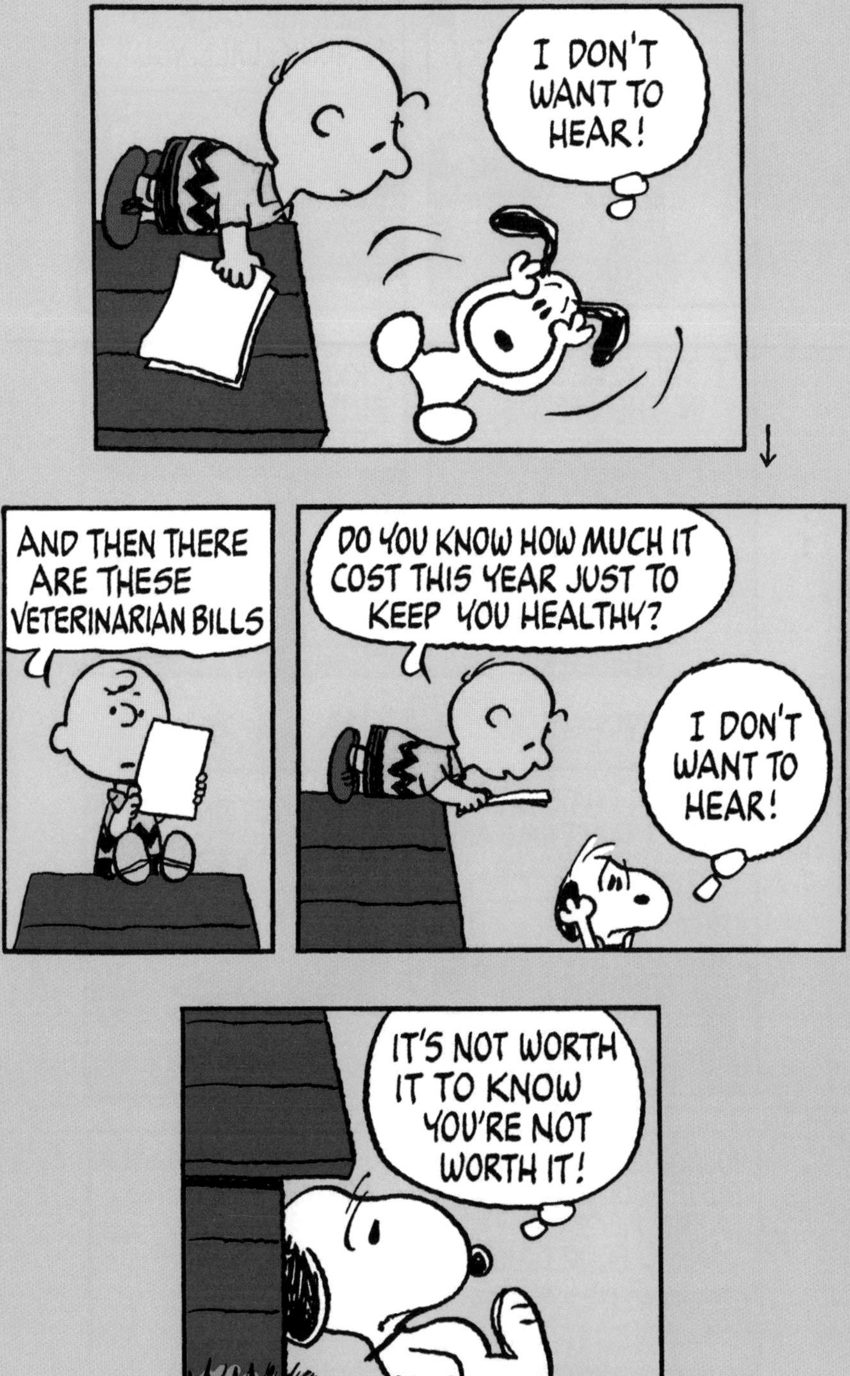
I DON'T WANT TO HEAR!
AND THEN THERE ARE THESE VETERINARIAN BILLS
DO YOU KNOW HOW MUCH IT COST THIS YEAR JUST TO KEEP YOU HEALTHY?
I DON'T WANT TO HEAR!
IT'S NOT WORTH IT TO KNOW YOU'RE NOT WORTH IT!
SCHULZ

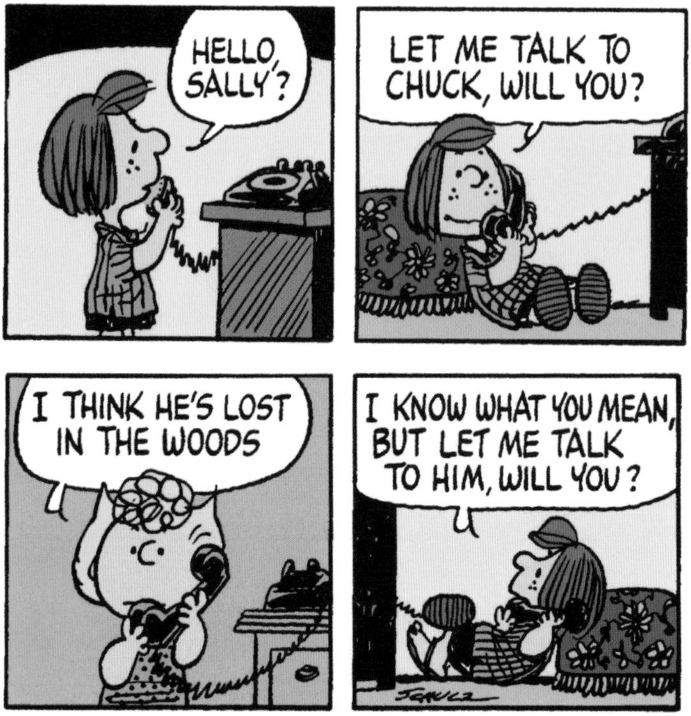
HELLO, SALLY?
LET ME TALK TO CHUCK, WILL YOU?
I THINK HE'S LOST IN THE WOODS
I KNOW WHAT YOU MEAN, BUT LET ME TALK TO HIM, WILL YOU?

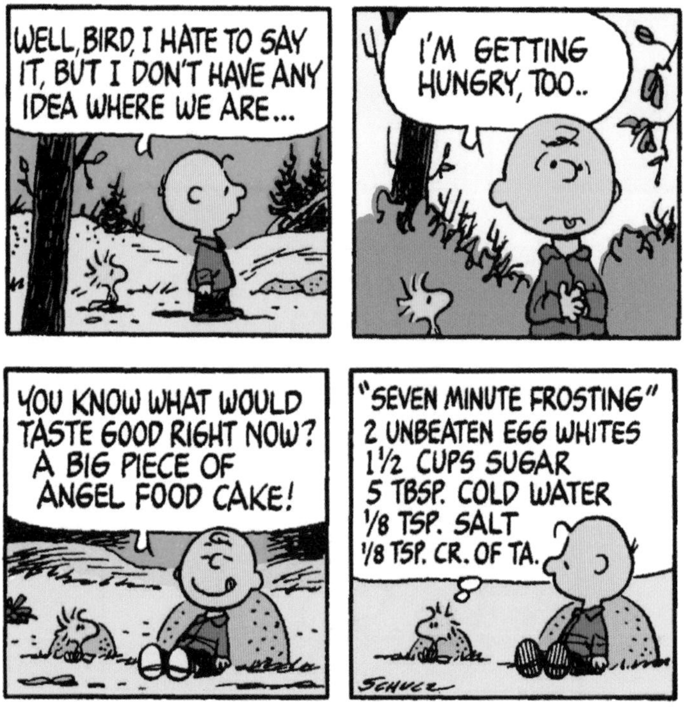
WELL, BIRD, I HATE TO SAY IT, BUT I DON'T HAVE ANY IDEA WHERE WE ARE...
I'M GETTING HUNGRY, TOO..
YOU KNOW WHAT WOULD TASTE GOOD RIGHT NOW? A BIG PIECE OF ANGEL FOOD CAKE!
"SEVEN MINUTE FROSTING"
2 UNBEATEN EGG WHITES
1½ CUPS SUGAR
5 TBSP. COLD WATER
⅛ TSP. SALT
⅛ TSP. CR. OF TA.

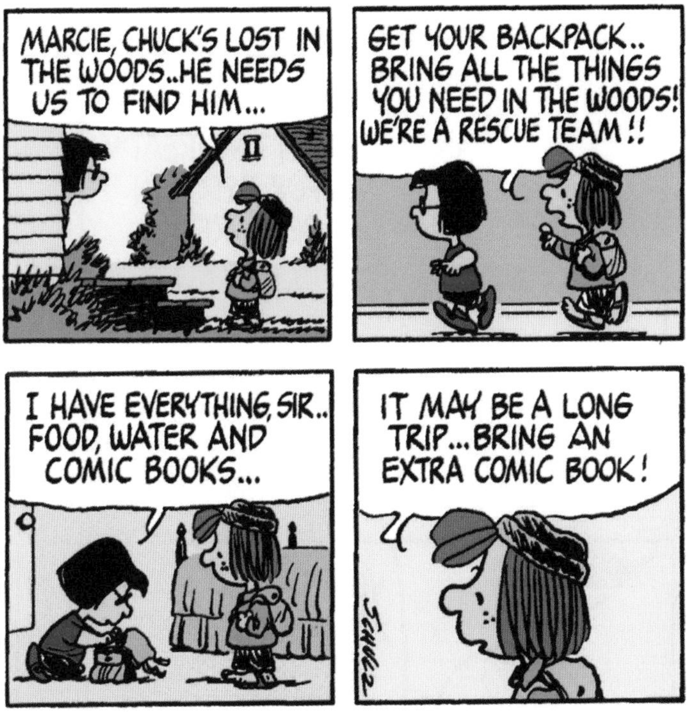
MARCIE, CHUCK'S LOST IN THE WOODS..HE NEEDS US TO FIND HIM...
GET YOUR BACKPACK.. BRING ALL THE THINGS YOU NEED IN THE WOODS! WE'RE A RESCUE TEAM!!
I HAVE EVERYTHING, SIR.. FOOD, WATER AND COMIC BOOKS...
IT MAY BE A LONG TRIP...BRING AN EXTRA COMIC BOOK!

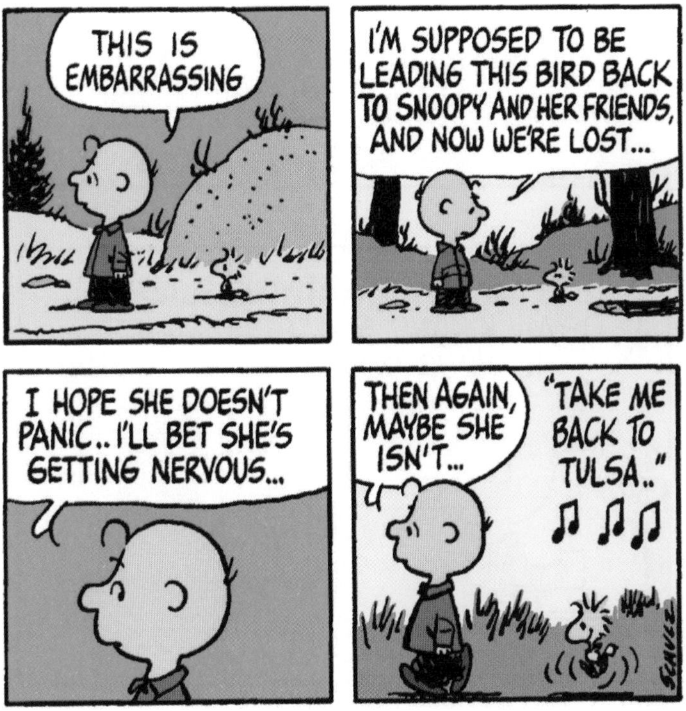
THIS IS EMBARRASSING
I'M SUPPOSED TO BE LEADING THIS BIRD BACK TO SNOOPY AND HER FRIENDS, AND NOW WE'RE LOST...
I HOPE SHE DOESN'T PANIC.. I'LL BET SHE'S GETTING NERVOUS...
THEN AGAIN, MAYBE SHE ISN'T...
"TAKE ME BACK TO TULSA.."

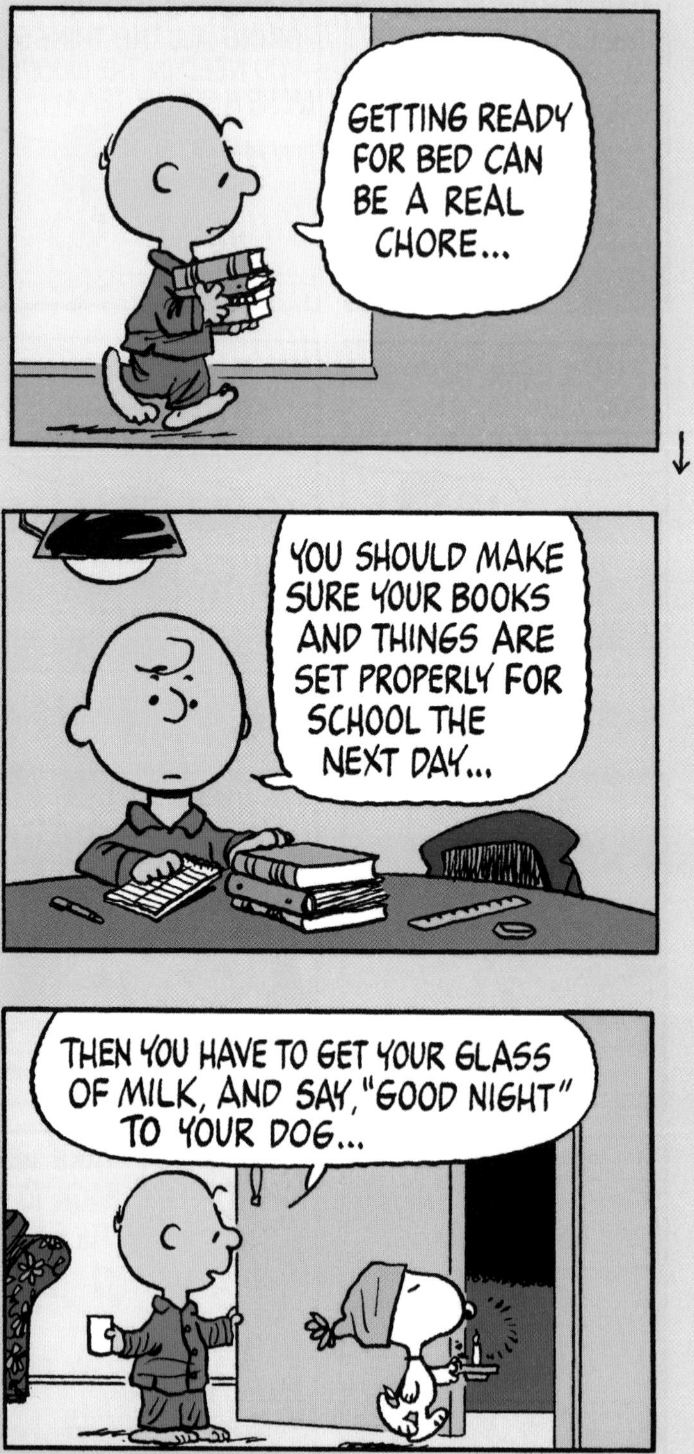
GETTING READY FOR BED CAN BE A REAL CHORE...
YOU SHOULD MAKE SURE YOUR BOOKS AND THINGS ARE SET PROPERLY FOR SCHOOL THE NEXT DAY...
THEN YOU HAVE TO GET YOUR GLASS OF MILK, AND SAY, "GOOD NIGHT" TO YOUR DOG...

AND THEN YOU HAVE TO BE ABSOLUTELY SURE THAT YOU'VE TAKEN ALL THE...
AAUGH!
...PINS OUT OF YOUR NEW PAJAMAS!
SCHULZ

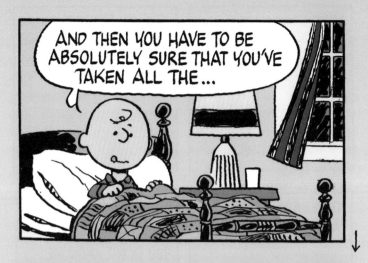

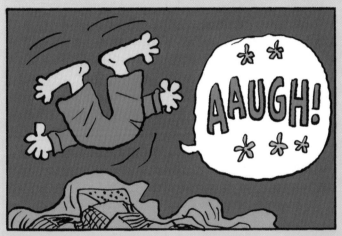

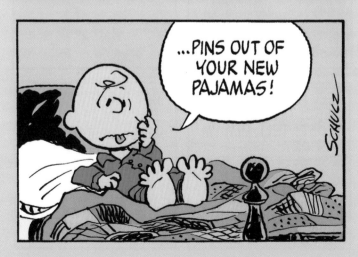

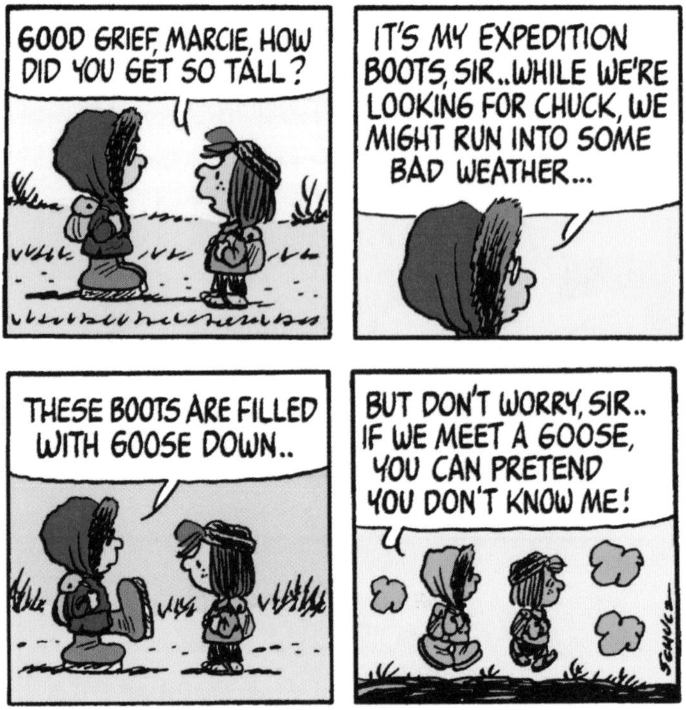
GOOD GRIEF, MARCIE, HOW DID YOU GET SO TALL?
IT'S MY EXPEDITION BOOTS, SIR..WHILE WE'RE LOOKING FOR CHUCK, WE MIGHT RUN INTO SOME BAD WEATHER...
THESE BOOTS ARE FILLED WITH GOOSE DOWN..
BUT DON'T WORRY, SIR.. IF WE MEET A GOOSE, YOU CAN PRETEND YOU DON'T KNOW ME!
SCHULZ

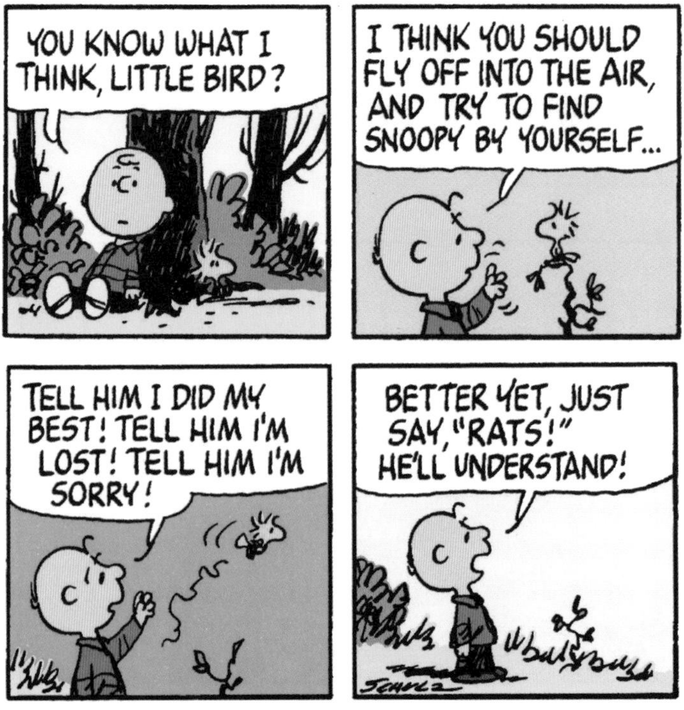
YOU KNOW WHAT I THINK, LITTLE BIRD?
I THINK YOU SHOULD FLY OFF INTO THE AIR, AND TRY TO FIND SNOOPY BY YOURSELF...
TELL HIM I DID MY BEST! TELL HIM I'M LOST! TELL HIM I'M SORRY!
BETTER YET, JUST SAY, "RATS!" HE'LL UNDERSTAND!
SCHULZ

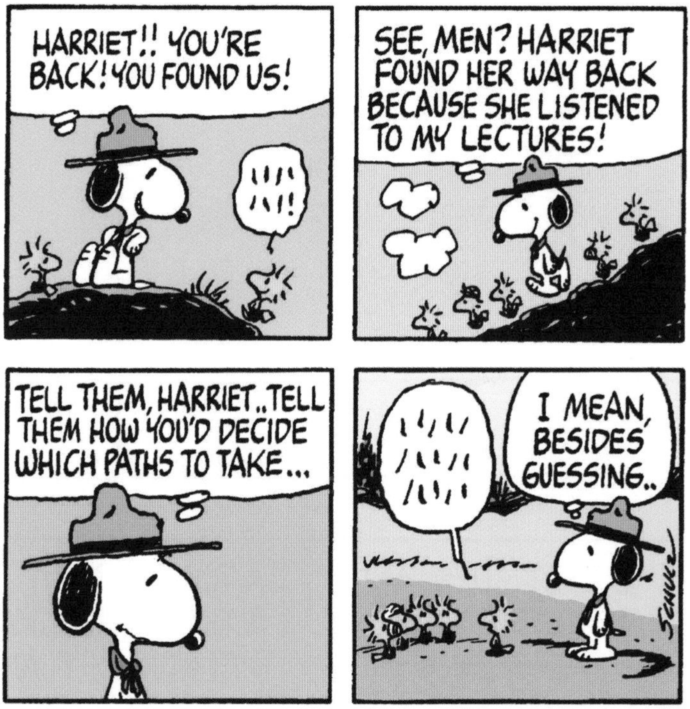
HARRIET!! YOU'RE BACK! YOU FOUND US!
SEE, MEN? HARRIET FOUND HER WAY BACK BECAUSE SHE LISTENED TO MY LECTURES!
TELL THEM, HARRIET..TELL THEM HOW YOU'D DECIDE WHICH PATHS TO TAKE...
I MEAN, BESIDES GUESSING..

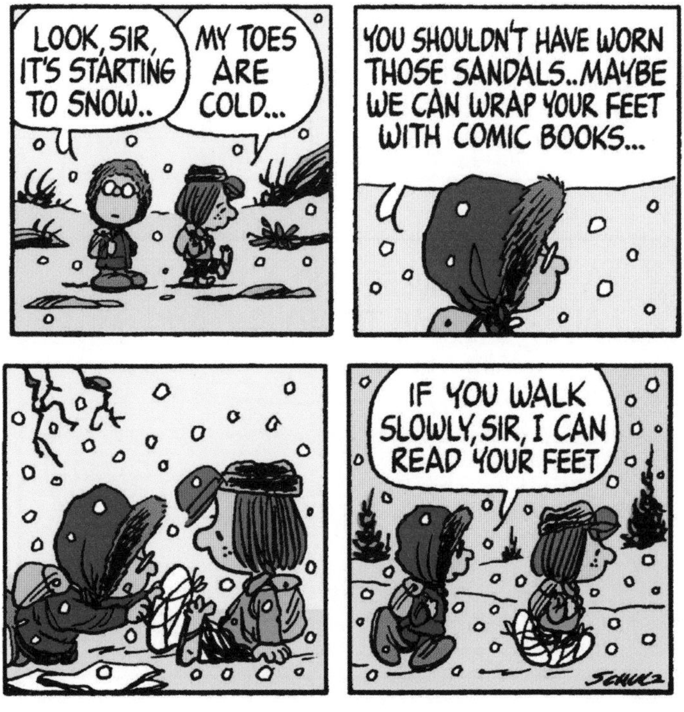
LOOK, SIR, IT'S STARTING TO SNOW..
MY TOES ARE COLD...
YOU SHOULDN'T HAVE WORN THOSE SANDALS..MAYBE WE CAN WRAP YOUR FEET WITH COMIC BOOKS...
IF YOU WALK SLOWLY, SIR, I CAN READ YOUR FEET

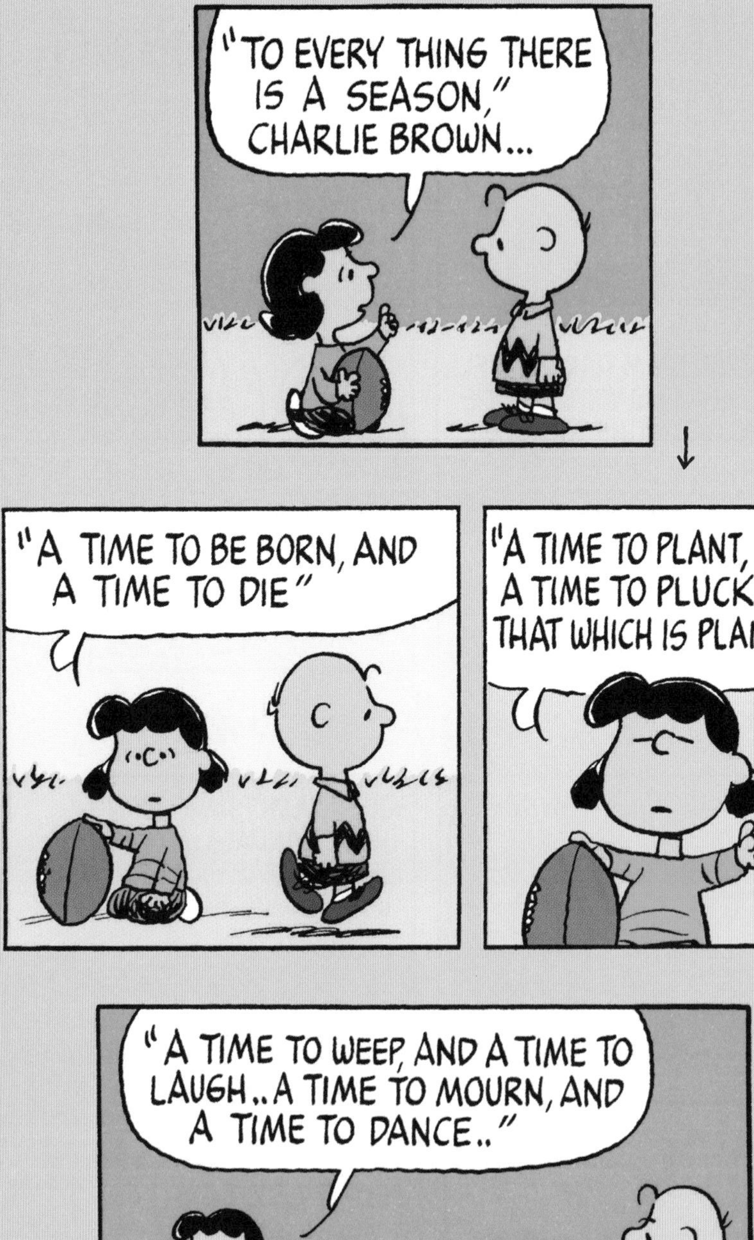
"TO EVERY THING THERE IS A SEASON," CHARLIE BROWN...
"A TIME TO BE BORN, AND A TIME TO DIE"
"A TIME TO PLANT, AND A TIME TO PLUCK UP THAT WHICH IS PLANTED"
"A TIME TO WEEP, AND A TIME TO LAUGH.. A TIME TO MOURN, AND A TIME TO DANCE.."

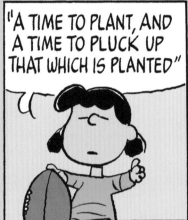

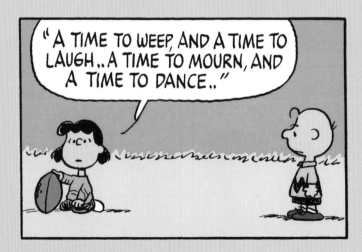

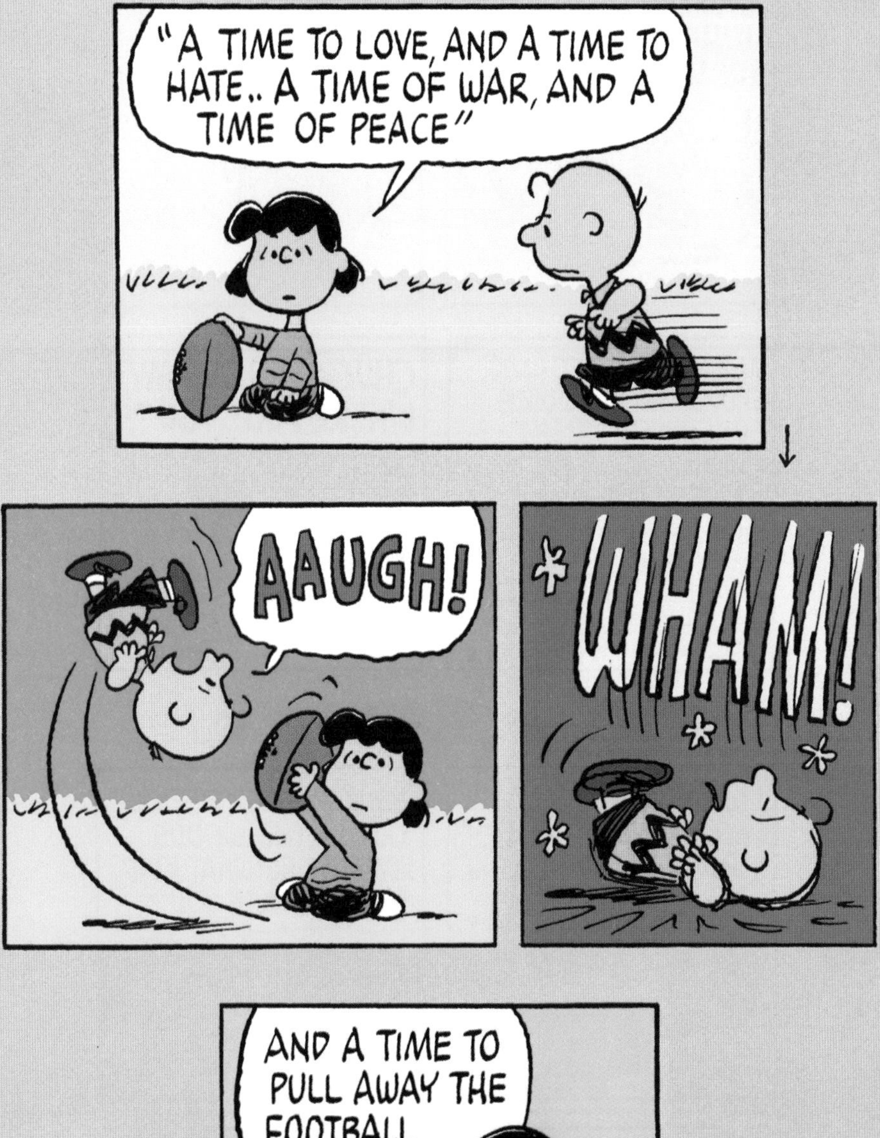
"A TIME TO LOVE, AND A TIME TO HATE.. A TIME OF WAR, AND A TIME OF PEACE"
AAUGH!
WHAM!
AND A TIME TO PULL AWAY THE FOOTBALL
SCHULZ

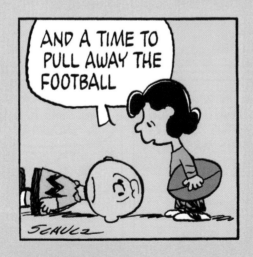

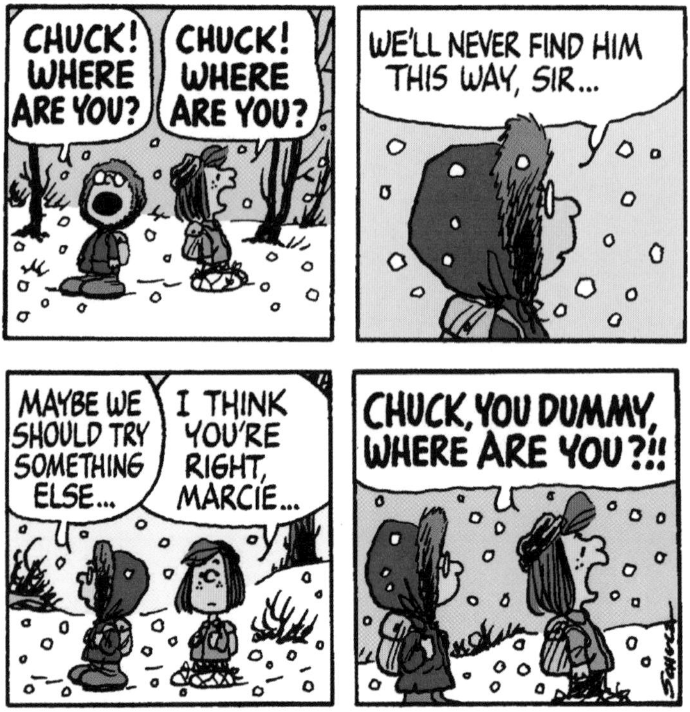
CHUCK! WHERE ARE YOU?
CHUCK! WHERE ARE YOU?
WE'LL NEVER FIND HIM THIS WAY, SIR...
MAYBE WE SHOULD TRY SOMETHING ELSE...
I THINK YOU'RE RIGHT, MARCIE...
CHUCK, YOU DUMMY, WHERE ARE YOU?!!
SCHULZ

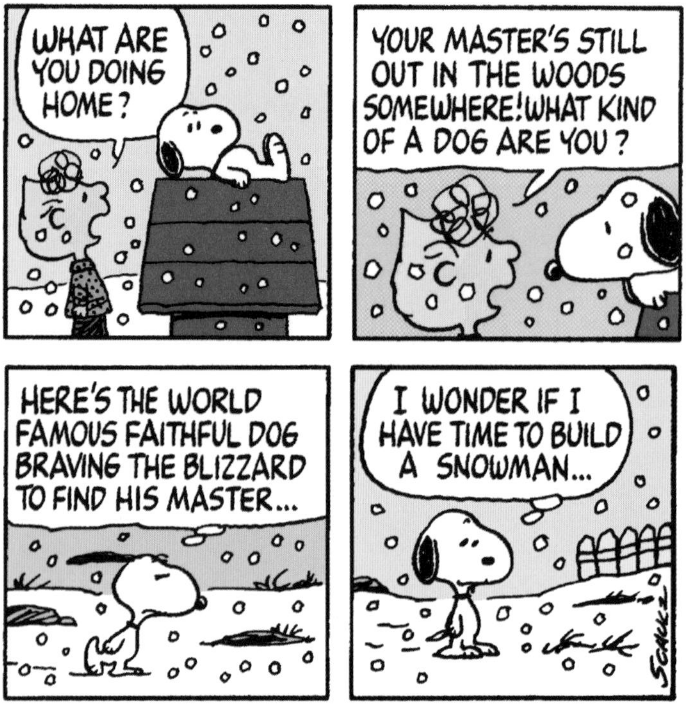
WHAT ARE YOU DOING HOME?
YOUR MASTER'S STILL OUT IN THE WOODS SOMEWHERE! WHAT KIND OF A DOG ARE YOU?
HERE'S THE WORLD FAMOUS FAITHFUL DOG BRAVING THE BLIZZARD TO FIND HIS MASTER...
I WONDER IF I HAVE TIME TO BUILD A SNOWMAN...
SCHULZ

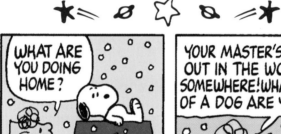

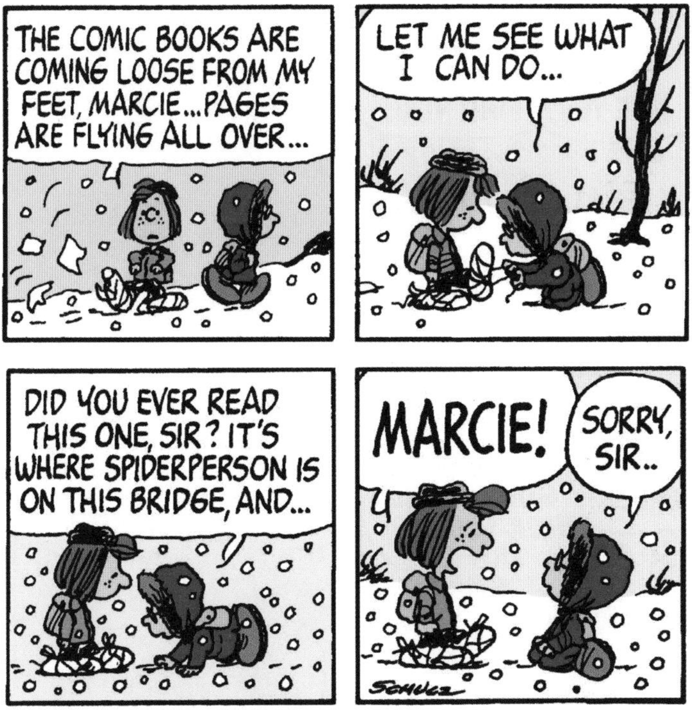
THE COMIC BOOKS ARE COMING LOOSE FROM MY FEET, MARCIE...PAGES ARE FLYING ALL OVER...
LET ME SEE WHAT I CAN DO...
DID YOU EVER READ THIS ONE, SIR? IT'S WHERE SPIDERPERSON IS ON THIS BRIDGE, AND...
MARCIE!
SORRY, SIR..

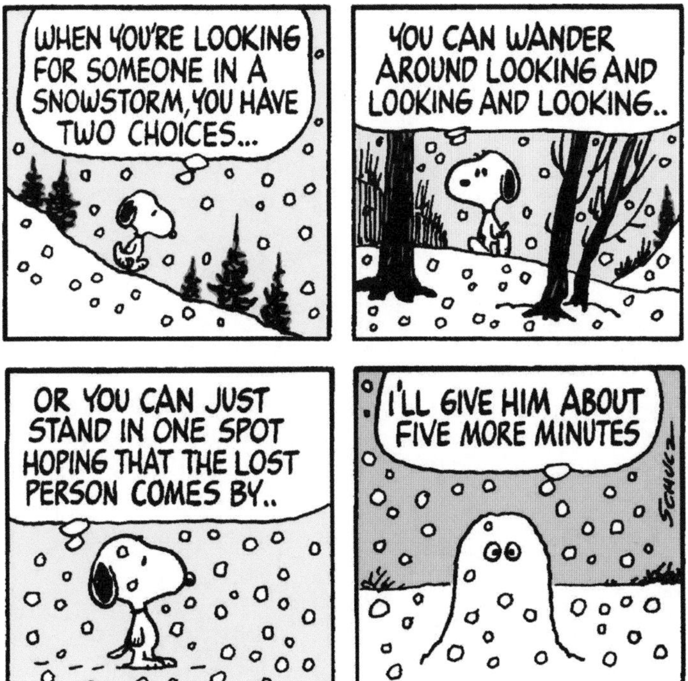
WHEN YOU'RE LOOKING FOR SOMEONE IN A SNOWSTORM, YOU HAVE TWO CHOICES...
YOU CAN WANDER AROUND LOOKING AND LOOKING AND LOOKING..
OR YOU CAN JUST STAND IN ONE SPOT HOPING THAT THE LOST PERSON COMES BY..
I'LL GIVE HIM ABOUT FIVE MORE MINUTES

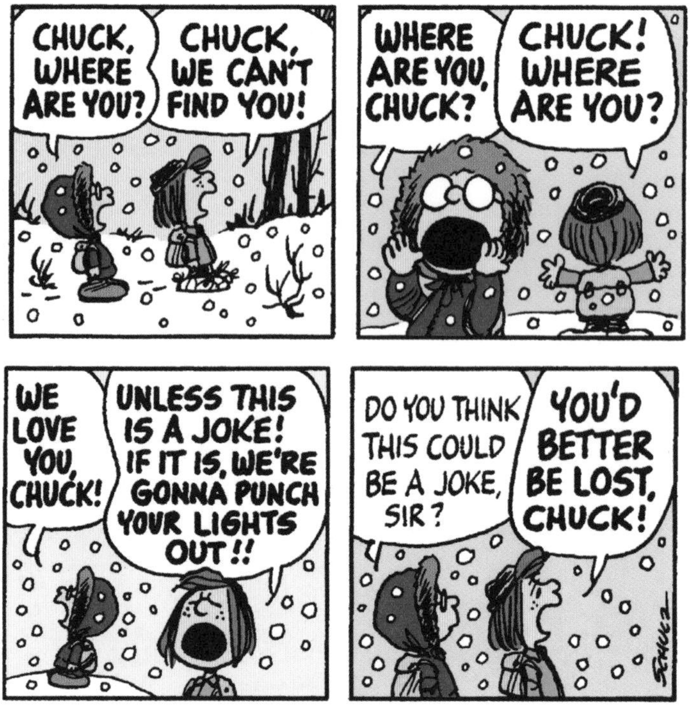
CHUCK, WHERE ARE YOU?
CHUCK, WE CAN'T FIND YOU!
WHERE ARE YOU, CHUCK?
CHUCK! WHERE ARE YOU?
WE LOVE YOU, CHUCK!
UNLESS THIS IS A JOKE! IF IT IS, WE'RE GONNA PUNCH YOUR LIGHTS OUT!!
DO YOU THINK THIS COULD BE A JOKE, SIR?
YOU'D BETTER BE LOST, CHUCK!

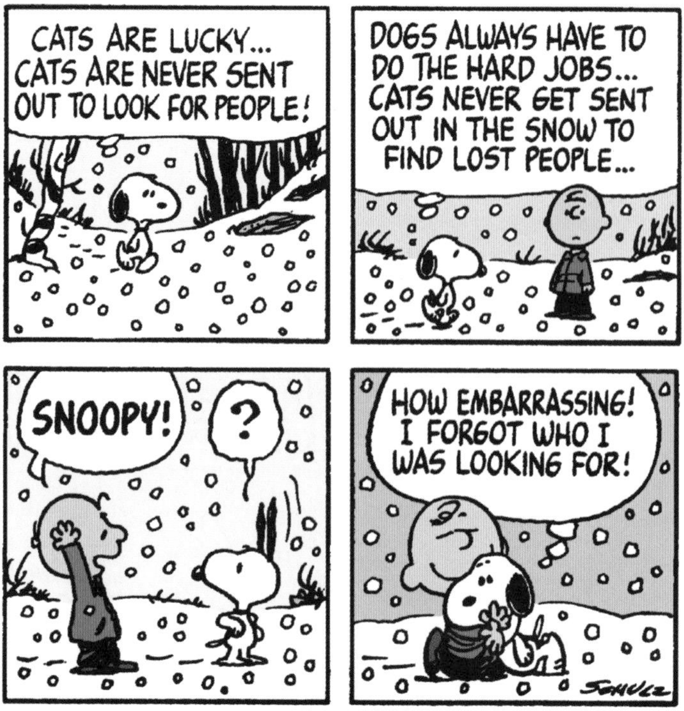
CATS ARE LUCKY... CATS ARE NEVER SENT OUT TO LOOK FOR PEOPLE!
DOGS ALWAYS HAVE TO DO THE HARD JOBS... CATS NEVER GET SENT OUT IN THE SNOW TO FIND LOST PEOPLE...
SNOOPY!
?
HOW EMBARRASSING! I FORGOT WHO I WAS LOOKING FOR!

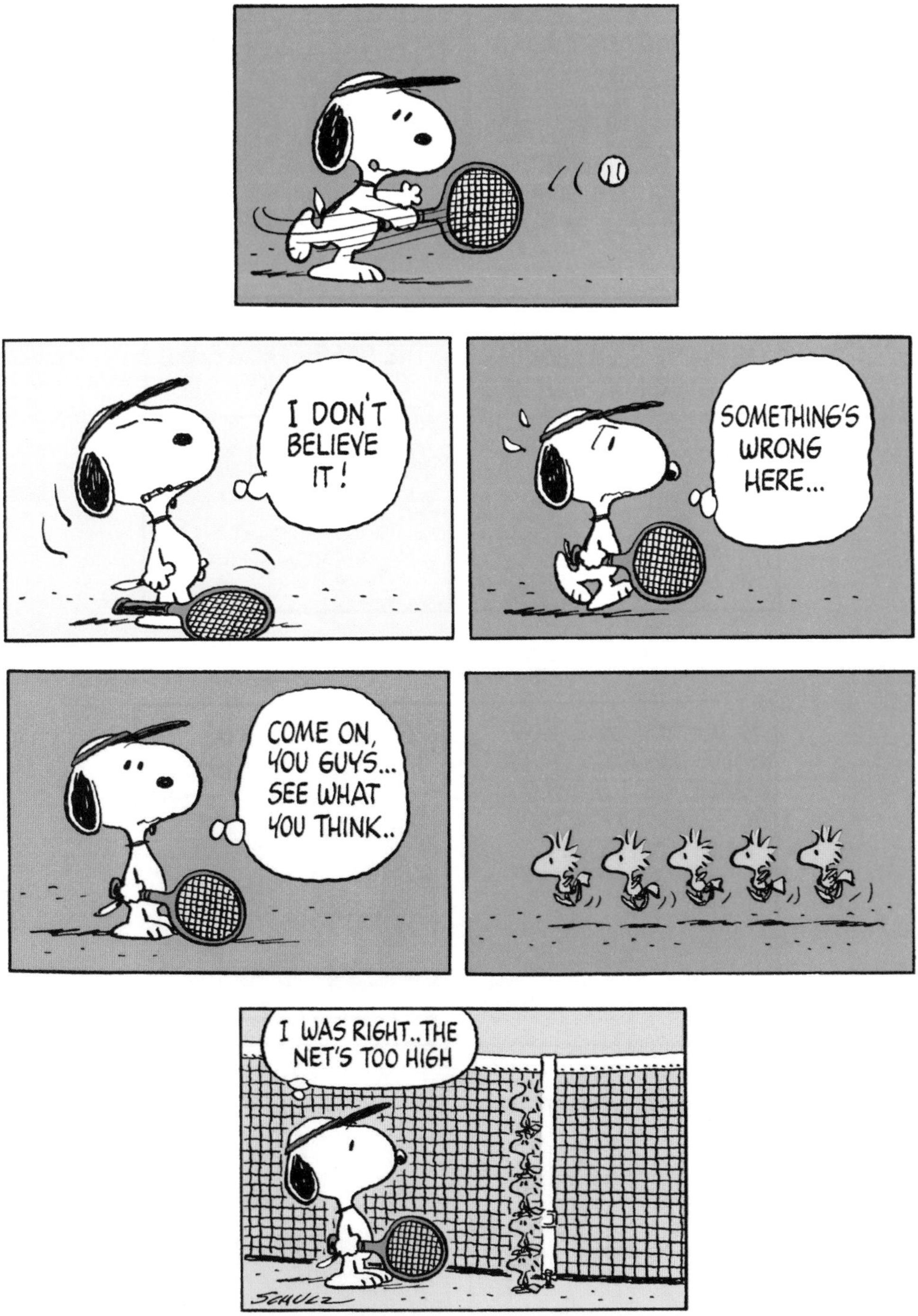
I DON'T BELIEVE IT!
SOMETHING'S WRONG HERE...
COME ON, YOU GUYS... SEE WHAT YOU THINK..
I WAS RIGHT..THE NET'S TOO HIGH
SCHULZ

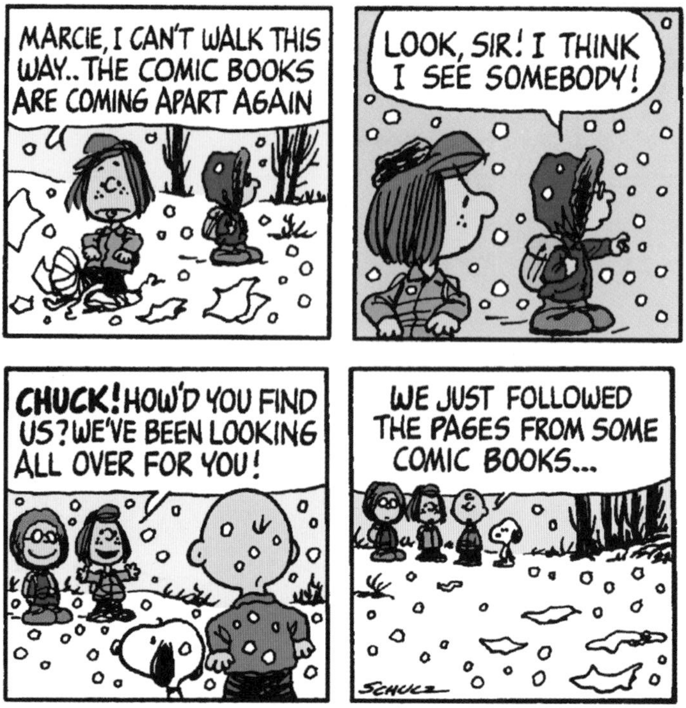
MARCIE, I CAN'T WALK THIS WAY.. THE COMIC BOOKS ARE COMING APART AGAIN
LOOK, SIR! I THINK I SEE SOMEBODY!
CHUCK! HOW'D YOU FIND US? WE'VE BEEN LOOKING ALL OVER FOR YOU!
WE JUST FOLLOWED THE PAGES FROM SOME COMIC BOOKS...
SCHULZ

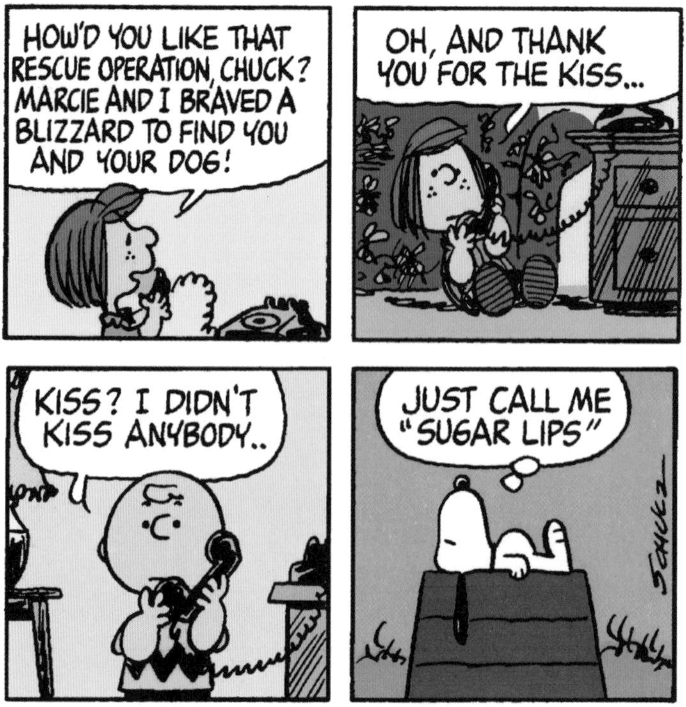
HOW'D YOU LIKE THAT RESCUE OPERATION, CHUCK? MARCIE AND I BRAVED A BLIZZARD TO FIND YOU AND YOUR DOG!
OH, AND THANK YOU FOR THE KISS...
KISS? I DIDN'T KISS ANYBODY..
JUST CALL ME "SUGAR LIPS"
SCHULZ

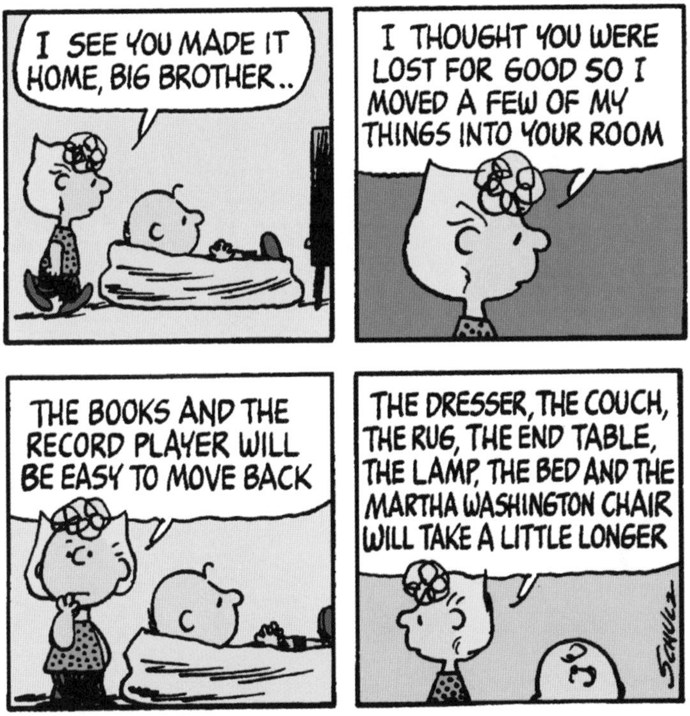
I SEE YOU MADE IT HOME, BIG BROTHER..
I THOUGHT YOU WERE LOST FOR GOOD SO I MOVED A FEW OF MY THINGS INTO YOUR ROOM
THE BOOKS AND THE RECORD PLAYER WILL BE EASY TO MOVE BACK
THE DRESSER, THE COUCH, THE RUG, THE END TABLE, THE LAMP, THE BED AND THE MARTHA WASHINGTON CHAIR WILL TAKE A LITTLE LONGER
SCHULZ

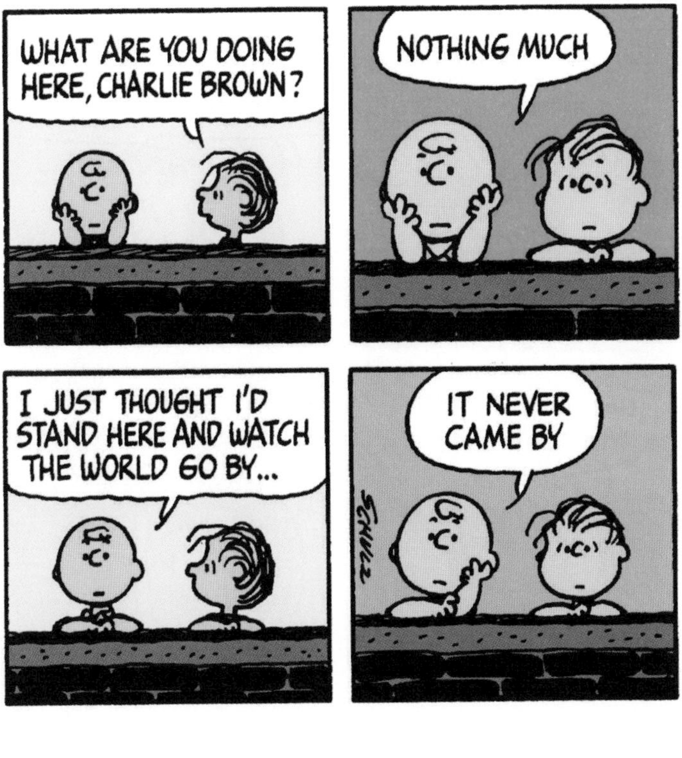
WHAT ARE YOU DOING HERE, CHARLIE BROWN?
NOTHING MUCH
I JUST THOUGHT I'D STAND HERE AND WATCH THE WORLD GO BY...
IT NEVER CAME BY
SCHULZ

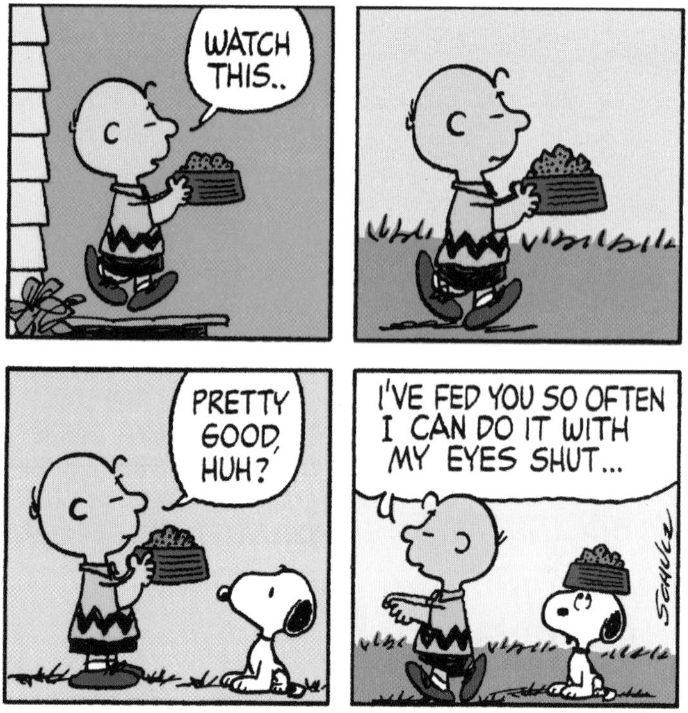
WATCH THIS..
PRETTY GOOD, HUH?
I'VE FED YOU SO OFTEN I CAN DO IT WITH MY EYES SHUT...

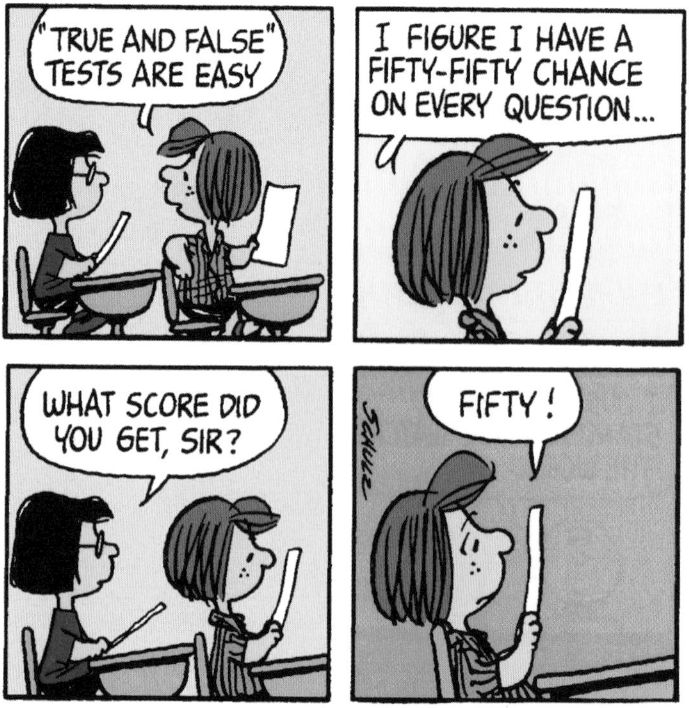
"TRUE AND FALSE" TESTS ARE EASY
I FIGURE I HAVE A FIFTY-FIFTY CHANCE ON EVERY QUESTION...
WHAT SCORE DID YOU GET, SIR?
FIFTY!

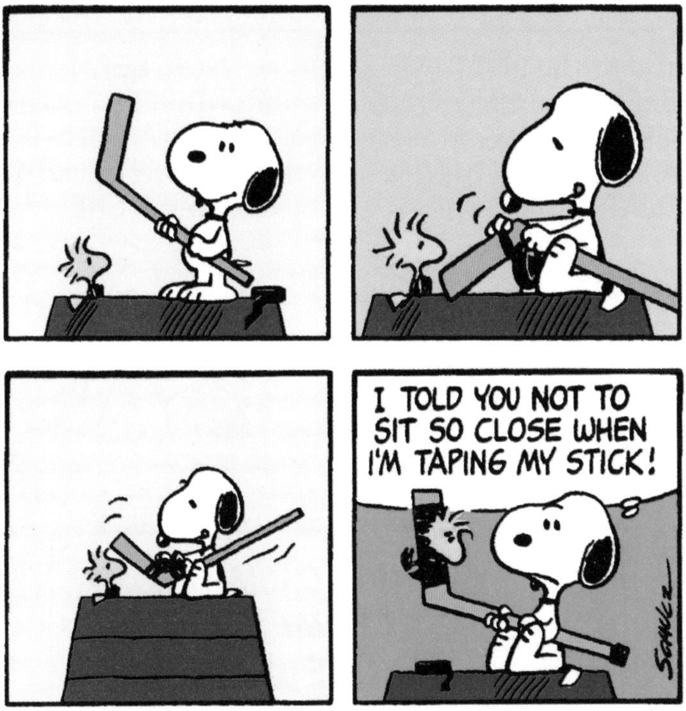
I TOLD YOU NOT TO SIT SO CLOSE WHEN I'M TAPING MY STICK!

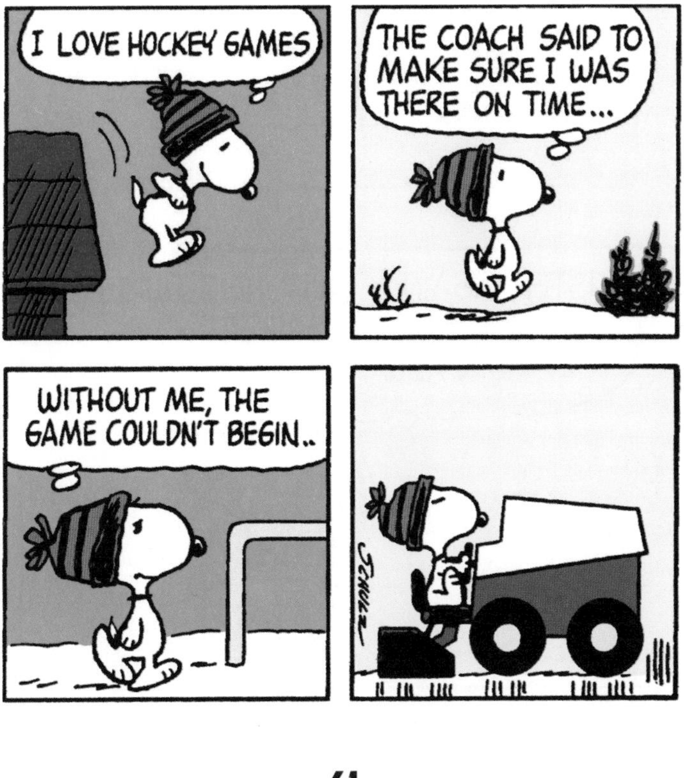
I LOVE HOCKEY GAMES
THE COACH SAID TO MAKE SURE I WAS THERE ON TIME...
WITHOUT ME, THE GAME COULDN'T BEGIN..

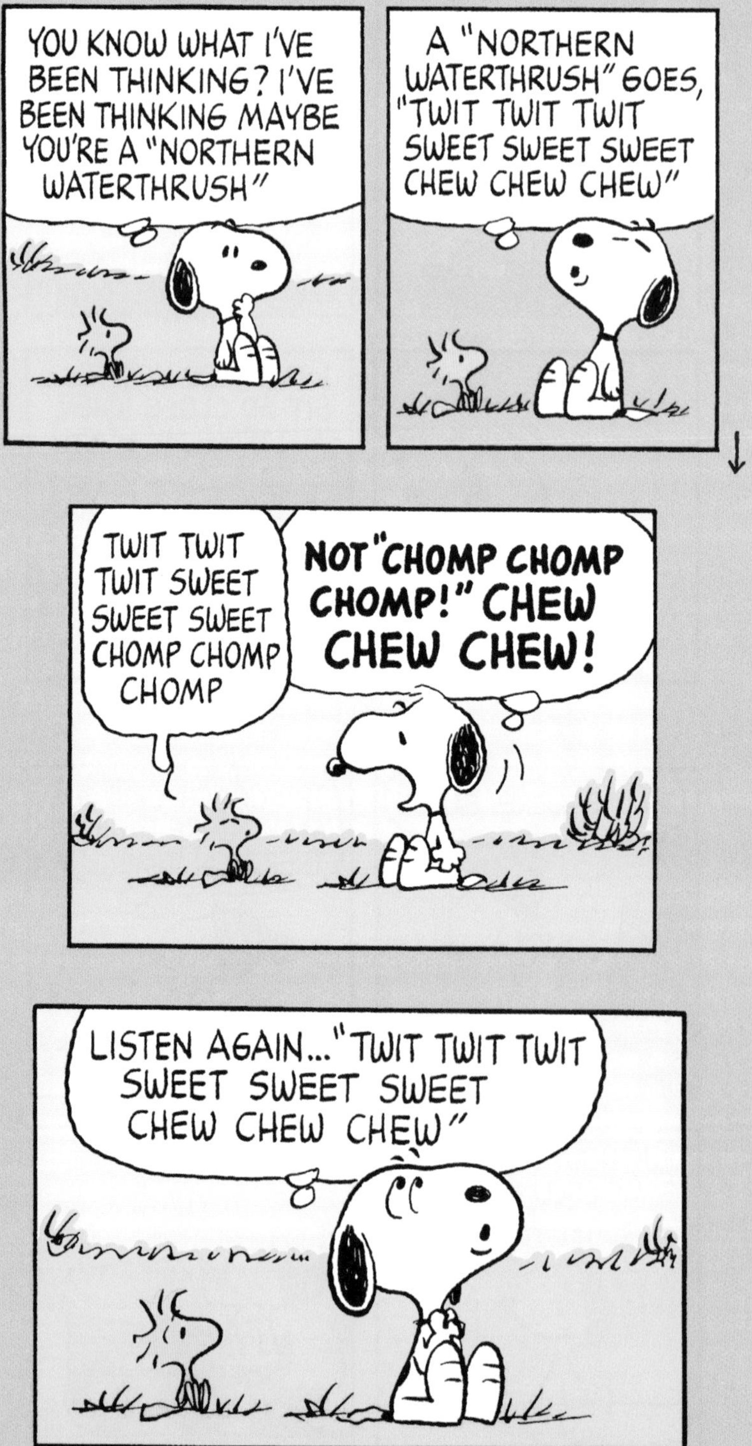
YOU KNOW WHAT I'VE BEEN THINKING? I'VE BEEN THINKING MAYBE YOU'RE A "NORTHERN WATERTHRUSH"
A "NORTHERN WATERTHRUSH" GOES, "TWIT TWIT TWIT SWEET SWEET SWEET CHEW CHEW CHEW"
TWIT TWIT TWIT SWEET SWEET SWEET CHOMP CHOMP CHOMP
NOT "CHOMP CHOMP CHOMP!" CHEW CHEW CHEW!
LISTEN AGAIN..."TWIT TWIT TWIT SWEET SWEET SWEET CHEW CHEW CHEW"

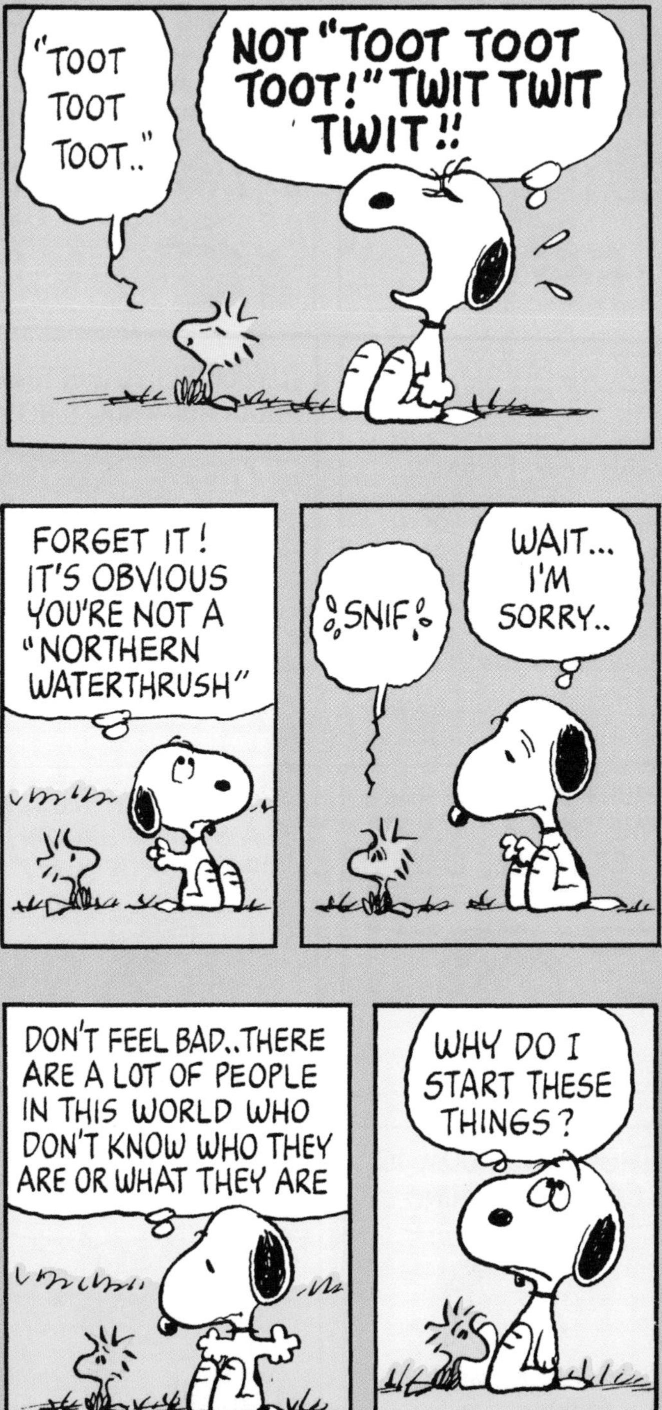
"TOOT TOOT TOOT.."
NOT "TOOT TOOT TOOT!" TWIT TWIT TWIT!!
FORGET IT! IT'S OBVIOUS YOU'RE NOT A "NORTHERN WATERTHRUSH"
SNIF
WAIT... I'M SORRY..
DON'T FEEL BAD..THERE ARE A LOT OF PEOPLE IN THIS WORLD WHO DON'T KNOW WHO THEY ARE OR WHAT THEY ARE
WHY DO I START THESE THINGS?
SCHULZ

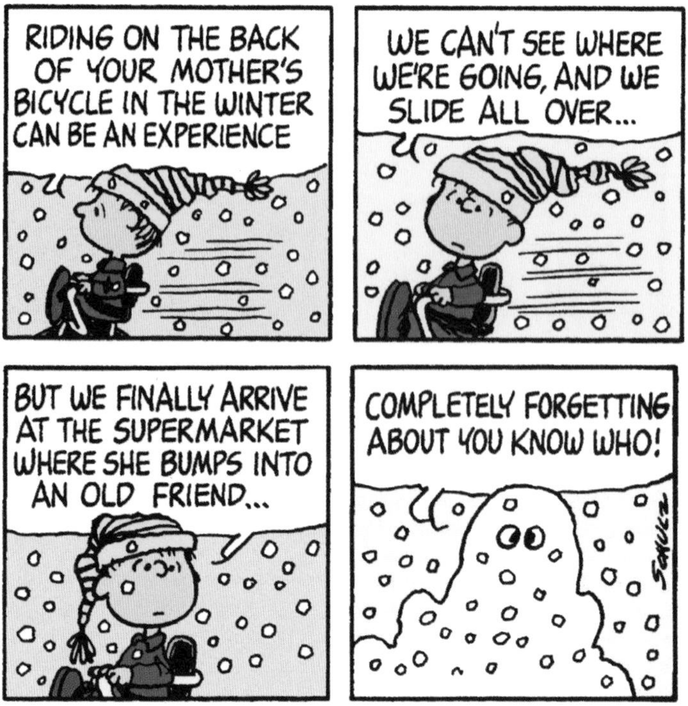
RIDING ON THE BACK OF YOUR MOTHER'S BICYCLE IN THE WINTER CAN BE AN EXPERIENCE
WE CAN'T SEE WHERE WE'RE GOING, AND WE SLIDE ALL OVER...
BUT WE FINALLY ARRIVE AT THE SUPERMARKET WHERE SHE BUMPS INTO AN OLD FRIEND...
COMPLETELY FORGETTING ABOUT YOU KNOW WHO!
SCHULZ

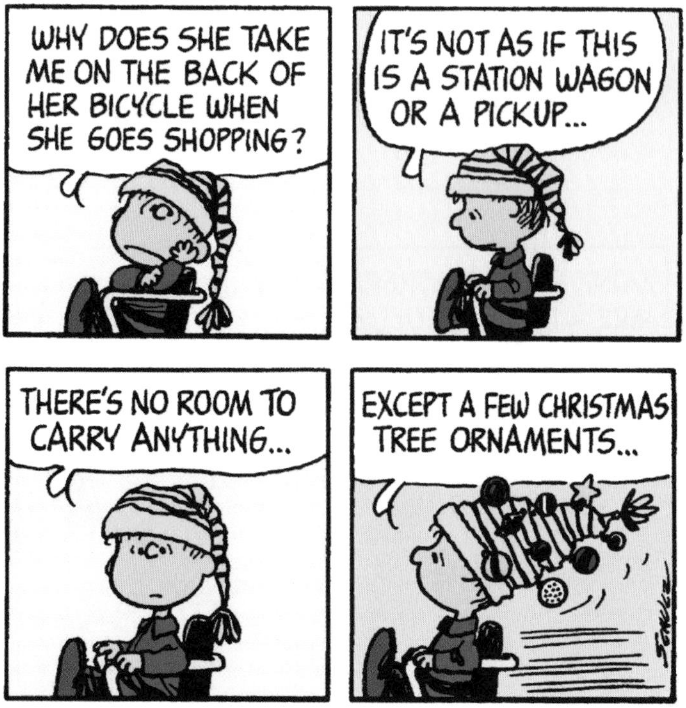
WHY DOES SHE TAKE ME ON THE BACK OF HER BICYCLE WHEN SHE GOES SHOPPING?
IT'S NOT AS IF THIS IS A STATION WAGON OR A PICKUP...
THERE'S NO ROOM TO CARRY ANYTHING...
EXCEPT A FEW CHRISTMAS TREE ORNAMENTS...
SCHULZ

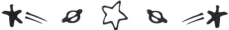

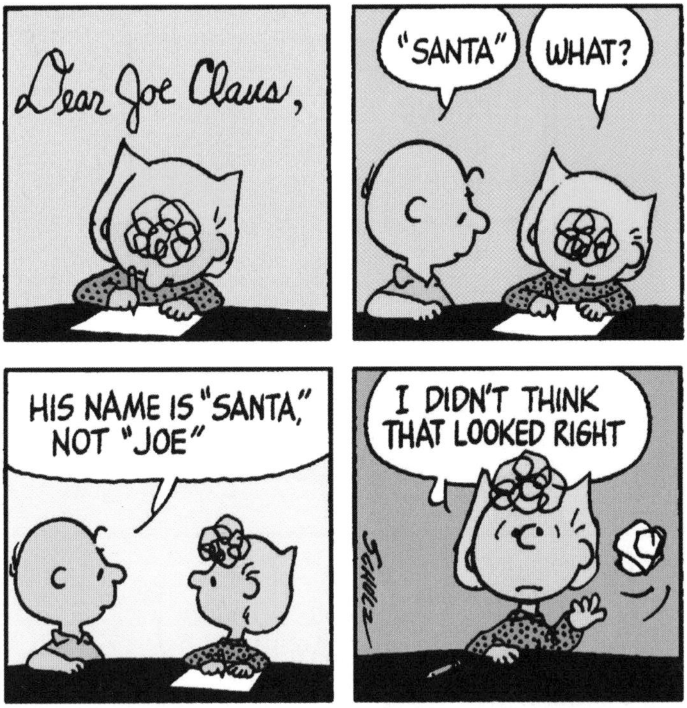
Dear Joe Claus,
"SANTA"
WHAT?
HIS NAME IS "SANTA," NOT "JOE"
I DIDN'T THINK THAT LOOKED RIGHT

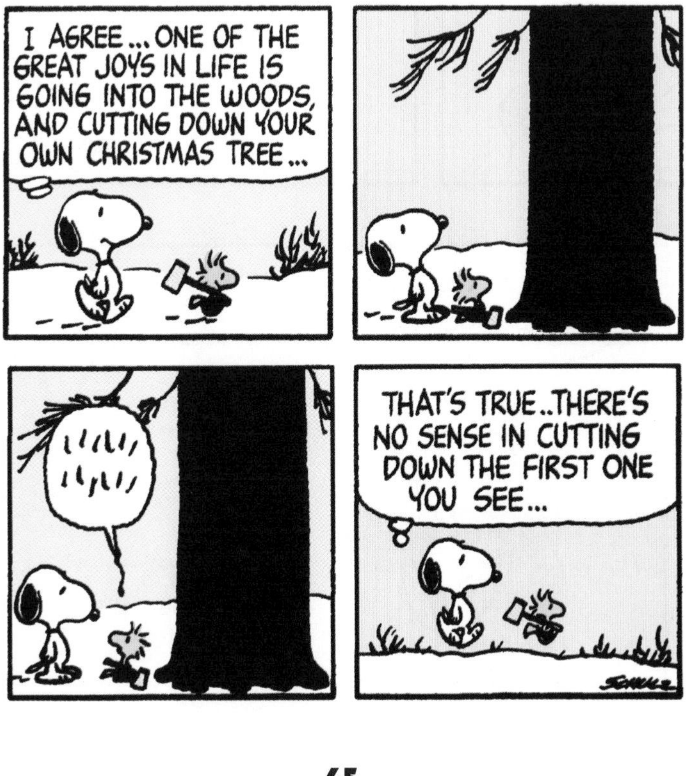
I AGREE... ONE OF THE GREAT JOYS IN LIFE IS GOING INTO THE WOODS, AND CUTTING DOWN YOUR OWN CHRISTMAS TREE...
THAT'S TRUE..THERE'S NO SENSE IN CUTTING DOWN THE FIRST ONE YOU SEE...

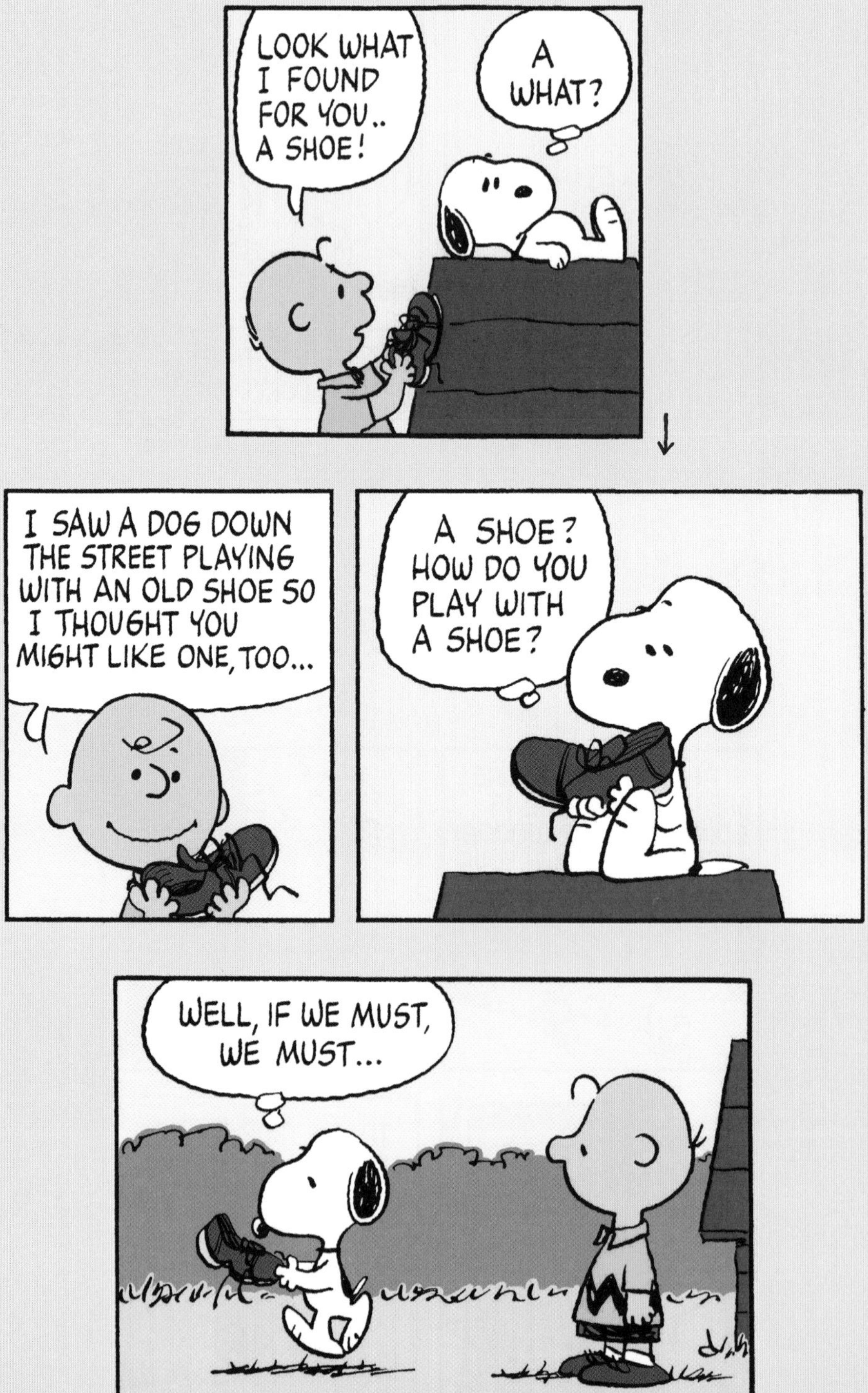
LOOK WHAT I FOUND FOR YOU.. A SHOE!
A WHAT?
I SAW A DOG DOWN THE STREET PLAYING WITH AN OLD SHOE SO I THOUGHT YOU MIGHT LIKE ONE, TOO...
A SHOE? HOW DO YOU PLAY WITH A SHOE?
WELL, IF WE MUST, WE MUST...

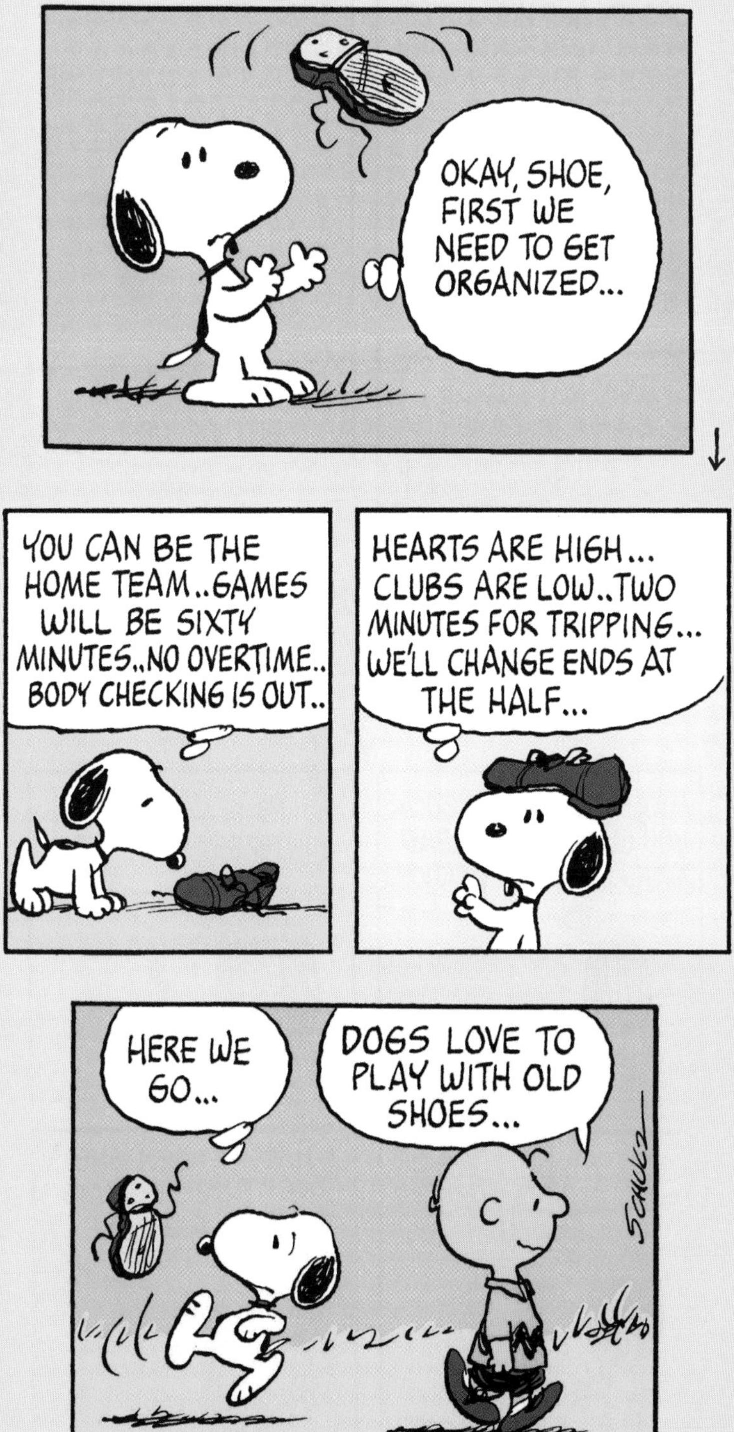
OKAY, SHOE, FIRST WE NEED TO GET ORGANIZED...
YOU CAN BE THE HOME TEAM..GAMES WILL BE SIXTY MINUTES..NO OVERTIME.. BODY CHECKING IS OUT..
HEARTS ARE HIGH... CLUBS ARE LOW..TWO MINUTES FOR TRIPPING... WE'LL CHANGE ENDS AT THE HALF...
HERE WE GO...
DOGS LOVE TO PLAY WITH OLD SHOES...
SCHULZ

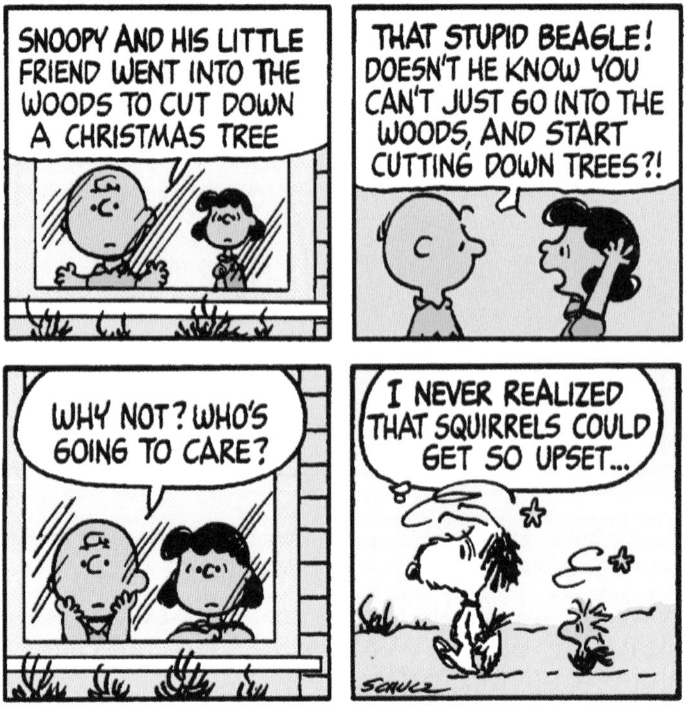
SNOOPY AND HIS LITTLE FRIEND WENT INTO THE WOODS TO CUT DOWN A CHRISTMAS TREE
THAT STUPID BEAGLE! DOESN'T HE KNOW YOU CAN'T JUST GO INTO THE WOODS, AND START CUTTING DOWN TREES?!
WHY NOT? WHO'S GOING TO CARE?
I NEVER REALIZED THAT SQUIRRELS COULD GET SO UPSET...

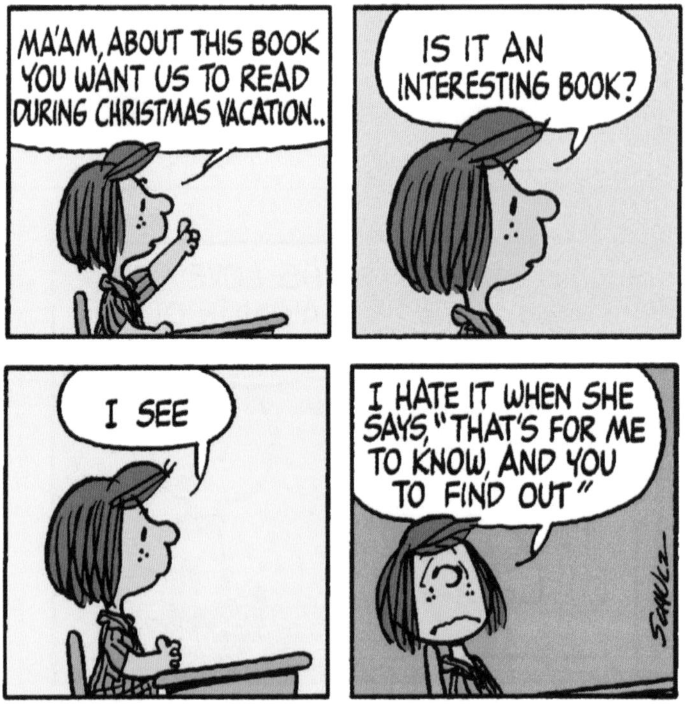
MA'AM, ABOUT THIS BOOK YOU WANT US TO READ DURING CHRISTMAS VACATION..
IS IT AN INTERESTING BOOK?
I SEE
I HATE IT WHEN SHE SAYS, "THAT'S FOR ME TO KNOW, AND YOU TO FIND OUT"

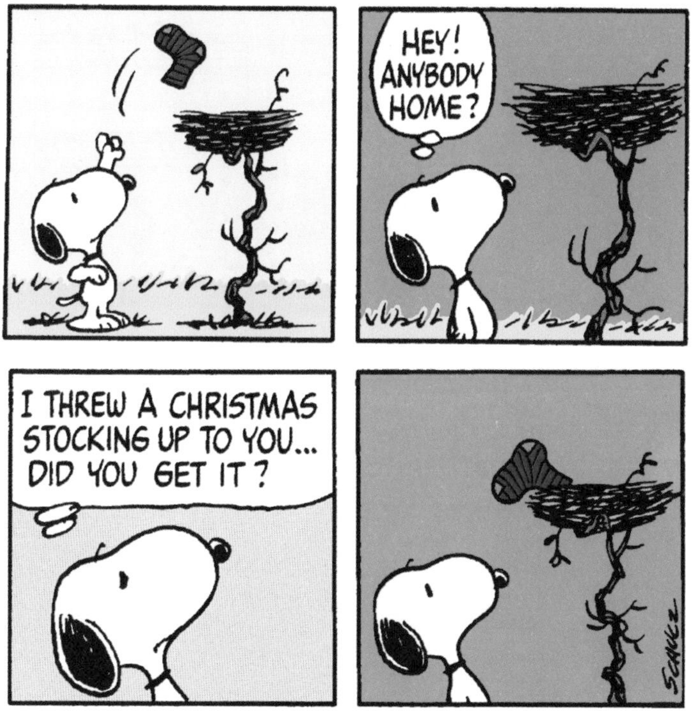
HEY! ANYBODY HOME?
I THREW A CHRISTMAS STOCKING UP TO YOU... DID YOU GET IT?

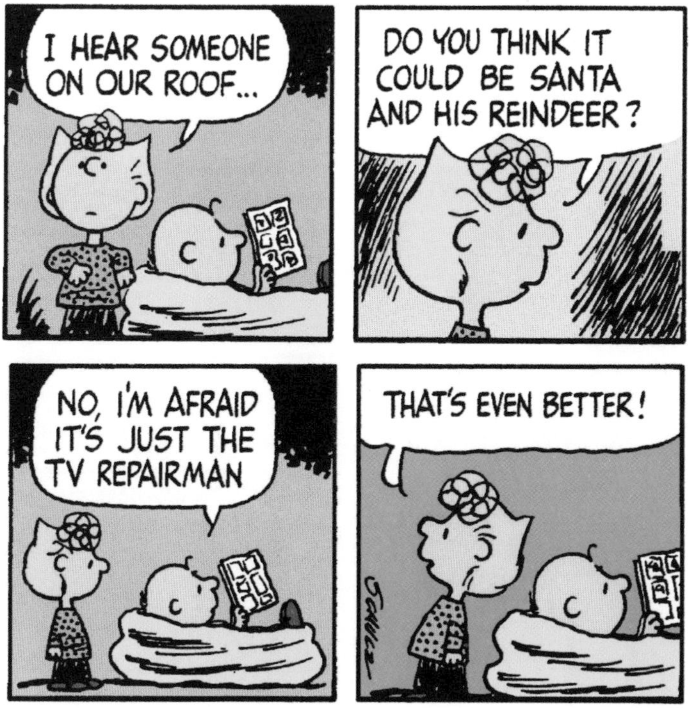
I HEAR SOMEONE ON OUR ROOF...
DO YOU THINK IT COULD BE SANTA AND HIS REINDEER?
NO, I'M AFRAID IT'S JUST THE TV REPAIRMAN
THAT'S EVEN BETTER!

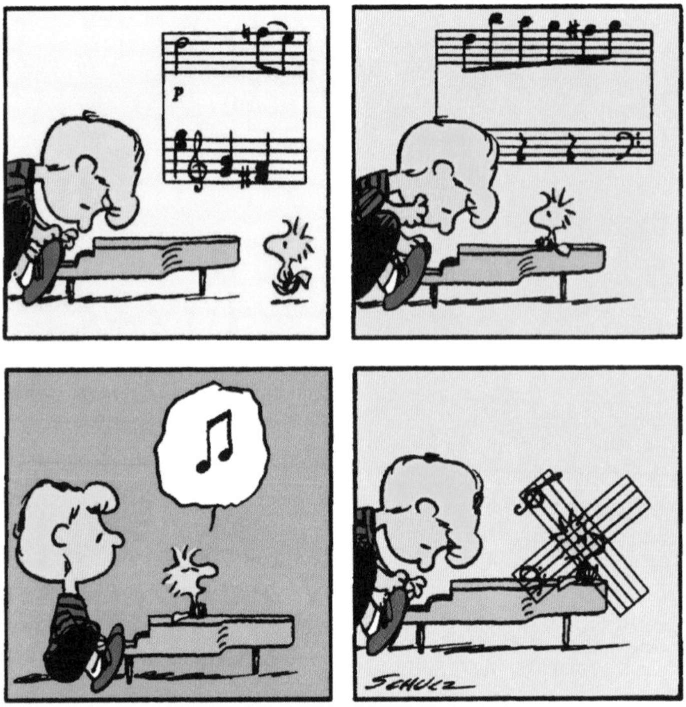

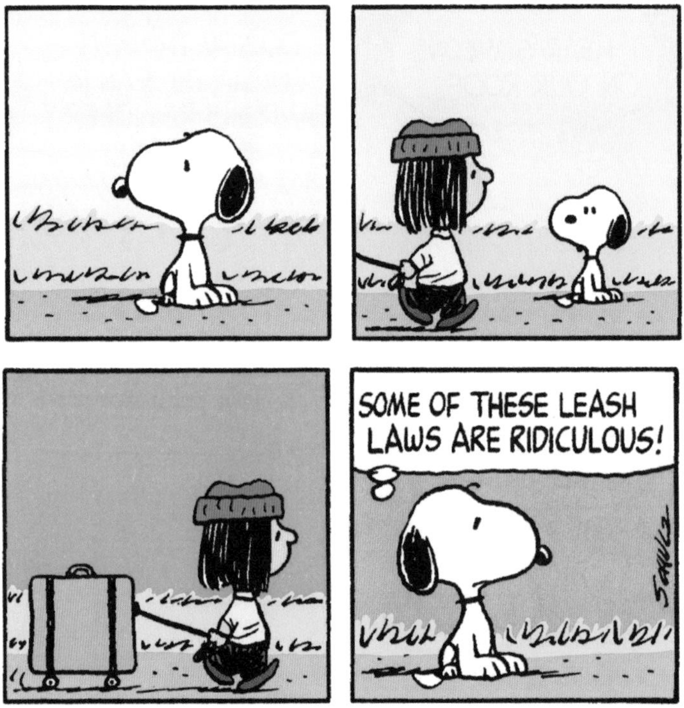
SOME OF THESE LEASH LAWS ARE RIDICULOUS!

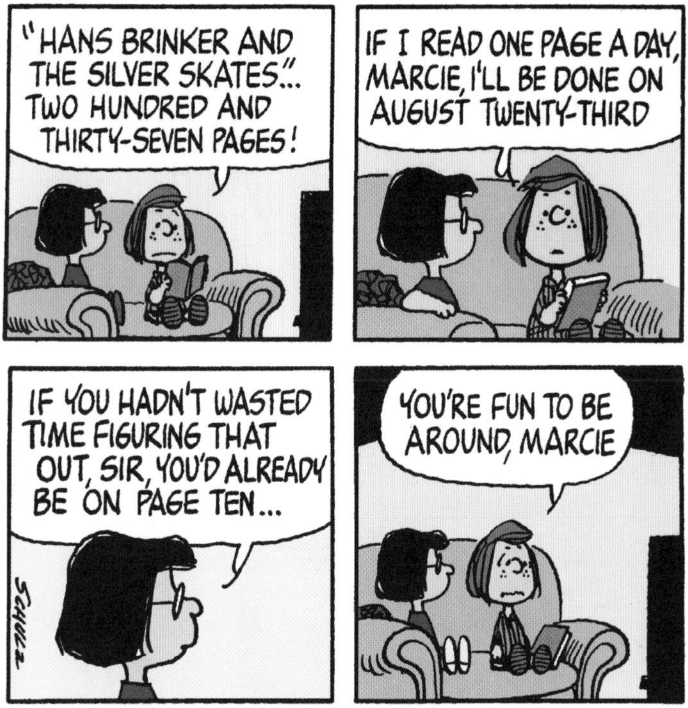
"HANS BRINKER AND THE SILVER SKATES."... TWO HUNDRED AND THIRTY-SEVEN PAGES!
IF I READ ONE PAGE A DAY, MARCIE, I'LL BE DONE ON AUGUST TWENTY-THIRD
IF YOU HADN'T WASTED TIME FIGURING THAT OUT, SIR, YOU'D ALREADY BE ON PAGE TEN...
YOU'RE FUN TO BE AROUND, MARCIE

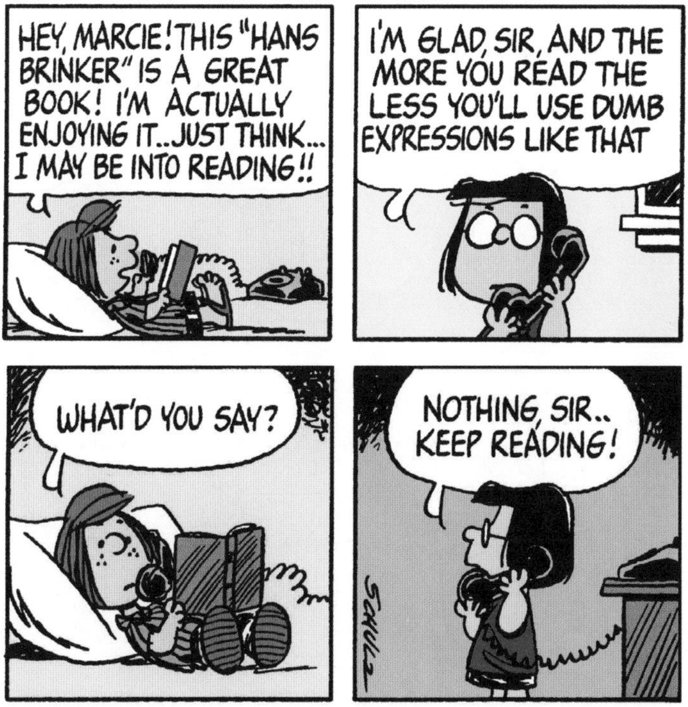
HEY, MARCIE! THIS "HANS BRINKER" IS A GREAT BOOK! I'M ACTUALLY ENJOYING IT...JUST THINK... I MAY BE INTO READING!!
I'M GLAD, SIR, AND THE MORE YOU READ THE LESS YOU'LL USE DUMB EXPRESSIONS LIKE THAT
WHAT'D YOU SAY?
NOTHING, SIR.. KEEP READING!

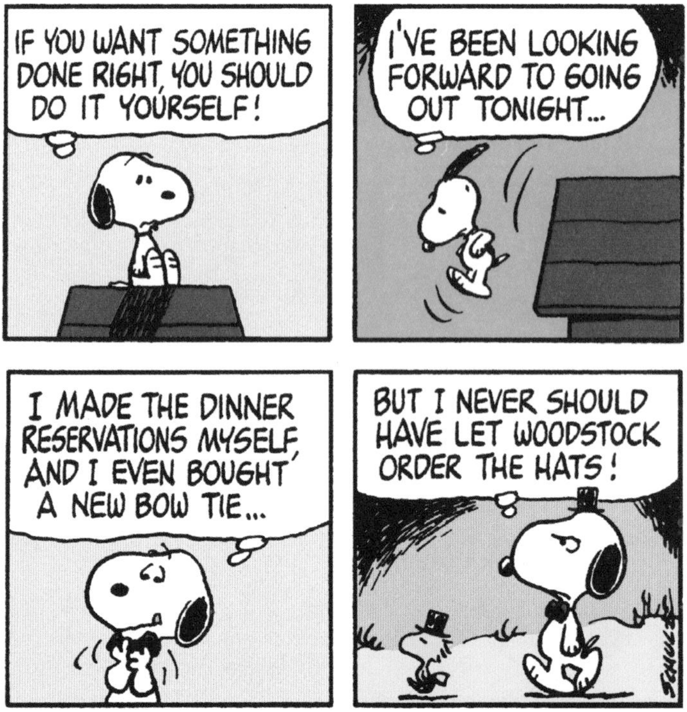
IF YOU WANT SOMETHING DONE RIGHT, YOU SHOULD DO IT YOURSELF!
I'VE BEEN LOOKING FORWARD TO GOING OUT TONIGHT...
I MADE THE DINNER RESERVATIONS MYSELF, AND I EVEN BOUGHT A NEW BOW TIE...
BUT I NEVER SHOULD HAVE LET WOODSTOCK ORDER THE HATS!

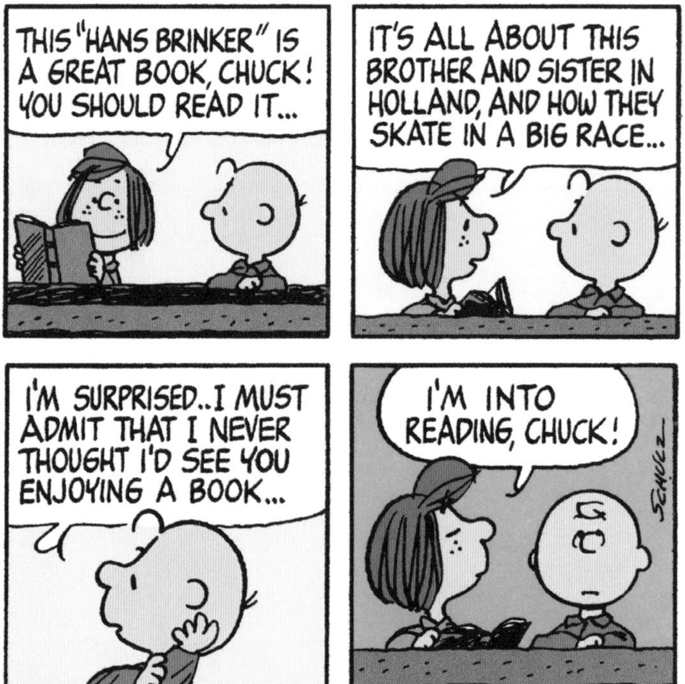
THIS "HANS BRINKER" IS A GREAT BOOK, CHUCK! YOU SHOULD READ IT...
IT'S ALL ABOUT THIS BROTHER AND SISTER IN HOLLAND, AND HOW THEY SKATE IN A BIG RACE...
I'M SURPRISED..I MUST ADMIT THAT I NEVER THOUGHT I'D SEE YOU ENJOYING A BOOK...
I'M INTO READING, CHUCK!

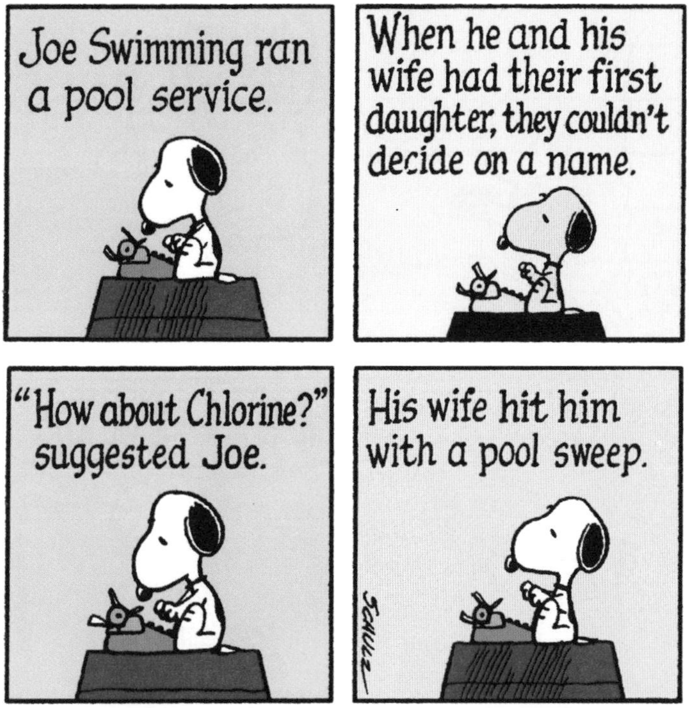
Joe Swimming ran a pool service.
When he and his wife had their first daughter, they couldn't decide on a name.
"How about Chlorine?" suggested Joe.
His wife hit him with a pool sweep.
SCHULZ

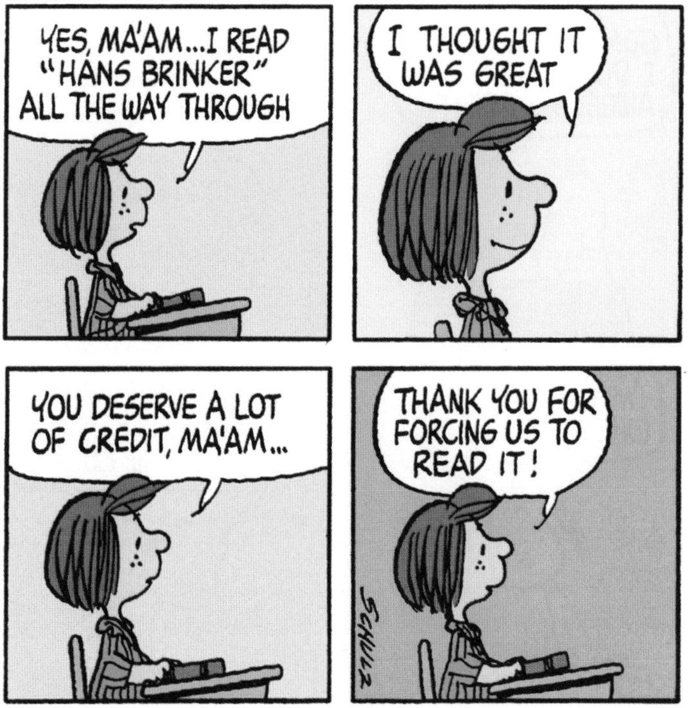
YES, MA'AM...I READ "HANS BRINKER" ALL THE WAY THROUGH
I THOUGHT IT WAS GREAT
YOU DESERVE A LOT OF CREDIT, MA'AM...
THANK YOU FOR FORCING US TO READ IT!
SCHULZ

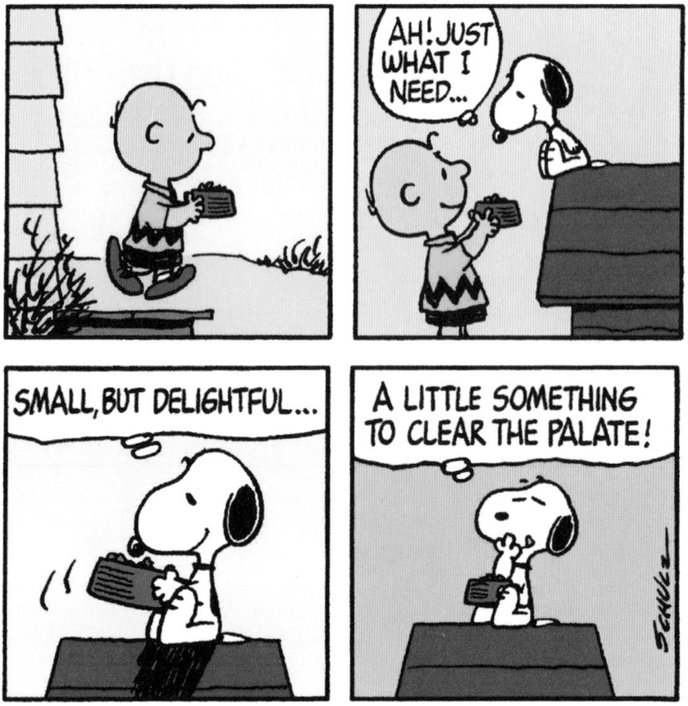
AH! JUST WHAT I NEED...
SMALL, BUT DELIGHTFUL...
A LITTLE SOMETHING TO CLEAR THE PALATE!

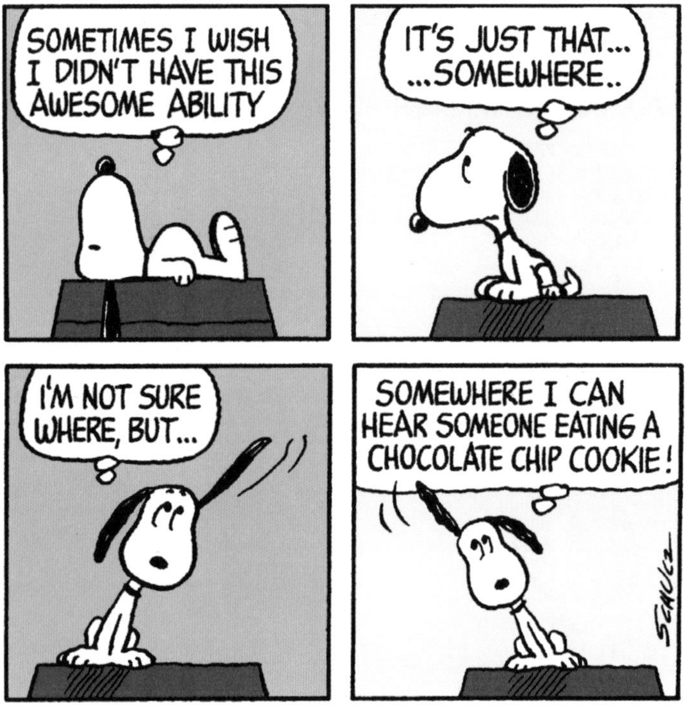
SOMETIMES I WISH I DIDN'T HAVE THIS AWESOME ABILITY
IT'S JUST THAT... ...SOMEWHERE..
I'M NOT SURE WHERE, BUT...
SOMEWHERE I CAN HEAR SOMEONE EATING A CHOCOLATE CHIP COOKIE!

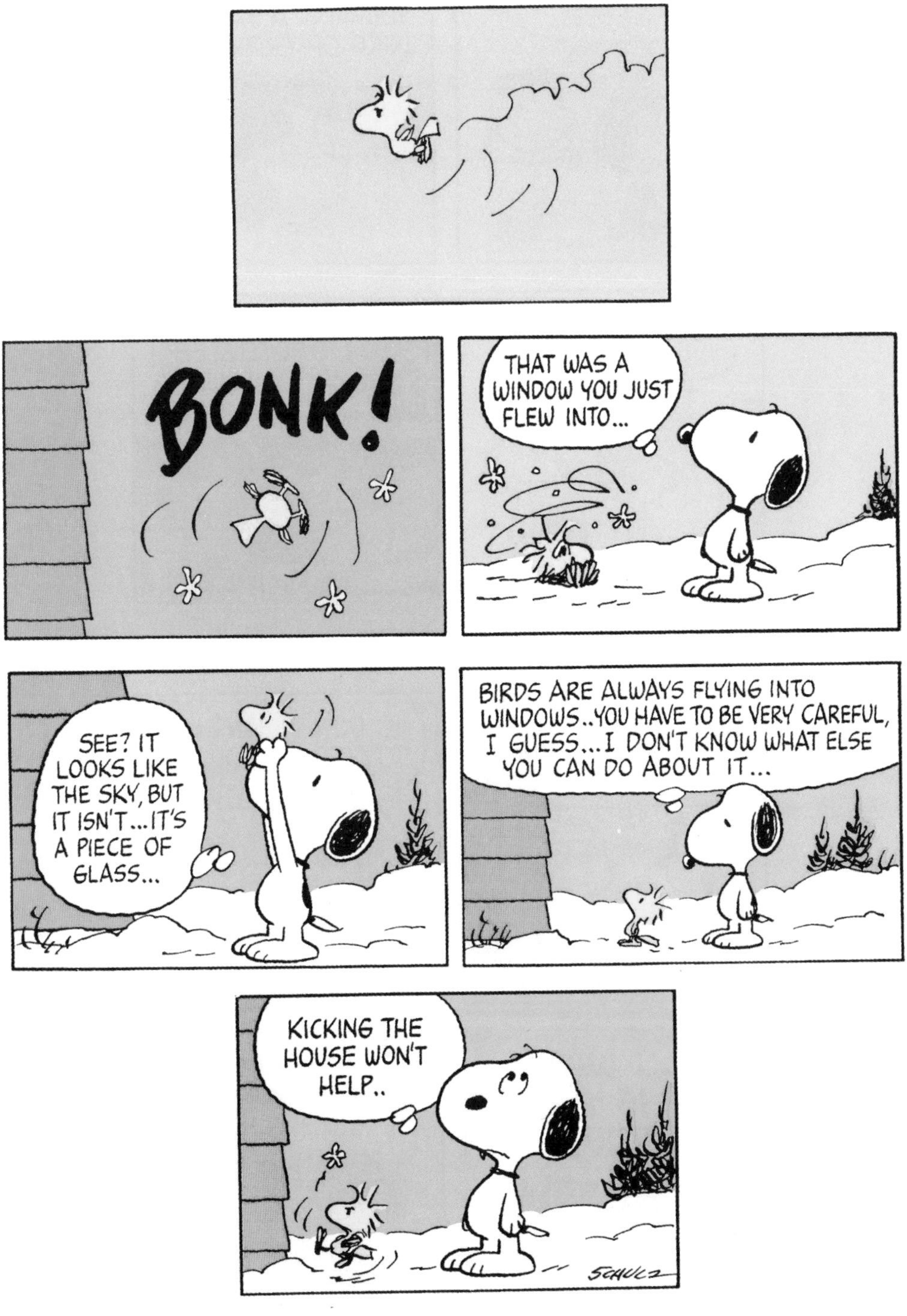
BONK!
THAT WAS A WINDOW YOU JUST FLEW INTO...
SEE? IT LOOKS LIKE THE SKY, BUT IT ISN'T...IT'S A PIECE OF GLASS...
BIRDS ARE ALWAYS FLYING INTO WINDOWS..YOU HAVE TO BE VERY CAREFUL, I GUESS...I DON'T KNOW WHAT ELSE YOU CAN DO ABOUT IT...
KICKING THE HOUSE WON'T HELP..
SCHULZ

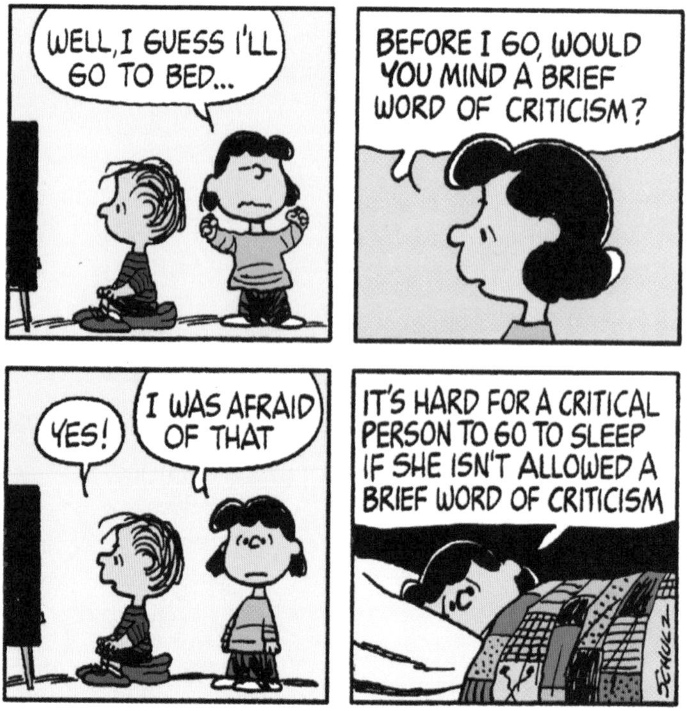
WELL, I GUESS I'LL GO TO BED...
BEFORE I GO, WOULD YOU MIND A BRIEF WORD OF CRITICISM?
YES!
I WAS AFRAID OF THAT
IT'S HARD FOR A CRITICAL PERSON TO GO TO SLEEP IF SHE ISN'T ALLOWED A BRIEF WORD OF CRITICISM
SCHULZ

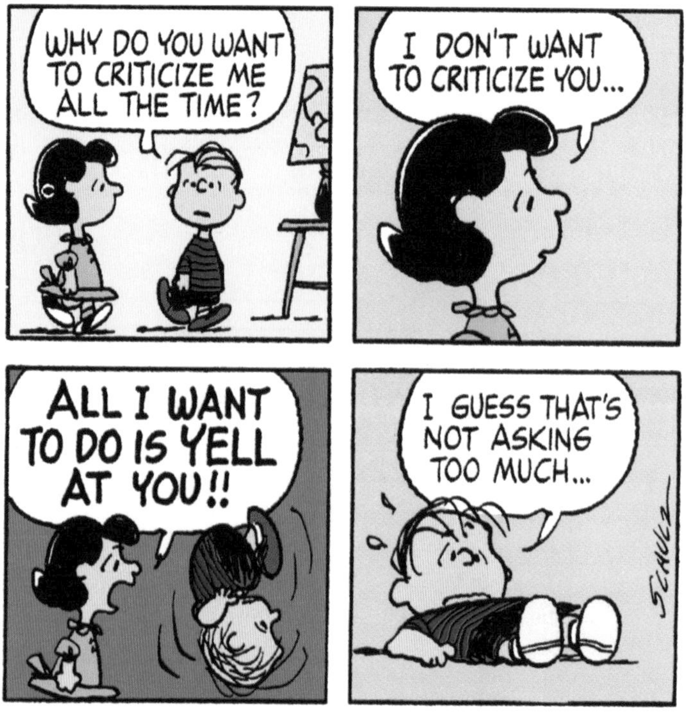
WHY DO YOU WANT TO CRITICIZE ME ALL THE TIME?
I DON'T WANT TO CRITICIZE YOU...
ALL I WANT TO DO IS YELL AT YOU!!
I GUESS THAT'S NOT ASKING TOO MUCH...
SCHULZ

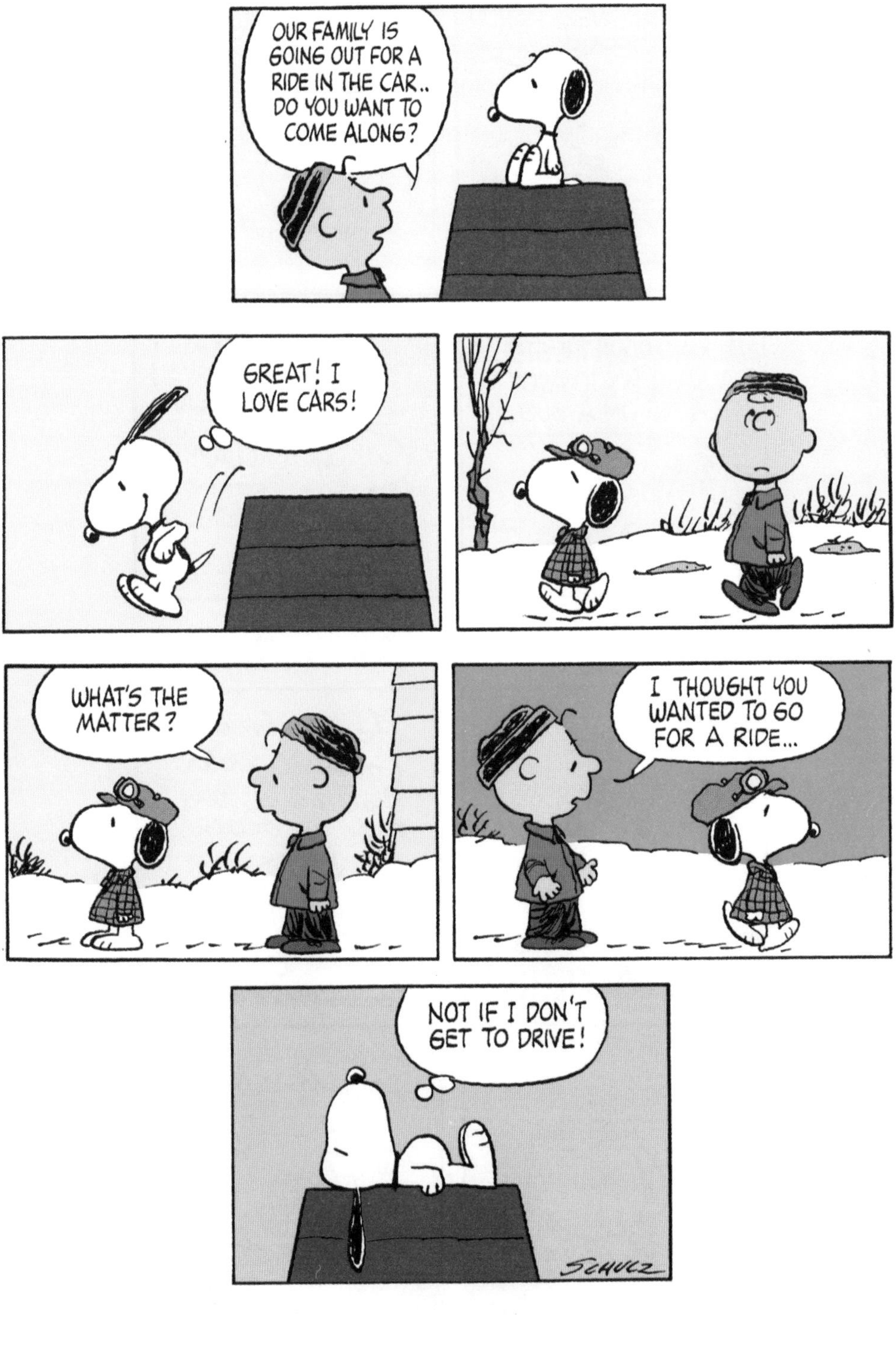
OUR FAMILY IS GOING OUT FOR A RIDE IN THE CAR.. DO YOU WANT TO COME ALONG?
GREAT! I LOVE CARS!
WHAT'S THE MATTER?
I THOUGHT YOU WANTED TO GO FOR A RIDE...
NOT IF I DON'T GET TO DRIVE!
SCHULZ

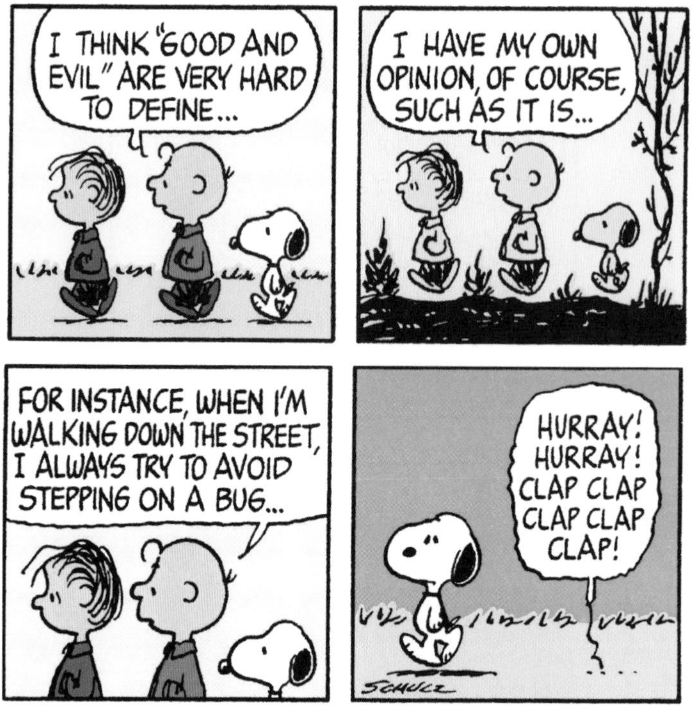
I THINK "GOOD AND EVIL" ARE VERY HARD TO DEFINE...
I HAVE MY OWN OPINION, OF COURSE, SUCH AS IT IS...
FOR INSTANCE, WHEN I'M WALKING DOWN THE STREET, I ALWAYS TRY TO AVOID STEPPING ON A BUG...
HURRAY! HURRAY! CLAP CLAP CLAP CLAP CLAP!
SCHULZ

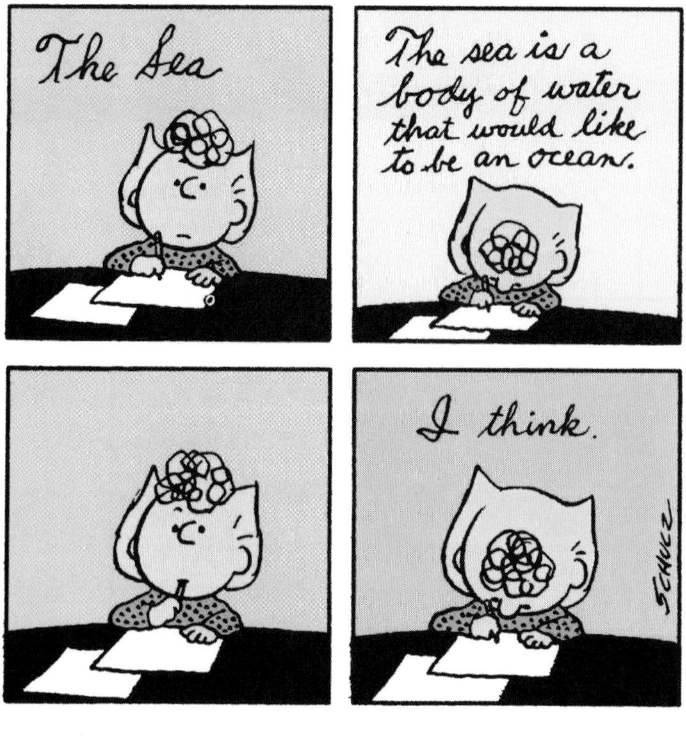
The Sea
The sea is a body of water that would like to be an ocean.
I think.
SCHULZ

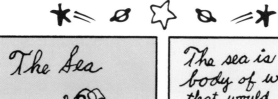

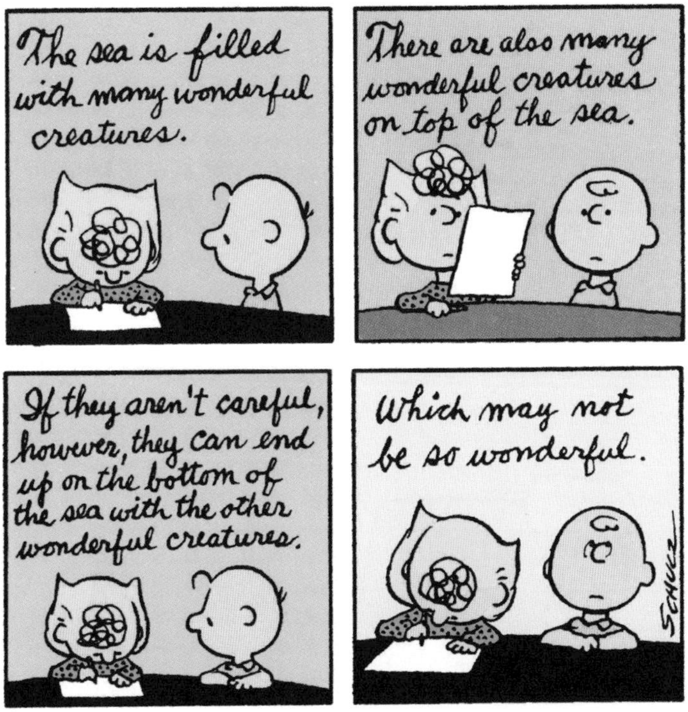
The sea is filled with many wonderful creatures.
There are also many wonderful creatures on top of the sea.
If they aren't careful, however, they can end up on the bottom of the sea with the other wonderful creatures.
Which may not be so wonderful.
SCHULZ

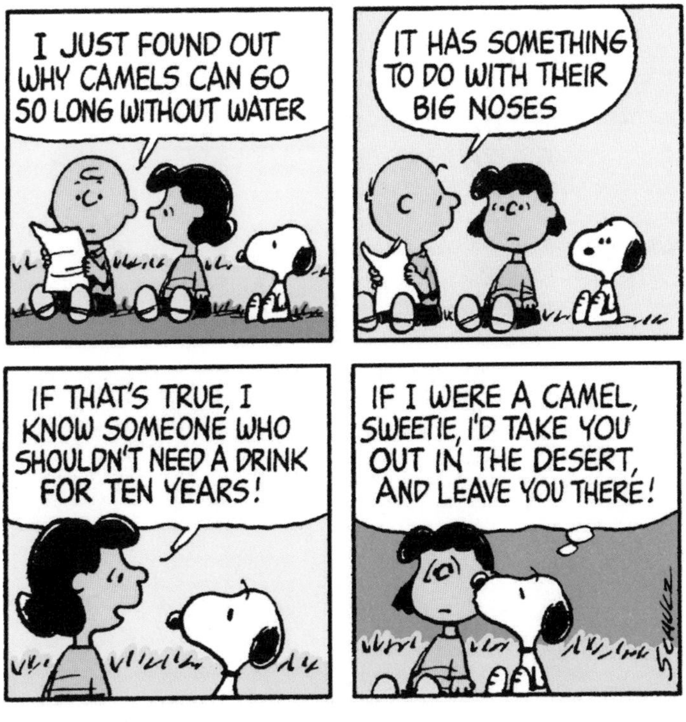
I JUST FOUND OUT WHY CAMELS CAN GO SO LONG WITHOUT WATER
IT HAS SOMETHING TO DO WITH THEIR BIG NOSES
IF THAT'S TRUE, I KNOW SOMEONE WHO SHOULDN'T NEED A DRINK FOR TEN YEARS!
IF I WERE A CAMEL, SWEETIE, I'D TAKE YOU OUT IN THE DESERT, AND LEAVE YOU THERE!
SCHULZ

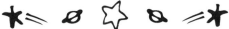

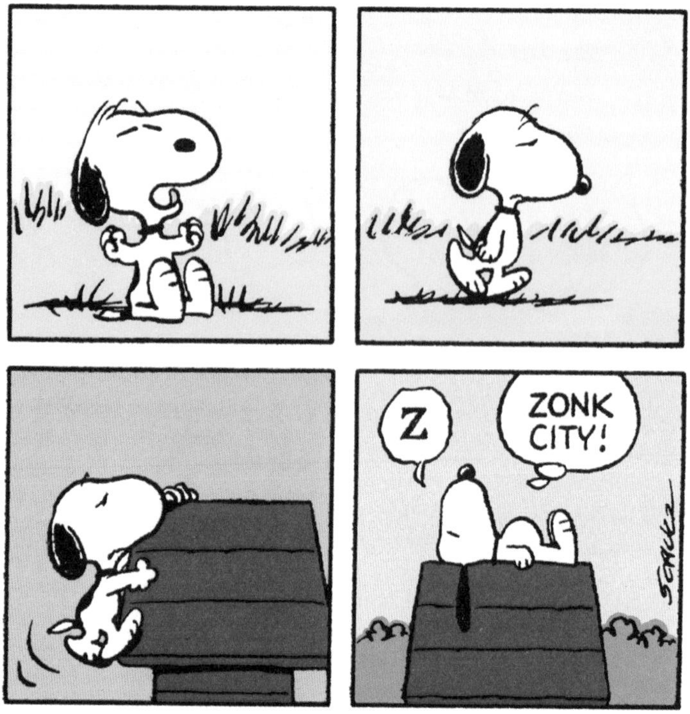
Z
ZONK CITY!

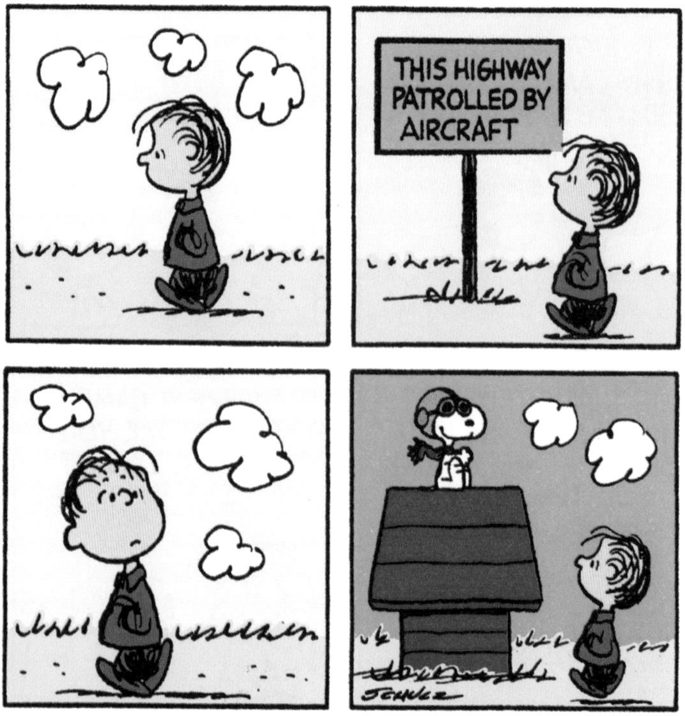
THIS HIGHWAY PATROLLED BY AIRCRAFT

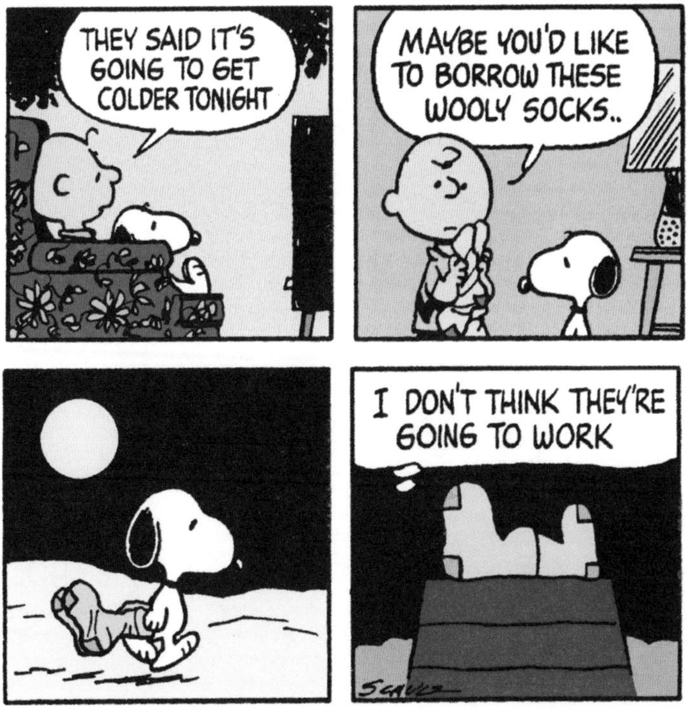
THEY SAID IT'S GOING TO GET COLDER TONIGHT
MAYBE YOU'D LIKE TO BORROW THESE WOOLY SOCKS..
I DON'T THINK THEY'RE GOING TO WORK

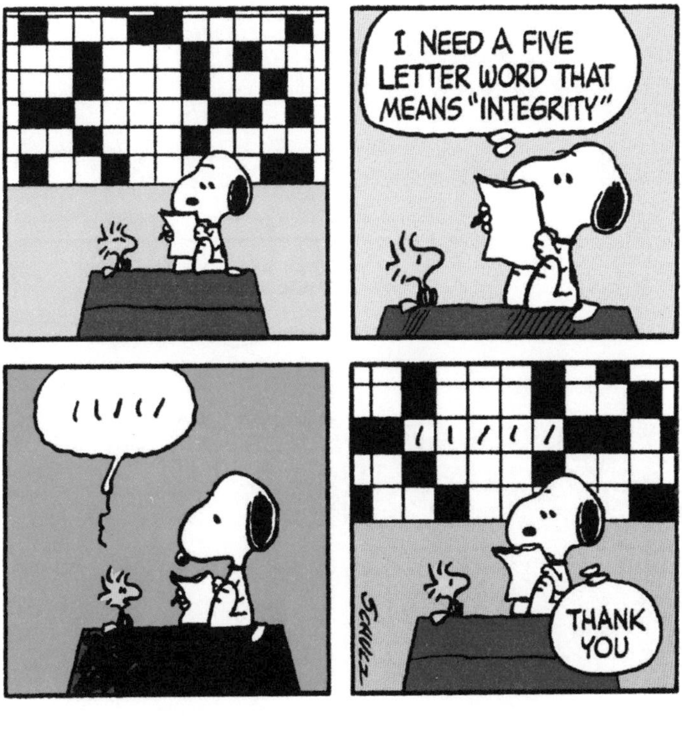
I NEED A FIVE LETTER WORD THAT MEANS "INTEGRITY"
THANK YOU

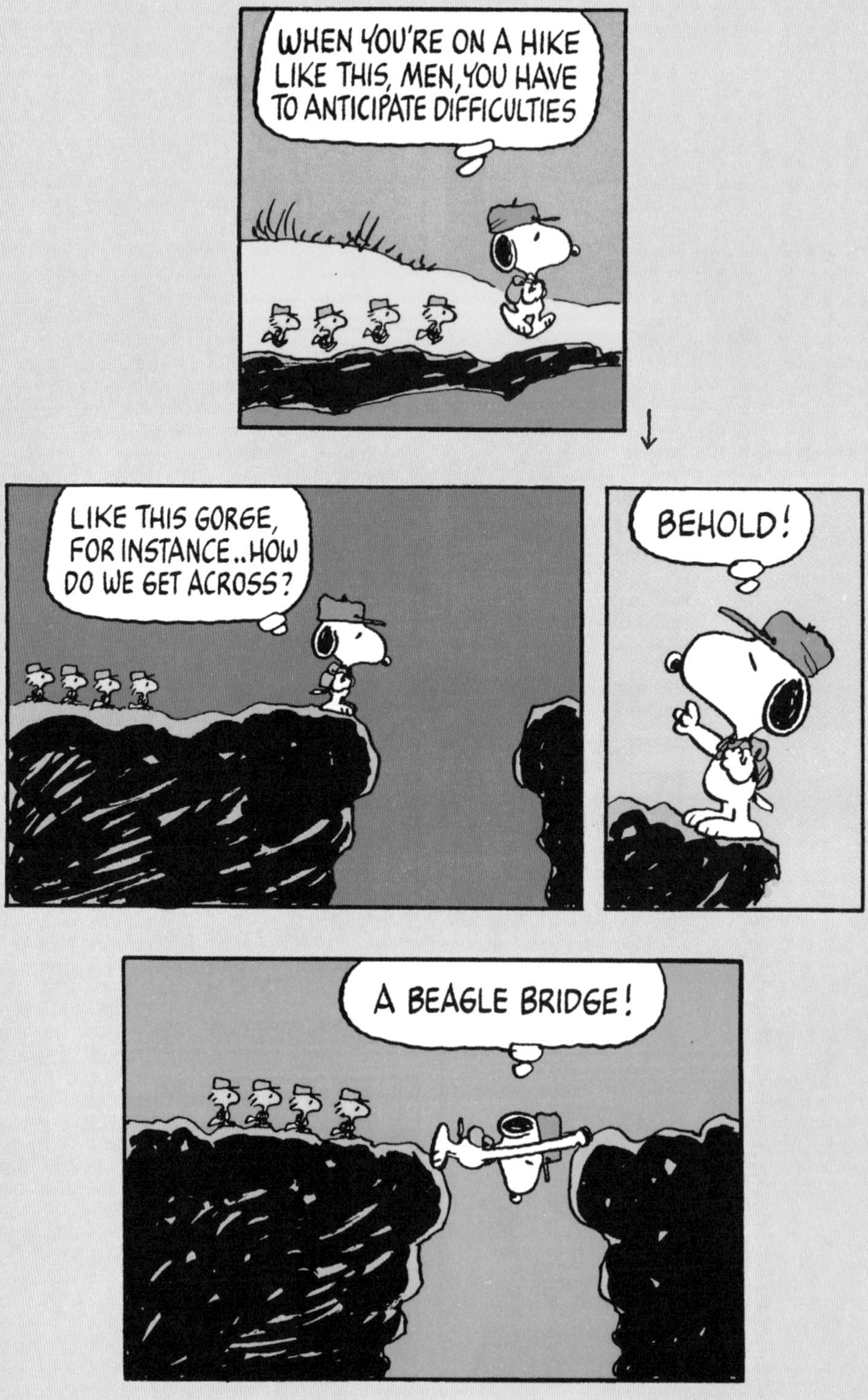
WHEN YOU'RE ON A HIKE LIKE THIS, MEN, YOU HAVE TO ANTICIPATE DIFFICULTIES
LIKE THIS GORGE, FOR INSTANCE..HOW DO WE GET ACROSS?
BEHOLD!
A BEAGLE BRIDGE!

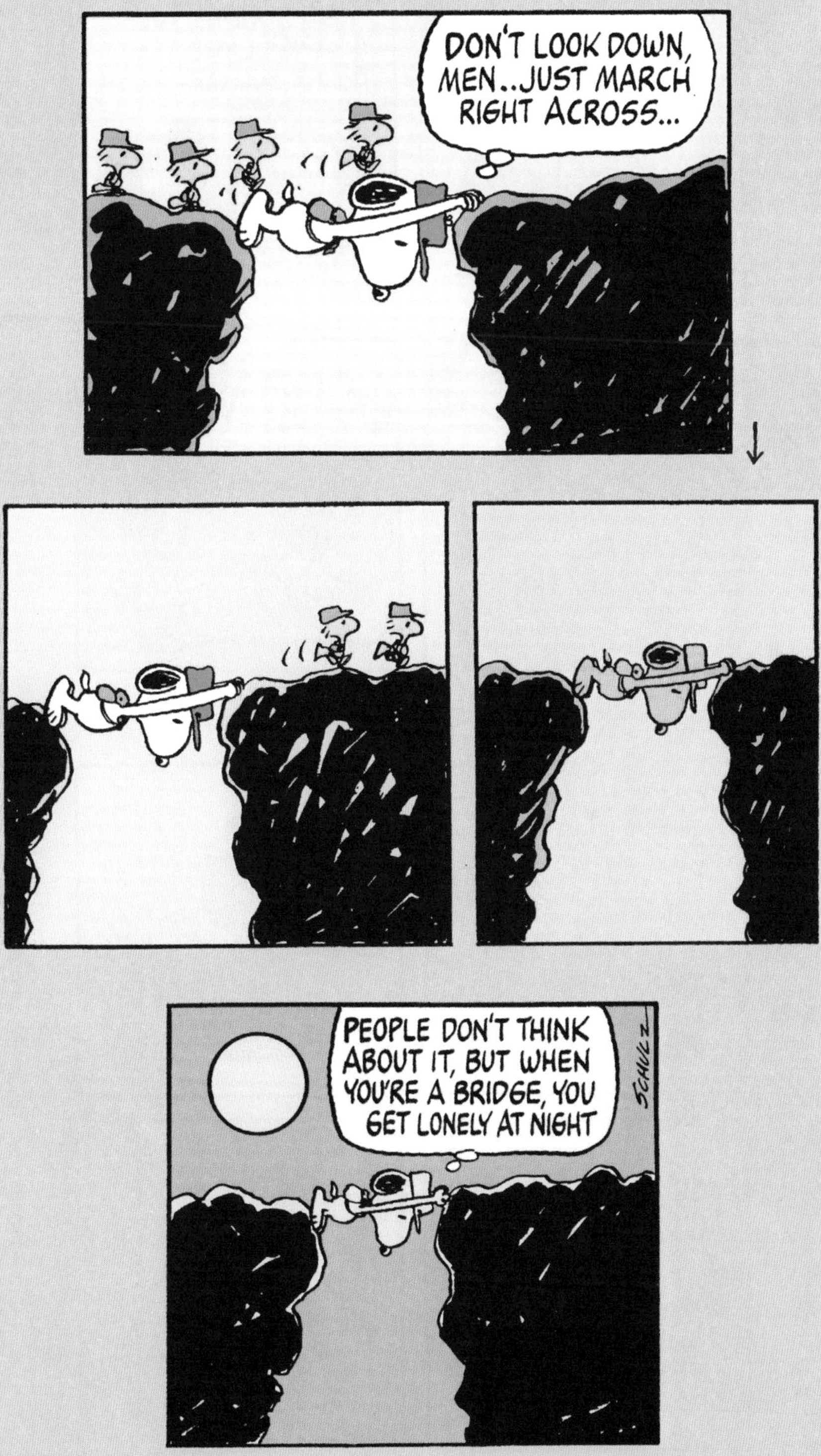
DON'T LOOK DOWN, MEN..JUST MARCH RIGHT ACROSS...
PEOPLE DON'T THINK ABOUT IT, BUT WHEN YOU'RE A BRIDGE, YOU GET LONELY AT NIGHT
SCHULZ

DO YOU REALIZE I HAVEN'T YELLED AT YOU ALL DAY ?
THAT'S RIGHT, AND I APPRECIATE IT... THANK YOU VERY MUCH
YOU'RE WELCOME
GOOD NIGHT!

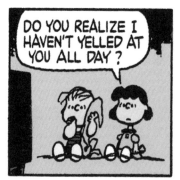

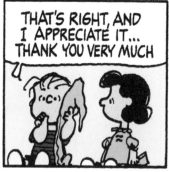

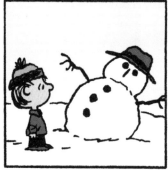

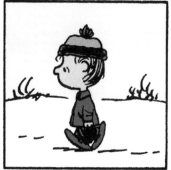

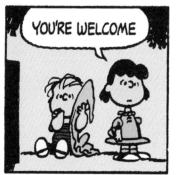

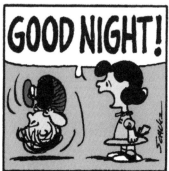

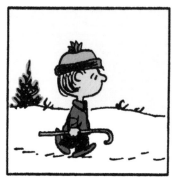

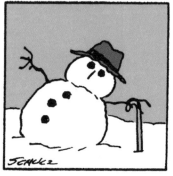

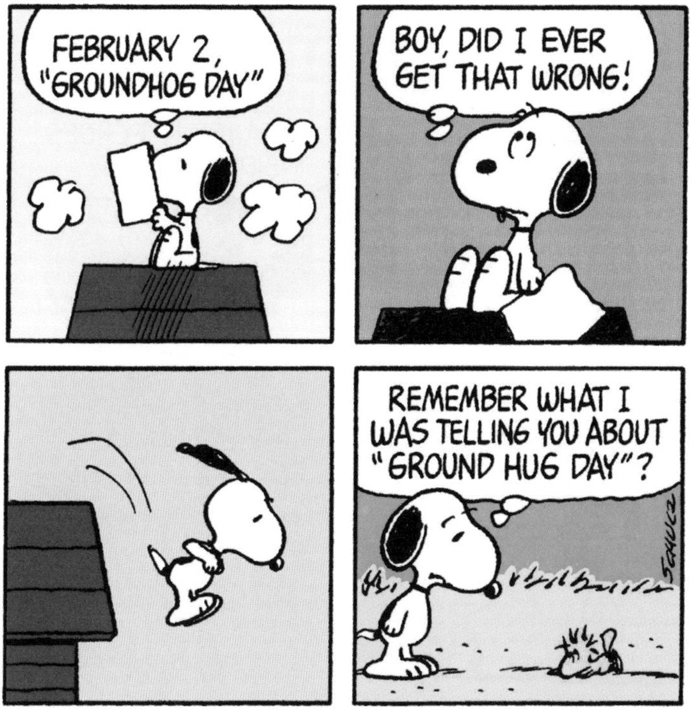
FEBRUARY 2, "GROUNDHOG DAY"
BOY, DID I EVER GET THAT WRONG!
REMEMBER WHAT I WAS TELLING YOU ABOUT "GROUND HUG DAY"?
SCHULZ

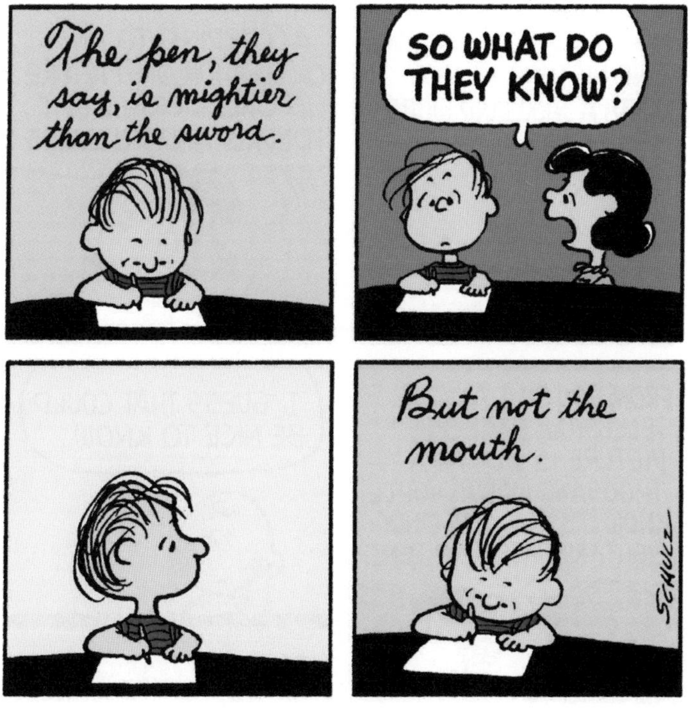
The pen, they say, is mightier than the sword.
SO WHAT DO THEY KNOW?
But not the mouth.
SCHULZ

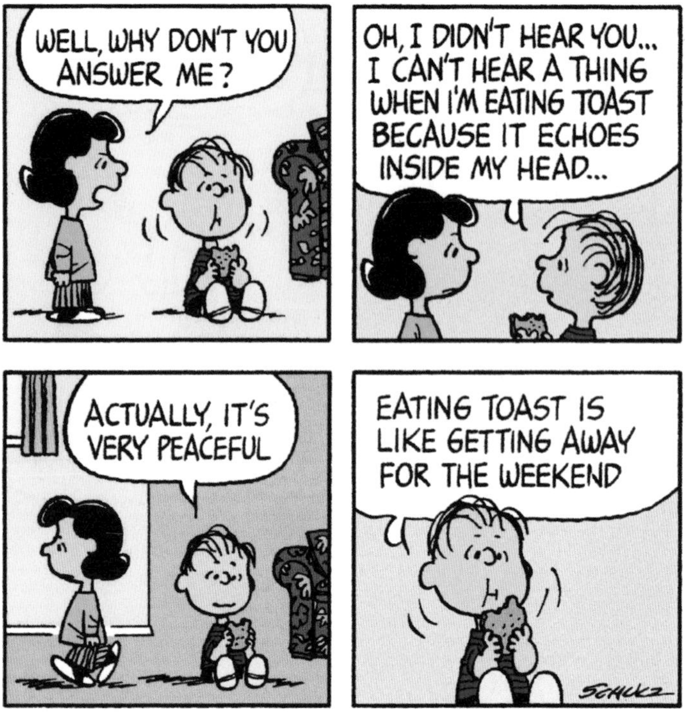
WELL, WHY DON'T YOU ANSWER ME?
OH, I DIDN'T HEAR YOU... I CAN'T HEAR A THING WHEN I'M EATING TOAST BECAUSE IT ECHOES INSIDE MY HEAD...
ACTUALLY, IT'S VERY PEACEFUL
EATING TOAST IS LIKE GETTING AWAY FOR THE WEEKEND

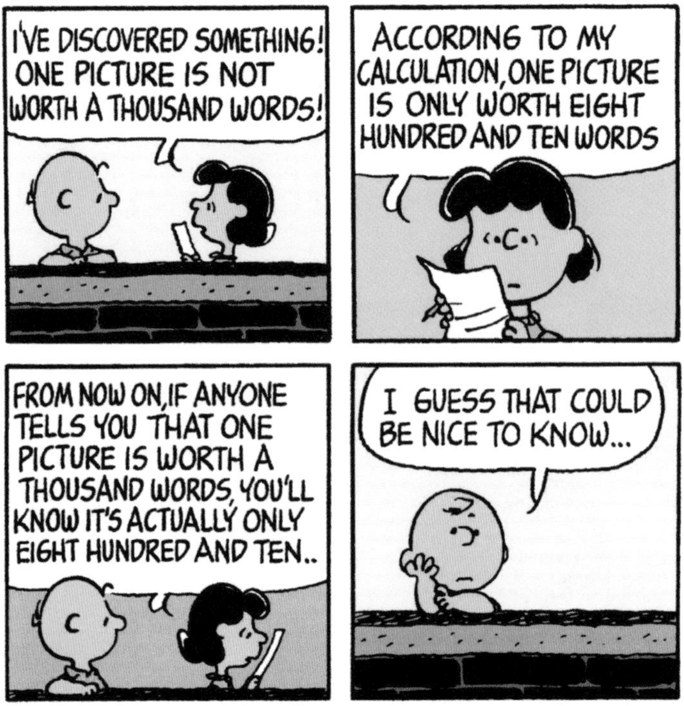
I'VE DISCOVERED SOMETHING! ONE PICTURE IS NOT WORTH A THOUSAND WORDS!
ACCORDING TO MY CALCULATION, ONE PICTURE IS ONLY WORTH EIGHT HUNDRED AND TEN WORDS
FROM NOW ON, IF ANYONE TELLS YOU THAT ONE PICTURE IS WORTH A THOUSAND WORDS, YOU'LL KNOW IT'S ACTUALLY ONLY EIGHT HUNDRED AND TEN..
I GUESS THAT COULD BE NICE TO KNOW...

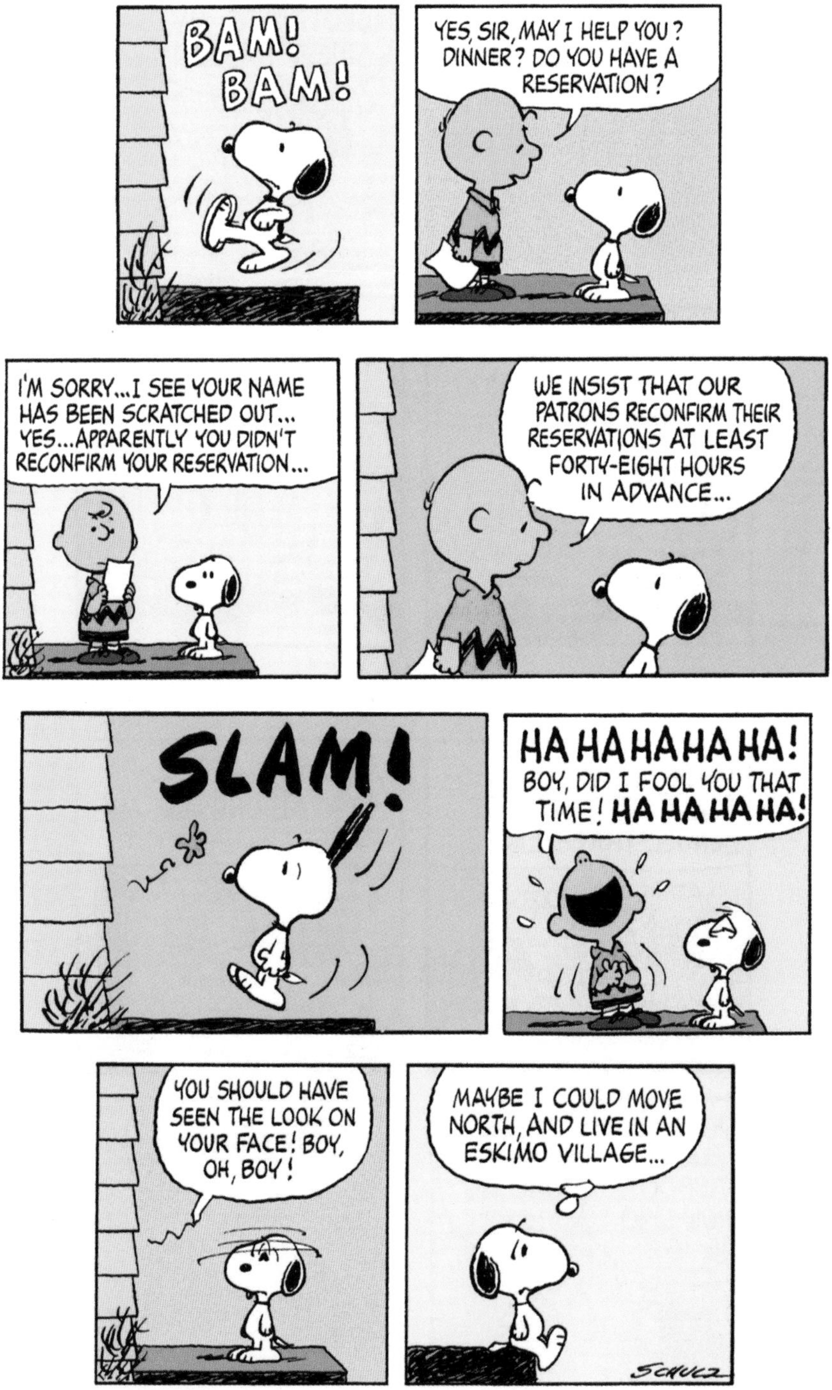
BAM! BAM!
YES, SIR, MAY I HELP YOU? DINNER? DO YOU HAVE A RESERVATION?
I'M SORRY...I SEE YOUR NAME HAS BEEN SCRATCHED OUT... YES...APPARENTLY YOU DIDN'T RECONFIRM YOUR RESERVATION...
WE INSIST THAT OUR PATRONS RECONFIRM THEIR RESERVATIONS AT LEAST FORTY-EIGHT HOURS IN ADVANCE...
SLAM!
HA HA HA HA HA! BOY, DID I FOOL YOU THAT TIME! HA HA HA HA!
YOU SHOULD HAVE SEEN THE LOOK ON YOUR FACE! BOY, OH, BOY!
MAYBE I COULD MOVE NORTH, AND LIVE IN AN ESKIMO VILLAGE...
SCHULZ

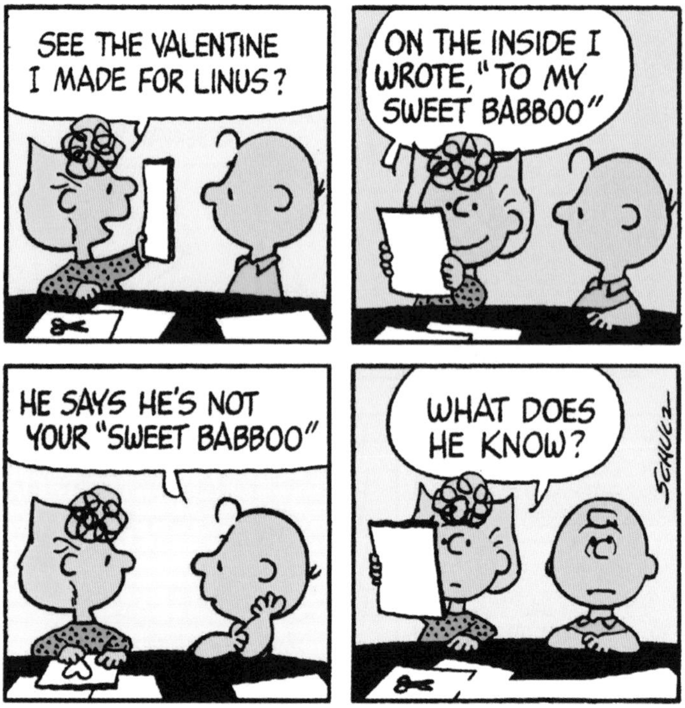
SEE THE VALENTINE I MADE FOR LINUS?
ON THE INSIDE I WROTE, "TO MY SWEET BABBOO"
HE SAYS HE'S NOT YOUR "SWEET BABBOO"
WHAT DOES HE KNOW?

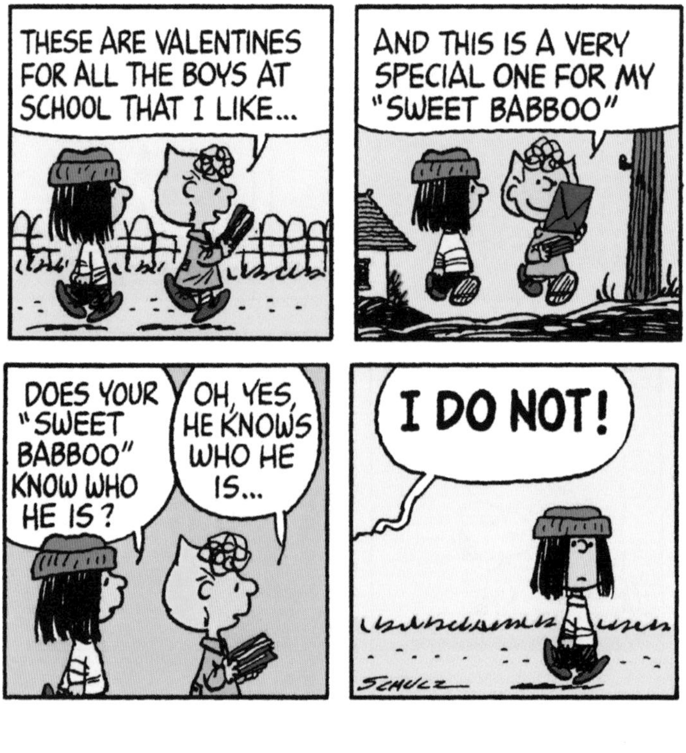
THESE ARE VALENTINES FOR ALL THE BOYS AT SCHOOL THAT I LIKE...
AND THIS IS A VERY SPECIAL ONE FOR MY "SWEET BABBOO"
DOES YOUR "SWEET BABBOO" KNOW WHO HE IS?
OH, YES, HE KNOWS WHO HE IS...
I DO NOT!

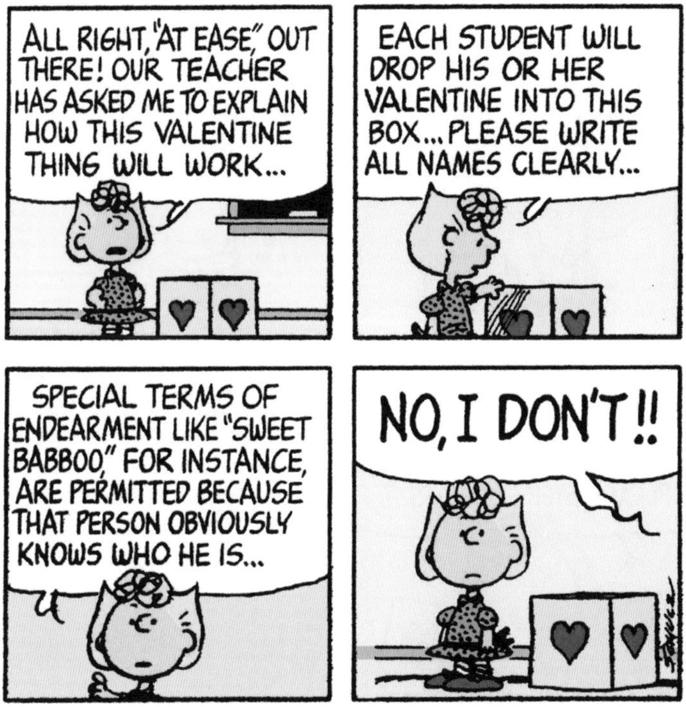
ALL RIGHT, "AT EASE" OUT THERE! OUR TEACHER HAS ASKED ME TO EXPLAIN HOW THIS VALENTINE THING WILL WORK...
EACH STUDENT WILL DROP HIS OR HER VALENTINE INTO THIS BOX... PLEASE WRITE ALL NAMES CLEARLY...
SPECIAL TERMS OF ENDEARMENT LIKE "SWEET BABBOO," FOR INSTANCE, ARE PERMITTED BECAUSE THAT PERSON OBVIOUSLY KNOWS WHO HE IS...
NO, I DON'T!!

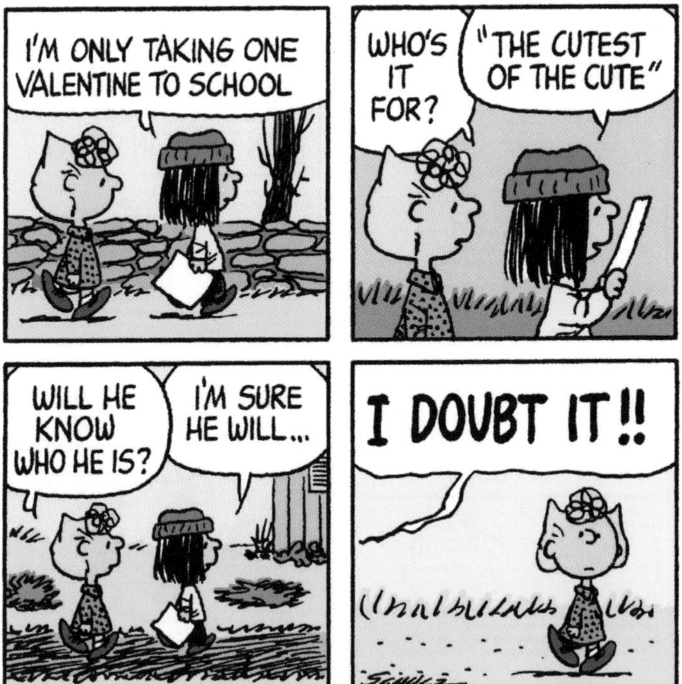
I'M ONLY TAKING ONE VALENTINE TO SCHOOL
WHO'S IT FOR?
"THE CUTEST OF THE CUTE"
WILL HE KNOW WHO HE IS?
I'M SURE HE WILL...
I DOUBT IT!!

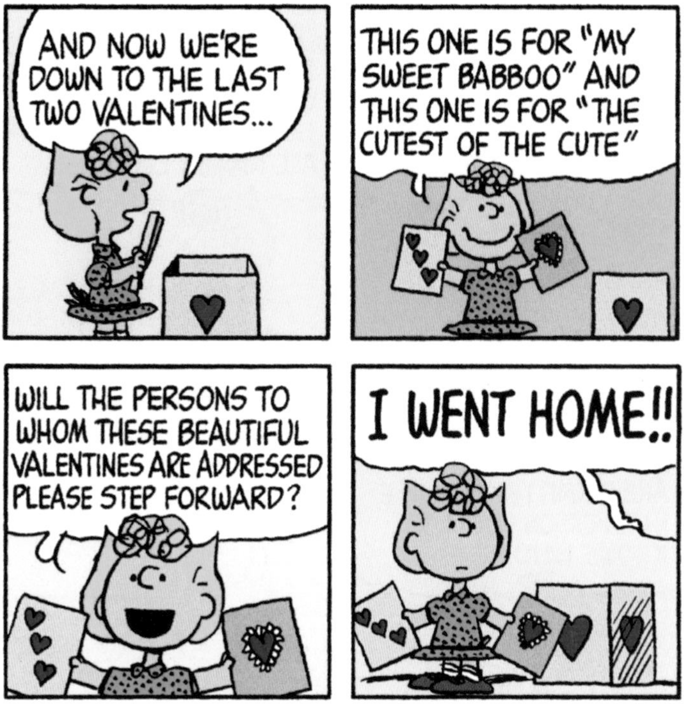
AND NOW WE'RE DOWN TO THE LAST TWO VALENTINES...
THIS ONE IS FOR "MY SWEET BABBOO" AND THIS ONE IS FOR "THE CUTEST OF THE CUTE"
WILL THE PERSONS TO WHOM THESE BEAUTIFUL VALENTINES ARE ADDRESSED PLEASE STEP FORWARD?
I WENT HOME!!

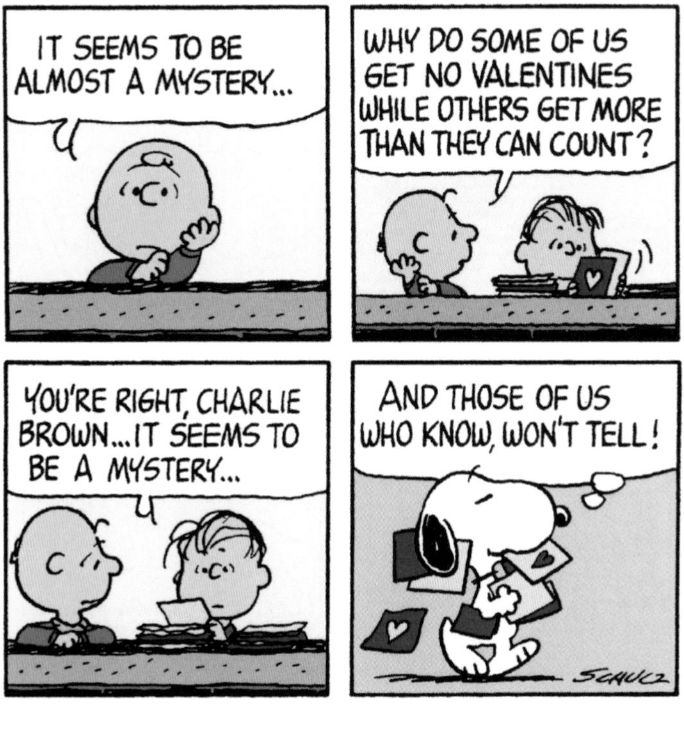
IT SEEMS TO BE ALMOST A MYSTERY...
WHY DO SOME OF US GET NO VALENTINES WHILE OTHERS GET MORE THAN THEY CAN COUNT?
YOU'RE RIGHT, CHARLIE BROWN...IT SEEMS TO BE A MYSTERY...
AND THOSE OF US WHO KNOW, WON'T TELL!
SCHULZ

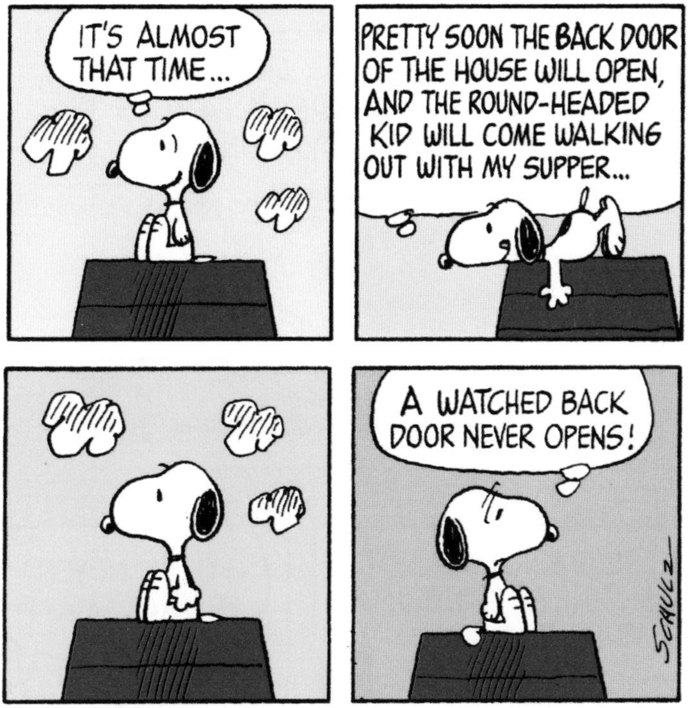
IT'S ALMOST THAT TIME...
PRETTY SOON THE BACK DOOR OF THE HOUSE WILL OPEN, AND THE ROUND-HEADED KID WILL COME WALKING OUT WITH MY SUPPER...
A WATCHED BACK DOOR NEVER OPENS!
SCHULZ

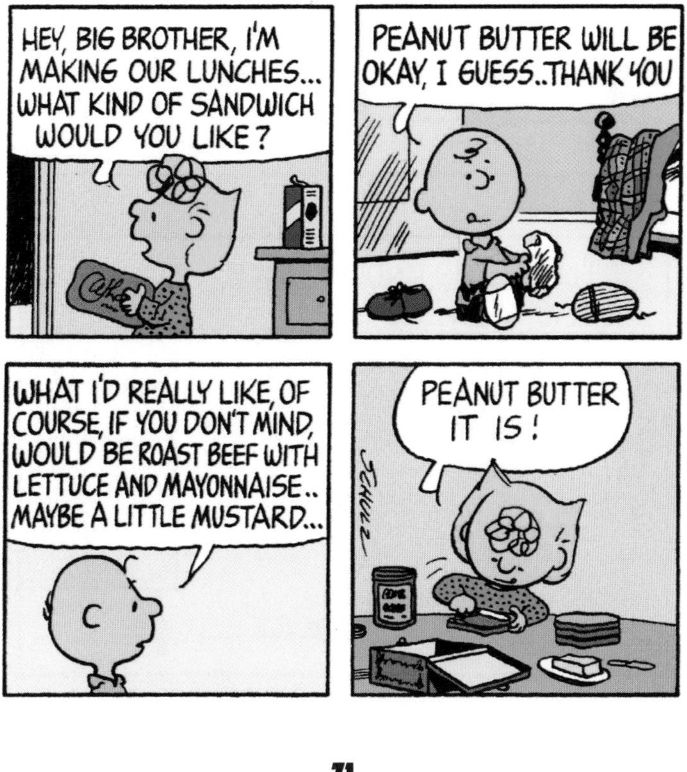
HEY, BIG BROTHER, I'M MAKING OUR LUNCHES... WHAT KIND OF SANDWICH WOULD YOU LIKE?
PEANUT BUTTER WILL BE OKAY, I GUESS..THANK YOU
WHAT I'D REALLY LIKE, OF COURSE, IF YOU DON'T MIND, WOULD BE ROAST BEEF WITH LETTUCE AND MAYONNAISE.. MAYBE A LITTLE MUSTARD...
PEANUT BUTTER IT IS!
SCHULZ

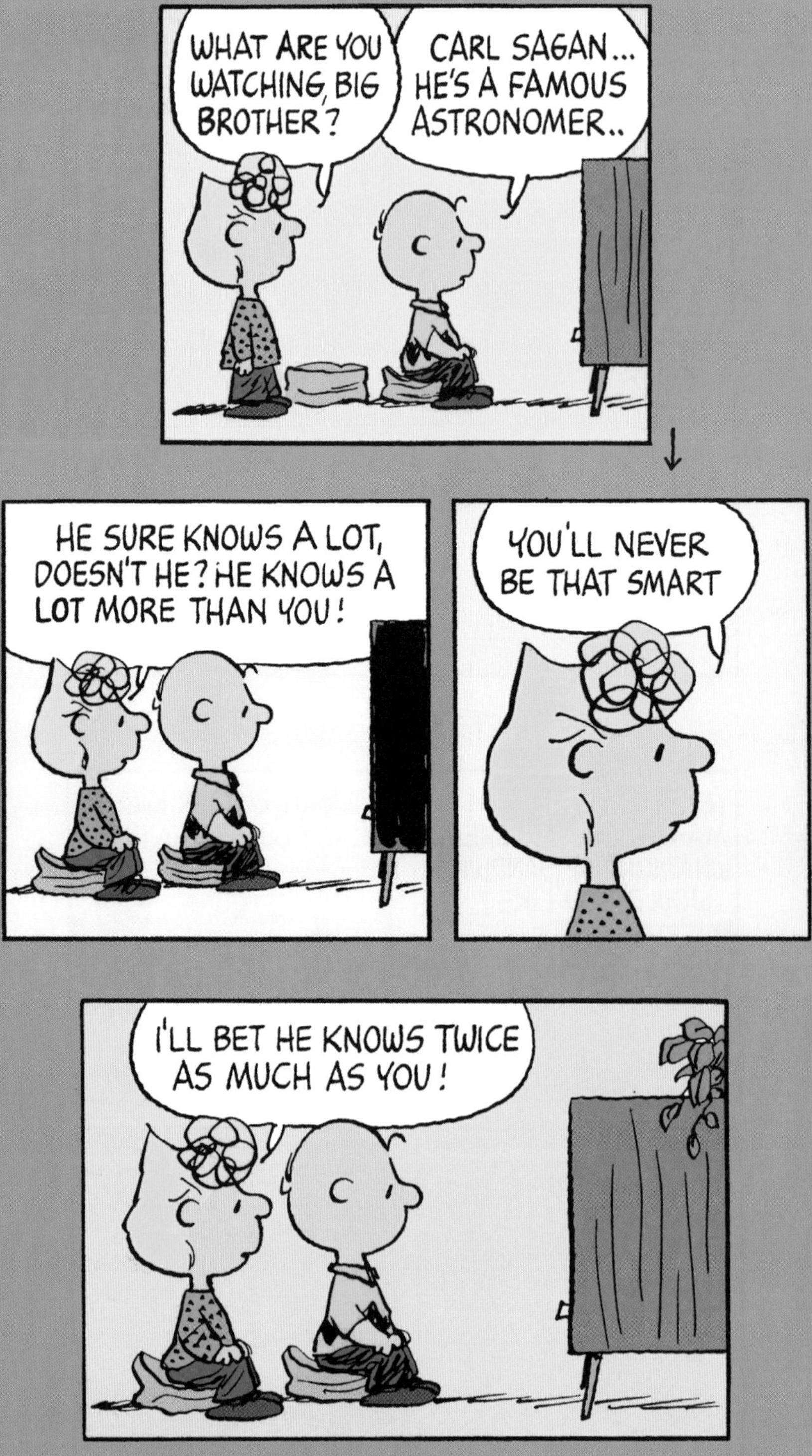
WHAT ARE YOU WATCHING, BIG BROTHER?
CARL SAGAN... HE'S A FAMOUS ASTRONOMER..
HE SURE KNOWS A LOT, DOESN'T HE? HE KNOWS A LOT MORE THAN YOU!
YOU'LL NEVER BE THAT SMART
I'LL BET HE KNOWS TWICE AS MUCH AS YOU!

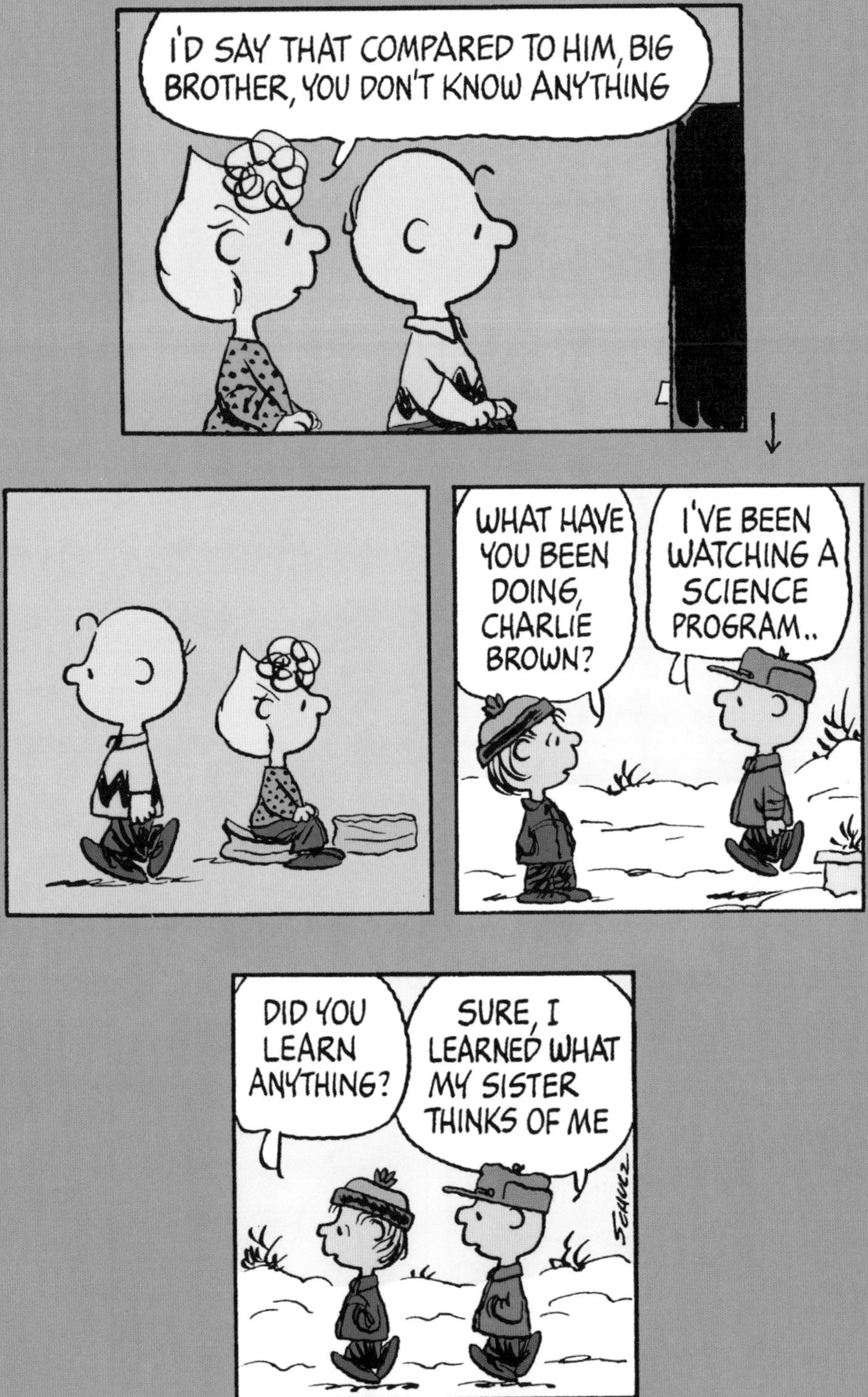
I'D SAY THAT COMPARED TO HIM, BIG BROTHER, YOU DON'T KNOW ANYTHING
WHAT HAVE YOU BEEN DOING, CHARLIE BROWN?
I'VE BEEN WATCHING A SCIENCE PROGRAM..
DID YOU LEARN ANYTHING?
SURE, I LEARNED WHAT MY SISTER THINKS OF ME
SCHULZ

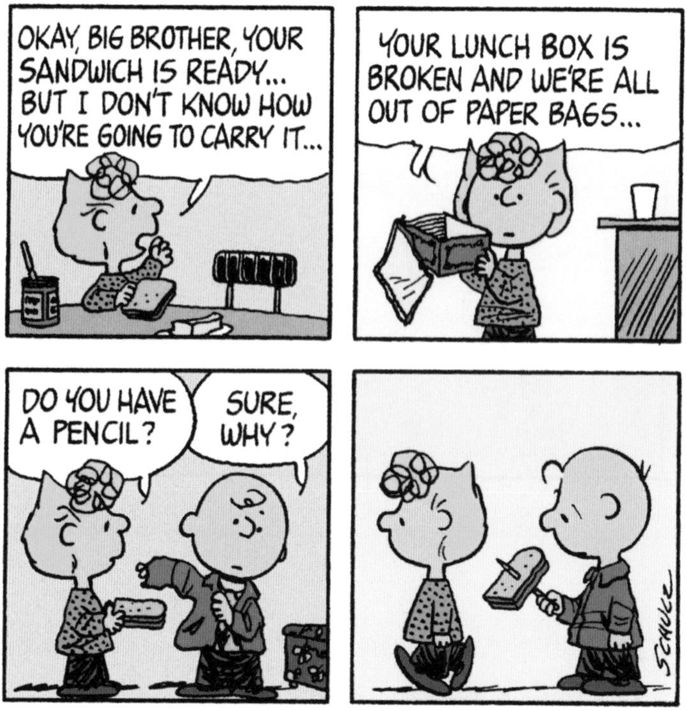
OKAY, BIG BROTHER, YOUR SANDWICH IS READY... BUT I DON'T KNOW HOW YOU'RE GOING TO CARRY IT...
YOUR LUNCH BOX IS BROKEN AND WE'RE ALL OUT OF PAPER BAGS...
DO YOU HAVE A PENCIL?
SURE, WHY?
SCHULZ

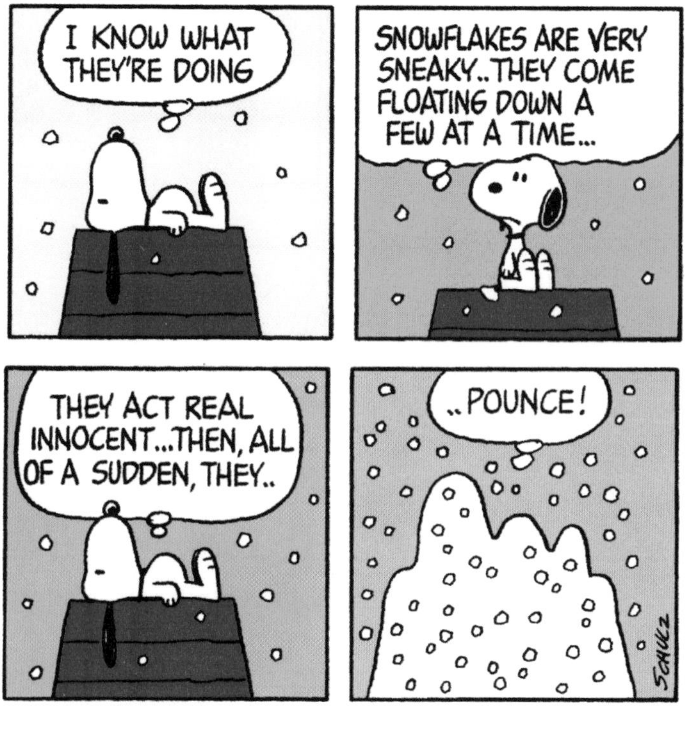
I KNOW WHAT THEY'RE DOING
SNOWFLAKES ARE VERY SNEAKY..THEY COME FLOATING DOWN A FEW AT A TIME...
THEY ACT REAL INNOCENT...THEN, ALL OF A SUDDEN, THEY..
..POUNCE!
SCHULZ

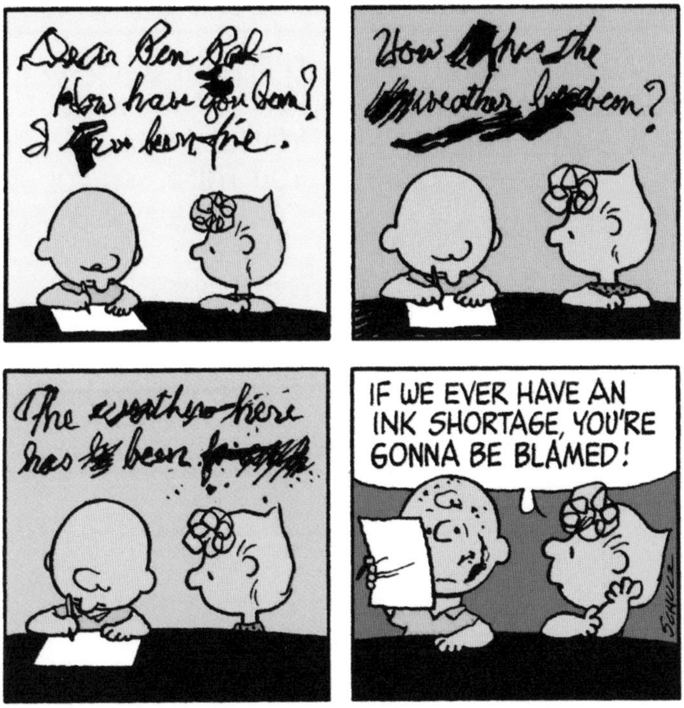
IF WE EVER HAVE AN INK SHORTAGE, YOU'RE GONNA BE BLAMED!

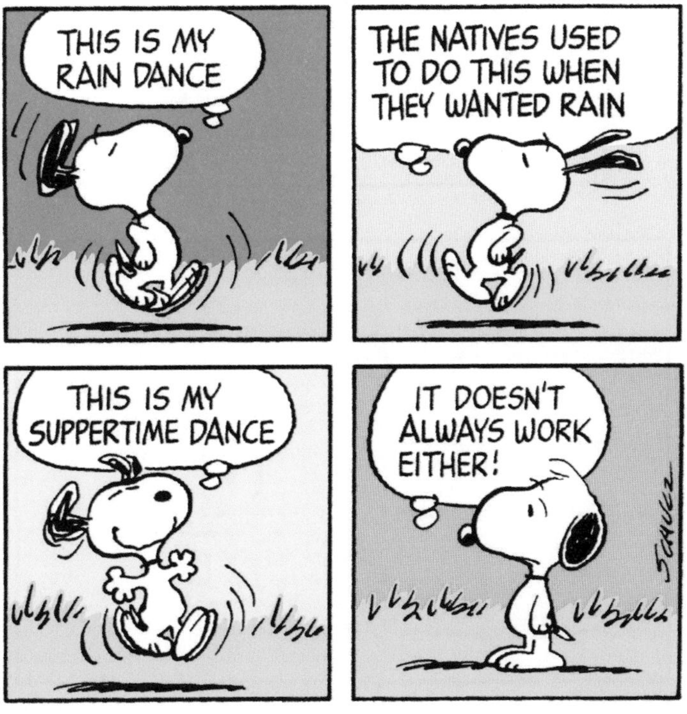
THIS IS MY RAIN DANCE
THE NATIVES USED TO DO THIS WHEN THEY WANTED RAIN
THIS IS MY SUPPERTIME DANCE
IT DOESN'T ALWAYS WORK EITHER!

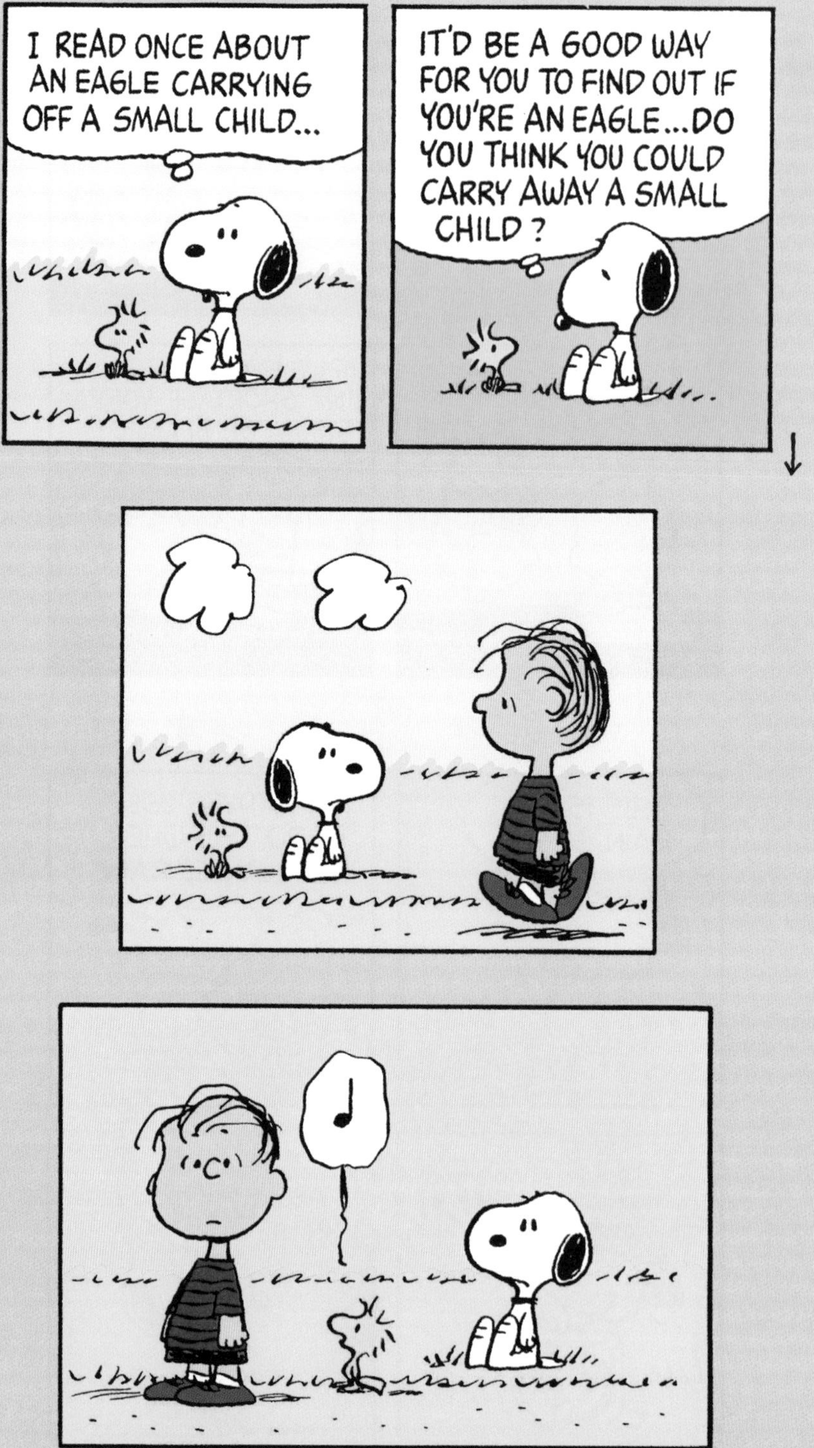
I READ ONCE ABOUT AN EAGLE CARRYING OFF A SMALL CHILD...
IT'D BE A GOOD WAY FOR YOU TO FIND OUT IF YOU'RE AN EAGLE...DO YOU THINK YOU COULD CARRY AWAY A SMALL CHILD?

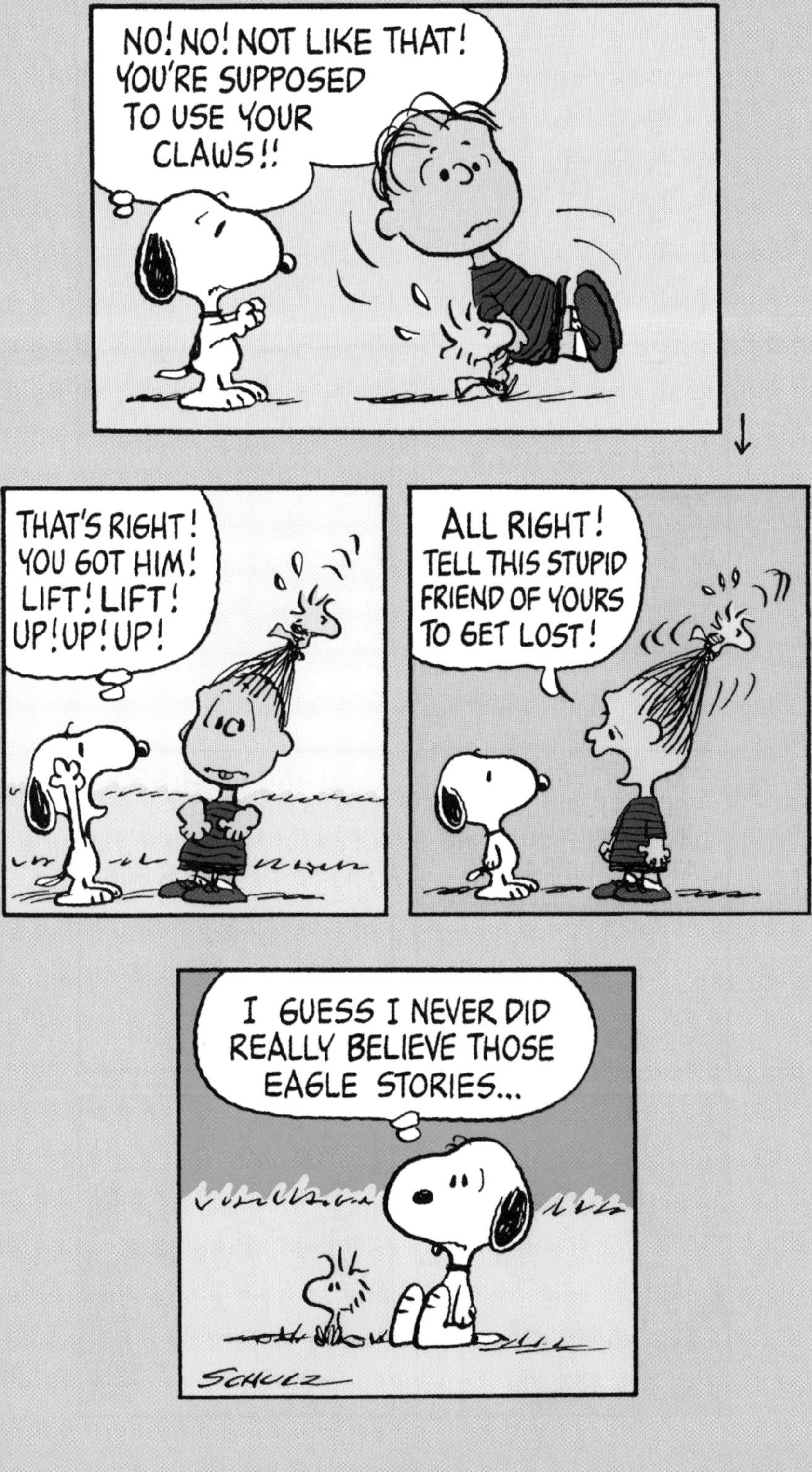
NO! NO! NOT LIKE THAT! YOU'RE SUPPOSED TO USE YOUR CLAWS!!
THAT'S RIGHT! YOU GOT HIM! LIFT! LIFT! UP! UP! UP!
ALL RIGHT! TELL THIS STUPID FRIEND OF YOURS TO GET LOST!
I GUESS I NEVER DID REALLY BELIEVE THOSE EAGLE STORIES...
SCHULZ

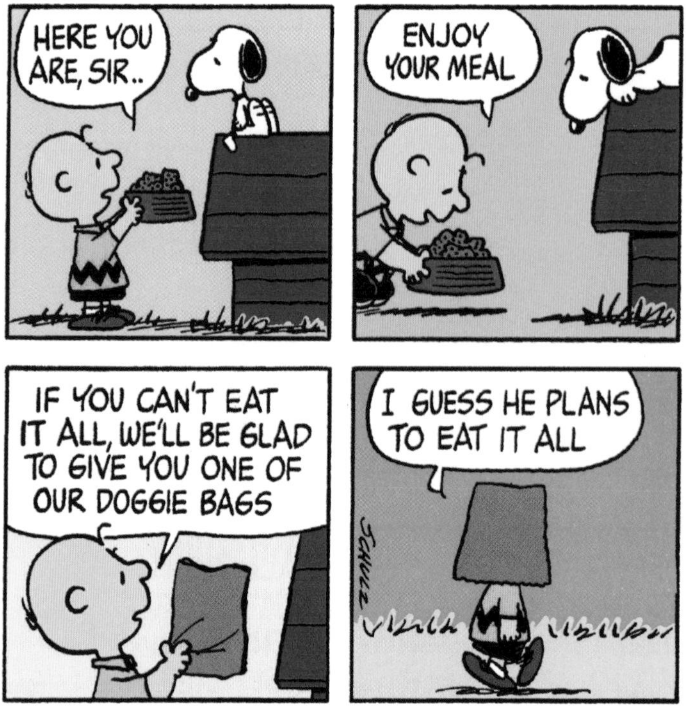
HERE YOU ARE, SIR..
ENJOY YOUR MEAL
IF YOU CAN'T EAT IT ALL, WE'LL BE GLAD TO GIVE YOU ONE OF OUR DOGGIE BAGS
I GUESS HE PLANS TO EAT IT ALL
SCHULZ

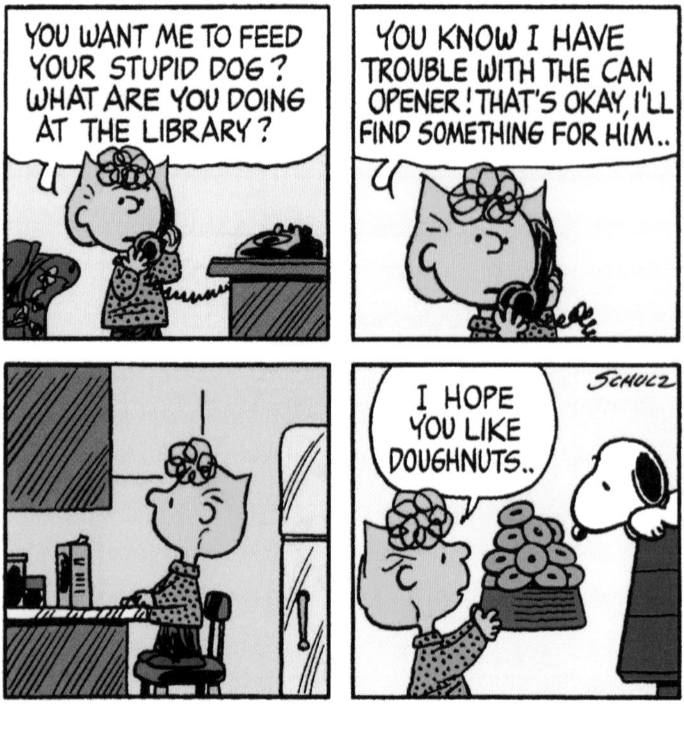
YOU WANT ME TO FEED YOUR STUPID DOG? WHAT ARE YOU DOING AT THE LIBRARY?
YOU KNOW I HAVE TROUBLE WITH THE CAN OPENER! THAT'S OKAY, I'LL FIND SOMETHING FOR HIM..
SCHULZ
I HOPE YOU LIKE DOUGHNUTS..

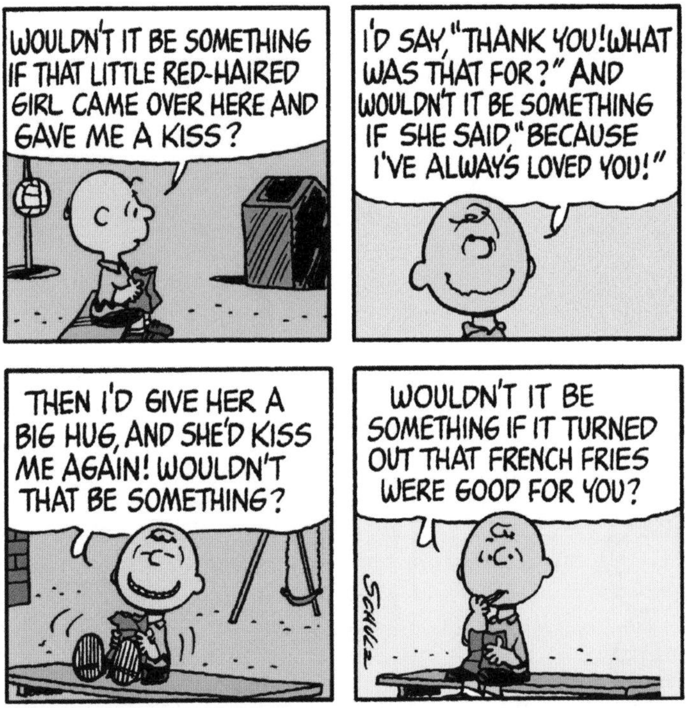
WOULDN'T IT BE SOMETHING IF THAT LITTLE RED-HAIRED GIRL CAME OVER HERE AND GAVE ME A KISS?
I'D SAY, "THANK YOU! WHAT WAS THAT FOR?" AND WOULDN'T IT BE SOMETHING IF SHE SAID, "BECAUSE I'VE ALWAYS LOVED YOU!"
THEN I'D GIVE HER A BIG HUG, AND SHE'D KISS ME AGAIN! WOULDN'T THAT BE SOMETHING?
WOULDN'T IT BE SOMETHING IF IT TURNED OUT THAT FRENCH FRIES WERE GOOD FOR YOU?
SCHULZ

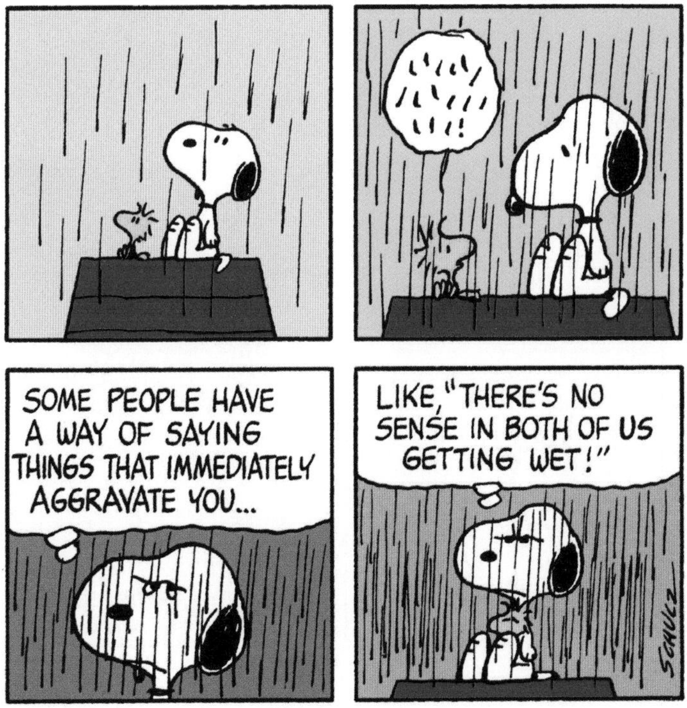
SOME PEOPLE HAVE A WAY OF SAYING THINGS THAT IMMEDIATELY AGGRAVATE YOU...
LIKE, "THERE'S NO SENSE IN BOTH OF US GETTING WET!"
SCHULZ

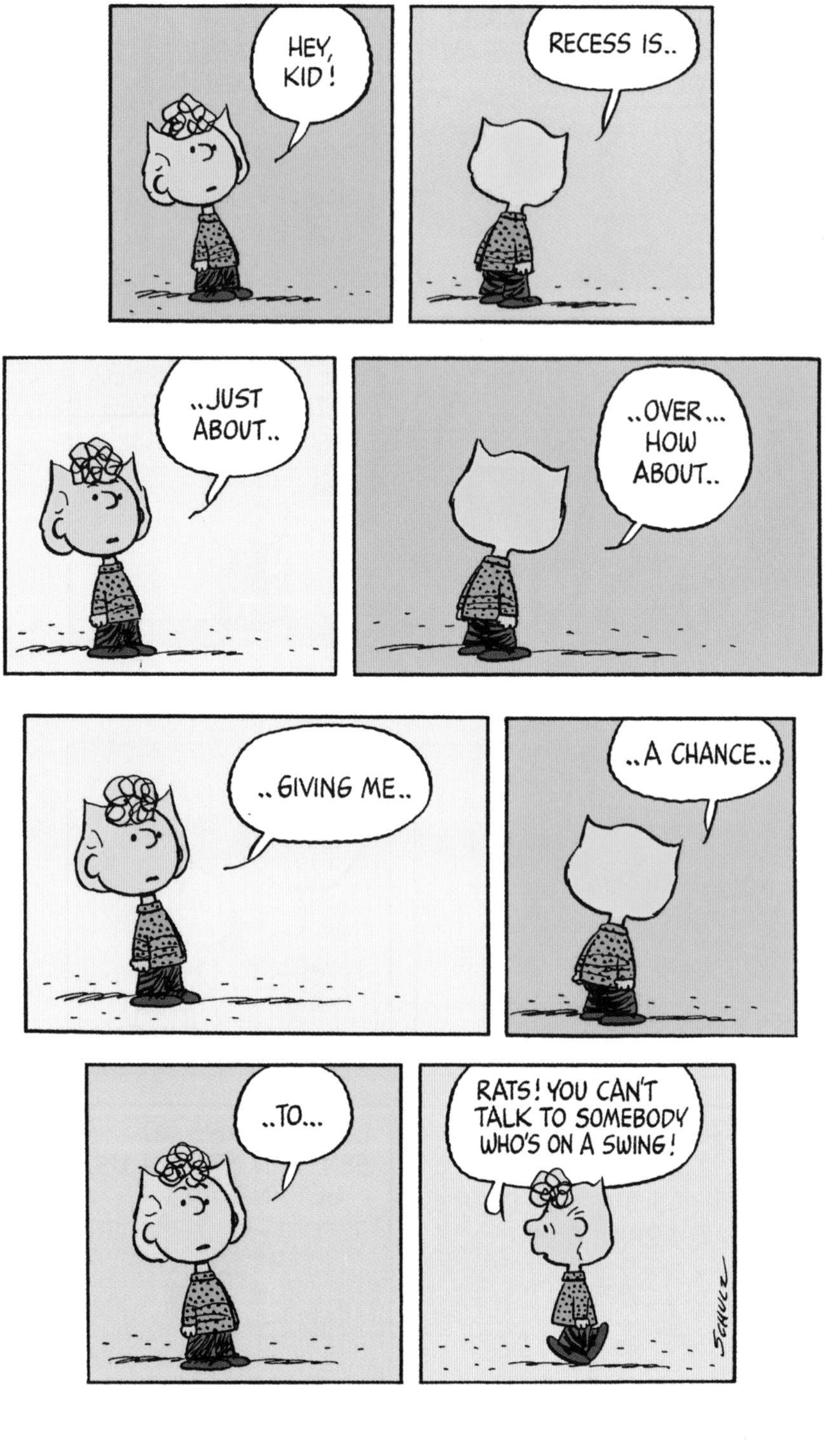
HEY, KID!
RECESS IS..
..JUST ABOUT..
..OVER... HOW ABOUT..
..GIVING ME..
..A CHANCE..
..TO...
RATS! YOU CAN'T TALK TO SOMEBODY WHO'S ON A SWING!
SCHULZ

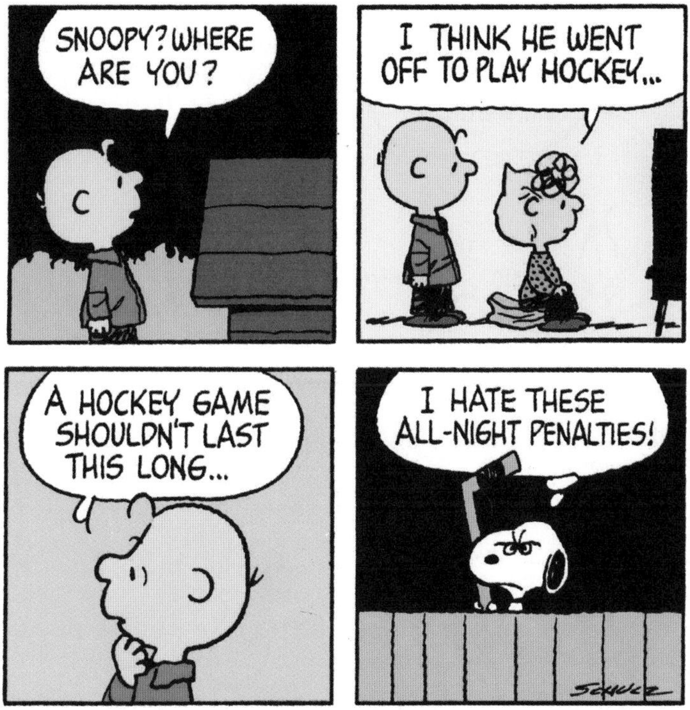
SNOOPY? WHERE ARE YOU?
I THINK HE WENT OFF TO PLAY HOCKEY...
A HOCKEY GAME SHOULDN'T LAST THIS LONG...
I HATE THESE ALL-NIGHT PENALTIES!

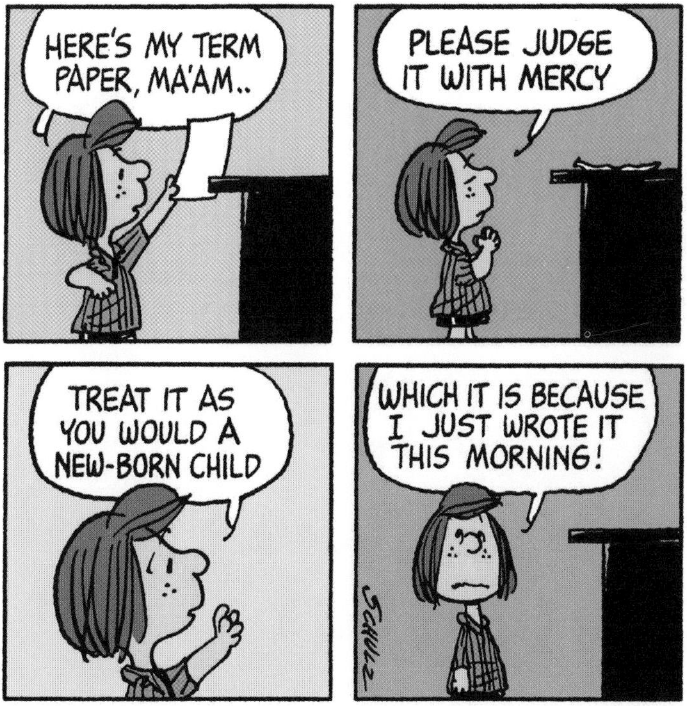
HERE'S MY TERM PAPER, MA'AM..
PLEASE JUDGE IT WITH MERCY
TREAT IT AS YOU WOULD A NEW-BORN CHILD
WHICH IT IS BECAUSE I JUST WROTE IT THIS MORNING!

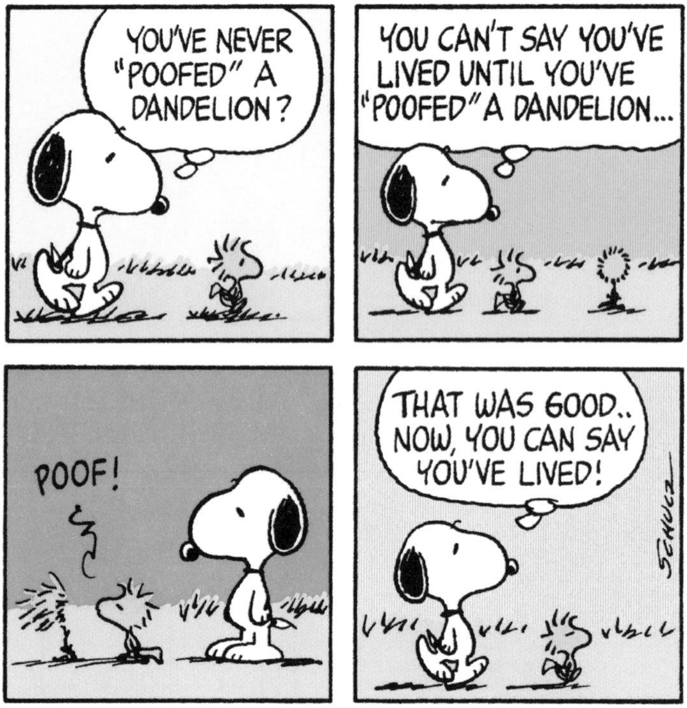
YOU'VE NEVER "POOFED" A DANDELION?
YOU CAN'T SAY YOU'VE LIVED UNTIL YOU'VE "POOFED" A DANDELION...
POOF!
THAT WAS GOOD.. NOW, YOU CAN SAY YOU'VE LIVED!
SCHULZ

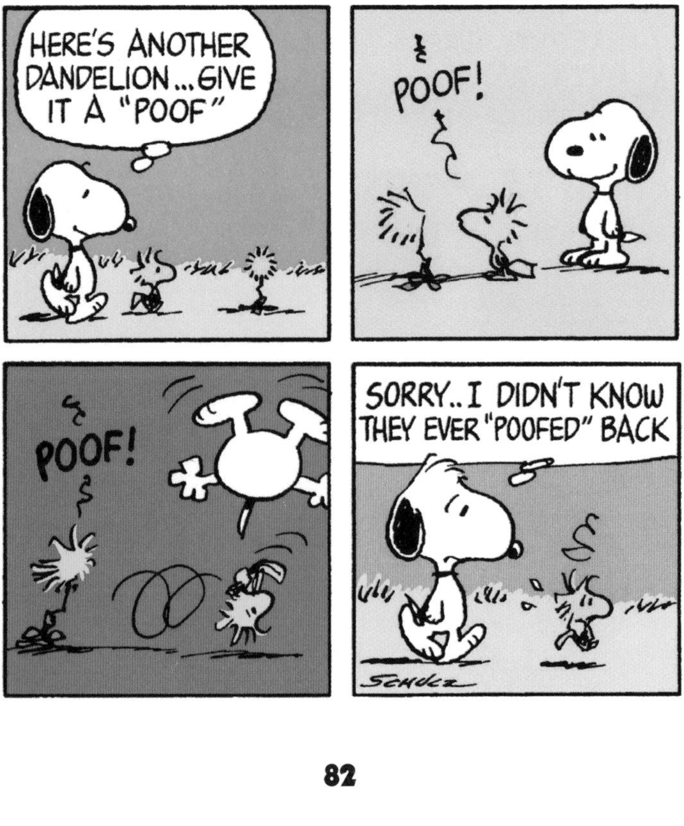
HERE'S ANOTHER DANDELION...GIVE IT A "POOF"
POOF!
POOF!
SORRY..I DIDN'T KNOW THEY EVER "POOFED" BACK
SCHULZ

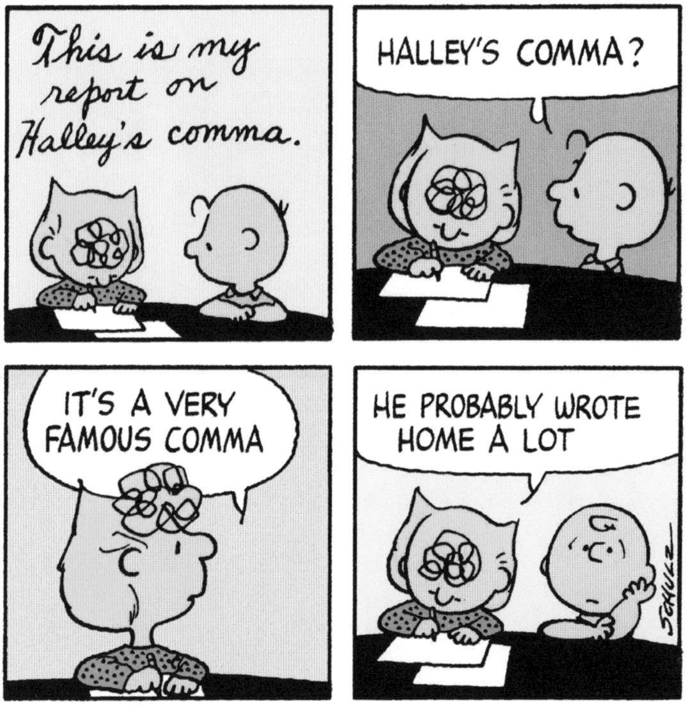
This is my report on Halley's comma.
HALLEY'S COMMA?
IT'S A VERY FAMOUS COMMA
HE PROBABLY WROTE HOME A LOT
SCHULZ

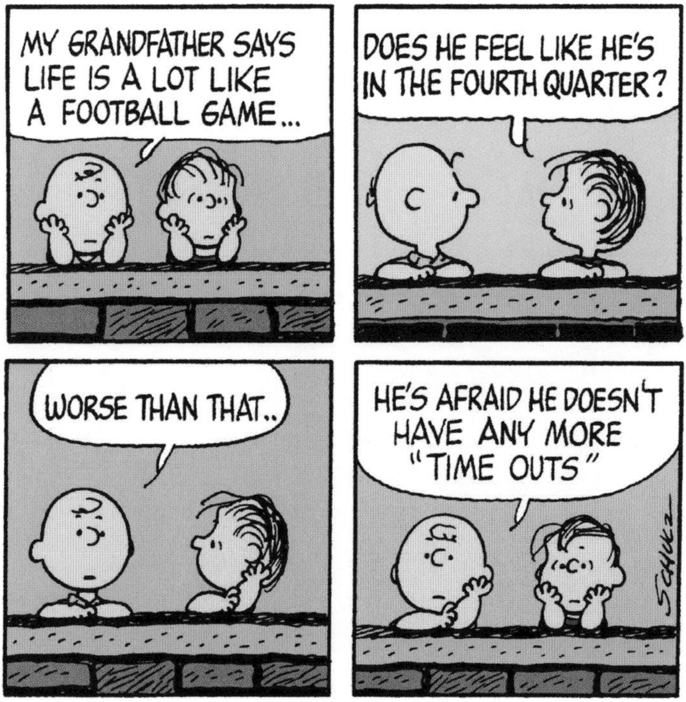
MY GRANDFATHER SAYS LIFE IS A LOT LIKE A FOOTBALL GAME...
DOES HE FEEL LIKE HE'S IN THE FOURTH QUARTER?
WORSE THAN THAT..
HE'S AFRAID HE DOESN'T HAVE ANY MORE "TIME OUTS"
SCHULZ

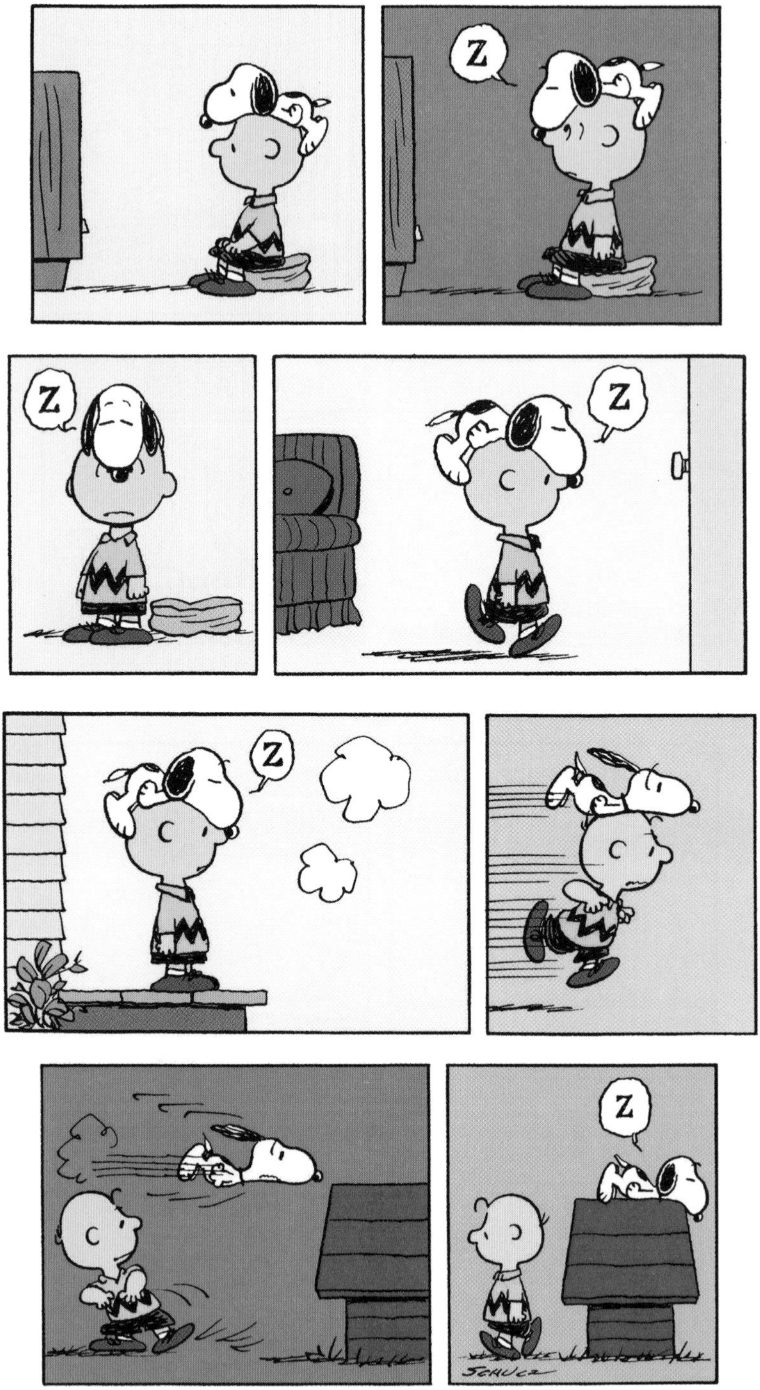
Z
Z
Z
Z
Z
SCHULZ

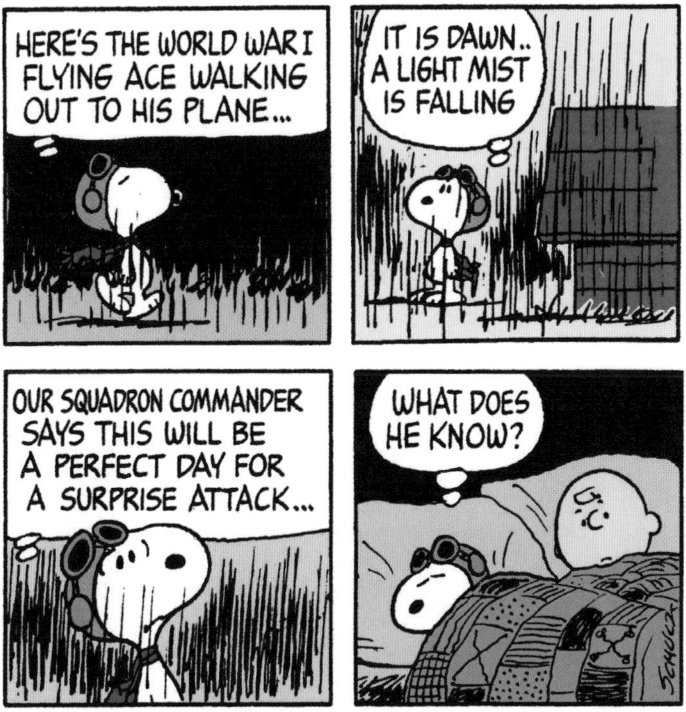
HERE'S THE WORLD WAR I FLYING ACE WALKING OUT TO HIS PLANE...
IT IS DAWN.. A LIGHT MIST IS FALLING
OUR SQUADRON COMMANDER SAYS THIS WILL BE A PERFECT DAY FOR A SURPRISE ATTACK...
WHAT DOES HE KNOW?
SCHULZ

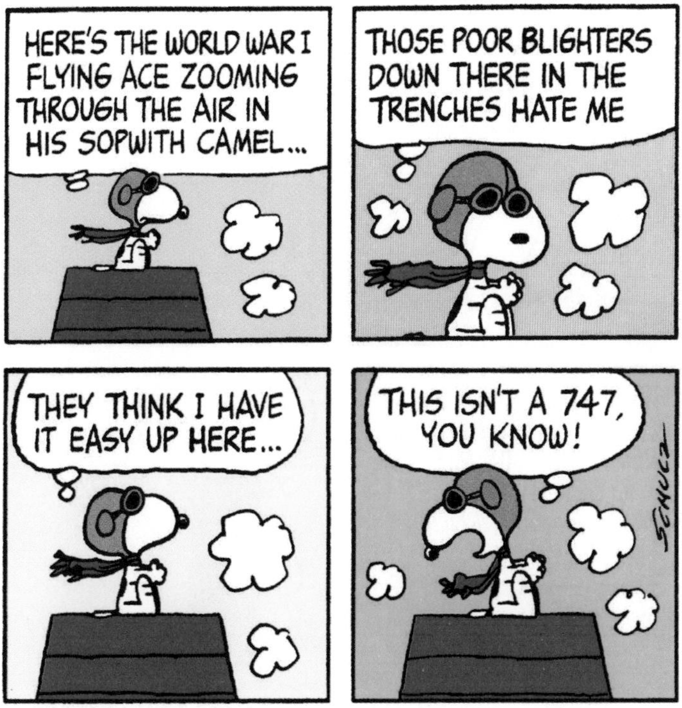
HERE'S THE WORLD WAR I FLYING ACE ZOOMING THROUGH THE AIR IN HIS SOPWITH CAMEL...
THOSE POOR BLIGHTERS DOWN THERE IN THE TRENCHES HATE ME
THEY THINK I HAVE IT EASY UP HERE...
THIS ISN'T A 747, YOU KNOW!
SCHULZ

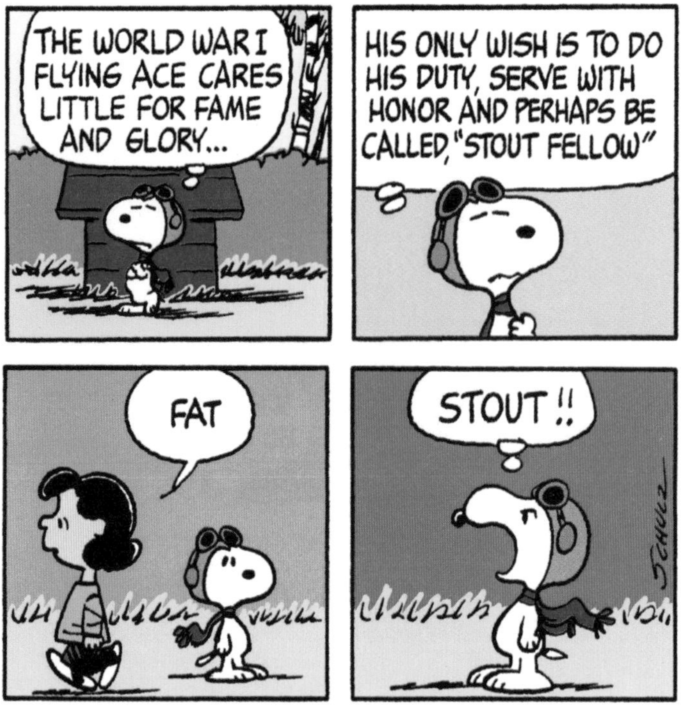
THE WORLD WAR I FLYING ACE CARES LITTLE FOR FAME AND GLORY...
HIS ONLY WISH IS TO DO HIS DUTY, SERVE WITH HONOR AND PERHAPS BE CALLED, "STOUT FELLOW"
FAT
STOUT !!
SCHULZ

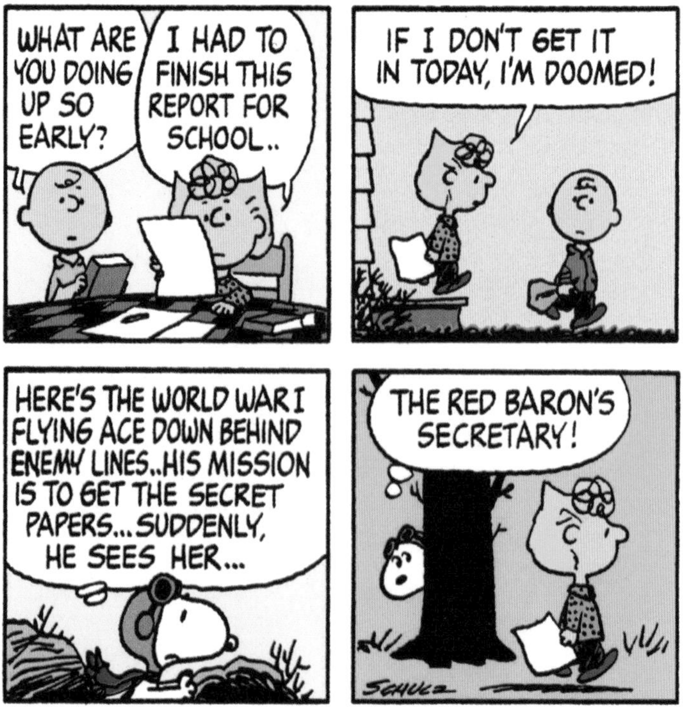
WHAT ARE YOU DOING UP SO EARLY?
I HAD TO FINISH THIS REPORT FOR SCHOOL..
IF I DON'T GET IT IN TODAY, I'M DOOMED!
HERE'S THE WORLD WAR I FLYING ACE DOWN BEHIND ENEMY LINES..HIS MISSION IS TO GET THE SECRET PAPERS...SUDDENLY, HE SEES HER...
THE RED BARON'S SECRETARY!
SCHULZ

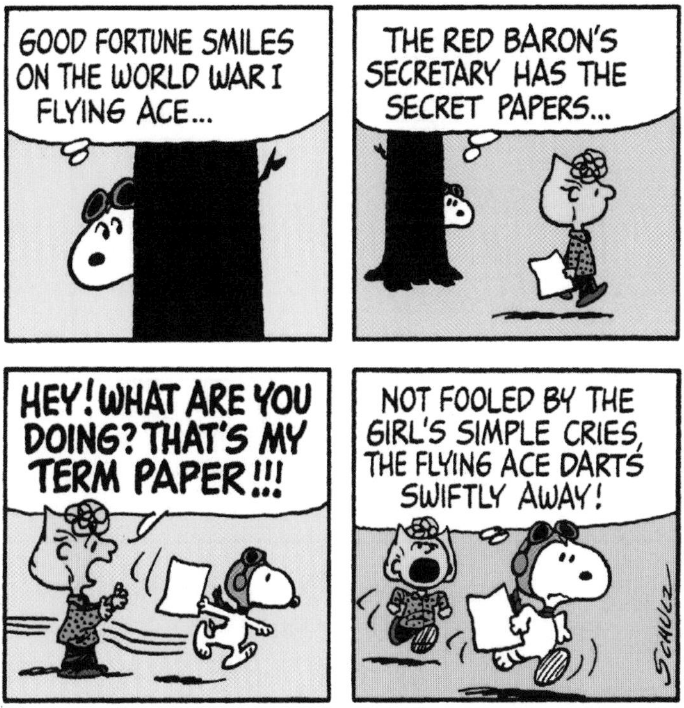
GOOD FORTUNE SMILES ON THE WORLD WAR I FLYING ACE...
THE RED BARON'S SECRETARY HAS THE SECRET PAPERS...
HEY! WHAT ARE YOU DOING? THAT'S MY TERM PAPER!!!
NOT FOOLED BY THE GIRL'S SIMPLE CRIES, THE FLYING ACE DARTS SWIFTLY AWAY!

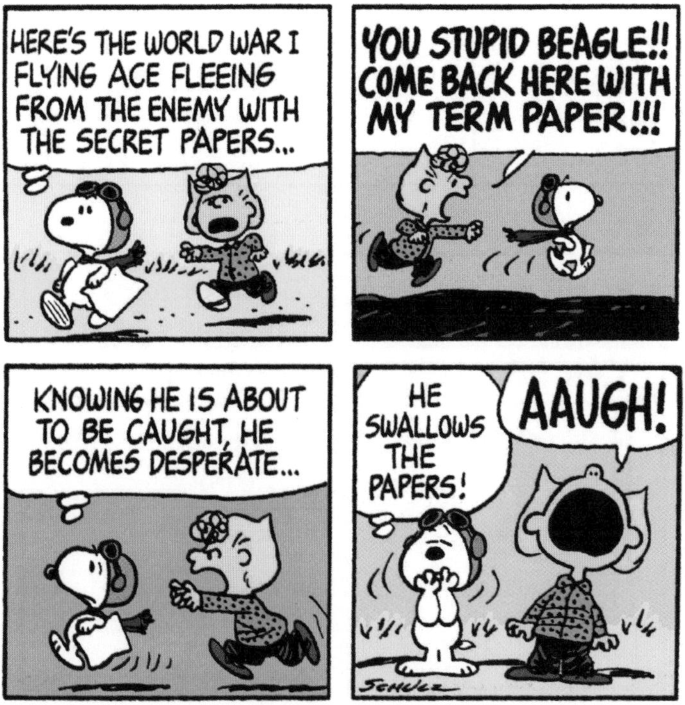
HERE'S THE WORLD WAR I FLYING ACE FLEEING FROM THE ENEMY WITH THE SECRET PAPERS...
YOU STUPID BEAGLE!! COME BACK HERE WITH MY TERM PAPER!!!
KNOWING HE IS ABOUT TO BE CAUGHT, HE BECOMES DESPERATE...
HE SWALLOWS THE PAPERS!
AAUGH!

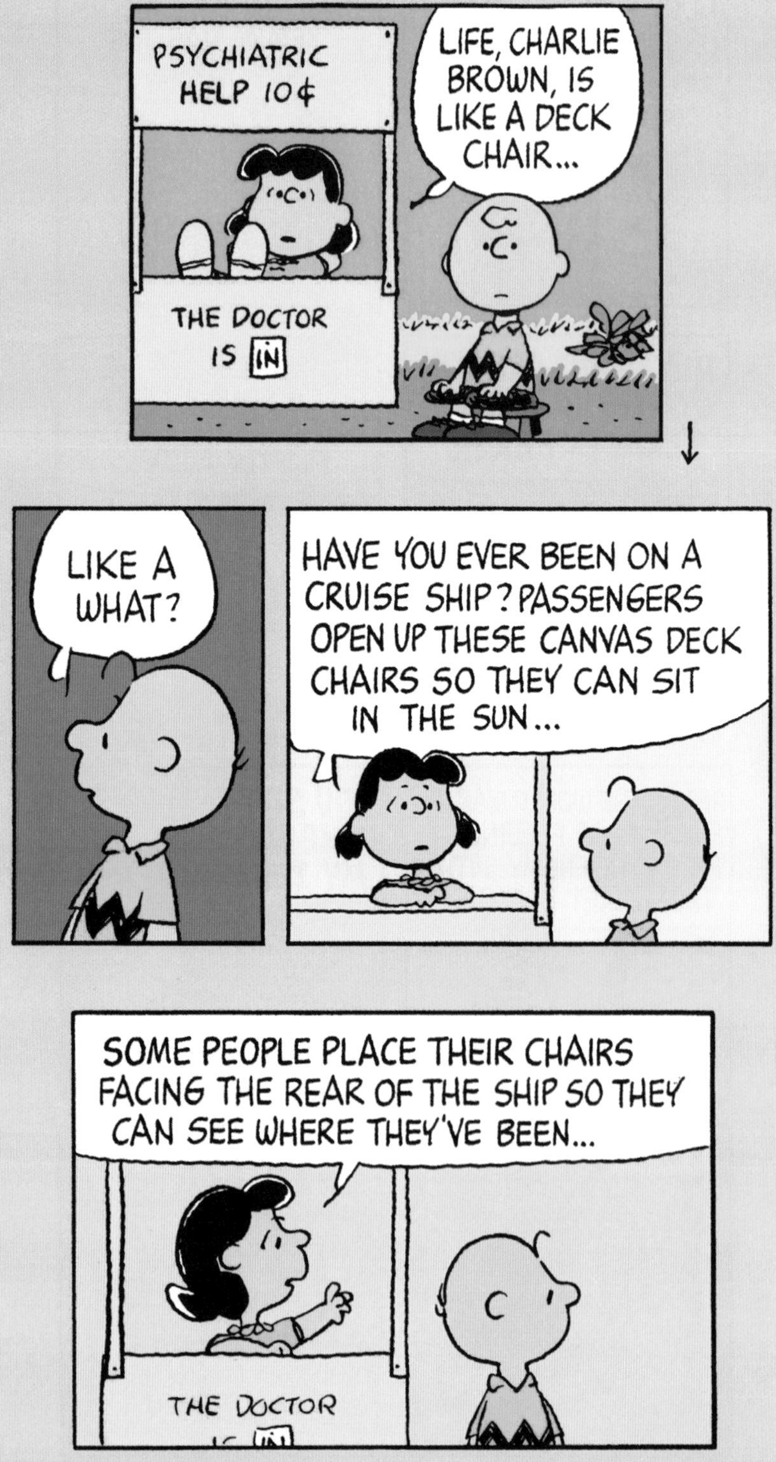
PSYCHIATRIC HELP 10¢
THE DOCTOR IS IN
LIFE, CHARLIE BROWN, IS LIKE A DECK CHAIR...
LIKE A WHAT?
HAVE YOU EVER BEEN ON A CRUISE SHIP? PASSENGERS OPEN UP THESE CANVAS DECK CHAIRS SO THEY CAN SIT IN THE SUN...
SOME PEOPLE PLACE THEIR CHAIRS FACING THE REAR OF THE SHIP SO THEY CAN SEE WHERE THEY'VE BEEN...
THE DOCTOR

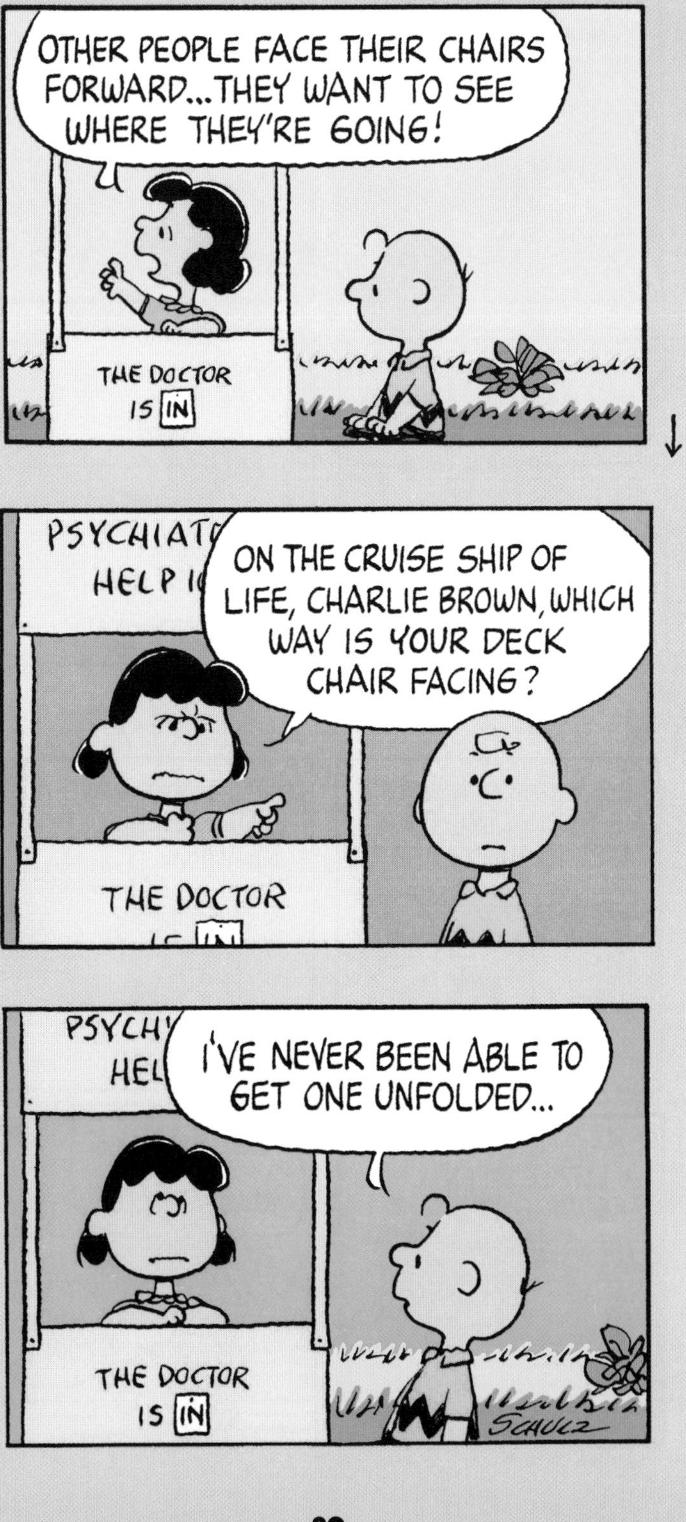
OTHER PEOPLE FACE THEIR CHAIRS FORWARD...THEY WANT TO SEE WHERE THEY'RE GOING!
THE DOCTOR IS IN
PSYCHIAT
HELP I
ON THE CRUISE SHIP OF LIFE, CHARLIE BROWN, WHICH WAY IS YOUR DECK CHAIR FACING?
THE DOCTOR
PSYCH
HEL
I'VE NEVER BEEN ABLE TO GET ONE UNFOLDED...
THE DOCTOR IS IN
SCHULZ

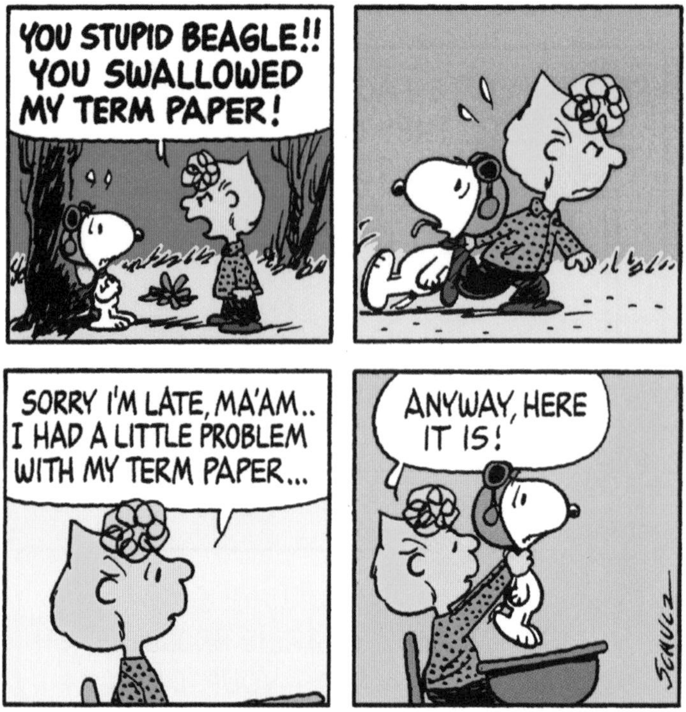
YOU STUPID BEAGLE!! YOU SWALLOWED MY TERM PAPER!
SORRY I'M LATE, MA'AM.. I HAD A LITTLE PROBLEM WITH MY TERM PAPER...
ANYWAY, HERE IT IS!

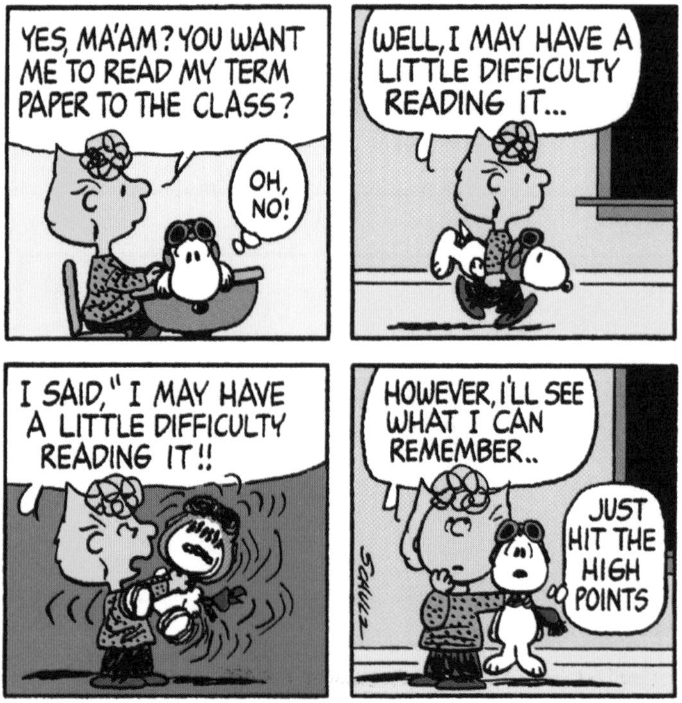
YES, MA'AM? YOU WANT ME TO READ MY TERM PAPER TO THE CLASS?
OH, NO!
WELL, I MAY HAVE A LITTLE DIFFICULTY READING IT...
I SAID, " I MAY HAVE A LITTLE DIFFICULTY READING IT!!
HOWEVER, I'LL SEE WHAT I CAN REMEMBER..
JUST HIT THE HIGH POINTS

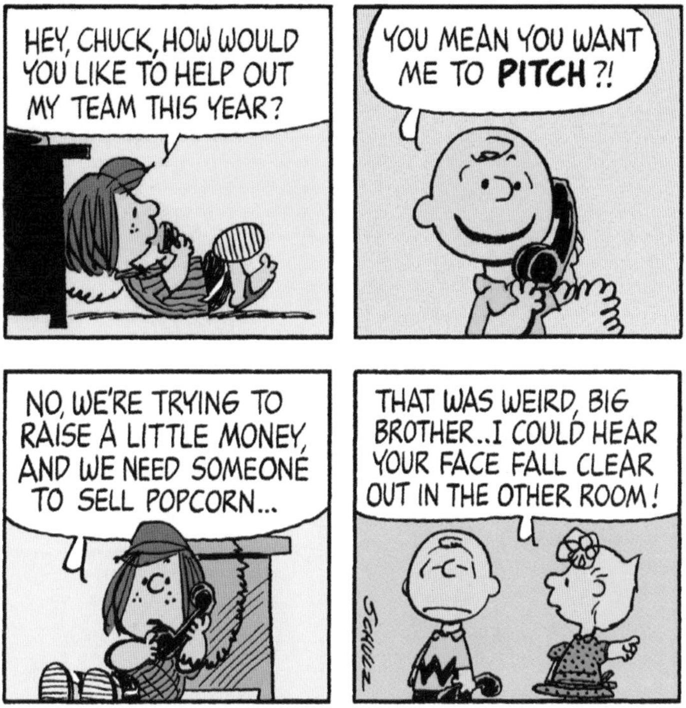
HEY, CHUCK, HOW WOULD YOU LIKE TO HELP OUT MY TEAM THIS YEAR?
YOU MEAN YOU WANT ME TO **PITCH**?!
NO, WE'RE TRYING TO RAISE A LITTLE MONEY, AND WE NEED SOMEONE TO SELL POPCORN...
THAT WAS WEIRD, BIG BROTHER..I COULD HEAR YOUR FACE FALL CLEAR OUT IN THE OTHER ROOM!

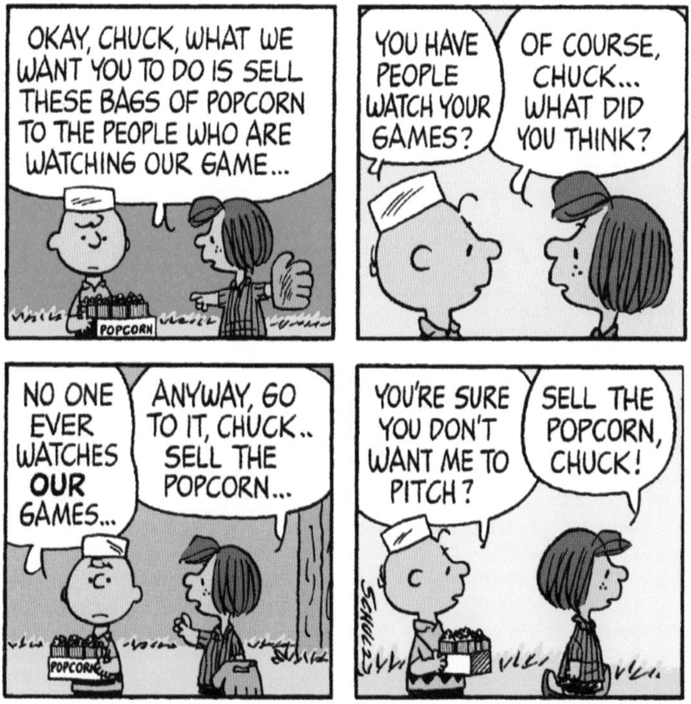
OKAY, CHUCK, WHAT WE WANT YOU TO DO IS SELL THESE BAGS OF POPCORN TO THE PEOPLE WHO ARE WATCHING OUR GAME...
POPCORN
YOU HAVE PEOPLE WATCH YOUR GAMES?
OF COURSE, CHUCK... WHAT DID YOU THINK?
NO ONE EVER WATCHES **OUR** GAMES...
ANYWAY, GO TO IT, CHUCK.. SELL THE POPCORN...
YOU'RE SURE YOU DON'T WANT ME TO PITCH?
SELL THE POPCORN, CHUCK!

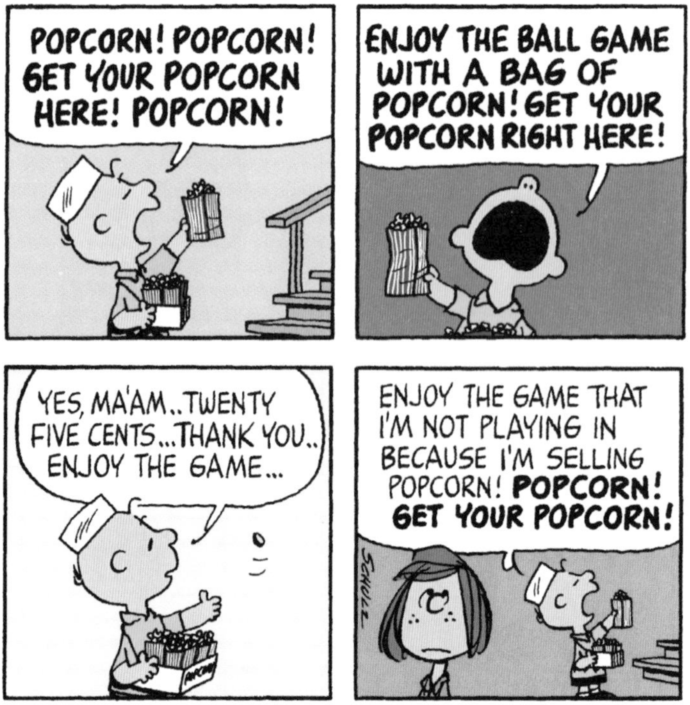
POPCORN! POPCORN! GET YOUR POPCORN HERE! POPCORN!
ENJOY THE BALL GAME WITH A BAG OF POPCORN! GET YOUR POPCORN RIGHT HERE!
YES, MA'AM..TWENTY FIVE CENTS...THANK YOU.. ENJOY THE GAME...
ENJOY THE GAME THAT I'M NOT PLAYING IN BECAUSE I'M SELLING POPCORN! POPCORN! GET YOUR POPCORN!
SCHULZ

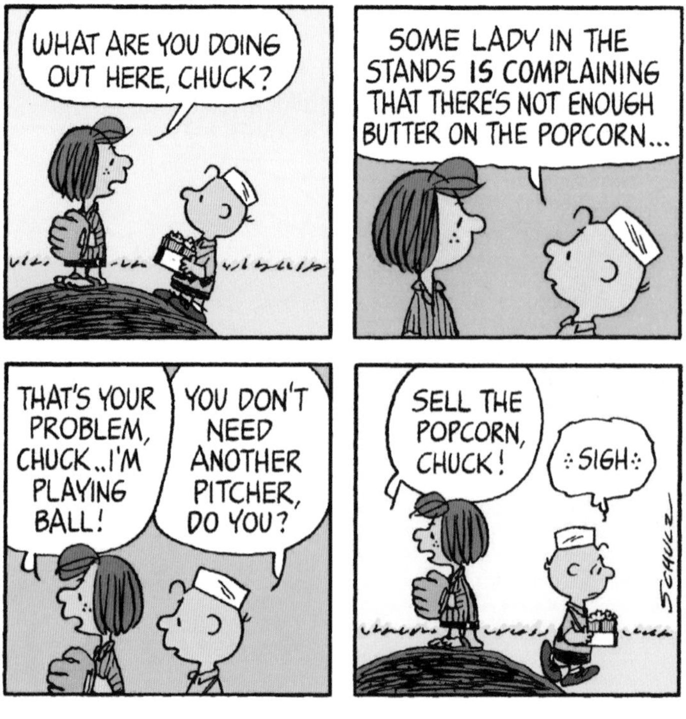
WHAT ARE YOU DOING OUT HERE, CHUCK?
SOME LADY IN THE STANDS IS COMPLAINING THAT THERE'S NOT ENOUGH BUTTER ON THE POPCORN...
THAT'S YOUR PROBLEM, CHUCK..I'M PLAYING BALL!
YOU DON'T NEED ANOTHER PITCHER, DO YOU?
SELL THE POPCORN, CHUCK!
SIGH
SCHULZ

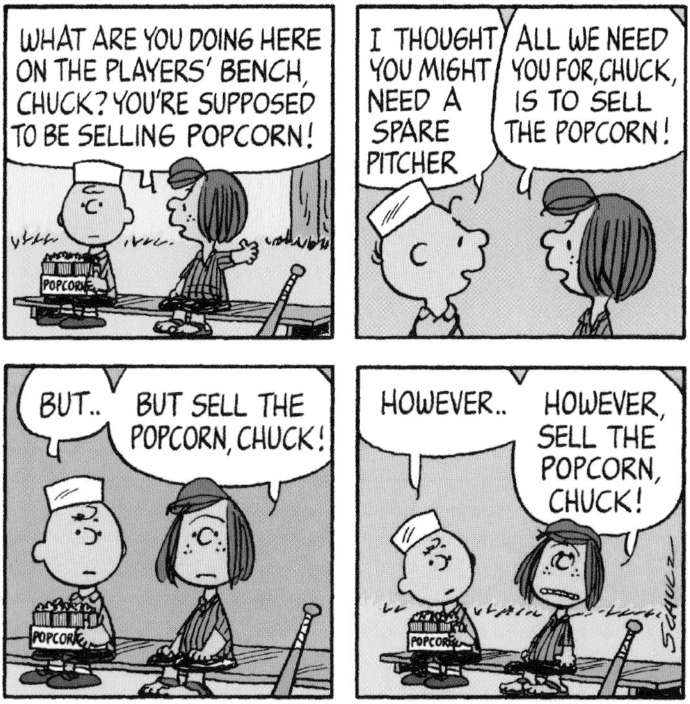
WHAT ARE YOU DOING HERE ON THE PLAYERS' BENCH, CHUCK? YOU'RE SUPPOSED TO BE SELLING POPCORN!
POPCORN
I THOUGHT YOU MIGHT NEED A SPARE PITCHER
ALL WE NEED YOU FOR, CHUCK, IS TO SELL THE POPCORN!
BUT..
BUT SELL THE POPCORN, CHUCK!
POPCORN
HOWEVER..
HOWEVER, SELL THE POPCORN, CHUCK!
POPCORN
SCHULZ

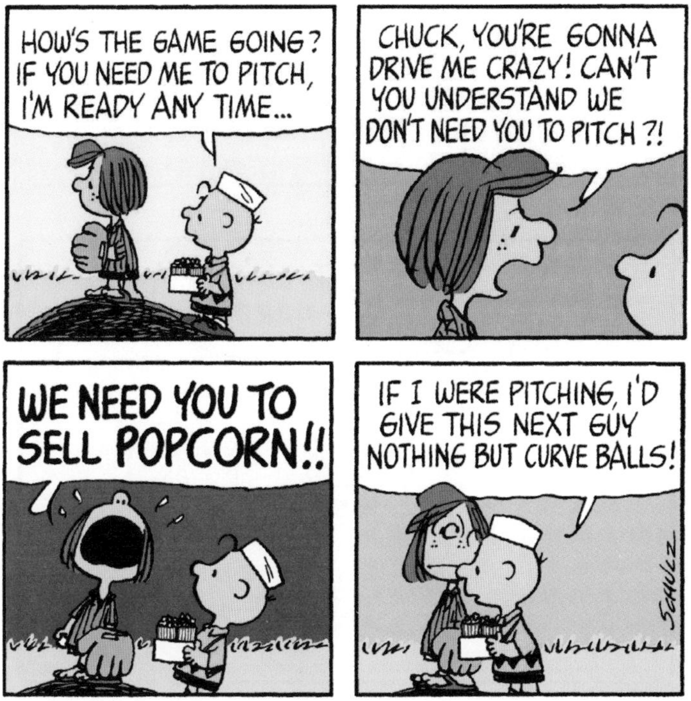
HOW'S THE GAME GOING? IF YOU NEED ME TO PITCH, I'M READY ANY TIME...
CHUCK, YOU'RE GONNA DRIVE ME CRAZY! CAN'T YOU UNDERSTAND WE DON'T NEED YOU TO PITCH?!
WE NEED YOU TO SELL POPCORN!!
IF I WERE PITCHING, I'D GIVE THIS NEXT GUY NOTHING BUT CURVE BALLS!
SCHULZ

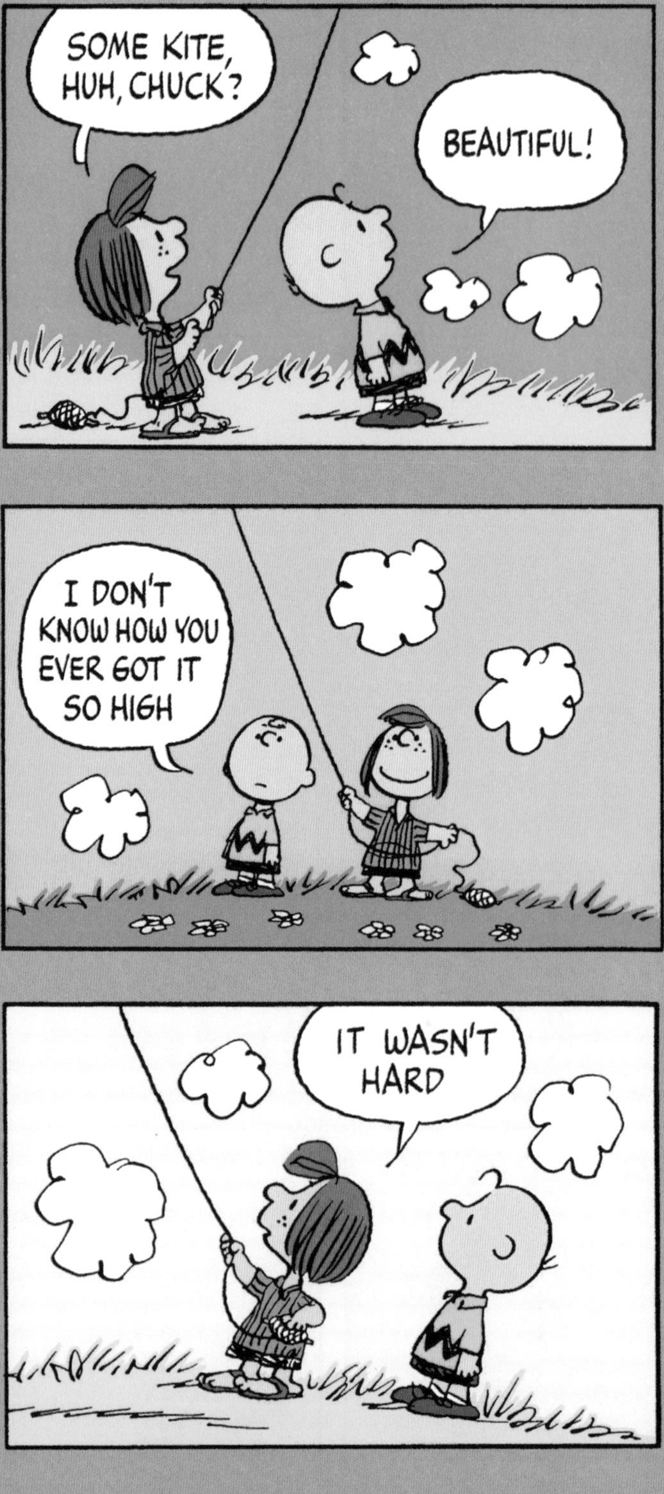
SOME KITE, HUH, CHUCK?
BEAUTIFUL!
I DON'T KNOW HOW YOU EVER GOT IT SO HIGH
IT WASN'T HARD

HERE, WOULD YOU LIKE TO HOLD THE STRING FOR A MINUTE?
ARE YOU SURE YOU WANT ME TO?
OF COURSE, CHUCK.. WHY WOULDN'T I?
NO REASON
SCHULZ

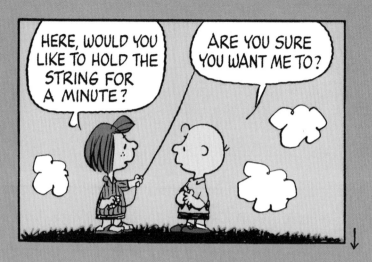

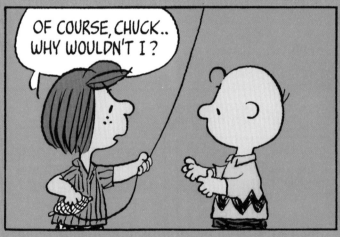

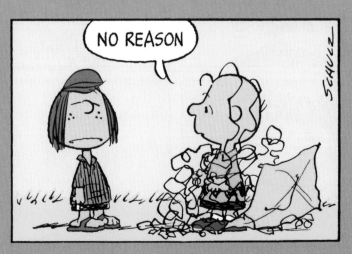

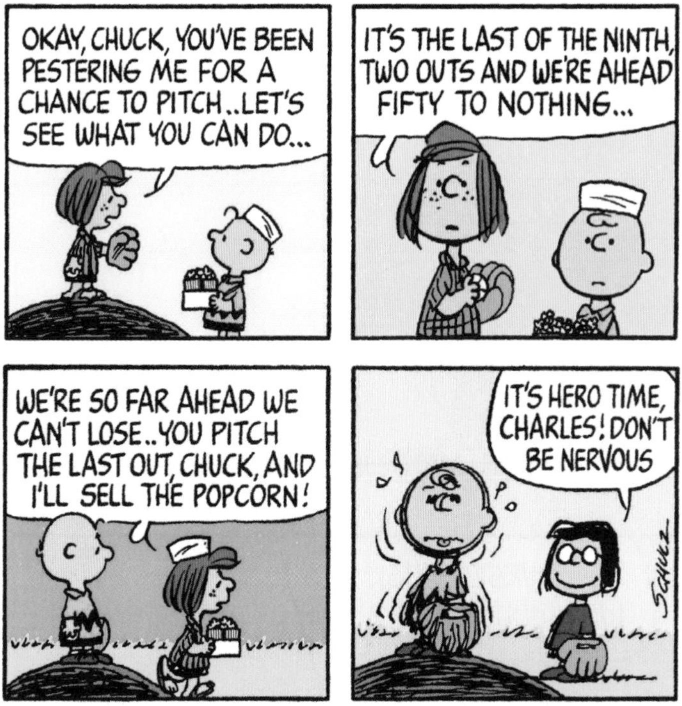
OKAY, CHUCK, YOU'VE BEEN PESTERING ME FOR A CHANCE TO PITCH..LET'S SEE WHAT YOU CAN DO...
IT'S THE LAST OF THE NINTH, TWO OUTS AND WE'RE AHEAD FIFTY TO NOTHING...
WE'RE SO FAR AHEAD WE CAN'T LOSE..YOU PITCH THE LAST OUT, CHUCK, AND I'LL SELL THE POPCORN!
IT'S HERO TIME, CHARLES! DON'T BE NERVOUS

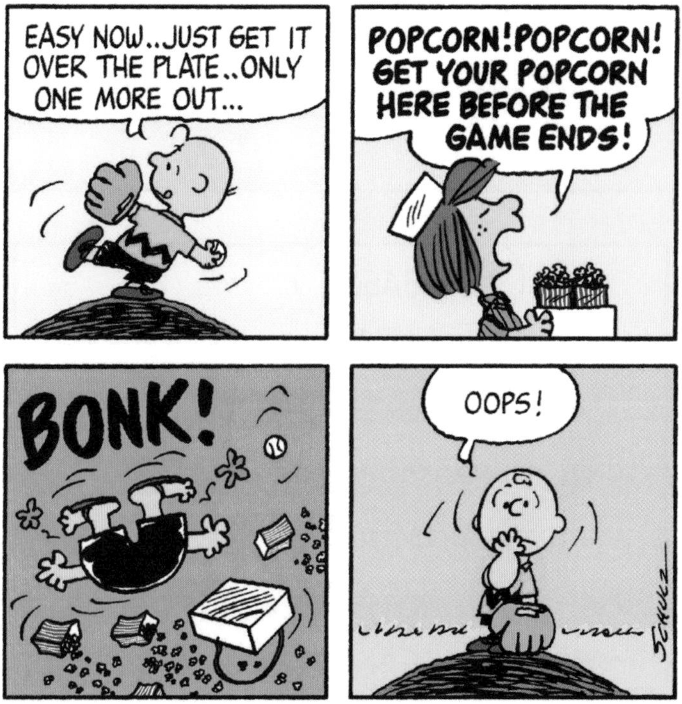
EASY NOW..JUST GET IT OVER THE PLATE..ONLY ONE MORE OUT...
POPCORN! POPCORN! GET YOUR POPCORN HERE BEFORE THE GAME ENDS!
BONK!
OOPS!

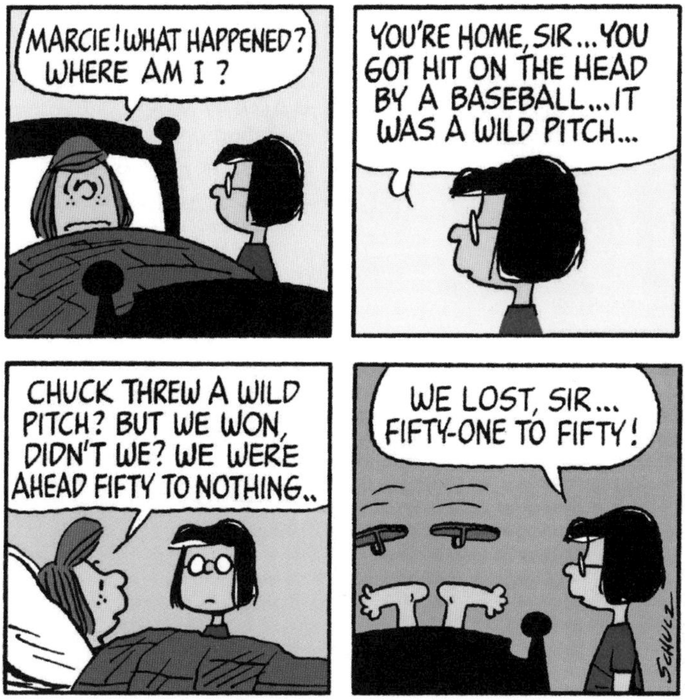
MARCIE! WHAT HAPPENED? WHERE AM I?
YOU'RE HOME, SIR... YOU GOT HIT ON THE HEAD BY A BASEBALL... IT WAS A WILD PITCH...
CHUCK THREW A WILD PITCH? BUT WE WON, DIDN'T WE? WE WERE AHEAD FIFTY TO NOTHING..
WE LOST, SIR... FIFTY-ONE TO FIFTY!
SCHULZ

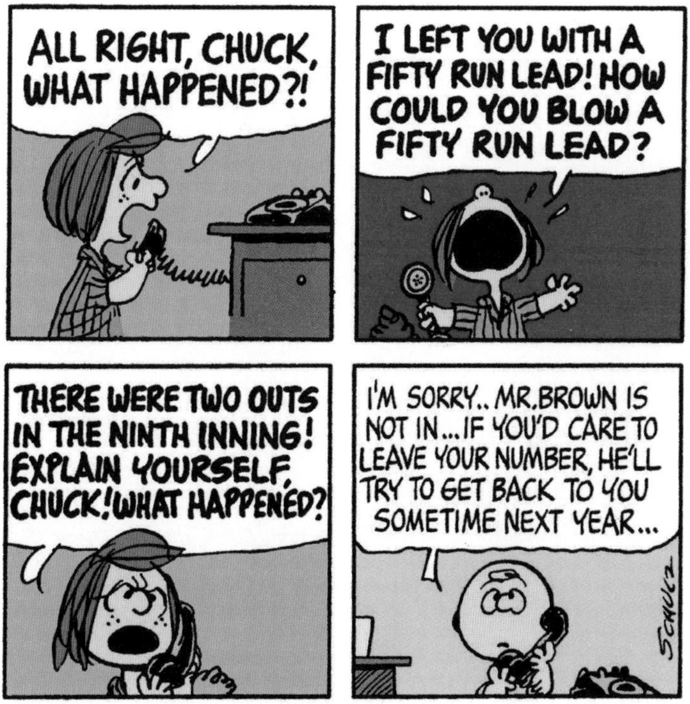
ALL RIGHT, CHUCK, WHAT HAPPENED?!
I LEFT YOU WITH A FIFTY RUN LEAD! HOW COULD YOU BLOW A FIFTY RUN LEAD?
THERE WERE TWO OUTS IN THE NINTH INNING! EXPLAIN YOURSELF, CHUCK! WHAT HAPPENED?
I'M SORRY.. MR. BROWN IS NOT IN... IF YOU'D CARE TO LEAVE YOUR NUMBER, HE'LL TRY TO GET BACK TO YOU SOMETIME NEXT YEAR...
SCHULZ

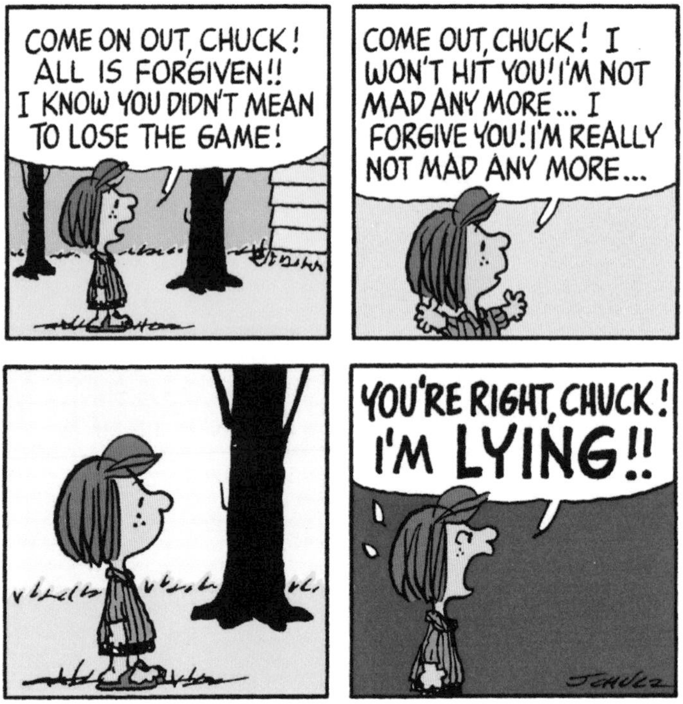
COME ON OUT, CHUCK! ALL IS FORGIVEN!! I KNOW YOU DIDN'T MEAN TO LOSE THE GAME!
COME OUT, CHUCK! I WON'T HIT YOU! I'M NOT MAD ANY MORE... I FORGIVE YOU! I'M REALLY NOT MAD ANY MORE...
YOU'RE RIGHT, CHUCK! I'M LYING!!
SCHULZ

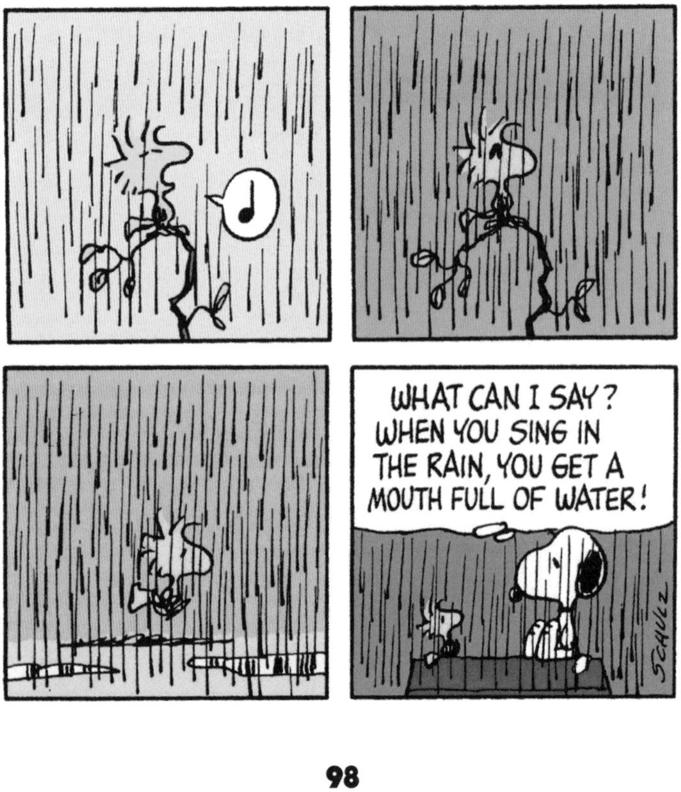
WHAT CAN I SAY? WHEN YOU SING IN THE RAIN, YOU GET A MOUTH FULL OF WATER!
SCHULZ

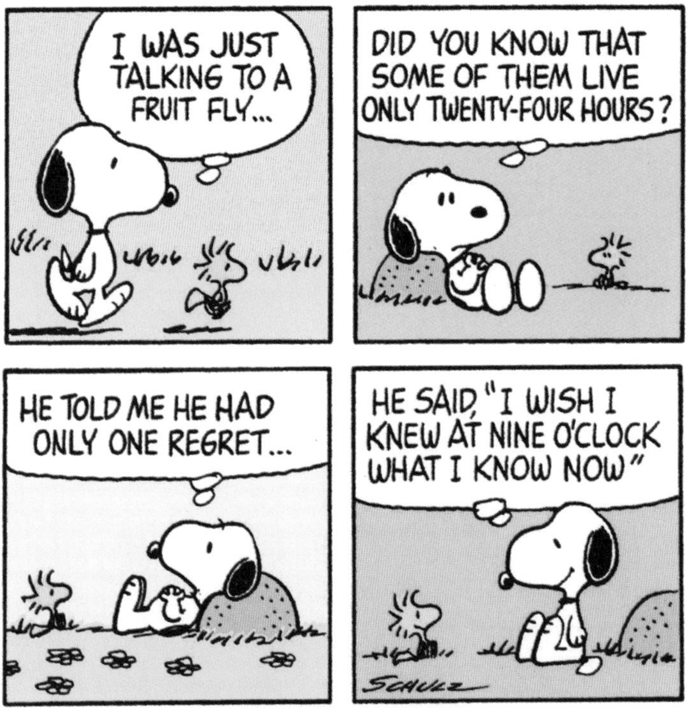
I WAS JUST TALKING TO A FRUIT FLY...
DID YOU KNOW THAT SOME OF THEM LIVE ONLY TWENTY-FOUR HOURS?
HE TOLD ME HE HAD ONLY ONE REGRET...
HE SAID, "I WISH I KNEW AT NINE O'CLOCK WHAT I KNOW NOW"

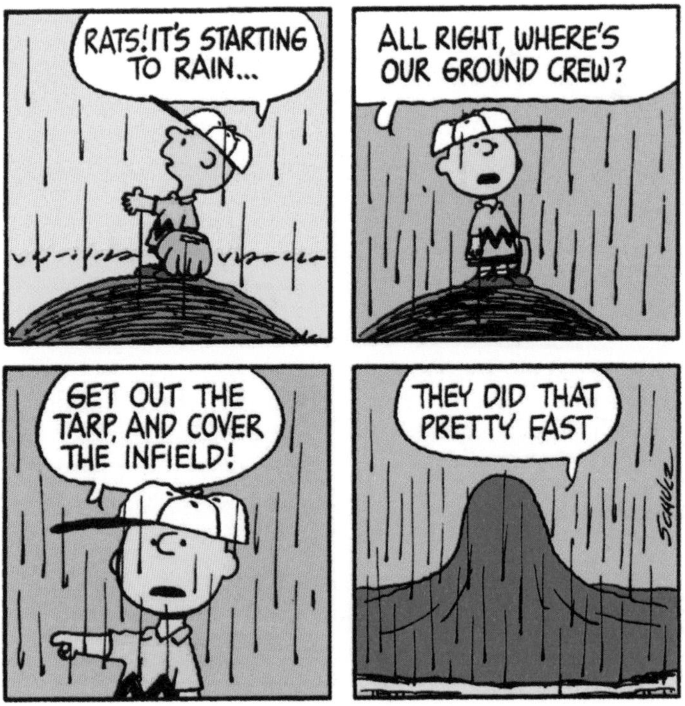
RATS! IT'S STARTING TO RAIN...
ALL RIGHT, WHERE'S OUR GROUND CREW?
GET OUT THE TARP, AND COVER THE INFIELD!
THEY DID THAT PRETTY FAST

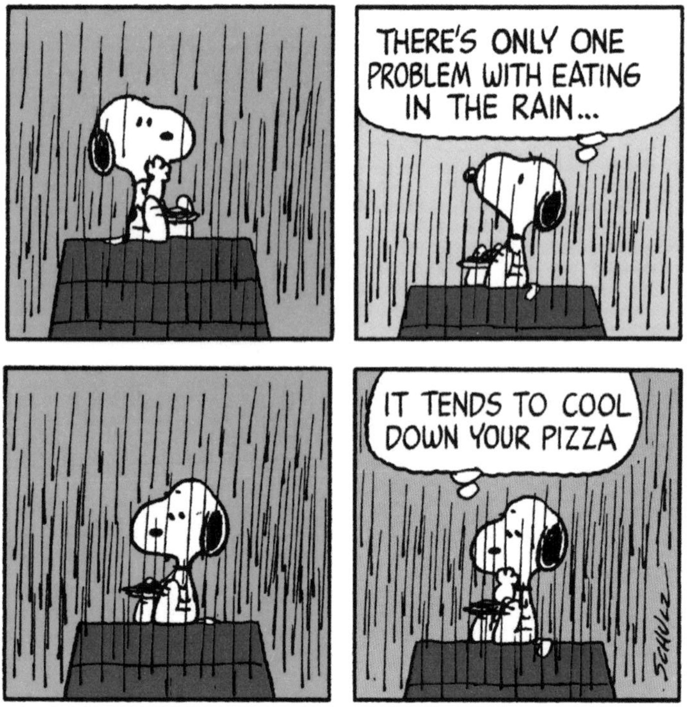
THERE'S ONLY ONE PROBLEM WITH EATING IN THE RAIN...
IT TENDS TO COOL DOWN YOUR PIZZA

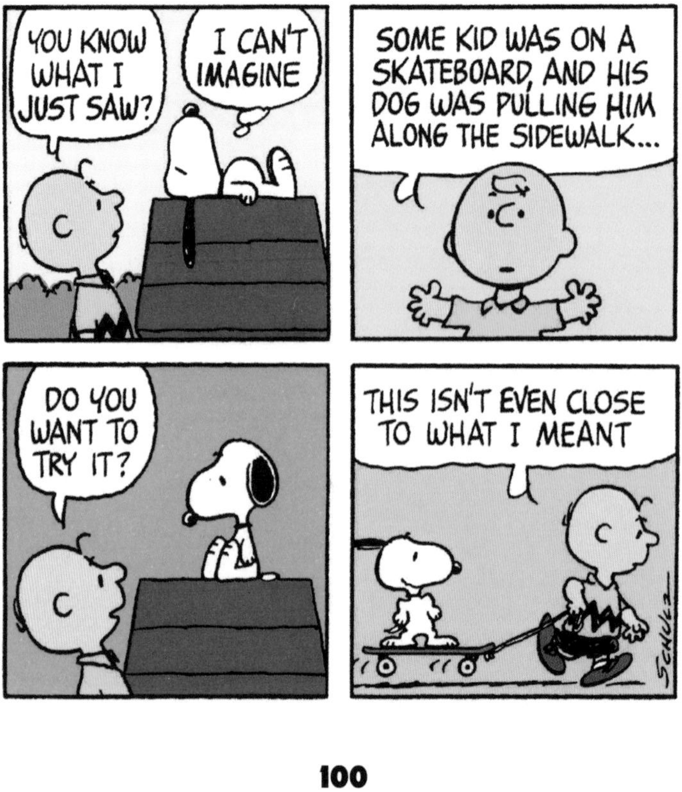
YOU KNOW WHAT I JUST SAW?
I CAN'T IMAGINE
SOME KID WAS ON A SKATEBOARD, AND HIS DOG WAS PULLING HIM ALONG THE SIDEWALK...
DO YOU WANT TO TRY IT?
THIS ISN'T EVEN CLOSE TO WHAT I MEANT

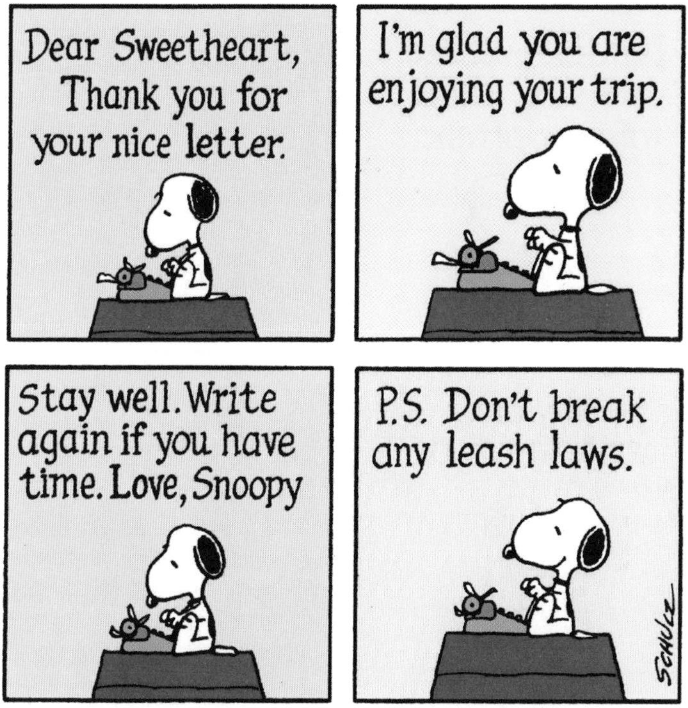
Dear Sweetheart, Thank you for your nice letter.
I'm glad you are enjoying your trip.
Stay well. Write again if you have time. Love, Snoopy
P.S. Don't break any leash laws.

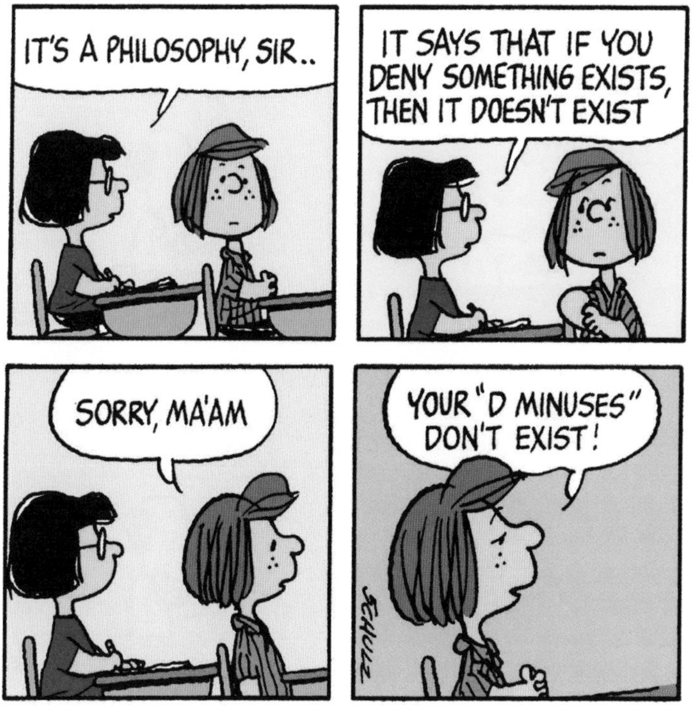
IT'S A PHILOSOPHY, SIR..
IT SAYS THAT IF YOU DENY SOMETHING EXISTS, THEN IT DOESN'T EXIST
SORRY, MA'AM
YOUR "D MINUSES" DON'T EXIST!

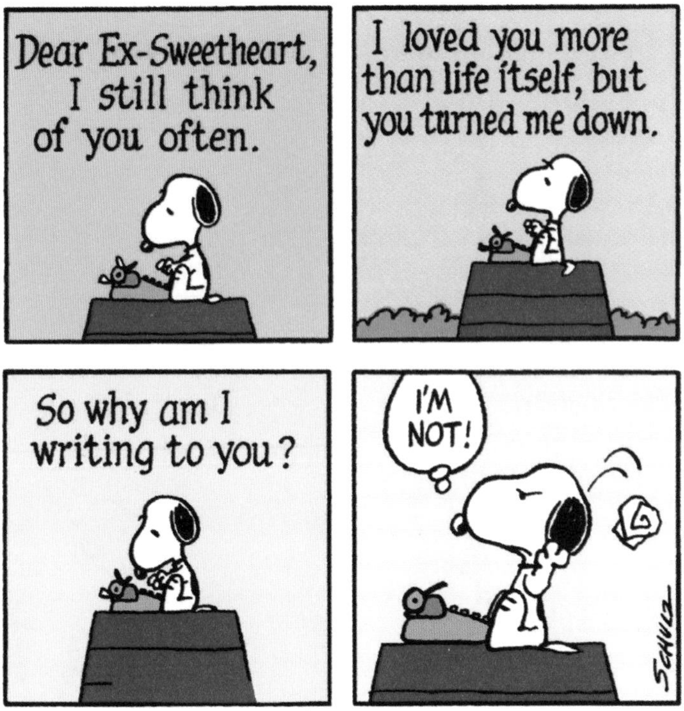
Dear Ex-Sweetheart, I still think of you often.
I loved you more than life itself, but you turned me down.
So why am I writing to you?
I'M NOT!
SCHULZ

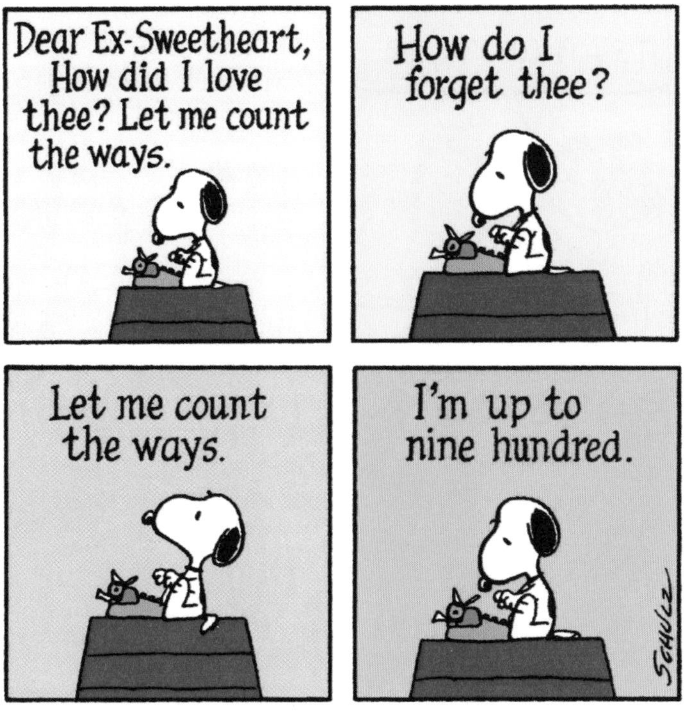
Dear Ex-Sweetheart, How did I love thee? Let me count the ways.
How do I forget thee?
Let me count the ways.
I'm up to nine hundred.
SCHULZ

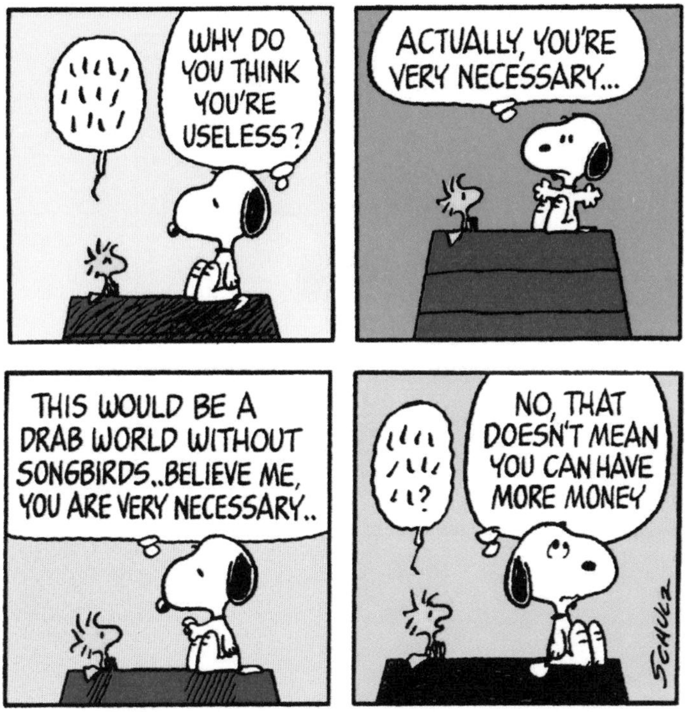
WHY DO YOU THINK YOU'RE USELESS?
ACTUALLY, YOU'RE VERY NECESSARY...
THIS WOULD BE A DRAB WORLD WITHOUT SONGBIRDS..BELIEVE ME, YOU ARE VERY NECESSARY..
NO, THAT DOESN'T MEAN YOU CAN HAVE MORE MONEY
SCHULZ

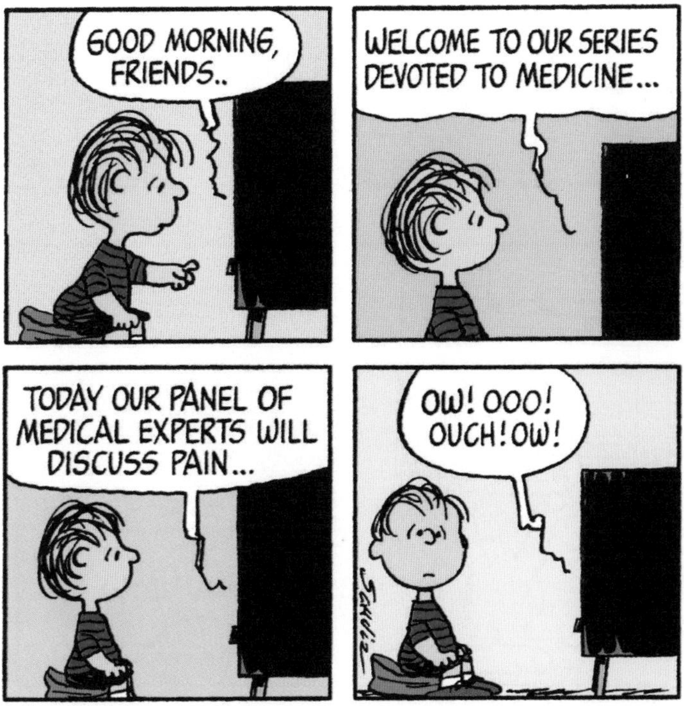
GOOD MORNING, FRIENDS..
WELCOME TO OUR SERIES DEVOTED TO MEDICINE...
TODAY OUR PANEL OF MEDICAL EXPERTS WILL DISCUSS PAIN...
OW! OOO! OUCH! OW!
SCHULZ

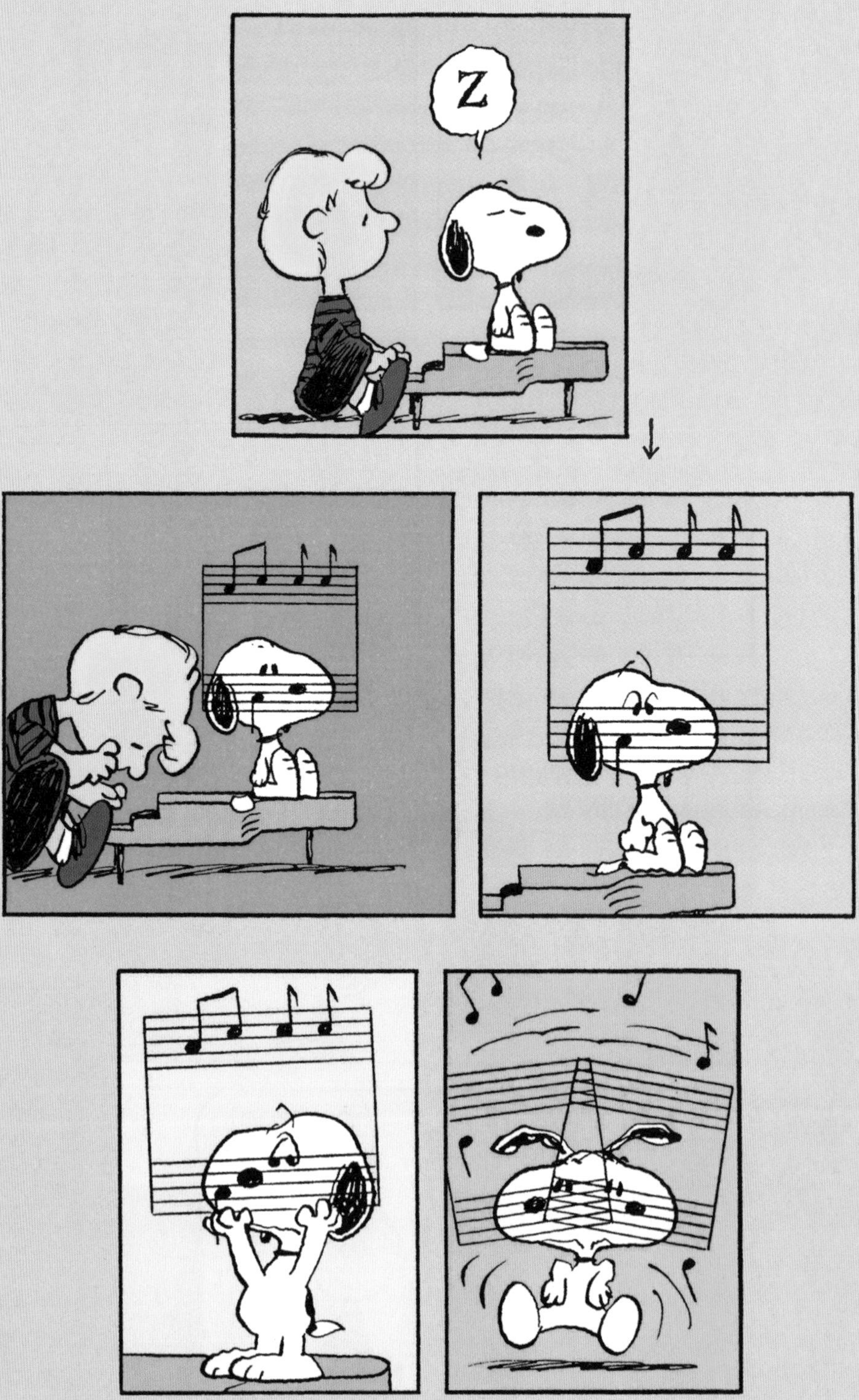
Z

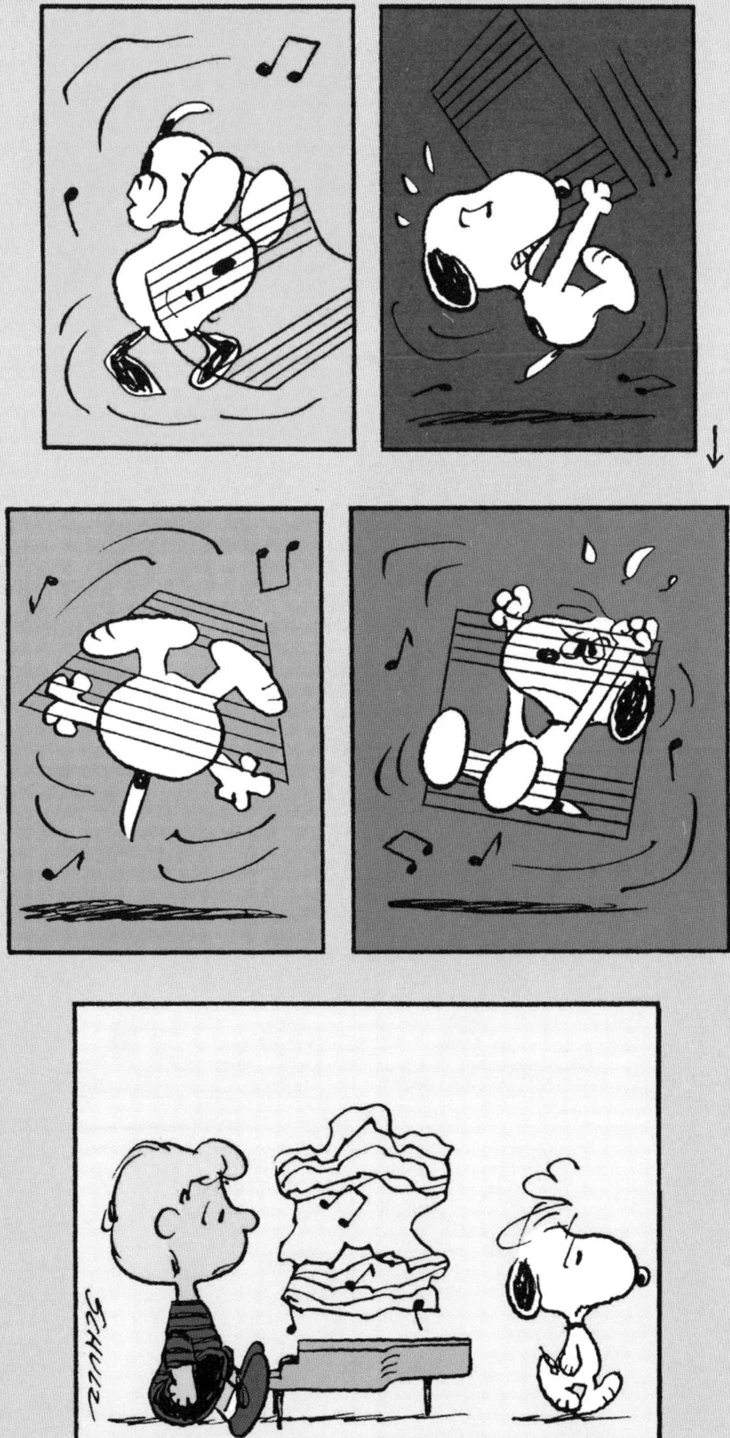
SCHULZ

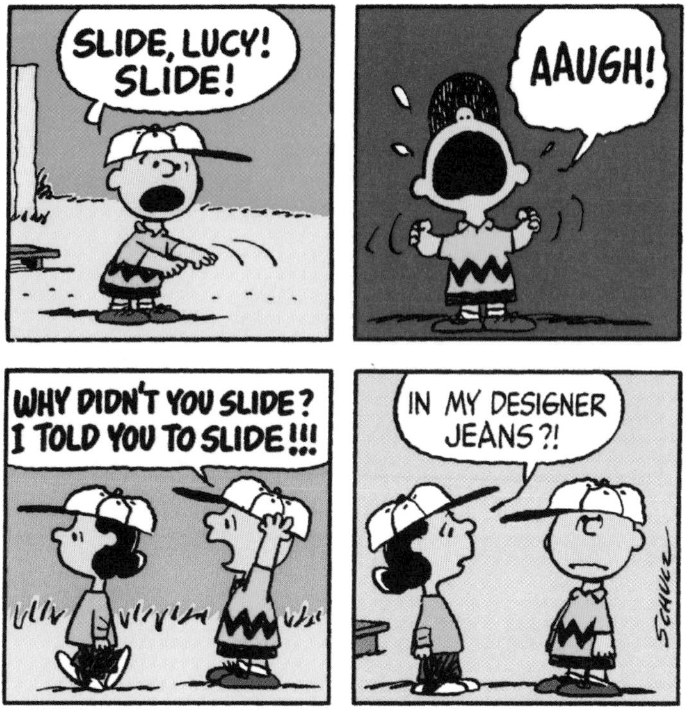
SLIDE, LUCY! SLIDE!
AAUGH!
WHY DIDN'T YOU SLIDE? I TOLD YOU TO SLIDE!!!
IN MY DESIGNER JEANS?!
SCHULZ

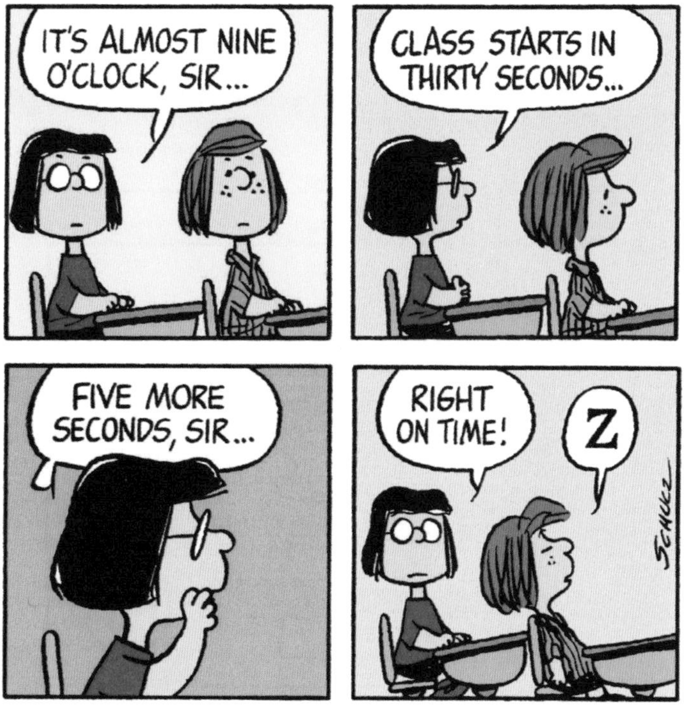
IT'S ALMOST NINE O'CLOCK, SIR...
CLASS STARTS IN THIRTY SECONDS...
FIVE MORE SECONDS, SIR...
RIGHT ON TIME!
Z
SCHULZ

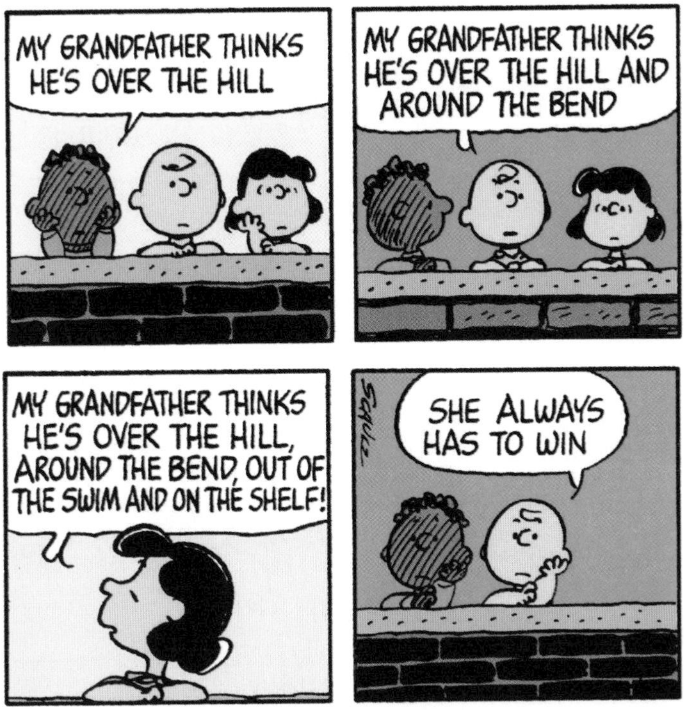
MY GRANDFATHER THINKS HE'S OVER THE HILL
MY GRANDFATHER THINKS HE'S OVER THE HILL AND AROUND THE BEND
MY GRANDFATHER THINKS HE'S OVER THE HILL, AROUND THE BEND, OUT OF THE SWIM AND ON THE SHELF!
SHE ALWAYS HAS TO WIN

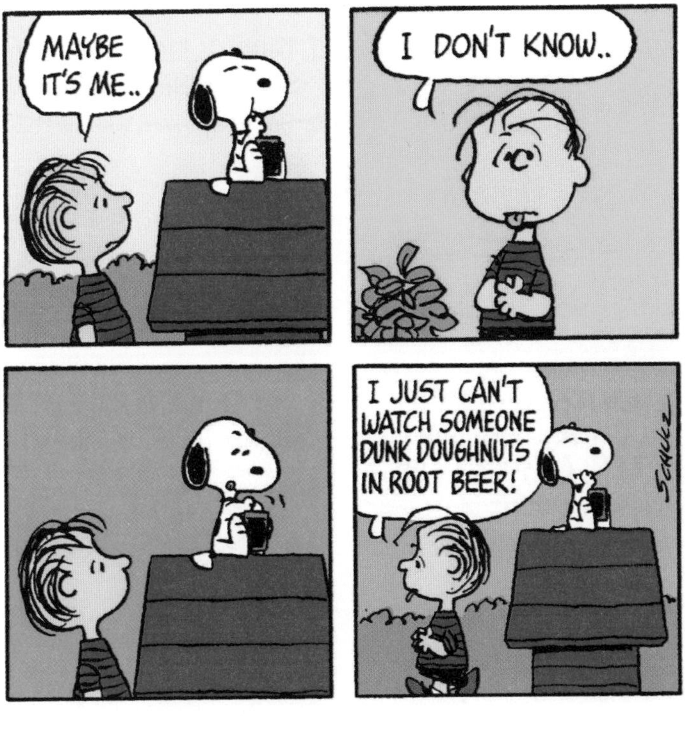
MAYBE IT'S ME..
I DON'T KNOW..
I JUST CAN'T WATCH SOMEONE DUNK DOUGHNUTS IN ROOT BEER!

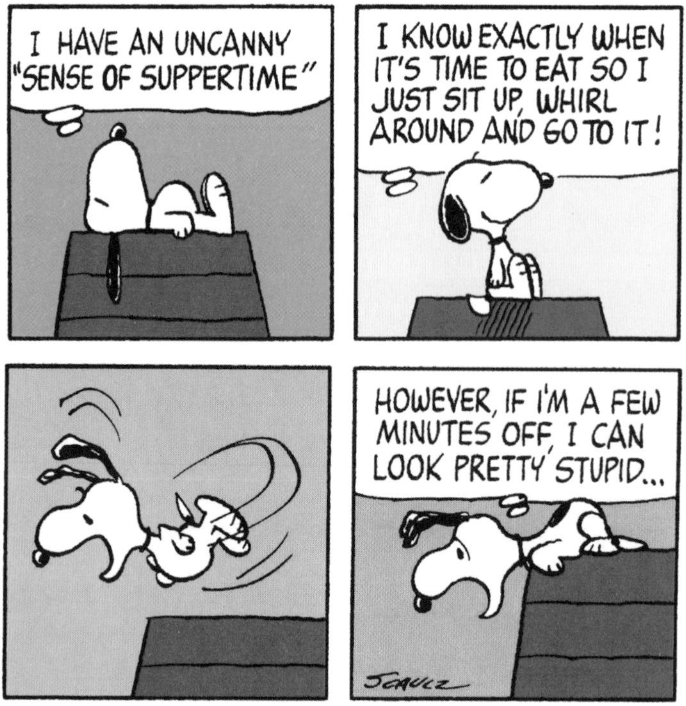
I HAVE AN UNCANNY "SENSE OF SUPPERTIME"
I KNOW EXACTLY WHEN IT'S TIME TO EAT SO I JUST SIT UP, WHIRL AROUND AND GO TO IT!
HOWEVER, IF I'M A FEW MINUTES OFF, I CAN LOOK PRETTY STUPID...

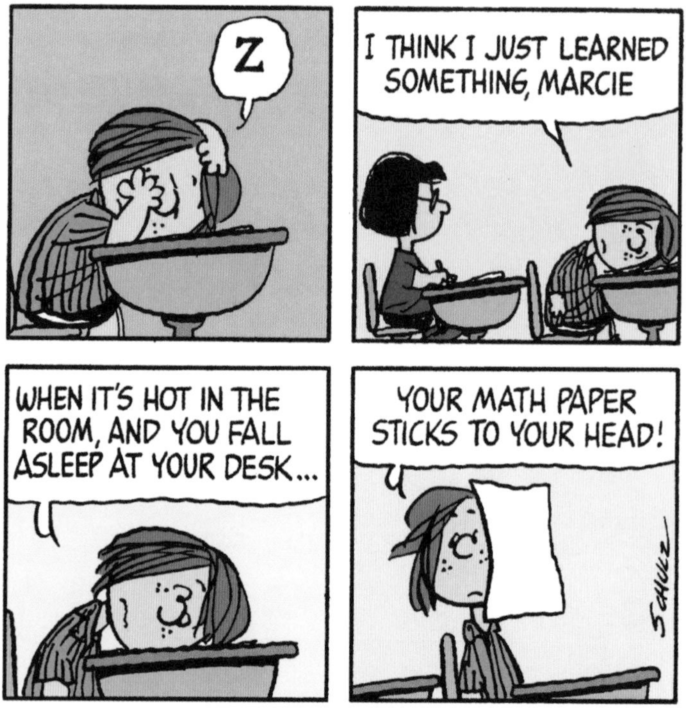
Z
I THINK I JUST LEARNED SOMETHING, MARCIE
WHEN IT'S HOT IN THE ROOM, AND YOU FALL ASLEEP AT YOUR DESK...
YOUR MATH PAPER STICKS TO YOUR HEAD!

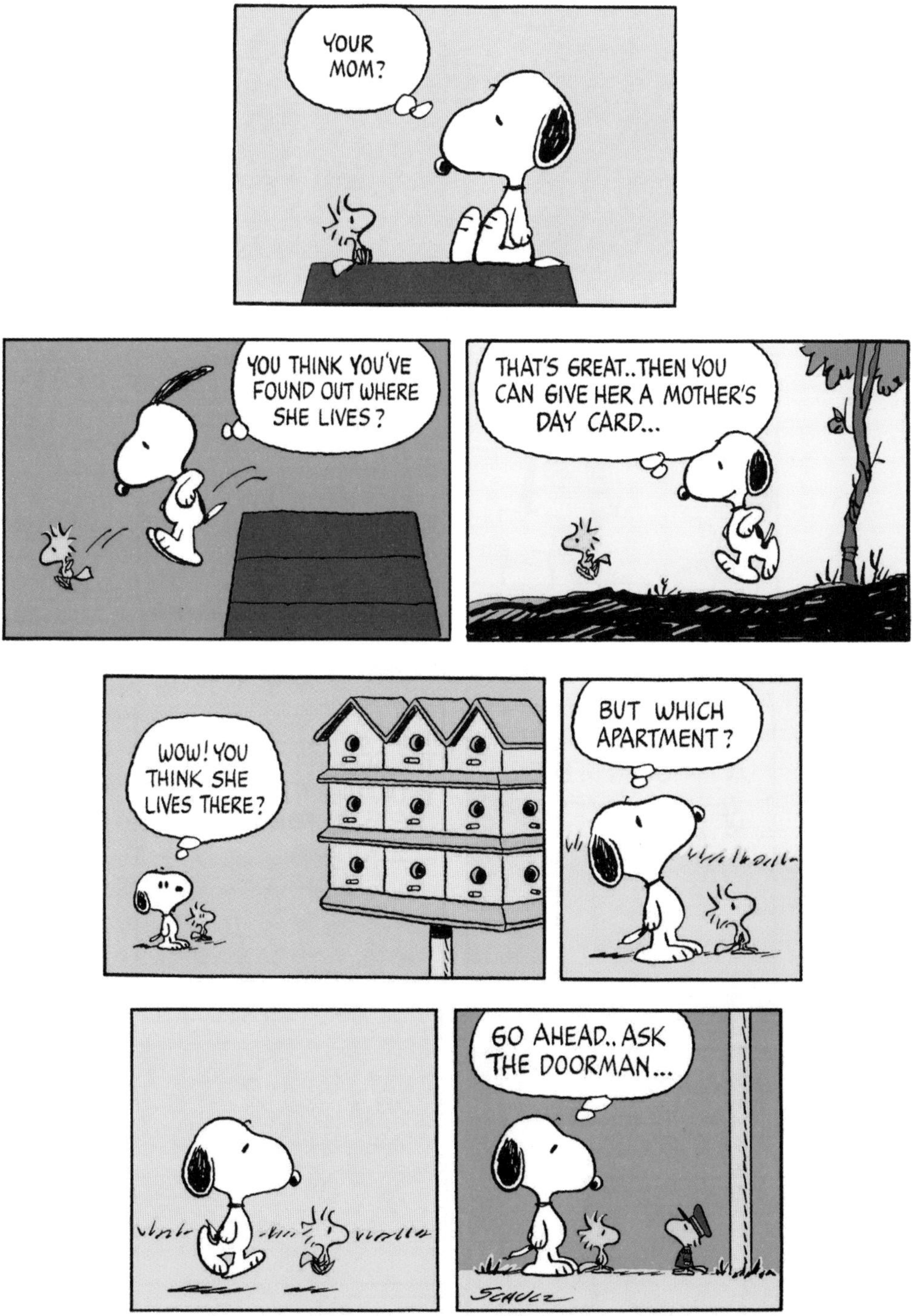
YOUR MOM?
YOU THINK YOU'VE FOUND OUT WHERE SHE LIVES?
THAT'S GREAT..THEN YOU CAN GIVE HER A MOTHER'S DAY CARD...
WOW! YOU THINK SHE LIVES THERE?
BUT WHICH APARTMENT?
GO AHEAD.. ASK THE DOORMAN...
SCHULZ

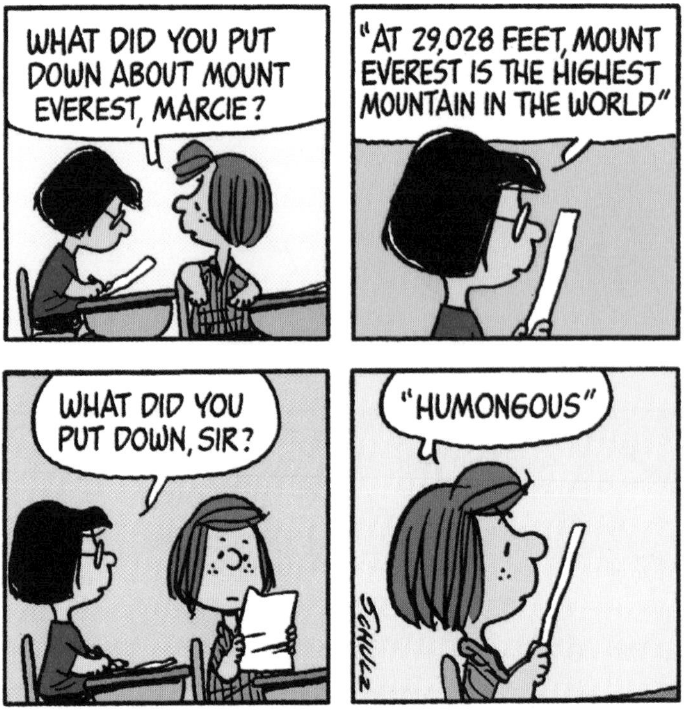
WHAT DID YOU PUT DOWN ABOUT MOUNT EVEREST, MARCIE?
"AT 29,028 FEET, MOUNT EVEREST IS THE HIGHEST MOUNTAIN IN THE WORLD"
WHAT DID YOU PUT DOWN, SIR?
"HUMONGOUS"

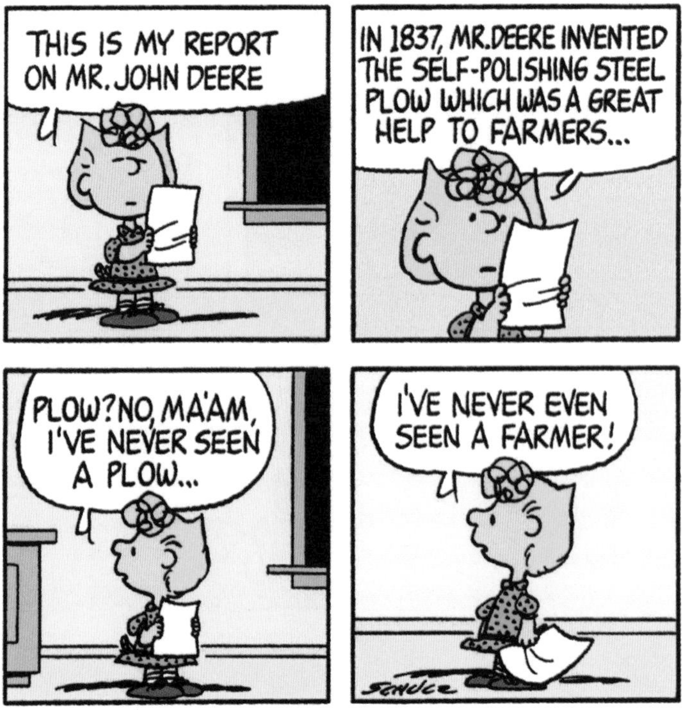
THIS IS MY REPORT ON MR. JOHN DEERE
IN 1837, MR. DEERE INVENTED THE SELF-POLISHING STEEL PLOW WHICH WAS A GREAT HELP TO FARMERS...
PLOW? NO, MA'AM, I'VE NEVER SEEN A PLOW...
I'VE NEVER EVEN SEEN A FARMER!

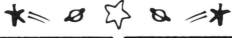

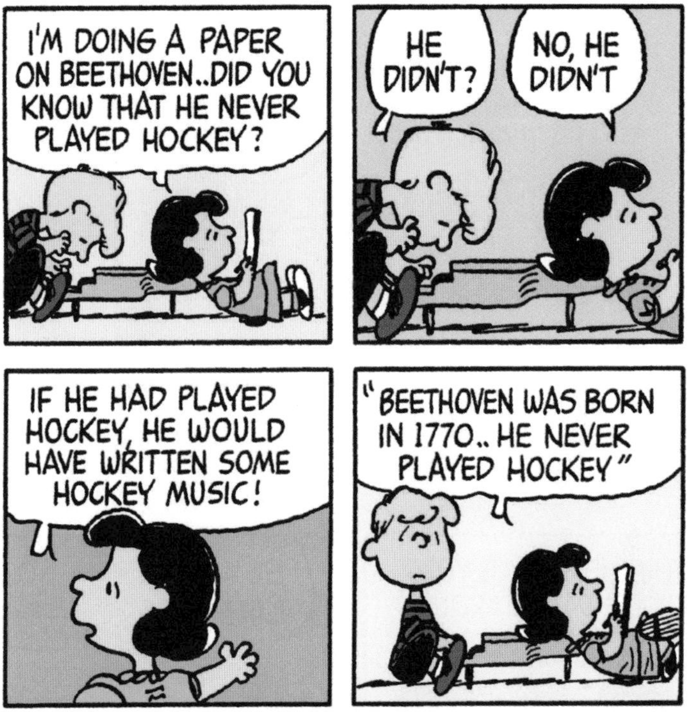
I'M DOING A PAPER ON BEETHOVEN..DID YOU KNOW THAT HE NEVER PLAYED HOCKEY?
HE DIDN'T?
NO, HE DIDN'T
IF HE HAD PLAYED HOCKEY, HE WOULD HAVE WRITTEN SOME HOCKEY MUSIC!
"BEETHOVEN WAS BORN IN 1770.. HE NEVER PLAYED HOCKEY"

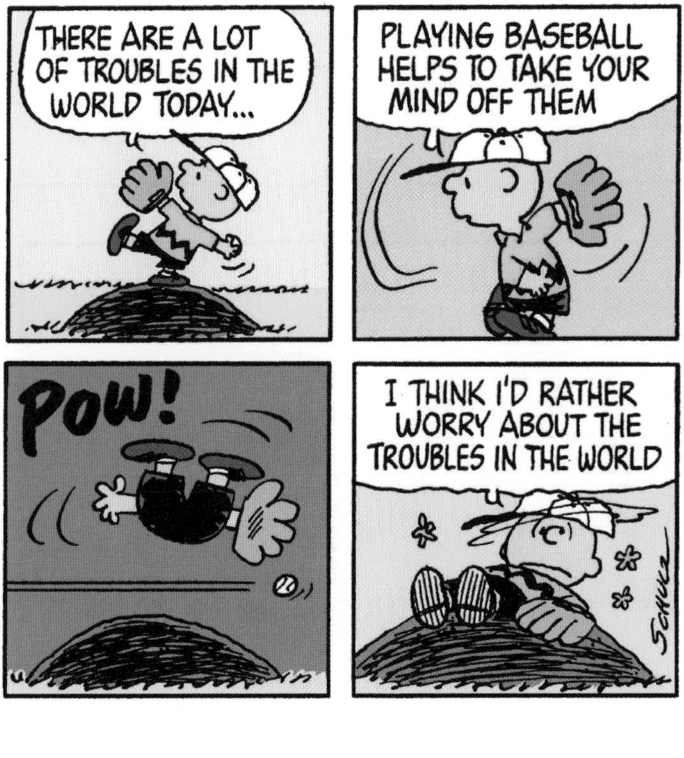
THERE ARE A LOT OF TROUBLES IN THE WORLD TODAY...
PLAYING BASEBALL HELPS TO TAKE YOUR MIND OFF THEM
POW!
I THINK I'D RATHER WORRY ABOUT THE TROUBLES IN THE WORLD
SCHULZ

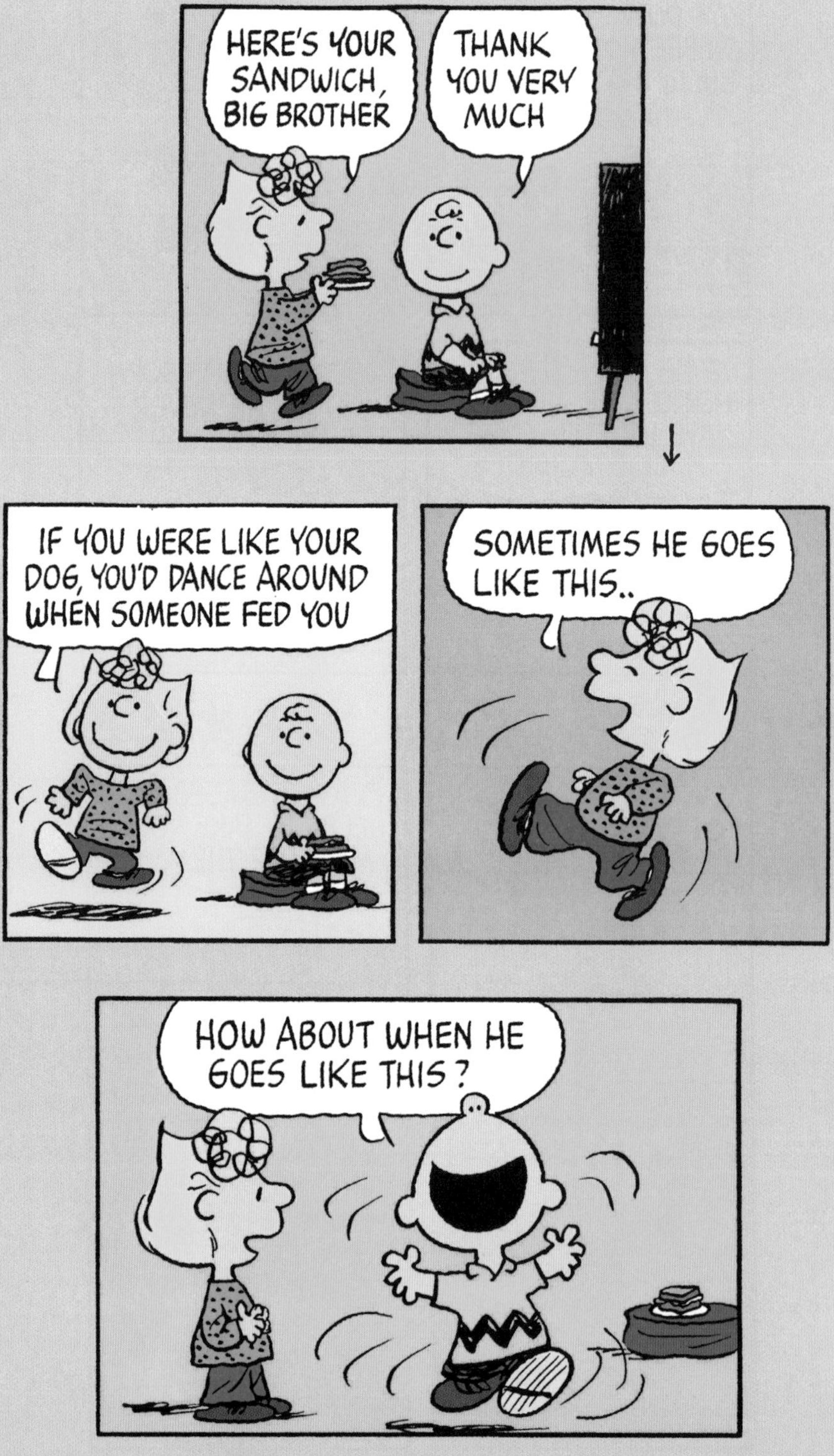
HERE'S YOUR SANDWICH, BIG BROTHER
THANK YOU VERY MUCH
IF YOU WERE LIKE YOUR DOG, YOU'D DANCE AROUND WHEN SOMEONE FED YOU
SOMETIMES HE GOES LIKE THIS..
HOW ABOUT WHEN HE GOES LIKE THIS ?

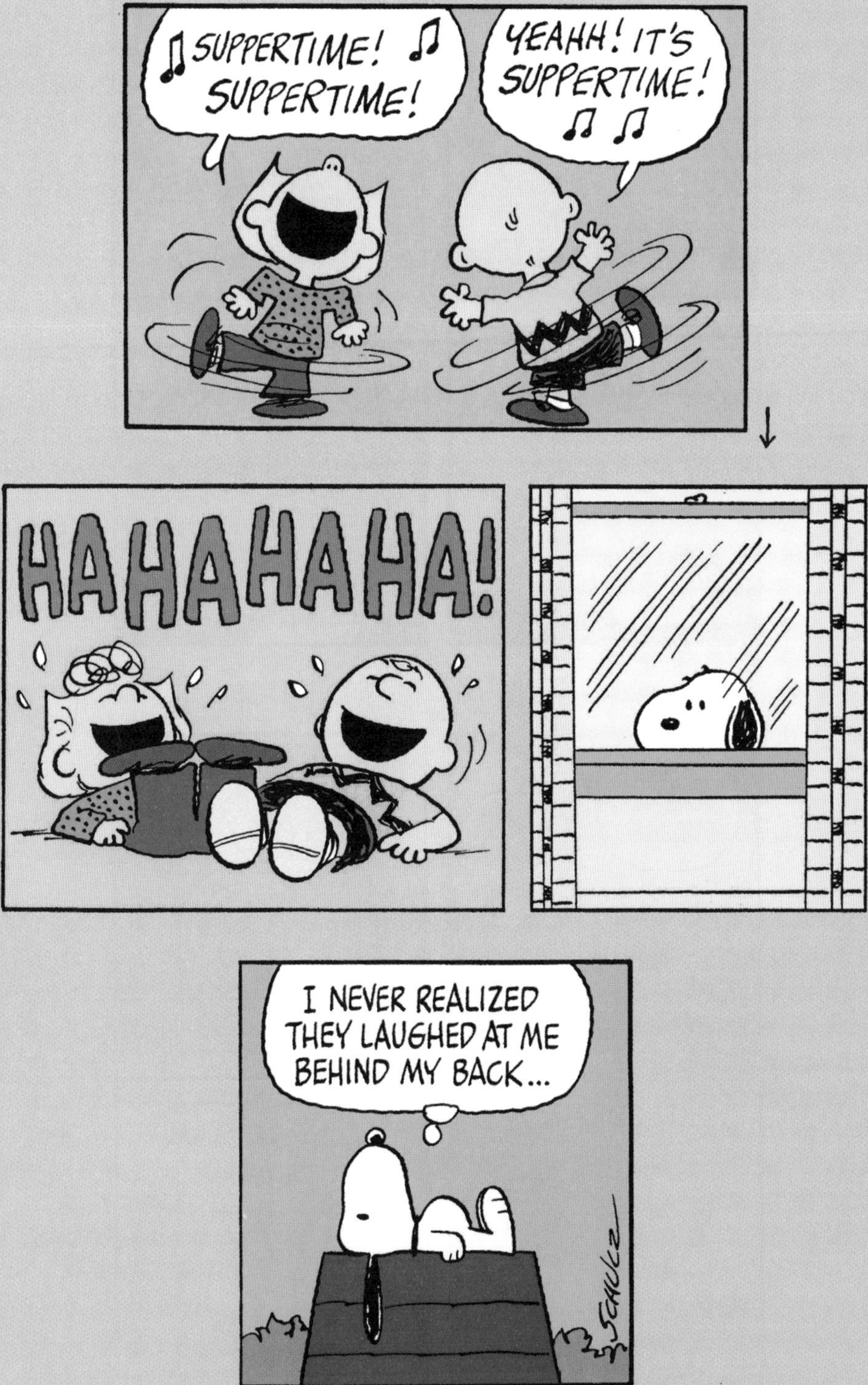
♫ SUPPERTIME! ♫ SUPPERTIME!
YEAHH! IT'S SUPPERTIME! ♫ ♫
HAHAHAHA!
I NEVER REALIZED THEY LAUGHED AT ME BEHIND MY BACK...
SCHULZ

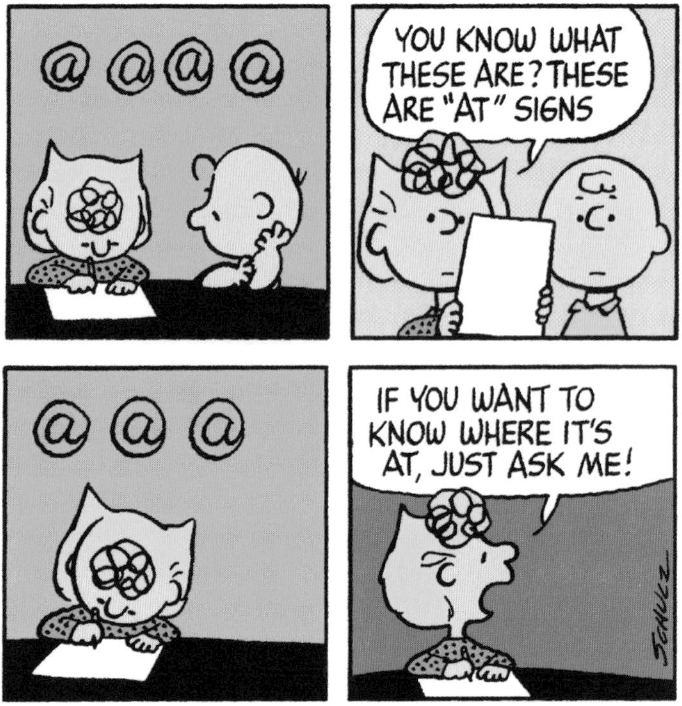
YOU KNOW WHAT THESE ARE? THESE ARE "AT" SIGNS
IF YOU WANT TO KNOW WHERE IT'S AT, JUST ASK ME!
SCHULZ

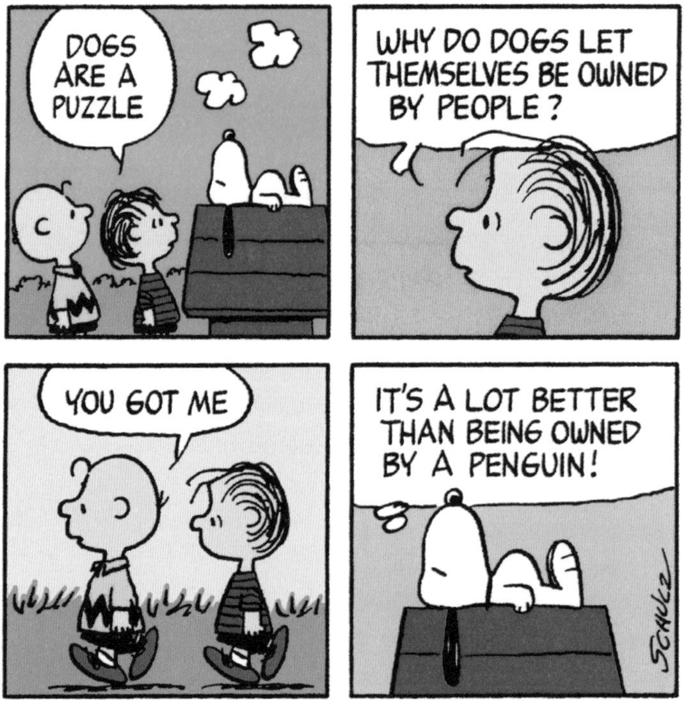
DOGS ARE A PUZZLE
WHY DO DOGS LET THEMSELVES BE OWNED BY PEOPLE?
YOU GOT ME
IT'S A LOT BETTER THAN BEING OWNED BY A PENGUIN!
SCHULZ

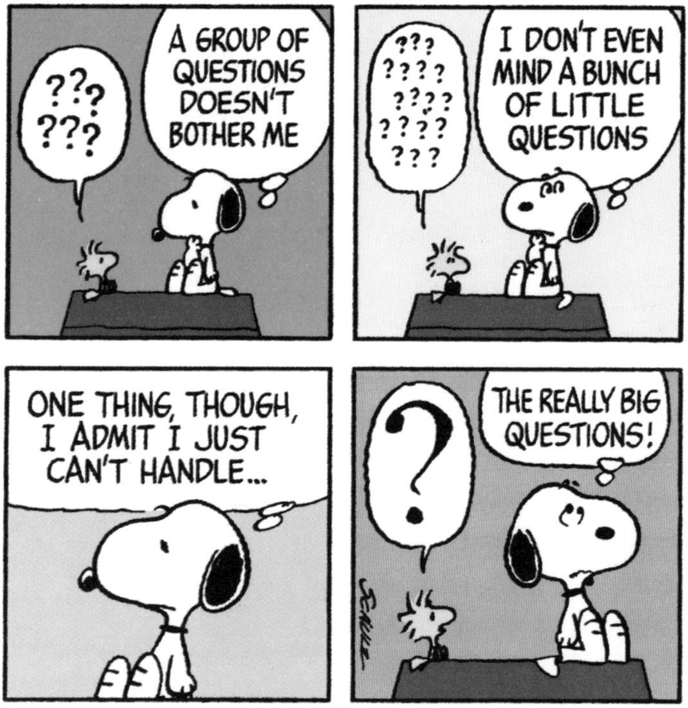
???
???
A GROUP OF QUESTIONS DOESN'T BOTHER ME
???
????
????
????
???
I DON'T EVEN MIND A BUNCH OF LITTLE QUESTIONS
ONE THING, THOUGH, I ADMIT I JUST CAN'T HANDLE...
?
THE REALLY BIG QUESTIONS!

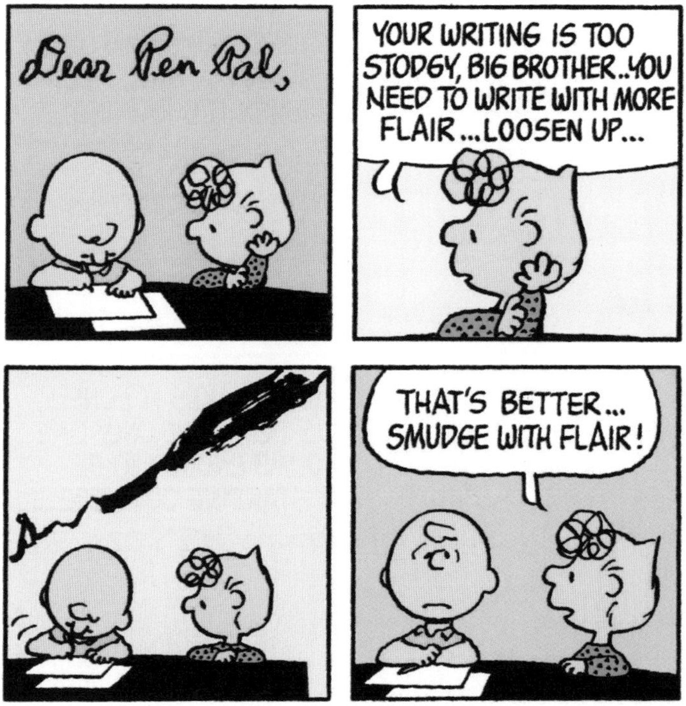
Dear Pen Pal,
YOUR WRITING IS TOO STODGY, BIG BROTHER..YOU NEED TO WRITE WITH MORE FLAIR...LOOSEN UP...
THAT'S BETTER... SMUDGE WITH FLAIR!

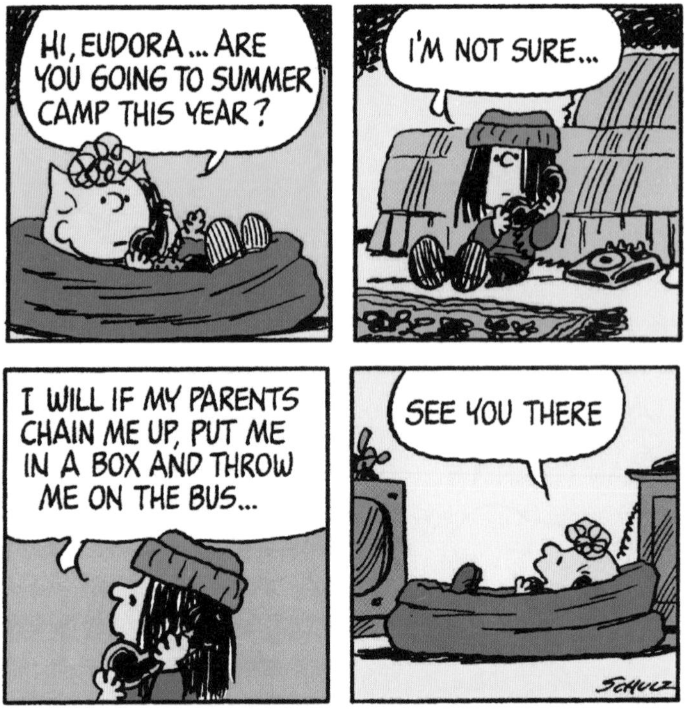
HI, EUDORA... ARE YOU GOING TO SUMMER CAMP THIS YEAR?
I'M NOT SURE...
I WILL IF MY PARENTS CHAIN ME UP, PUT ME IN A BOX AND THROW ME ON THE BUS...
SEE YOU THERE
SCHULZ

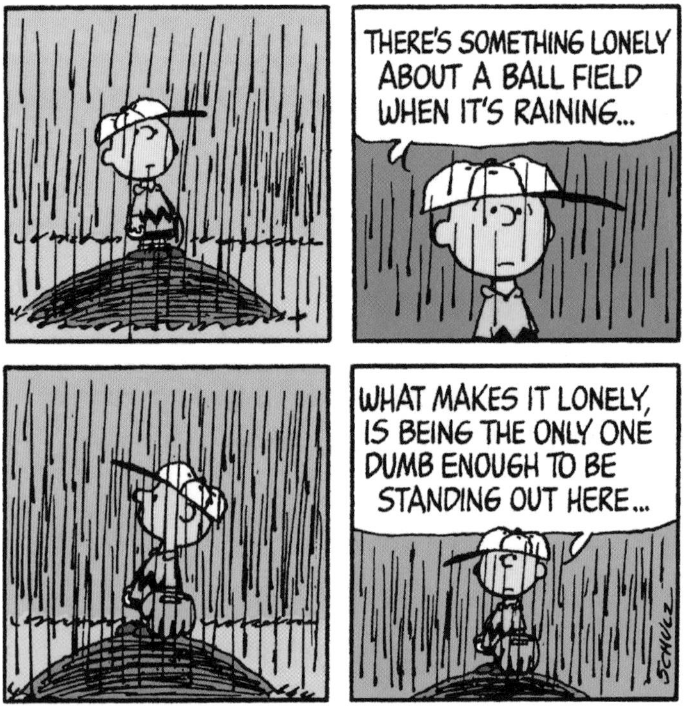
THERE'S SOMETHING LONELY ABOUT A BALL FIELD WHEN IT'S RAINING...
WHAT MAKES IT LONELY, IS BEING THE ONLY ONE DUMB ENOUGH TO BE STANDING OUT HERE...
SCHULZ

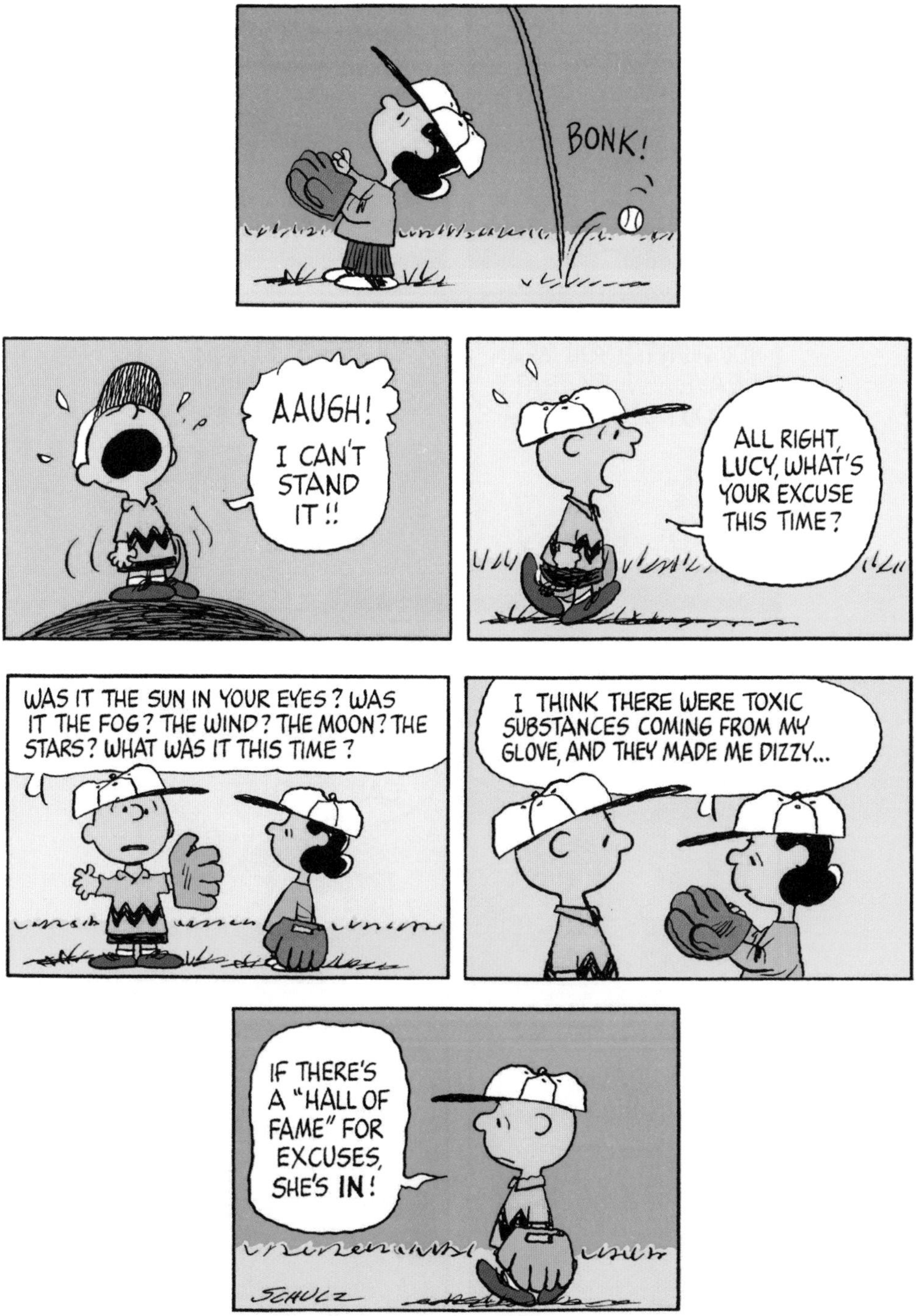
BONK!
AAUGH! I CAN'T STAND IT!!
ALL RIGHT, LUCY, WHAT'S YOUR EXCUSE THIS TIME?
WAS IT THE SUN IN YOUR EYES? WAS IT THE FOG? THE WIND? THE MOON? THE STARS? WHAT WAS IT THIS TIME?
I THINK THERE WERE TOXIC SUBSTANCES COMING FROM MY GLOVE, AND THEY MADE ME DIZZY...
IF THERE'S A "HALL OF FAME" FOR EXCUSES, SHE'S IN!
SCHULZ

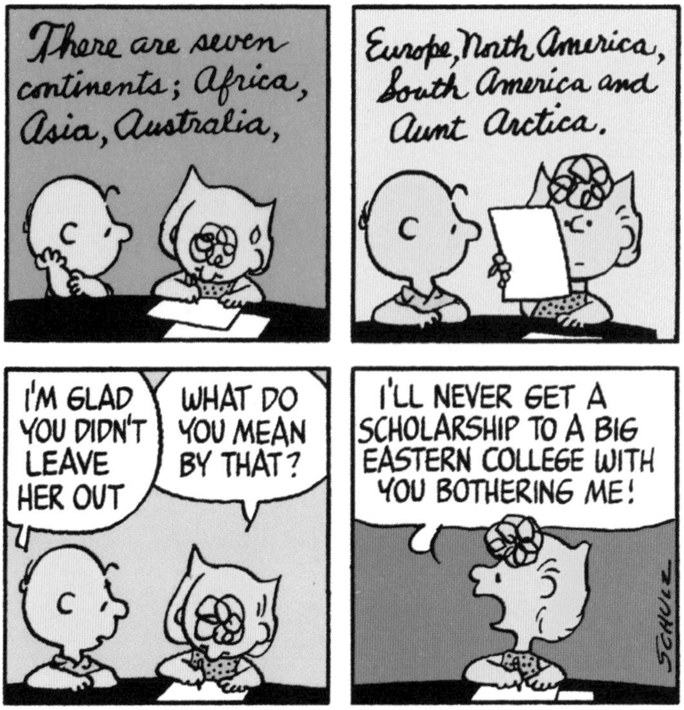
There are seven continents; Africa, Asia, Australia,
Europe, North America, South America and Aunt Arctica.
I'M GLAD YOU DIDN'T LEAVE HER OUT
WHAT DO YOU MEAN BY THAT?
I'LL NEVER GET A SCHOLARSHIP TO A BIG EASTERN COLLEGE WITH YOU BOTHERING ME!
SCHULZ

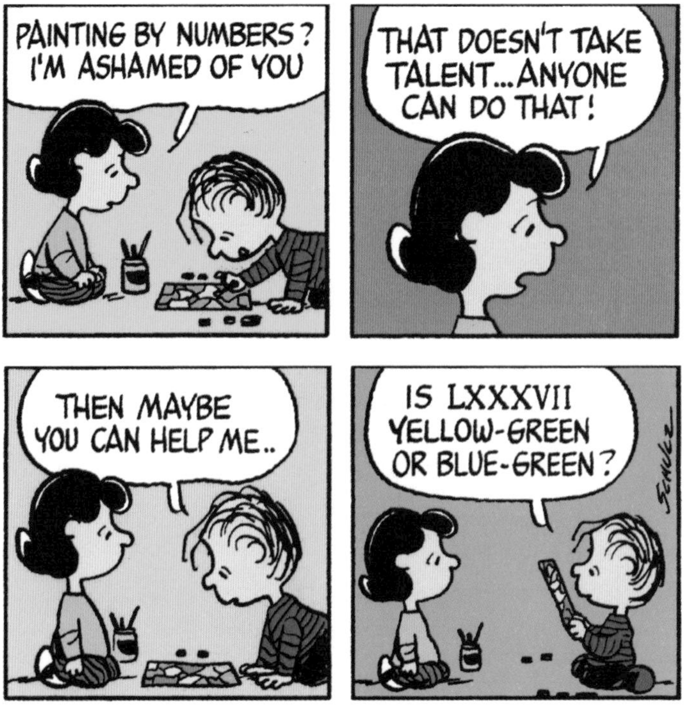
PAINTING BY NUMBERS? I'M ASHAMED OF YOU
THAT DOESN'T TAKE TALENT...ANYONE CAN DO THAT!
THEN MAYBE YOU CAN HELP ME..
IS LXXXVII YELLOW-GREEN OR BLUE-GREEN?
SCHULZ

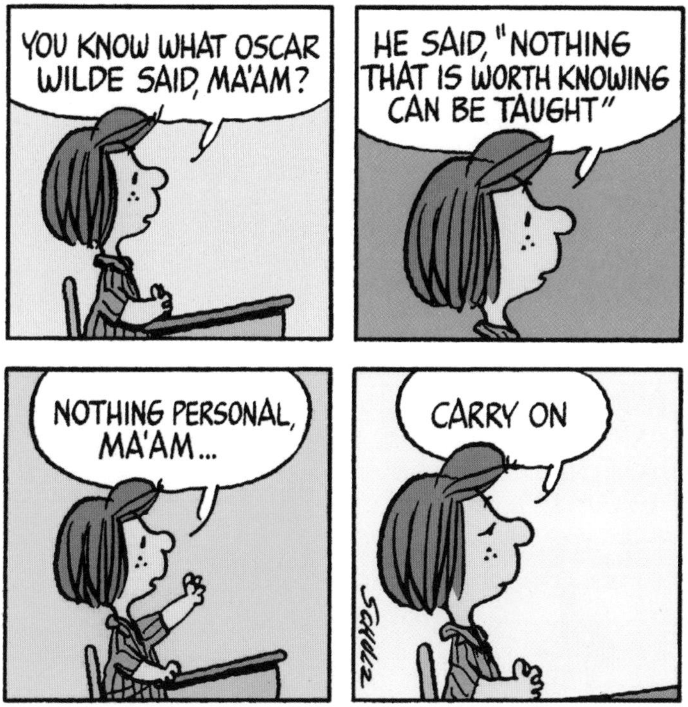
YOU KNOW WHAT OSCAR WILDE SAID, MA'AM?
HE SAID, "NOTHING THAT IS WORTH KNOWING CAN BE TAUGHT"
NOTHING PERSONAL, MA'AM...
CARRY ON
SCHULZ

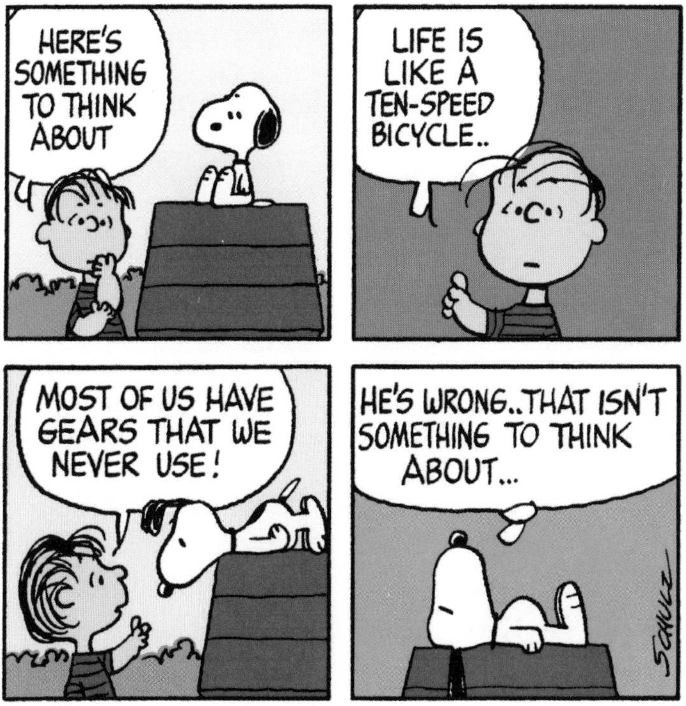
HERE'S SOMETHING TO THINK ABOUT
LIFE IS LIKE A TEN-SPEED BICYCLE..
MOST OF US HAVE GEARS THAT WE NEVER USE!
HE'S WRONG..THAT ISN'T SOMETHING TO THINK ABOUT...
SCHULZ

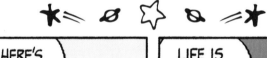

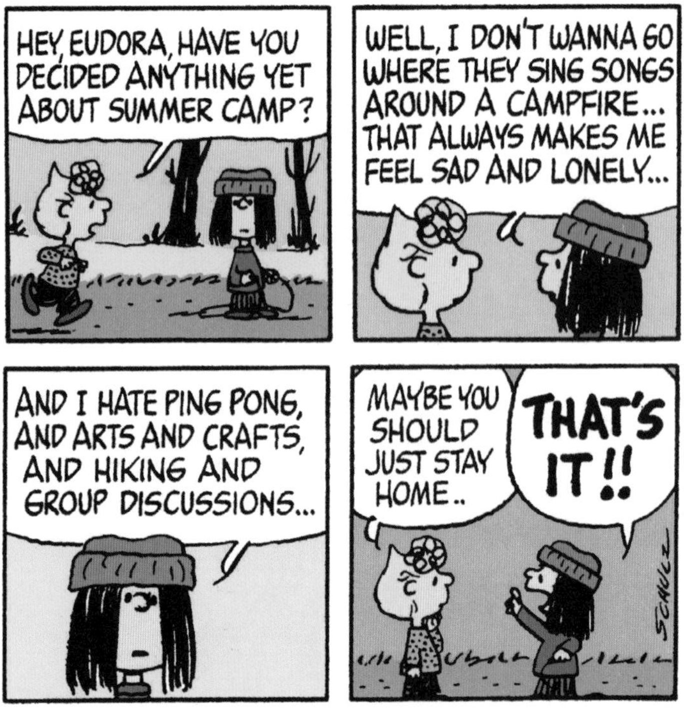
HEY, EUDORA, HAVE YOU DECIDED ANYTHING YET ABOUT SUMMER CAMP?
WELL, I DON'T WANNA GO WHERE THEY SING SONGS AROUND A CAMPFIRE... THAT ALWAYS MAKES ME FEEL SAD AND LONELY...
AND I HATE PING PONG, AND ARTS AND CRAFTS, AND HIKING AND GROUP DISCUSSIONS...
MAYBE YOU SHOULD JUST STAY HOME..
THAT'S IT!!
SCHULZ

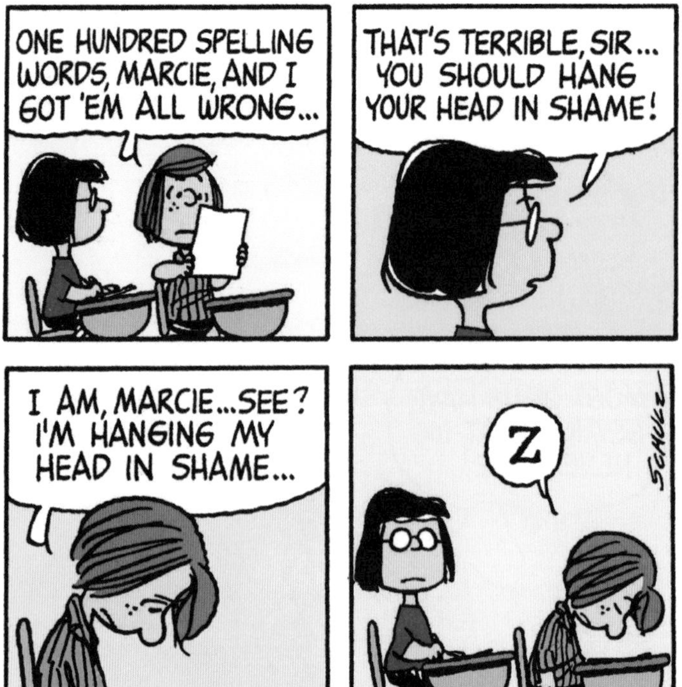
ONE HUNDRED SPELLING WORDS, MARCIE, AND I GOT 'EM ALL WRONG...
THAT'S TERRIBLE, SIR... YOU SHOULD HANG YOUR HEAD IN SHAME!
I AM, MARCIE...SEE? I'M HANGING MY HEAD IN SHAME...
Z
SCHULZ

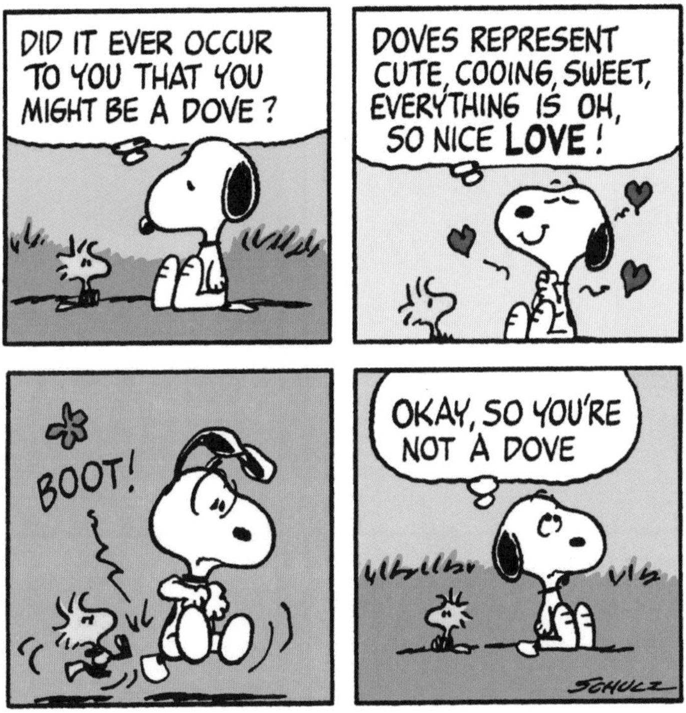
DID IT EVER OCCUR TO YOU THAT YOU MIGHT BE A DOVE?
DOVES REPRESENT CUTE, COOING, SWEET, EVERYTHING IS OH, SO NICE LOVE!
BOOT!
OKAY, SO YOU'RE NOT A DOVE
SCHULZ

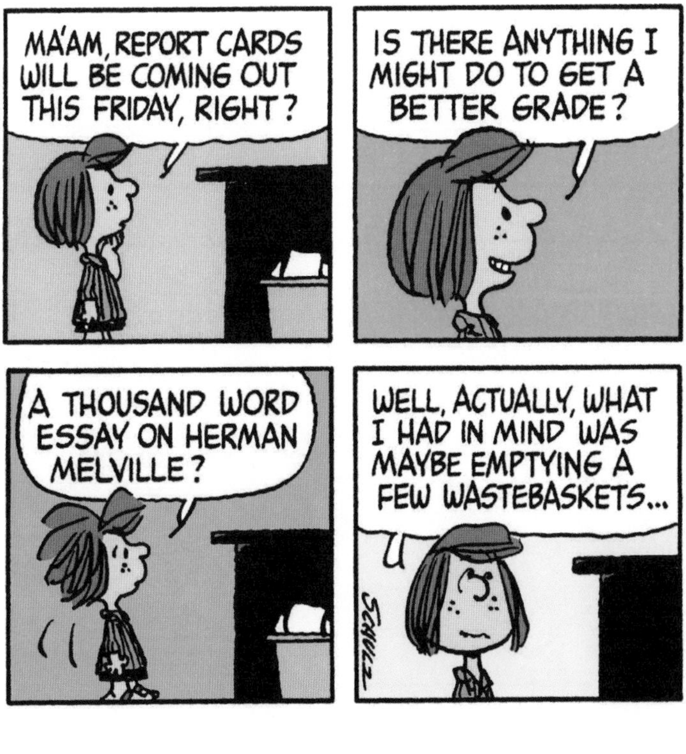
MA'AM, REPORT CARDS WILL BE COMING OUT THIS FRIDAY, RIGHT?
IS THERE ANYTHING I MIGHT DO TO GET A BETTER GRADE?
A THOUSAND WORD ESSAY ON HERMAN MELVILLE?
WELL, ACTUALLY, WHAT I HAD IN MIND WAS MAYBE EMPTYING A FEW WASTEBASKETS...
SCHULZ

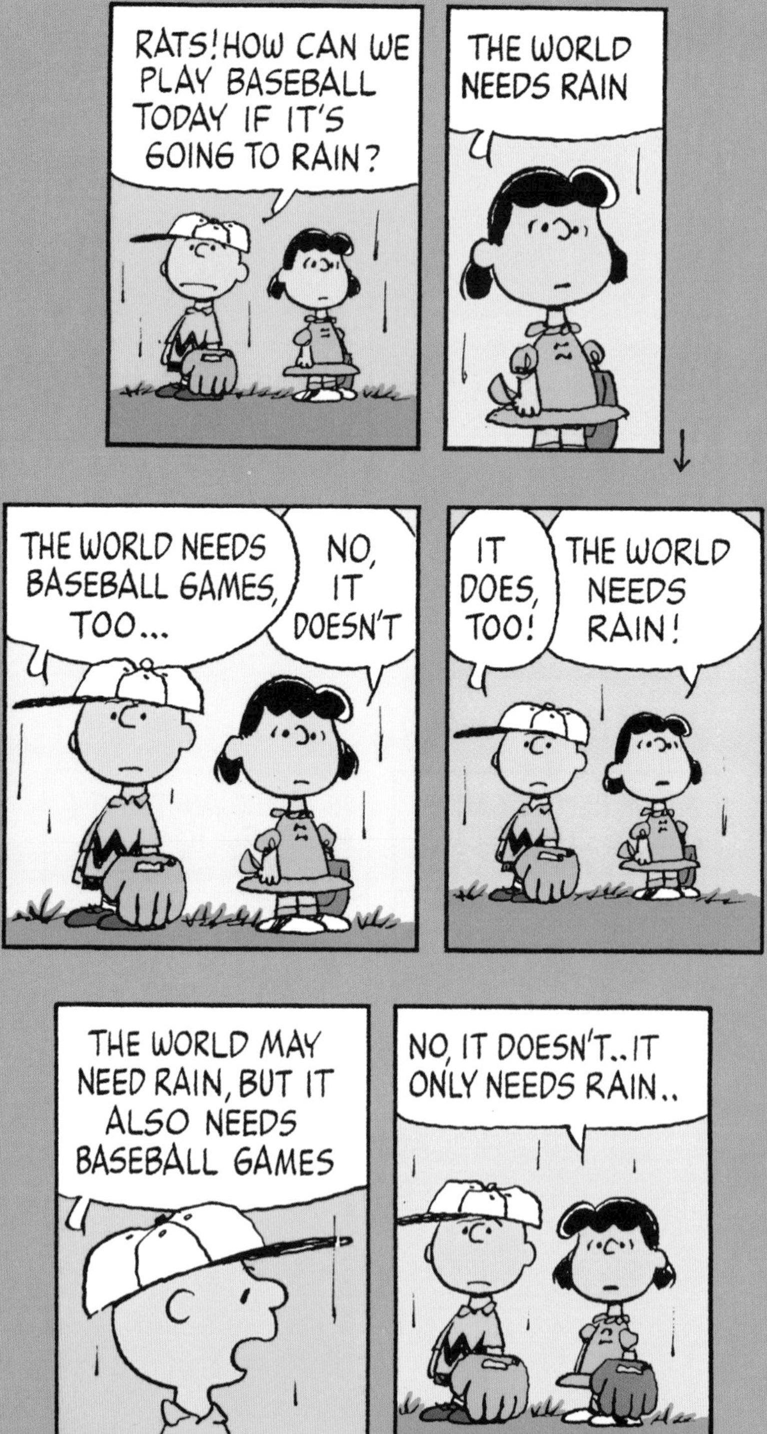
RATS! HOW CAN WE PLAY BASEBALL TODAY IF IT'S GOING TO RAIN?
THE WORLD NEEDS RAIN
THE WORLD NEEDS BASEBALL GAMES, TOO...
NO, IT DOESN'T
IT DOES, TOO!
THE WORLD NEEDS RAIN!
THE WORLD MAY NEED RAIN, BUT IT ALSO NEEDS BASEBALL GAMES
NO, IT DOESN'T.. IT ONLY NEEDS RAIN..

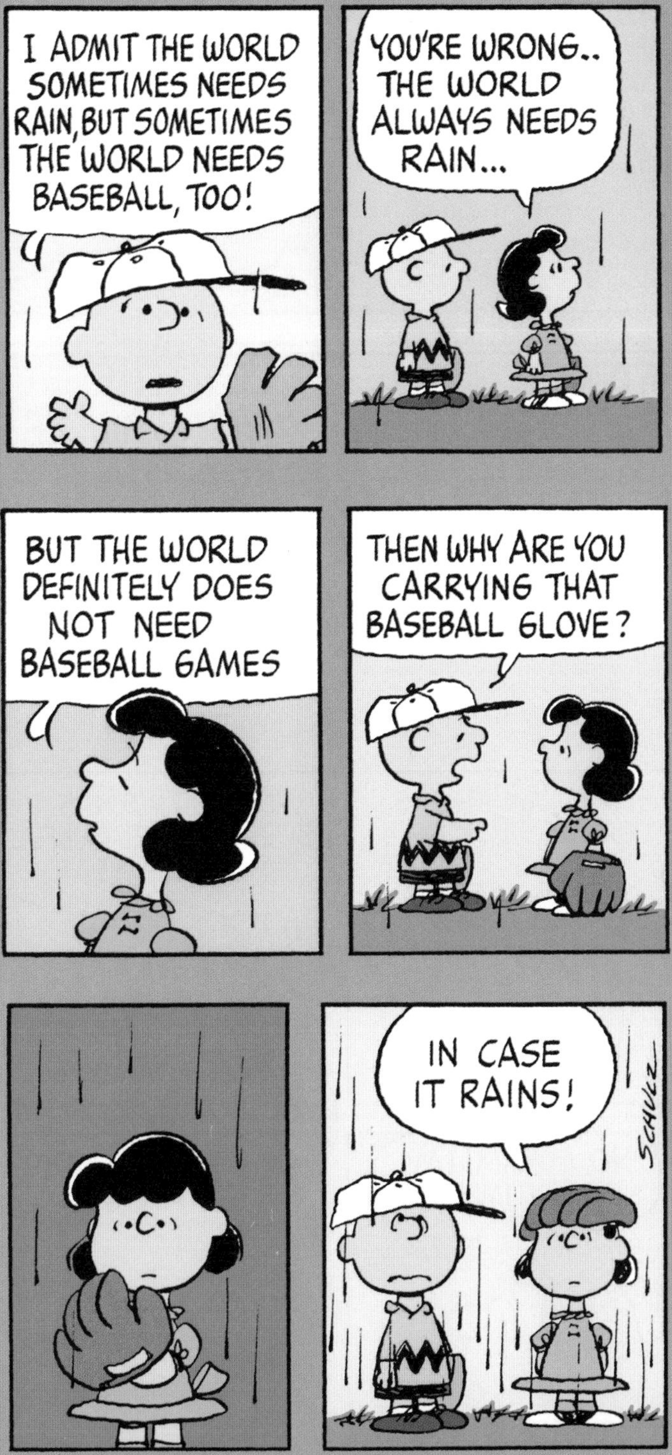
I ADMIT THE WORLD SOMETIMES NEEDS RAIN, BUT SOMETIMES THE WORLD NEEDS BASEBALL, TOO!
YOU'RE WRONG.. THE WORLD ALWAYS NEEDS RAIN...
BUT THE WORLD DEFINITELY DOES NOT NEED BASEBALL GAMES
THEN WHY ARE YOU CARRYING THAT BASEBALL GLOVE?
IN CASE IT RAINS!
SCHULZ

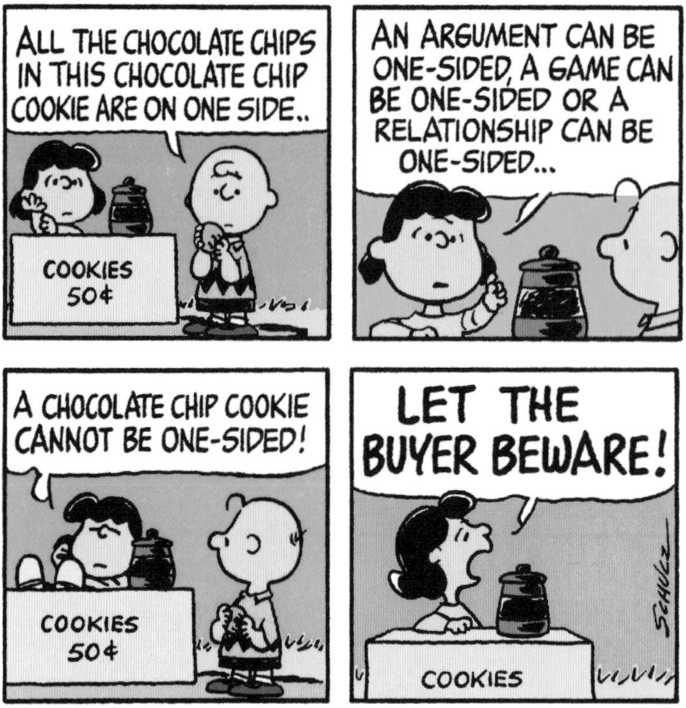
ALL THE CHOCOLATE CHIPS IN THIS CHOCOLATE CHIP COOKIE ARE ON ONE SIDE..
COOKIES 50¢
AN ARGUMENT CAN BE ONE-SIDED, A GAME CAN BE ONE-SIDED OR A RELATIONSHIP CAN BE ONE-SIDED...
A CHOCOLATE CHIP COOKIE CANNOT BE ONE-SIDED!
COOKIES 50¢
LET THE BUYER BEWARE!
COOKIES
SCHULZ

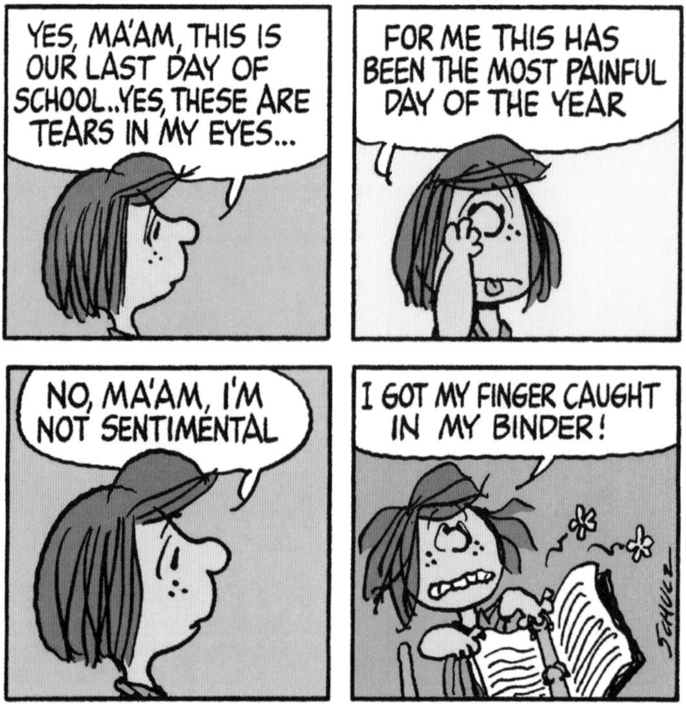
YES, MA'AM, THIS IS OUR LAST DAY OF SCHOOL..YES, THESE ARE TEARS IN MY EYES...
FOR ME THIS HAS BEEN THE MOST PAINFUL DAY OF THE YEAR
NO, MA'AM, I'M NOT SENTIMENTAL
I GOT MY FINGER CAUGHT IN MY BINDER!
SCHULZ

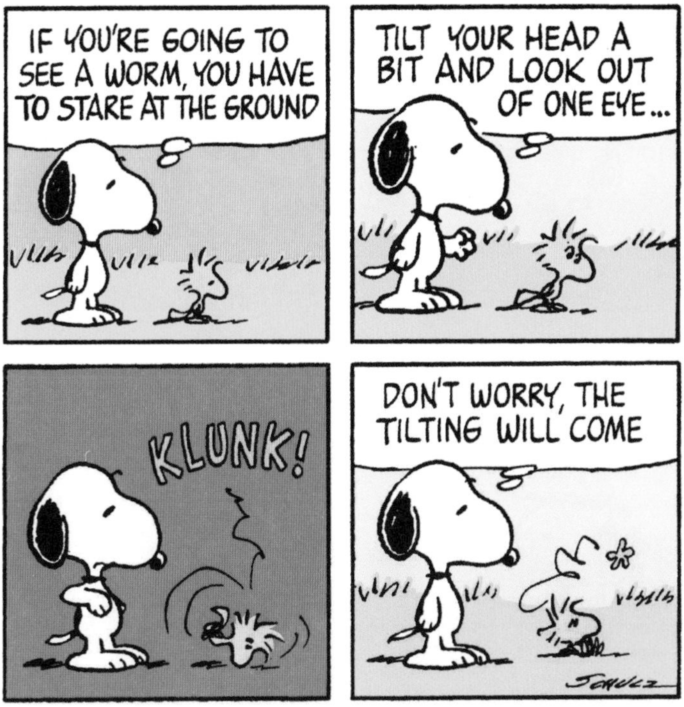
IF YOU'RE GOING TO SEE A WORM, YOU HAVE TO STARE AT THE GROUND
TILT YOUR HEAD A BIT AND LOOK OUT OF ONE EYE...
KLUNK!
DON'T WORRY, THE TILTING WILL COME

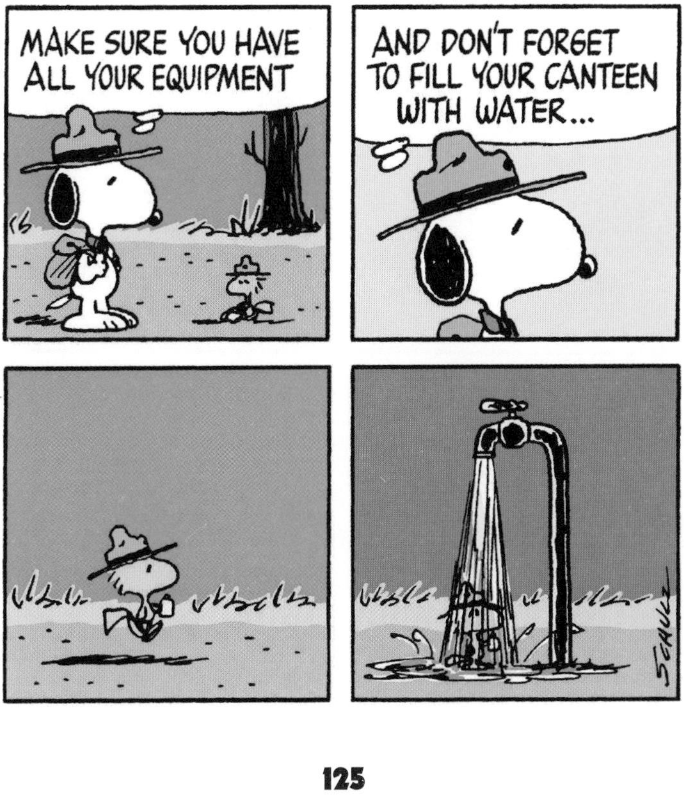
MAKE SURE YOU HAVE ALL YOUR EQUIPMENT
AND DON'T FORGET TO FILL YOUR CANTEEN WITH WATER...

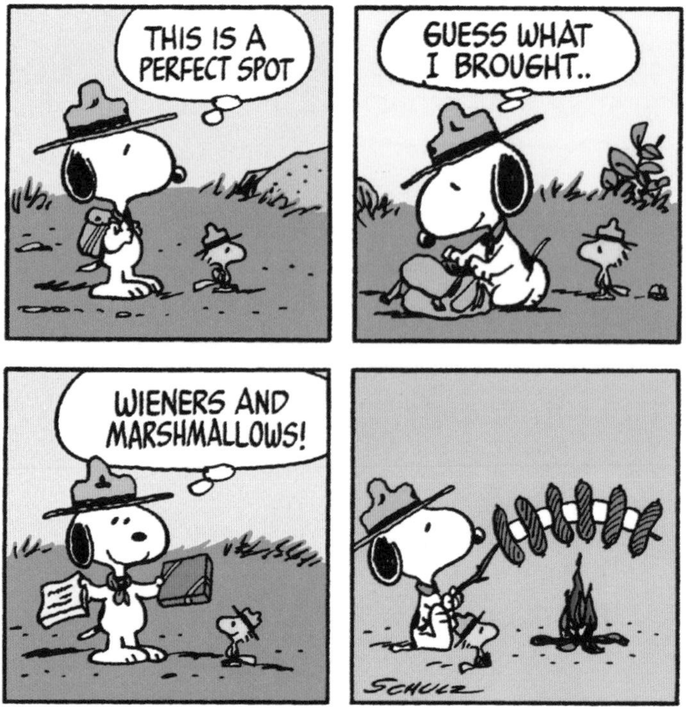
THIS IS A PERFECT SPOT
GUESS WHAT I BROUGHT..
WIENERS AND MARSHMALLOWS!
SCHULZ

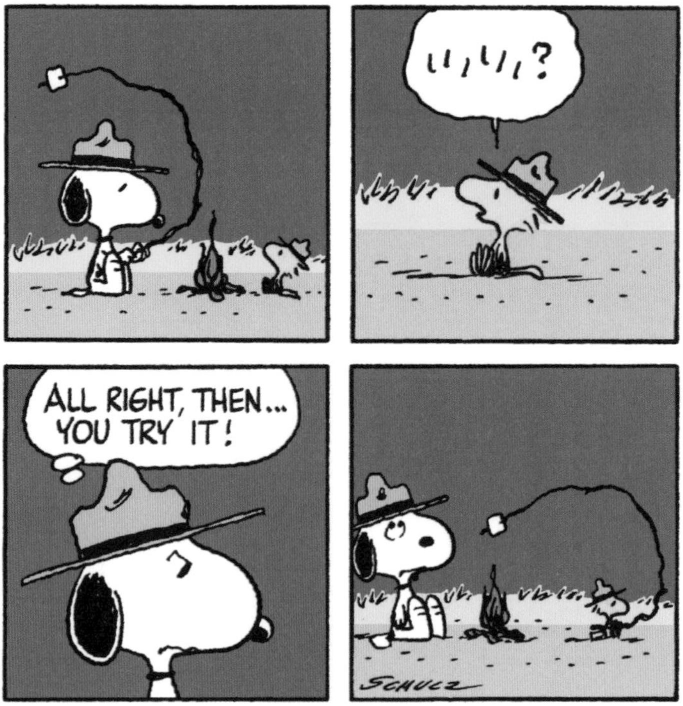
ALL RIGHT, THEN... YOU TRY IT!
SCHULZ

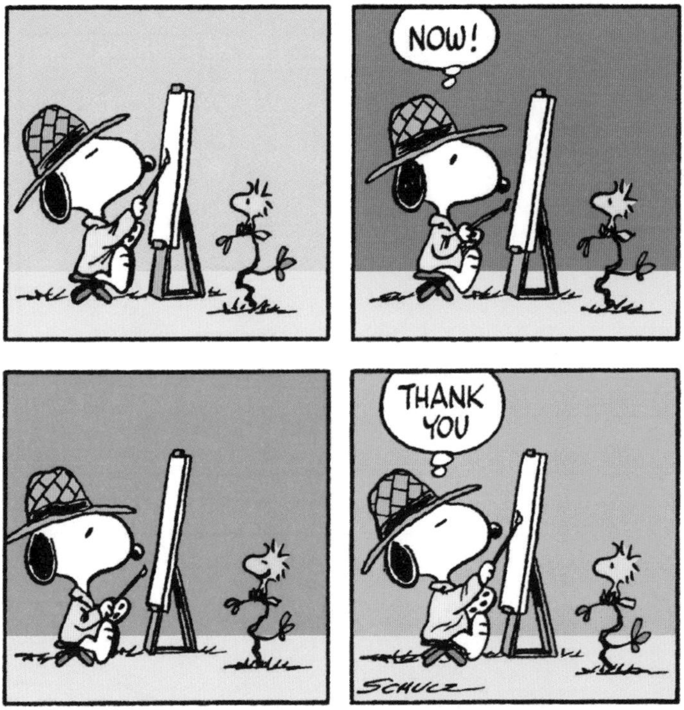
NOW!
THANK YOU
SCHULZ

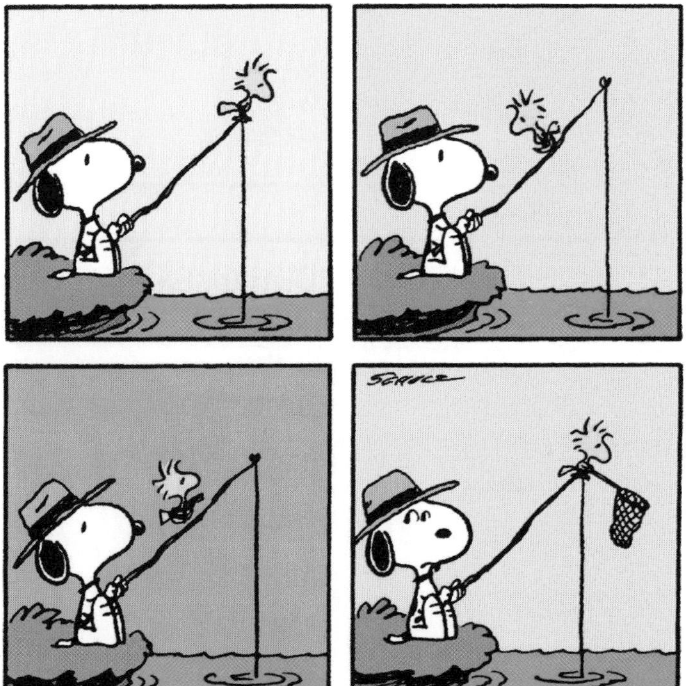
SCHULZ

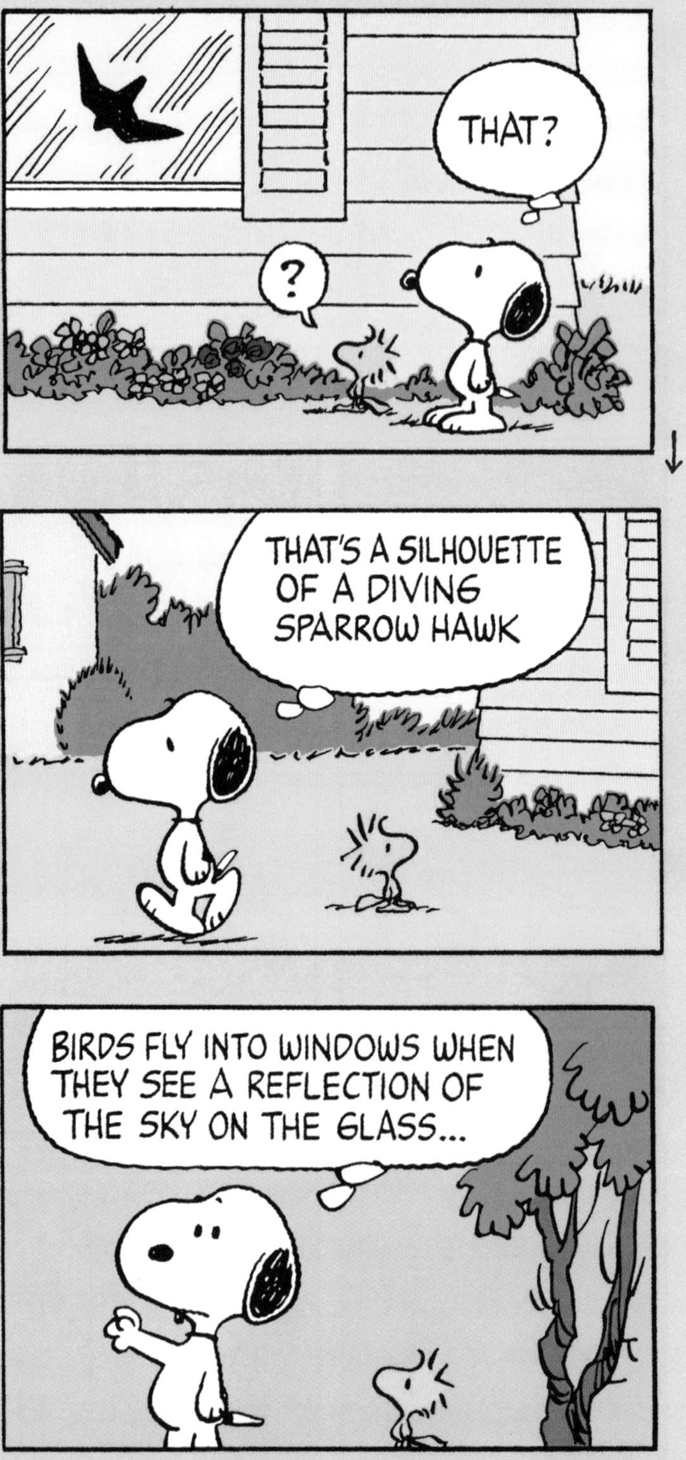
THAT?
?
THAT'S A SILHOUETTE OF A DIVING SPARROW HAWK
BIRDS FLY INTO WINDOWS WHEN THEY SEE A REFLECTION OF THE SKY ON THE GLASS...

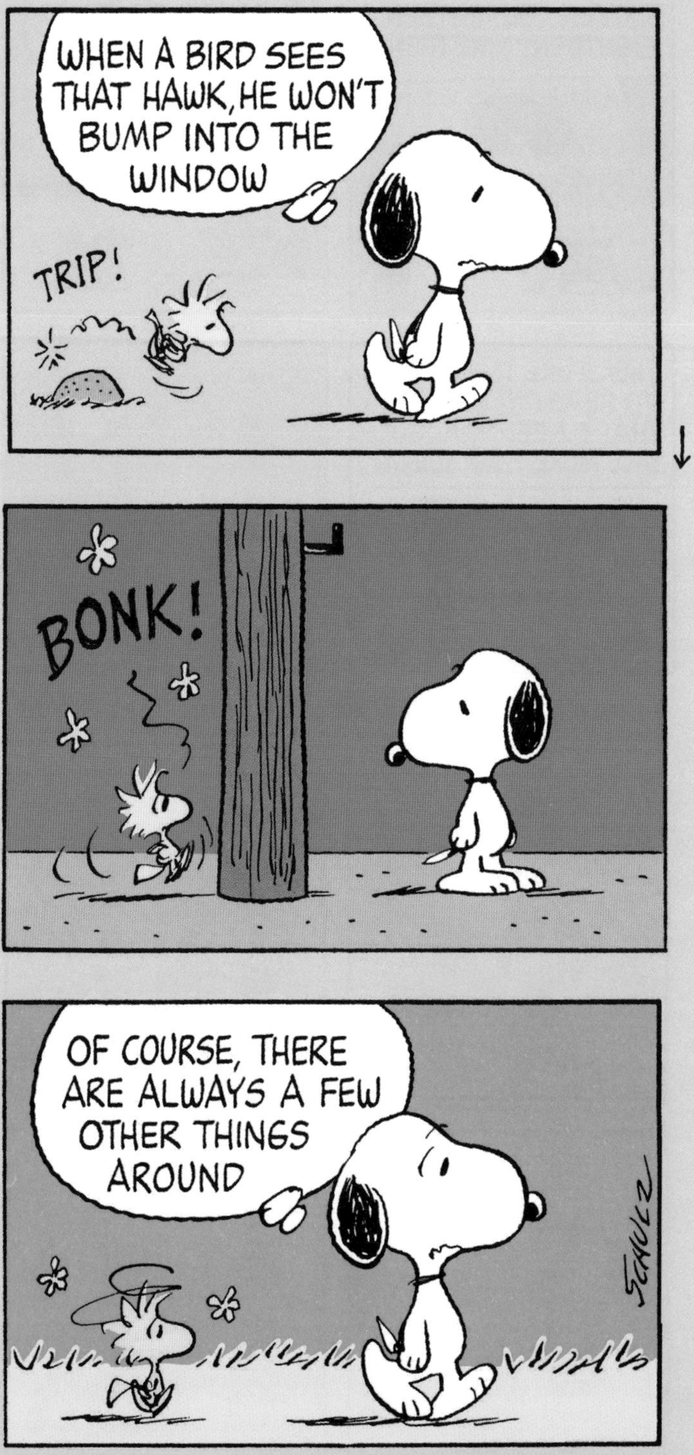
WHEN A BIRD SEES THAT HAWK, HE WON'T BUMP INTO THE WINDOW
TRIP!
BONK!
OF COURSE, THERE ARE ALWAYS A FEW OTHER THINGS AROUND
SCHULZ

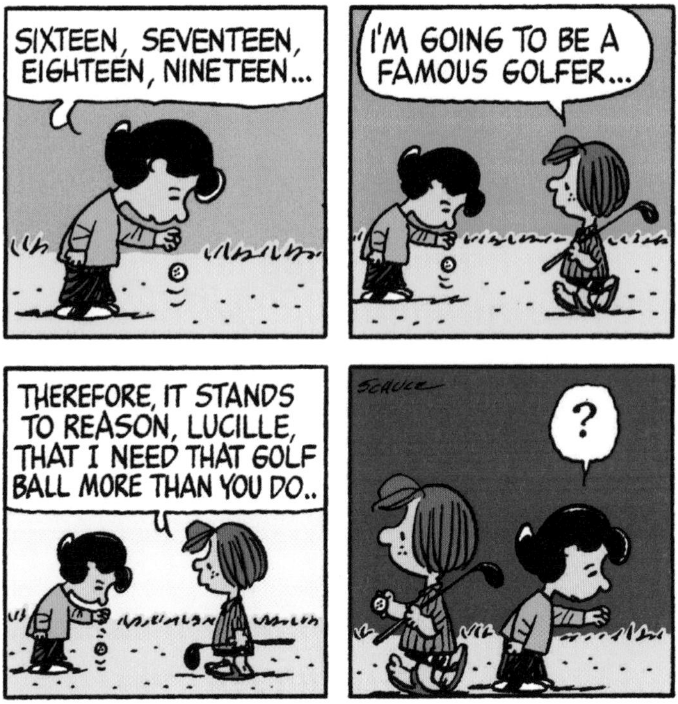
SIXTEEN, SEVENTEEN, EIGHTEEN, NINETEEN...
I'M GOING TO BE A FAMOUS GOLFER...
THEREFORE, IT STANDS TO REASON, LUCILLE, THAT I NEED THAT GOLF BALL MORE THAN YOU DO..
?

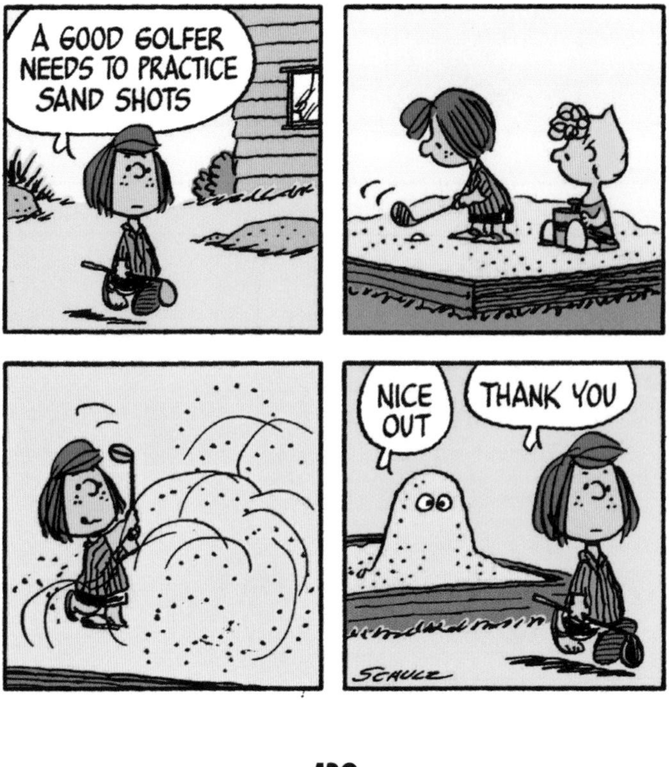
A GOOD GOLFER NEEDS TO PRACTICE SAND SHOTS
NICE OUT
THANK YOU

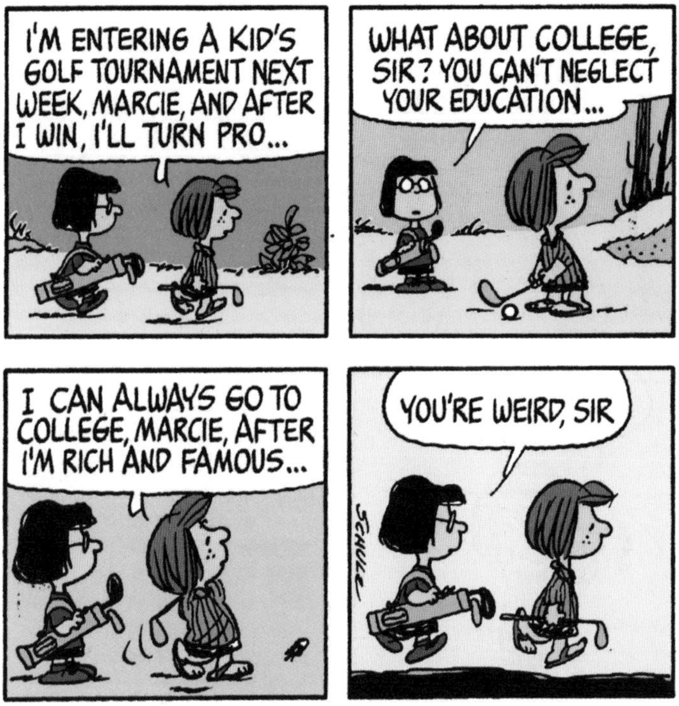
I'M ENTERING A KID'S GOLF TOURNAMENT NEXT WEEK, MARCIE, AND AFTER I WIN, I'LL TURN PRO...
WHAT ABOUT COLLEGE, SIR? YOU CAN'T NEGLECT YOUR EDUCATION...
I CAN ALWAYS GO TO COLLEGE, MARCIE, AFTER I'M RICH AND FAMOUS...
YOU'RE WEIRD, SIR

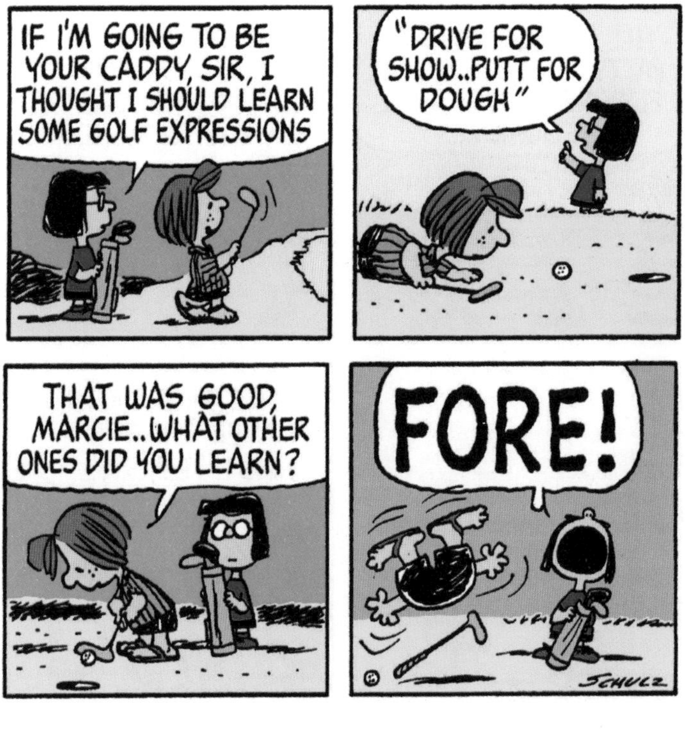
IF I'M GOING TO BE YOUR CADDY, SIR, I THOUGHT I SHOULD LEARN SOME GOLF EXPRESSIONS
"DRIVE FOR SHOW..PUTT FOR DOUGH"
THAT WAS GOOD, MARCIE..WHAT OTHER ONES DID YOU LEARN?
FORE!

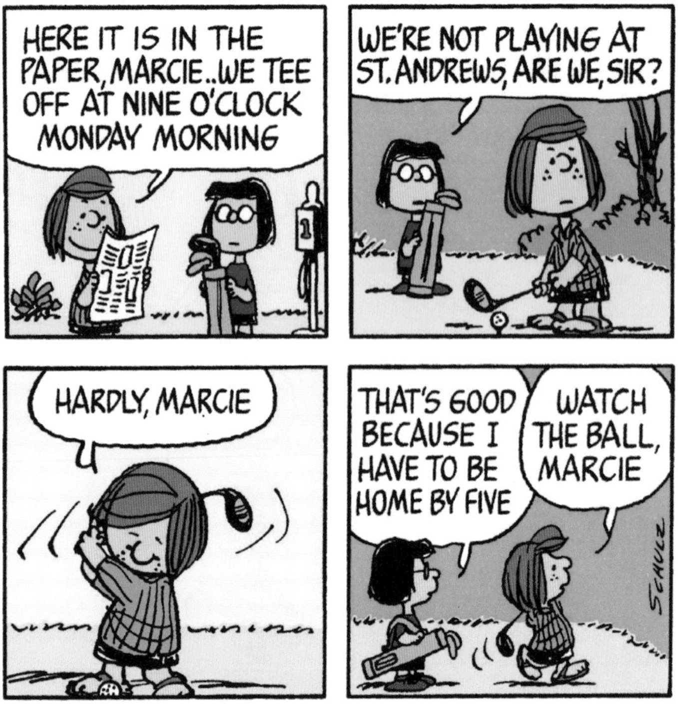
HERE IT IS IN THE PAPER, MARCIE..WE TEE OFF AT NINE O'CLOCK MONDAY MORNING
WE'RE NOT PLAYING AT ST. ANDREWS, ARE WE, SIR?
HARDLY, MARCIE
THAT'S GOOD BECAUSE I HAVE TO BE HOME BY FIVE
WATCH THE BALL, MARCIE
SCHULZ

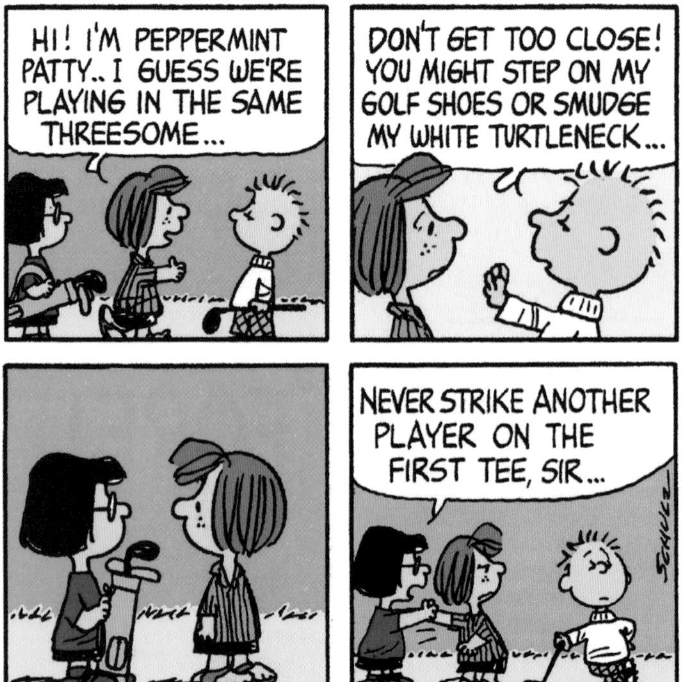
HI! I'M PEPPERMINT PATTY.. I GUESS WE'RE PLAYING IN THE SAME THREESOME...
DON'T GET TOO CLOSE! YOU MIGHT STEP ON MY GOLF SHOES OR SMUDGE MY WHITE TURTLENECK...
NEVER STRIKE ANOTHER PLAYER ON THE FIRST TEE, SIR...
SCHULZ

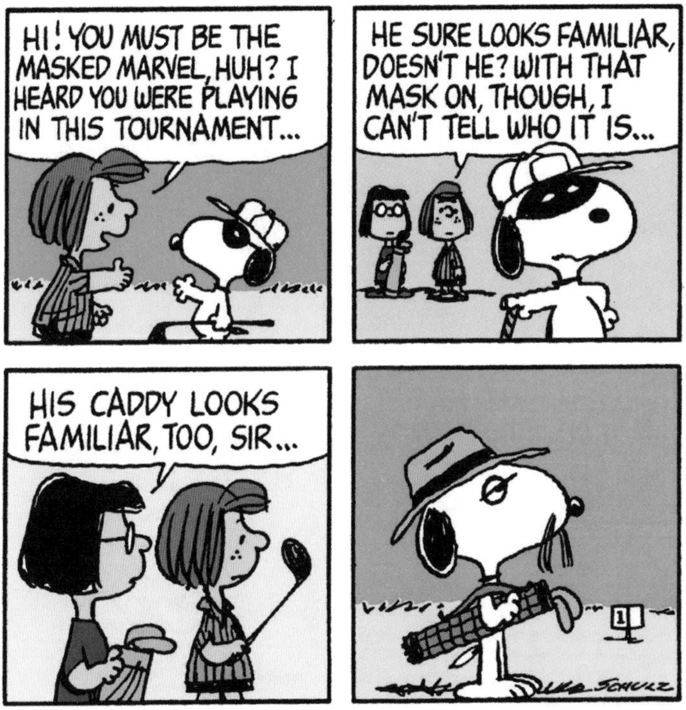
HI! YOU MUST BE THE MASKED MARVEL, HUH? I HEARD YOU WERE PLAYING IN THIS TOURNAMENT...
HE SURE LOOKS FAMILIAR, DOESN'T HE? WITH THAT MASK ON, THOUGH, I CAN'T TELL WHO IT IS...
HIS CADDY LOOKS FAMILIAR, TOO, SIR...

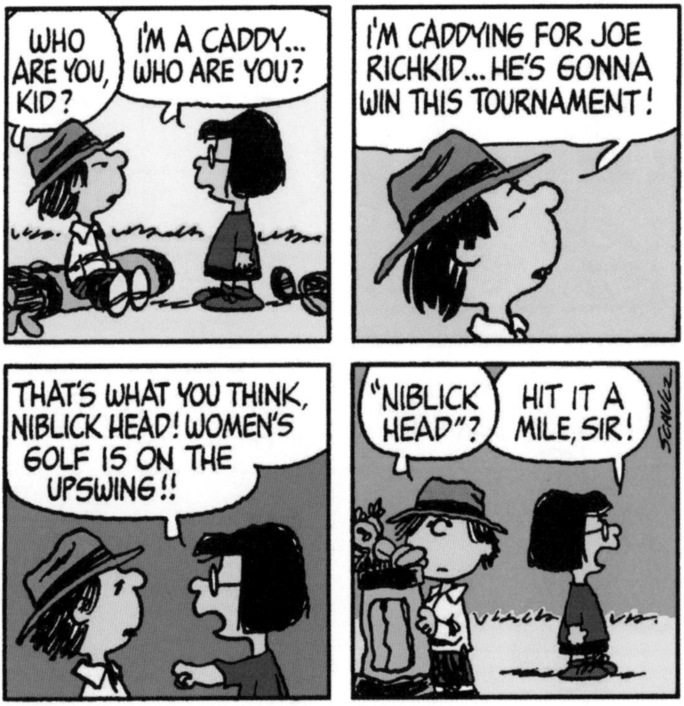
WHO ARE YOU, KID?
I'M A CADDY... WHO ARE YOU?
I'M CADDYING FOR JOE RICHKID... HE'S GONNA WIN THIS TOURNAMENT!
THAT'S WHAT YOU THINK, NIBLICK HEAD! WOMEN'S GOLF IS ON THE UPSWING!!
"NIBLICK HEAD"?
HIT IT A MILE, SIR!

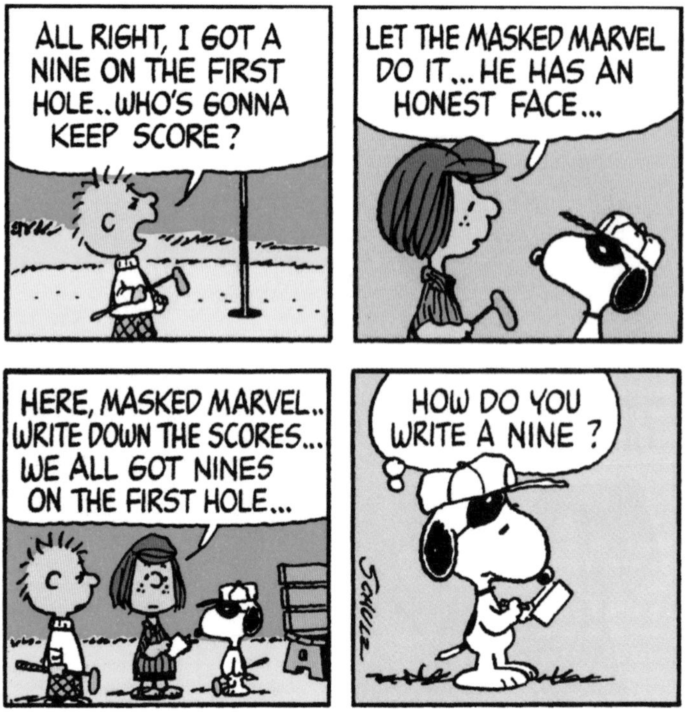
ALL RIGHT, I GOT A NINE ON THE FIRST HOLE..WHO'S GONNA KEEP SCORE?
LET THE MASKED MARVEL DO IT... HE HAS AN HONEST FACE...
HERE, MASKED MARVEL.. WRITE DOWN THE SCORES... WE ALL GOT NINES ON THE FIRST HOLE...
HOW DO YOU WRITE A NINE?
SCHULZ

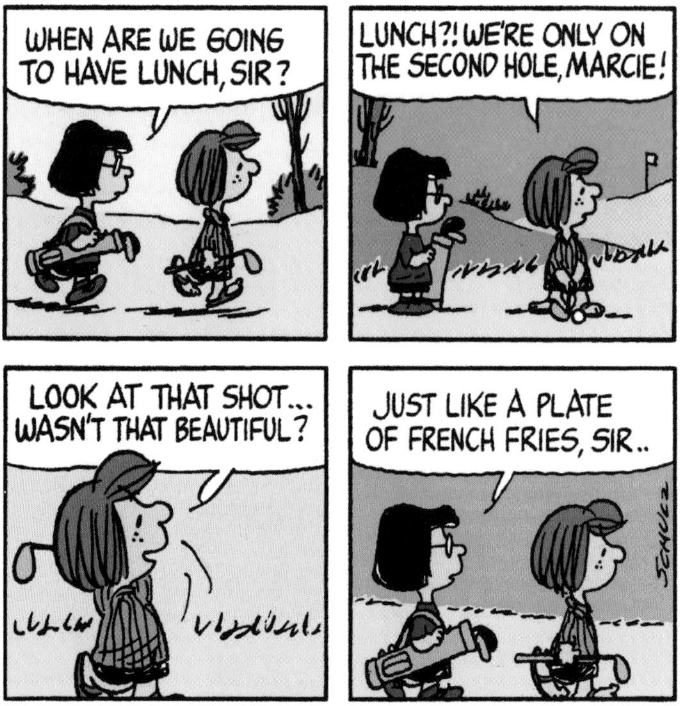
WHEN ARE WE GOING TO HAVE LUNCH, SIR?
LUNCH?! WE'RE ONLY ON THE SECOND HOLE, MARCIE!
LOOK AT THAT SHOT... WASN'T THAT BEAUTIFUL?
JUST LIKE A PLATE OF FRENCH FRIES, SIR..
SCHULZ

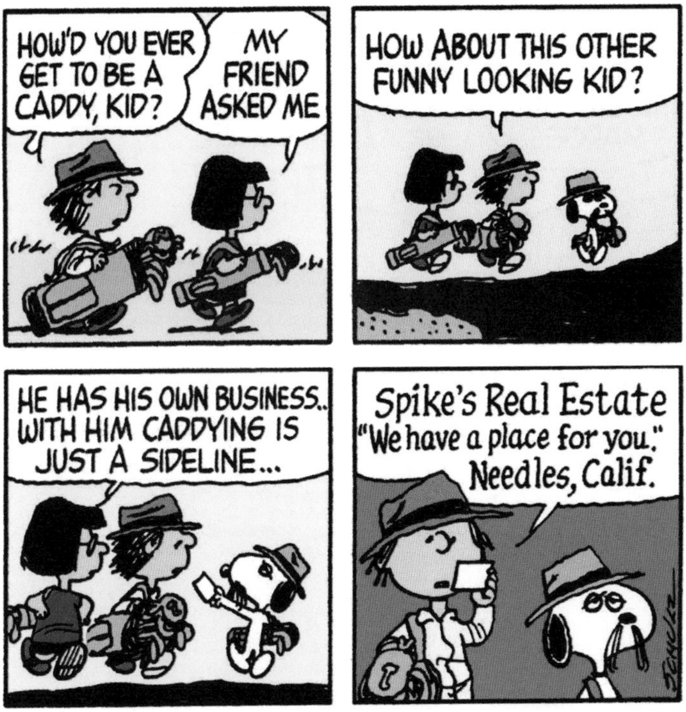
HOW'D YOU EVER GET TO BE A CADDY, KID?
MY FRIEND ASKED ME
HOW ABOUT THIS OTHER FUNNY LOOKING KID?
HE HAS HIS OWN BUSINESS.. WITH HIM CADDYING IS JUST A SIDELINE...
Spike's Real Estate
"We have a place for you."
Needles, Calif.
SCHULZ

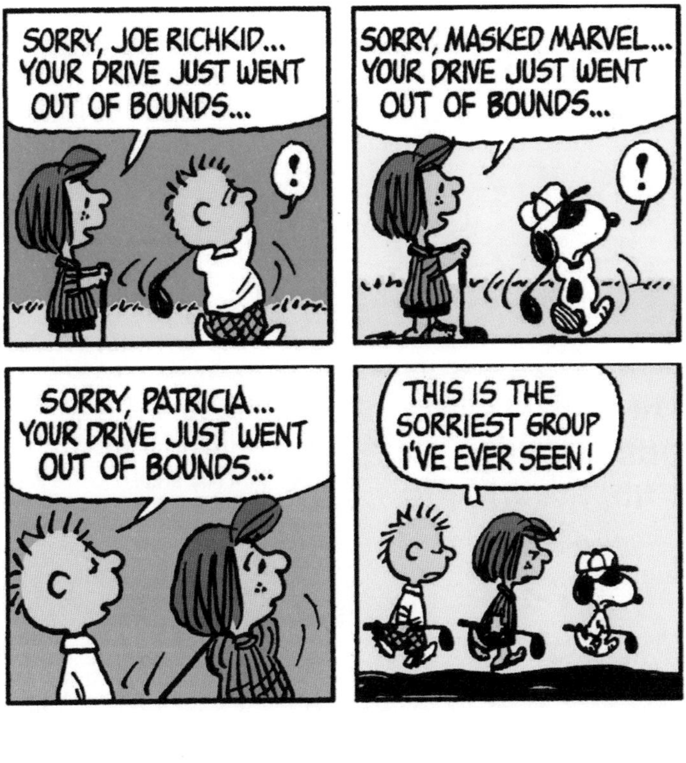
SORRY, JOE RICHKID... YOUR DRIVE JUST WENT OUT OF BOUNDS...
!
SORRY, MASKED MARVEL... YOUR DRIVE JUST WENT OUT OF BOUNDS...
!
SORRY, PATRICIA... YOUR DRIVE JUST WENT OUT OF BOUNDS...
THIS IS THE SORRIEST GROUP I'VE EVER SEEN!

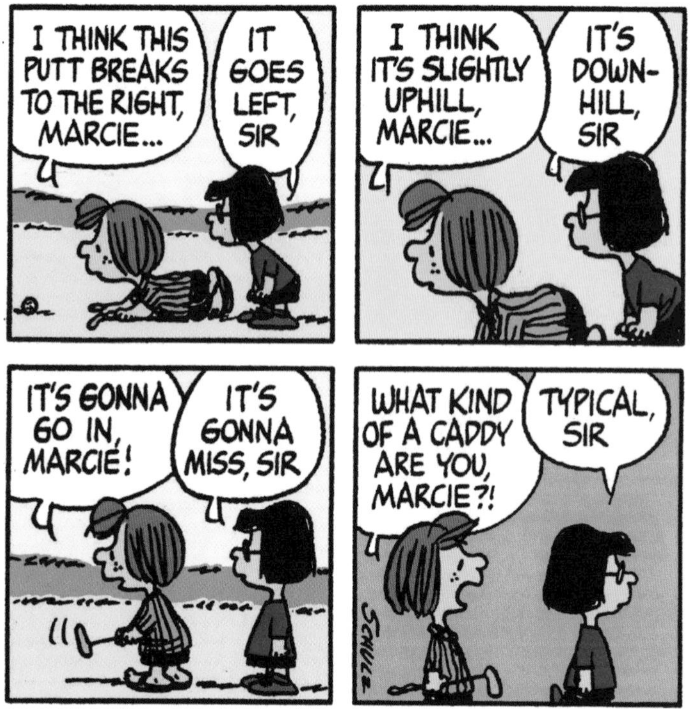
I THINK THIS PUTT BREAKS TO THE RIGHT, MARCIE...
IT GOES LEFT, SIR
I THINK IT'S SLIGHTLY UPHILL, MARCIE...
IT'S DOWN-HILL, SIR
IT'S GONNA GO IN, MARCIE!
IT'S GONNA MISS, SIR
WHAT KIND OF A CADDY ARE YOU, MARCIE?!
TYPICAL, SIR
SCHULZ

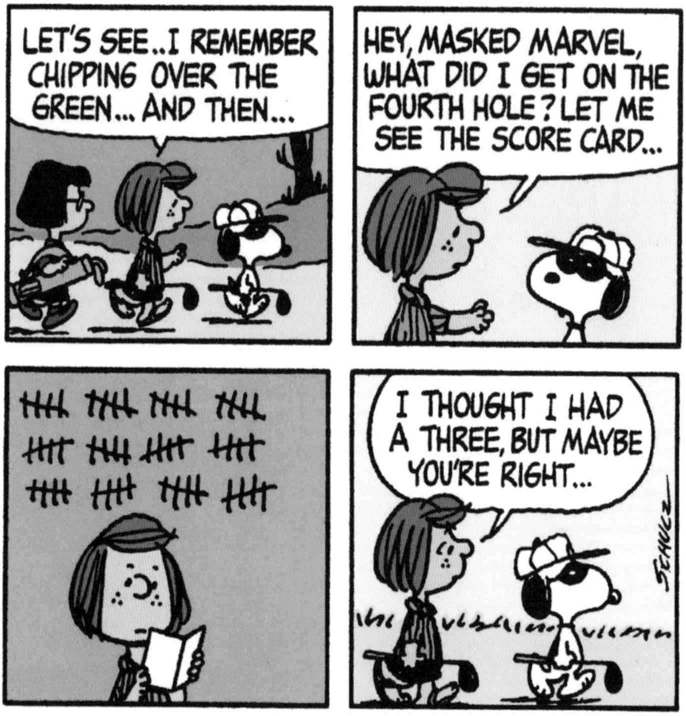
LET'S SEE..I REMEMBER CHIPPING OVER THE GREEN... AND THEN...
HEY, MASKED MARVEL, WHAT DID I GET ON THE FOURTH HOLE? LET ME SEE THE SCORE CARD...
I THOUGHT I HAD A THREE, BUT MAYBE YOU'RE RIGHT...
SCHULZ

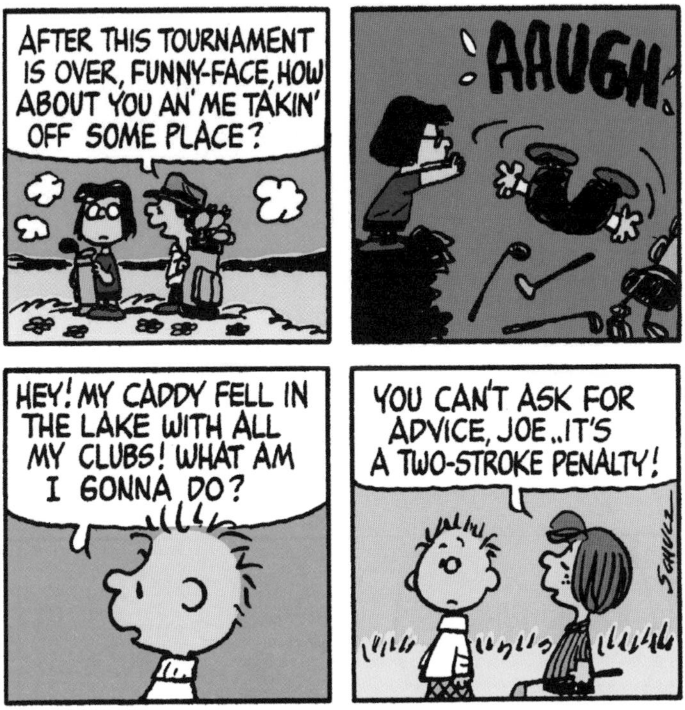
AFTER THIS TOURNAMENT IS OVER, FUNNY-FACE, HOW ABOUT YOU AN' ME TAKIN' OFF SOME PLACE?
AAUGH
HEY! MY CADDY FELL IN THE LAKE WITH ALL MY CLUBS! WHAT AM I GONNA DO?
YOU CAN'T ASK FOR ADVICE, JOE..IT'S A TWO-STROKE PENALTY!
SCHULZ

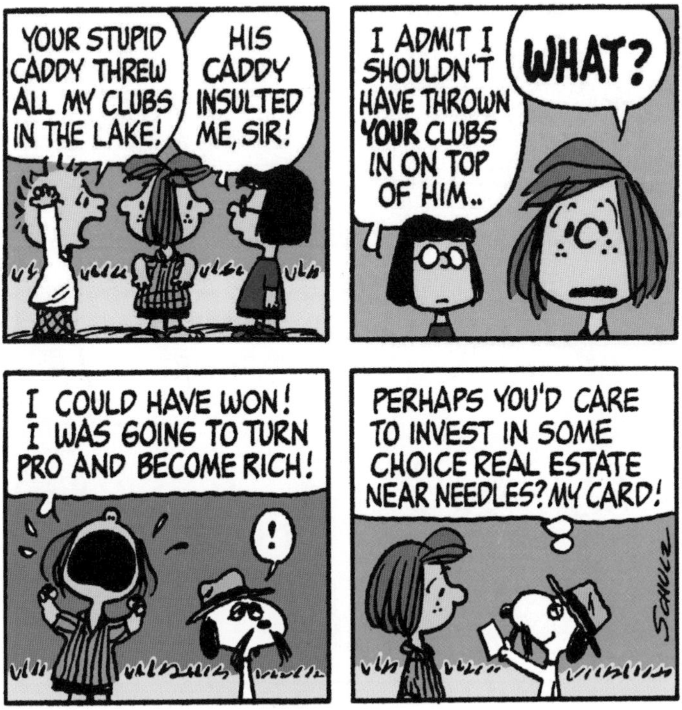
YOUR STUPID CADDY THREW ALL MY CLUBS IN THE LAKE!
HIS CADDY INSULTED ME, SIR!
I ADMIT I SHOULDN'T HAVE THROWN **YOUR** CLUBS IN ON TOP OF HIM..
WHAT?
I COULD HAVE WON! I WAS GOING TO TURN PRO AND BECOME RICH!
!
PERHAPS YOU'D CARE TO INVEST IN SOME CHOICE REAL ESTATE NEAR NEEDLES? MY CARD!
SCHULZ

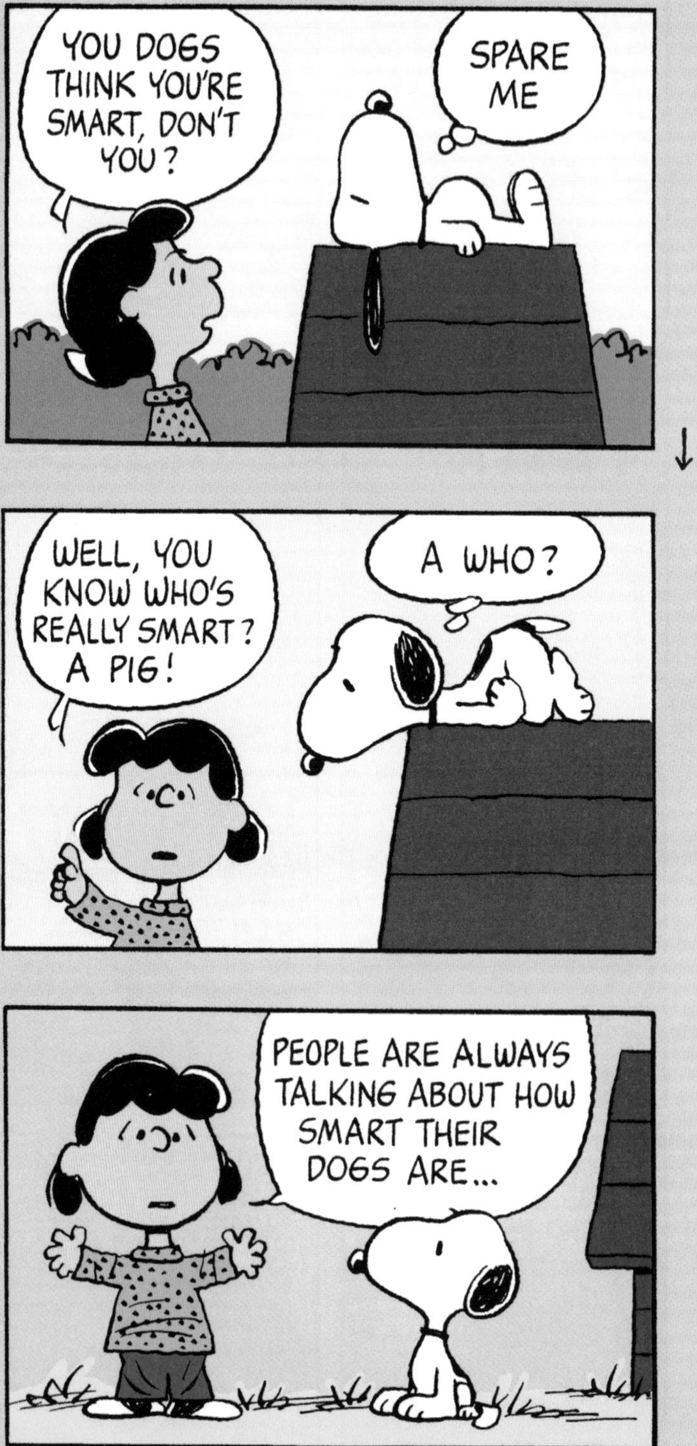
YOU DOGS THINK YOU'RE SMART, DON'T YOU?
SPARE ME
WELL, YOU KNOW WHO'S REALLY SMART? A PIG!
A WHO?
PEOPLE ARE ALWAYS TALKING ABOUT HOW SMART THEIR DOGS ARE...

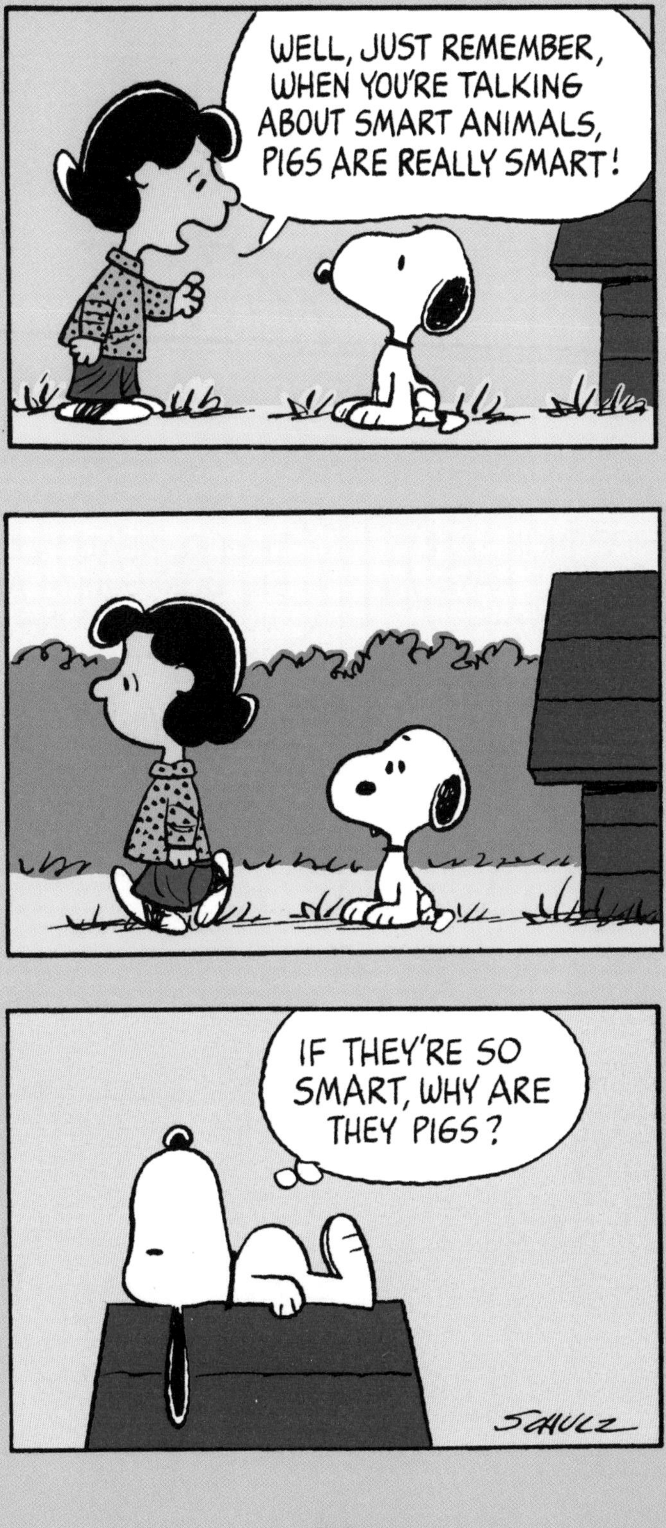
WELL, JUST REMEMBER, WHEN YOU'RE TALKING ABOUT SMART ANIMALS, PIGS ARE REALLY SMART!
IF THEY'RE SO SMART, WHY ARE THEY PIGS?
SCHULZ

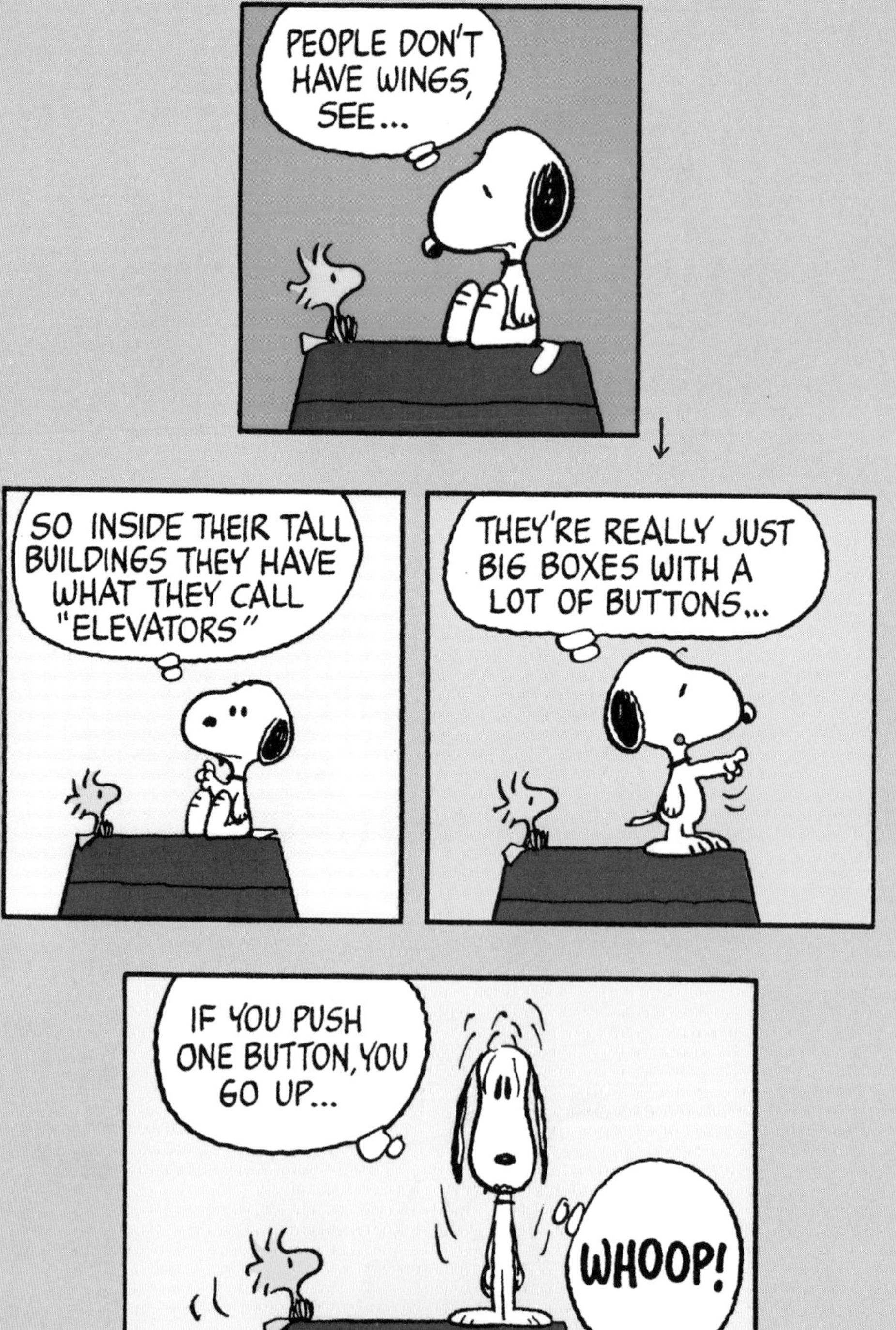
PEOPLE DON'T HAVE WINGS, SEE...
SO INSIDE THEIR TALL BUILDINGS THEY HAVE WHAT THEY CALL "ELEVATORS"
THEY'RE REALLY JUST BIG BOXES WITH A LOT OF BUTTONS...
IF YOU PUSH ONE BUTTON, YOU GO UP...
WHOOP!

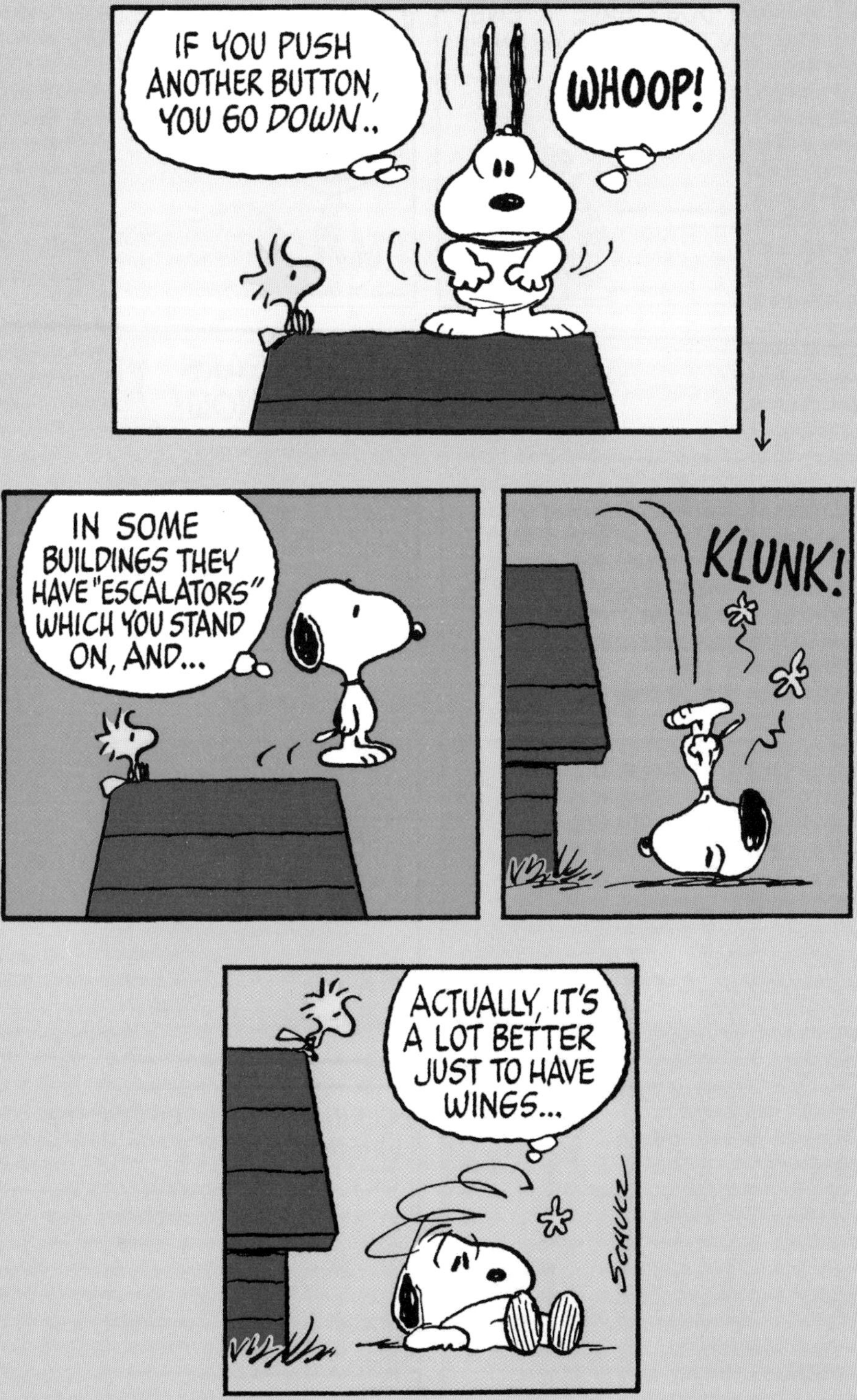
IF YOU PUSH ANOTHER BUTTON, YOU GO DOWN..
WHOOP!
IN SOME BUILDINGS THEY HAVE "ESCALATORS" WHICH YOU STAND ON, AND...
KLUNK!
ACTUALLY, IT'S A LOT BETTER JUST TO HAVE WINGS...
SCHULZ

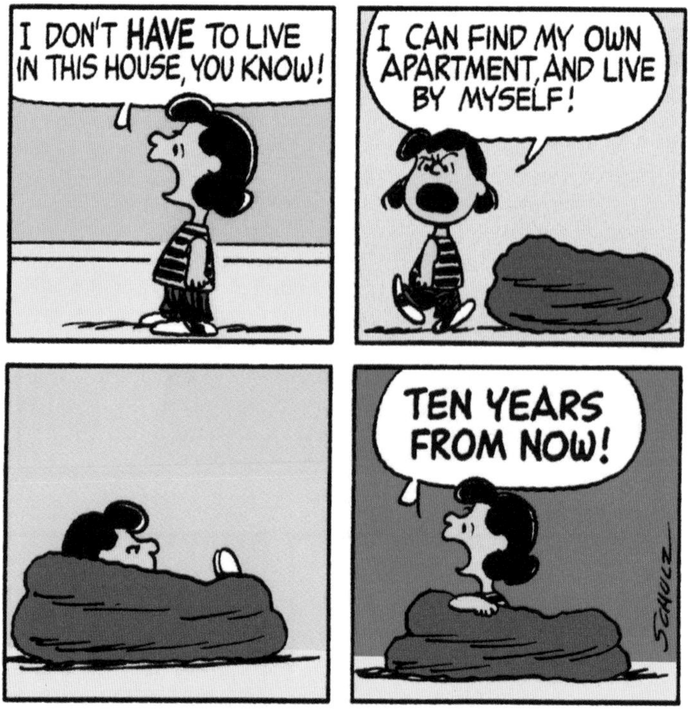
I DON'T HAVE TO LIVE IN THIS HOUSE, YOU KNOW!
I CAN FIND MY OWN APARTMENT, AND LIVE BY MYSELF!
TEN YEARS FROM NOW!
SCHULZ

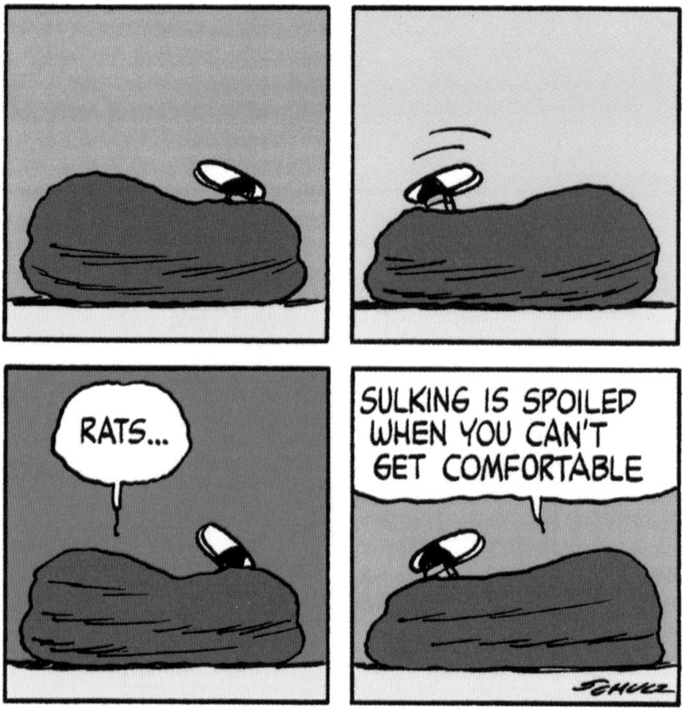
RATS...
SULKING IS SPOILED WHEN YOU CAN'T GET COMFORTABLE
SCHULZ

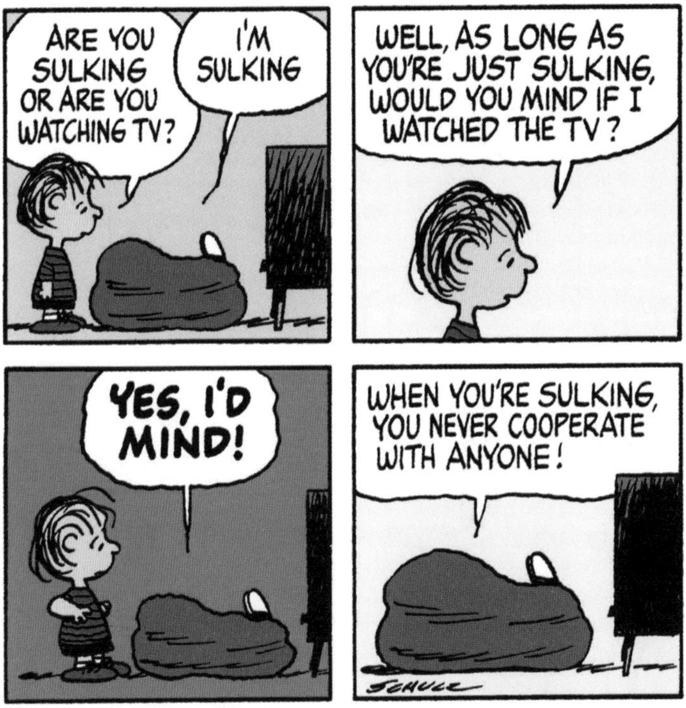
ARE YOU SULKING OR ARE YOU WATCHING TV?
I'M SULKING
WELL, AS LONG AS YOU'RE JUST SULKING, WOULD YOU MIND IF I WATCHED THE TV?
YES, I'D MIND!
WHEN YOU'RE SULKING, YOU NEVER COOPERATE WITH ANYONE!
SCHULZ

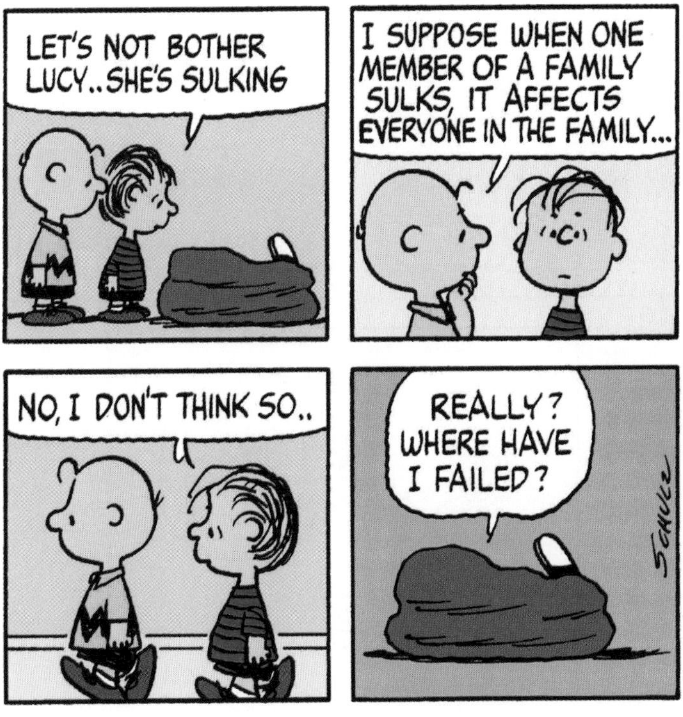
LET'S NOT BOTHER LUCY..SHE'S SULKING
I SUPPOSE WHEN ONE MEMBER OF A FAMILY SULKS, IT AFFECTS EVERYONE IN THE FAMILY...
NO, I DON'T THINK SO..
REALLY? WHERE HAVE I FAILED?
SCHULZ

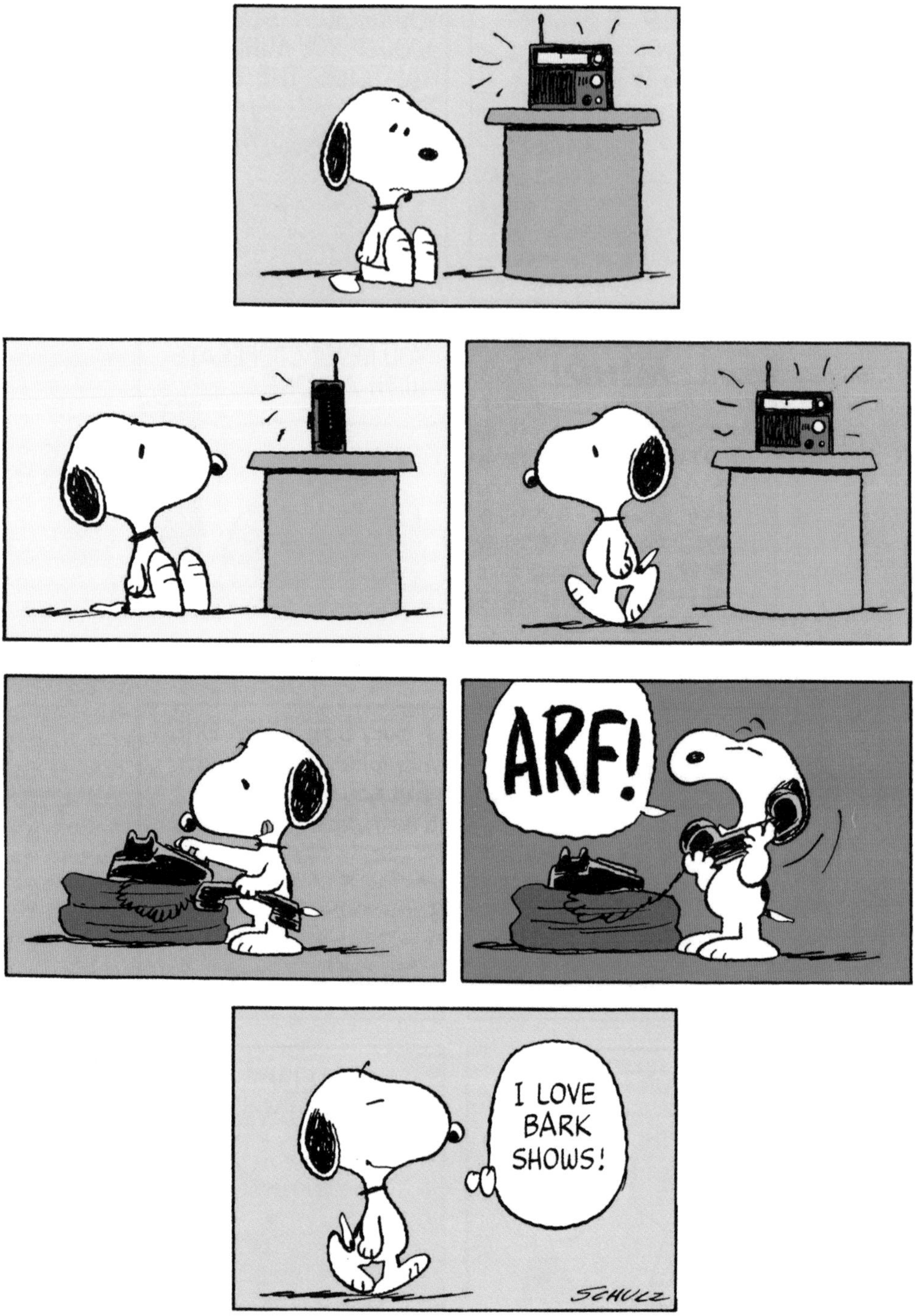
ARF!
I LOVE BARK SHOWS!
SCHULZ

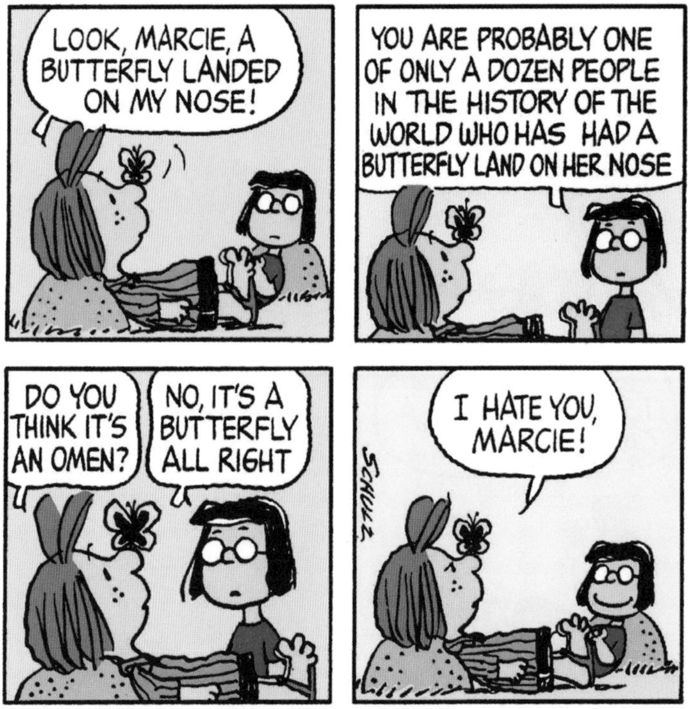
LOOK, MARCIE, A BUTTERFLY LANDED ON MY NOSE!
YOU ARE PROBABLY ONE OF ONLY A DOZEN PEOPLE IN THE HISTORY OF THE WORLD WHO HAS HAD A BUTTERFLY LAND ON HER NOSE
DO YOU THINK IT'S AN OMEN?
NO, IT'S A BUTTERFLY ALL RIGHT
I HATE YOU, MARCIE!
SCHULZ

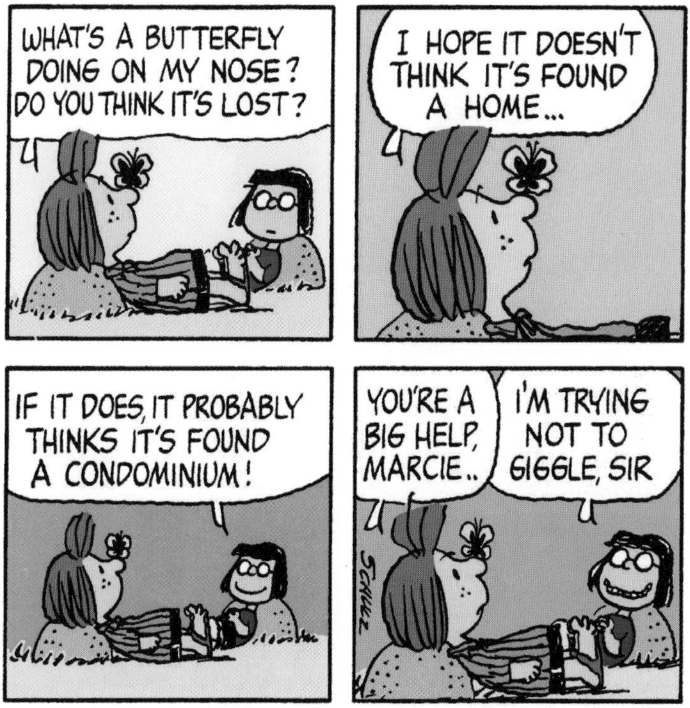
WHAT'S A BUTTERFLY DOING ON MY NOSE? DO YOU THINK IT'S LOST?
I HOPE IT DOESN'T THINK IT'S FOUND A HOME...
IF IT DOES, IT PROBABLY THINKS IT'S FOUND A CONDOMINIUM!
YOU'RE A BIG HELP, MARCIE..
I'M TRYING NOT TO GIGGLE, SIR
SCHULZ

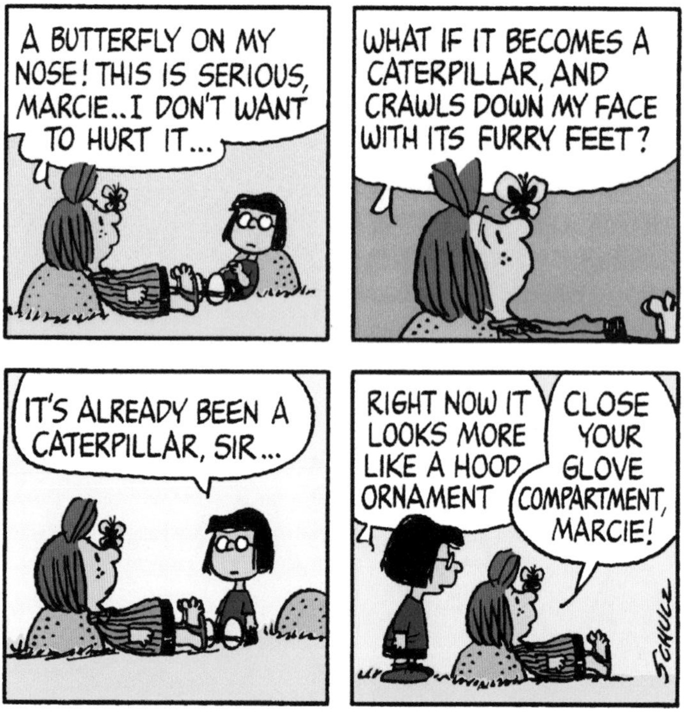
A BUTTERFLY ON MY NOSE! THIS IS SERIOUS, MARCIE..I DON'T WANT TO HURT IT...
WHAT IF IT BECOMES A CATERPILLAR, AND CRAWLS DOWN MY FACE WITH ITS FURRY FEET?
IT'S ALREADY BEEN A CATERPILLAR, SIR...
RIGHT NOW IT LOOKS MORE LIKE A HOOD ORNAMENT
CLOSE YOUR GLOVE COMPARTMENT, MARCIE!
SCHULZ

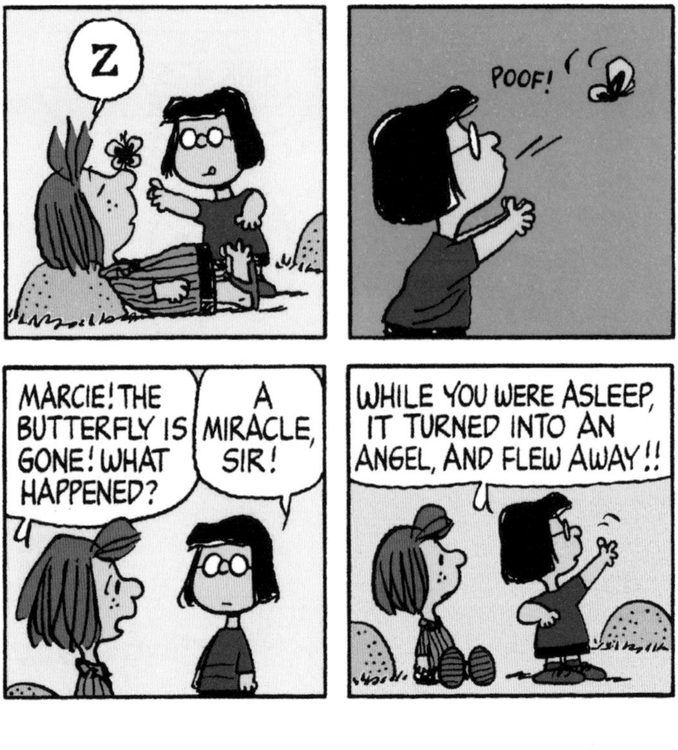
Z
POOF!
MARCIE! THE BUTTERFLY IS GONE! WHAT HAPPENED?
A MIRACLE, SIR!
WHILE YOU WERE ASLEEP, IT TURNED INTO AN ANGEL, AND FLEW AWAY!!

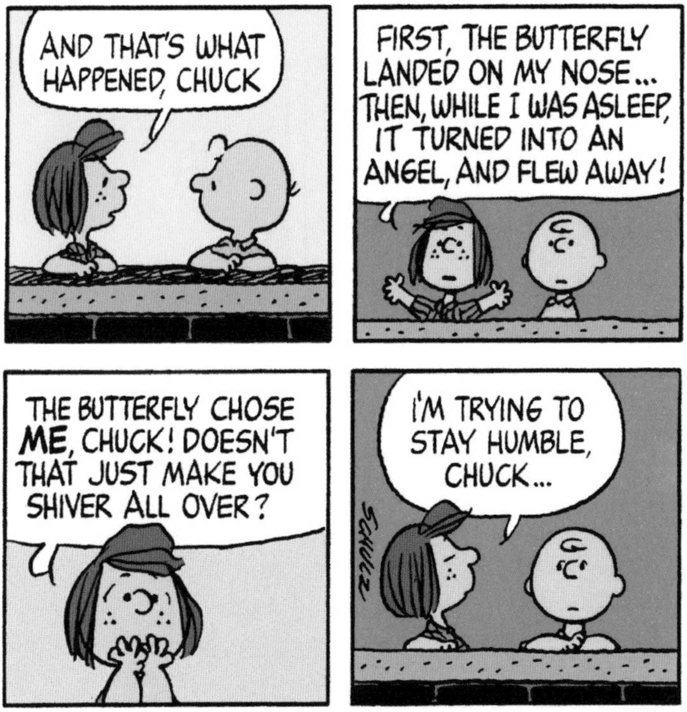
AND THAT'S WHAT HAPPENED, CHUCK
FIRST, THE BUTTERFLY LANDED ON MY NOSE... THEN, WHILE I WAS ASLEEP, IT TURNED INTO AN ANGEL, AND FLEW AWAY!
THE BUTTERFLY CHOSE **ME**, CHUCK! DOESN'T THAT JUST MAKE YOU SHIVER ALL OVER?
I'M TRYING TO STAY HUMBLE, CHUCK...
SCHULZ

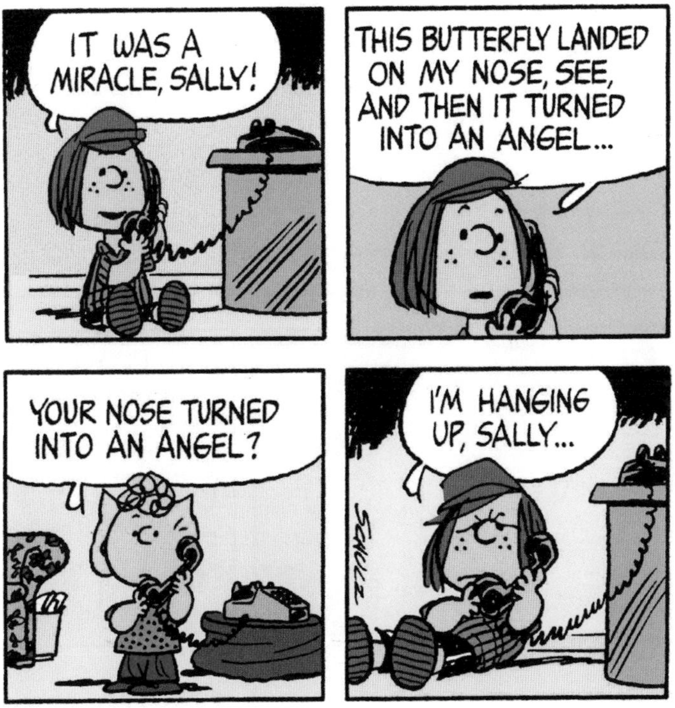
IT WAS A MIRACLE, SALLY!
THIS BUTTERFLY LANDED ON MY NOSE, SEE, AND THEN IT TURNED INTO AN ANGEL...
YOUR NOSE TURNED INTO AN ANGEL?
I'M HANGING UP, SALLY...
SCHULZ

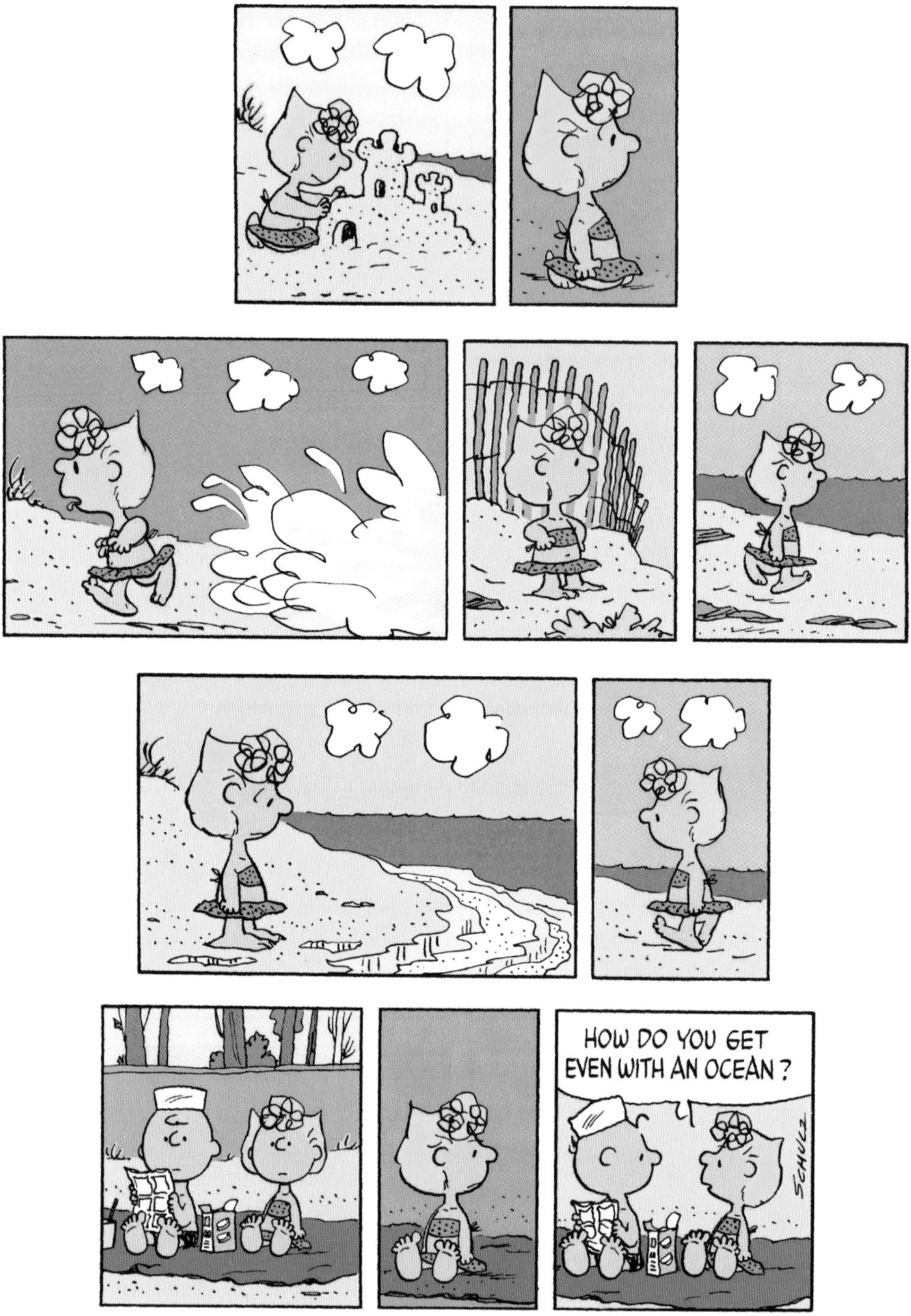
HOW DO YOU GET EVEN WITH AN OCEAN ?
SCHULZ

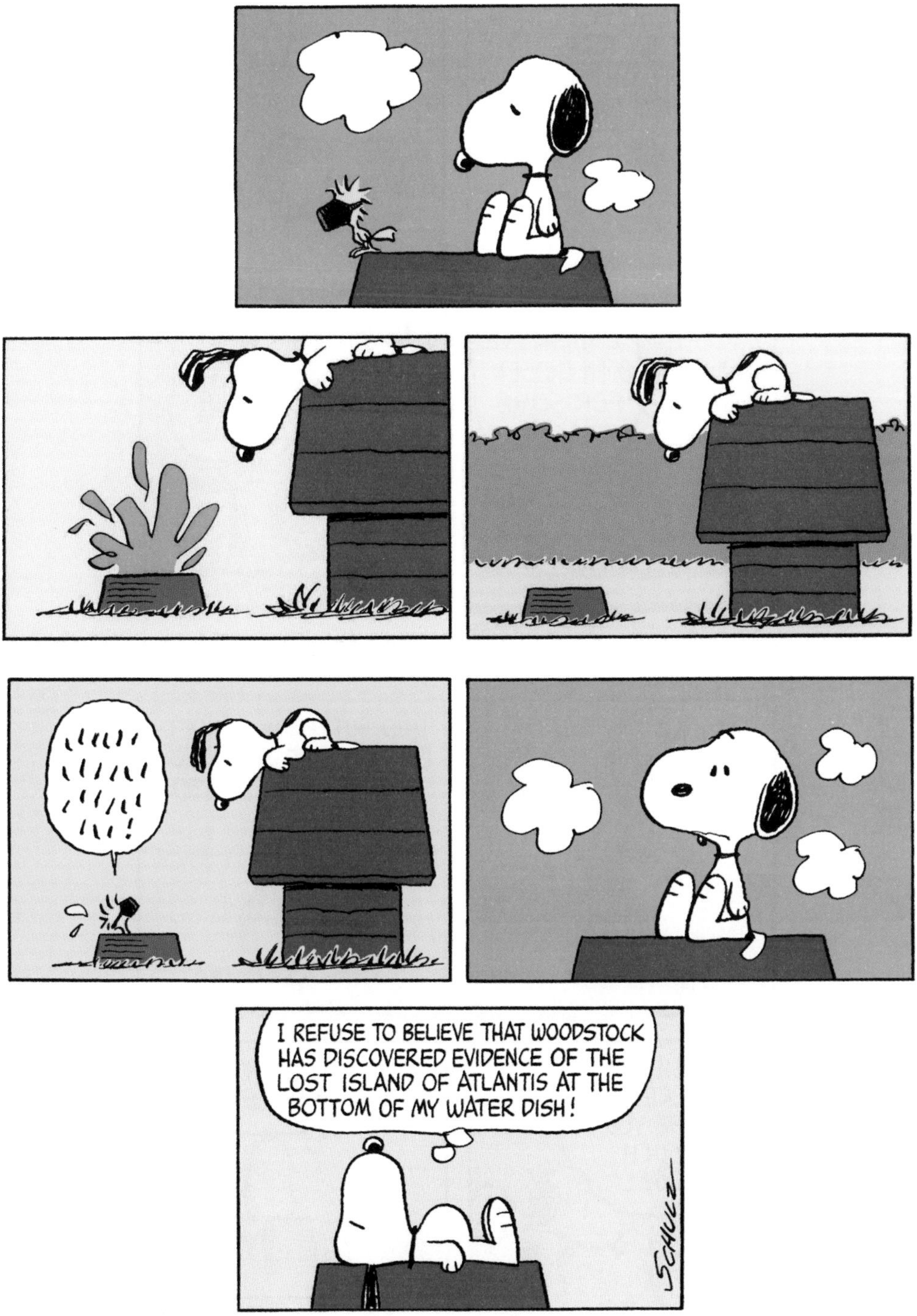
I REFUSE TO BELIEVE THAT WOODSTOCK HAS DISCOVERED EVIDENCE OF THE LOST ISLAND OF ATLANTIS AT THE BOTTOM OF MY WATER DISH!
SCHULZ

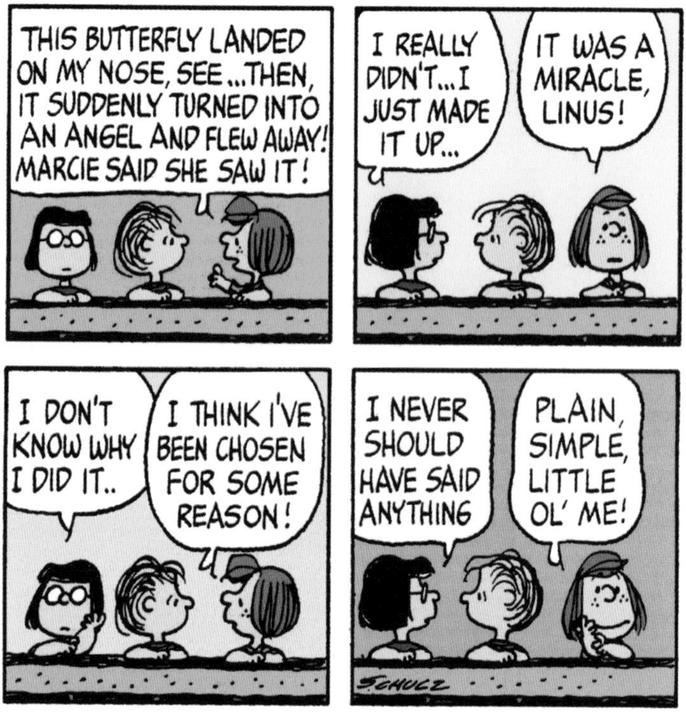
THIS BUTTERFLY LANDED ON MY NOSE, SEE...THEN, IT SUDDENLY TURNED INTO AN ANGEL AND FLEW AWAY! MARCIE SAID SHE SAW IT!
I REALLY DIDN'T...I JUST MADE IT UP...
IT WAS A MIRACLE, LINUS!
I DON'T KNOW WHY I DID IT..
I THINK I'VE BEEN CHOSEN FOR SOME REASON!
I NEVER SHOULD HAVE SAID ANYTHING
PLAIN, SIMPLE, LITTLE OL' ME!
SCHULZ

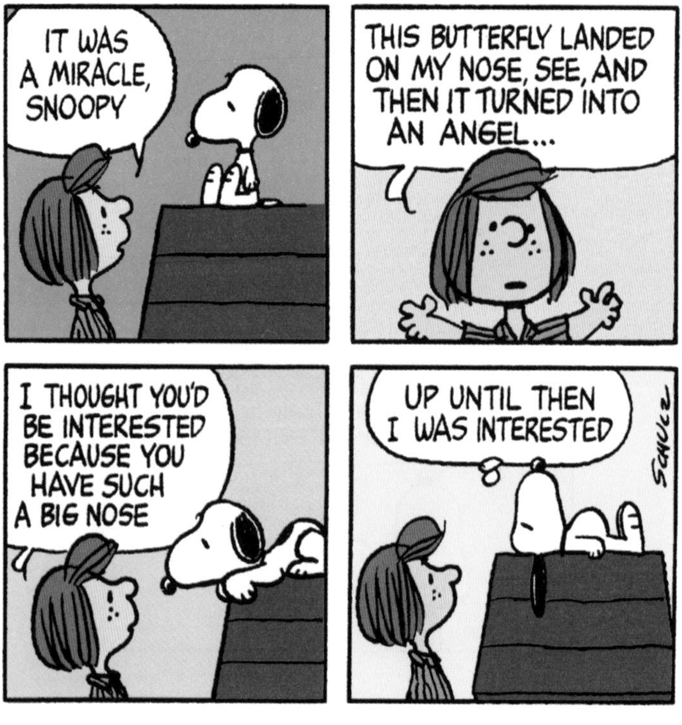
IT WAS A MIRACLE, SNOOPY
THIS BUTTERFLY LANDED ON MY NOSE, SEE, AND THEN IT TURNED INTO AN ANGEL...
I THOUGHT YOU'D BE INTERESTED BECAUSE YOU HAVE SUCH A BIG NOSE
UP UNTIL THEN I WAS INTERESTED
SCHULZ

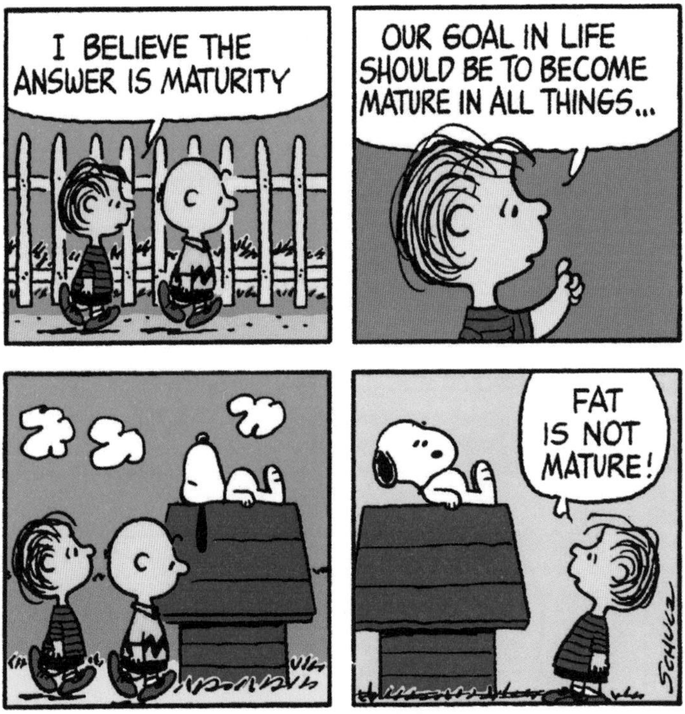
I BELIEVE THE ANSWER IS MATURITY
OUR GOAL IN LIFE SHOULD BE TO BECOME MATURE IN ALL THINGS...
FAT IS NOT MATURE!
SCHULZ

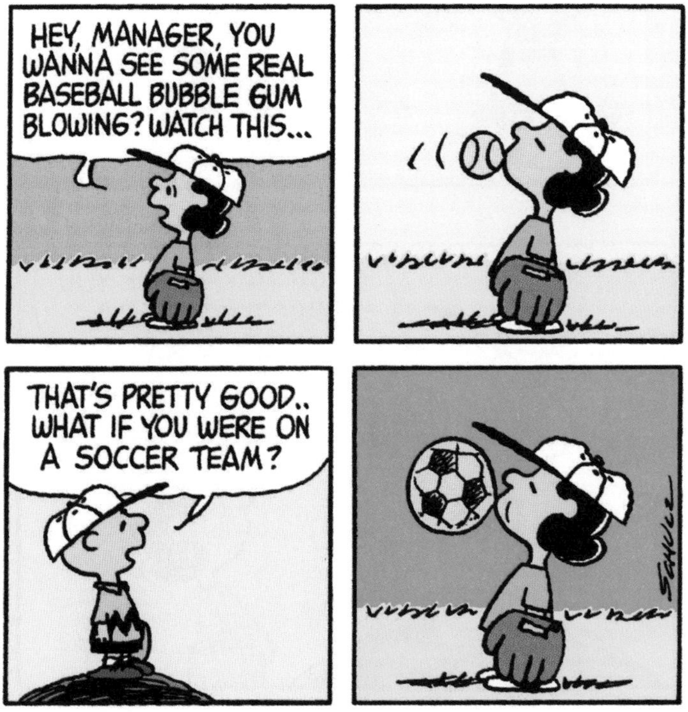
HEY, MANAGER, YOU WANNA SEE SOME REAL BASEBALL BUBBLE GUM BLOWING? WATCH THIS...
THAT'S PRETTY GOOD.. WHAT IF YOU WERE ON A SOCCER TEAM?
SCHULZ

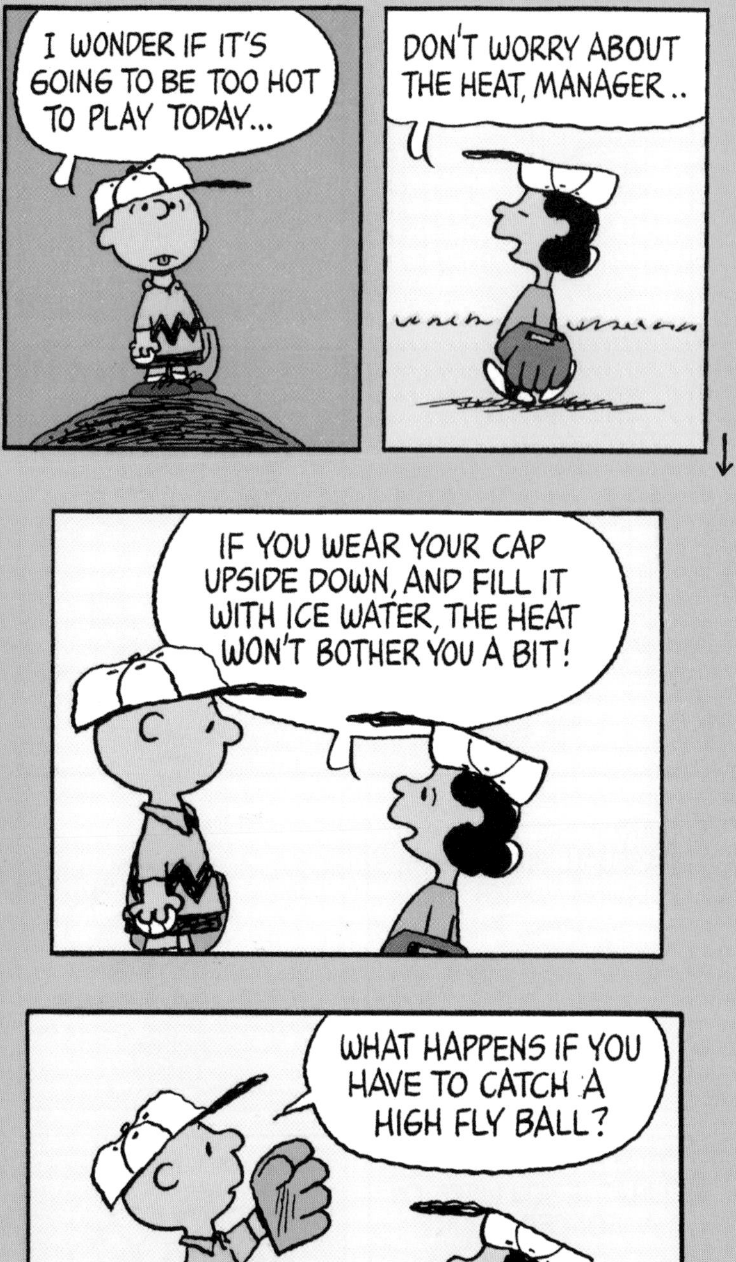
I WONDER IF IT'S GOING TO BE TOO HOT TO PLAY TODAY...
DON'T WORRY ABOUT THE HEAT, MANAGER..
IF YOU WEAR YOUR CAP UPSIDE DOWN, AND FILL IT WITH ICE WATER, THE HEAT WON'T BOTHER YOU A BIT!
WHAT HAPPENS IF YOU HAVE TO CATCH A HIGH FLY BALL?

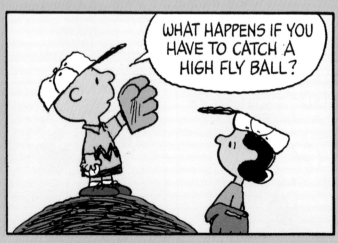

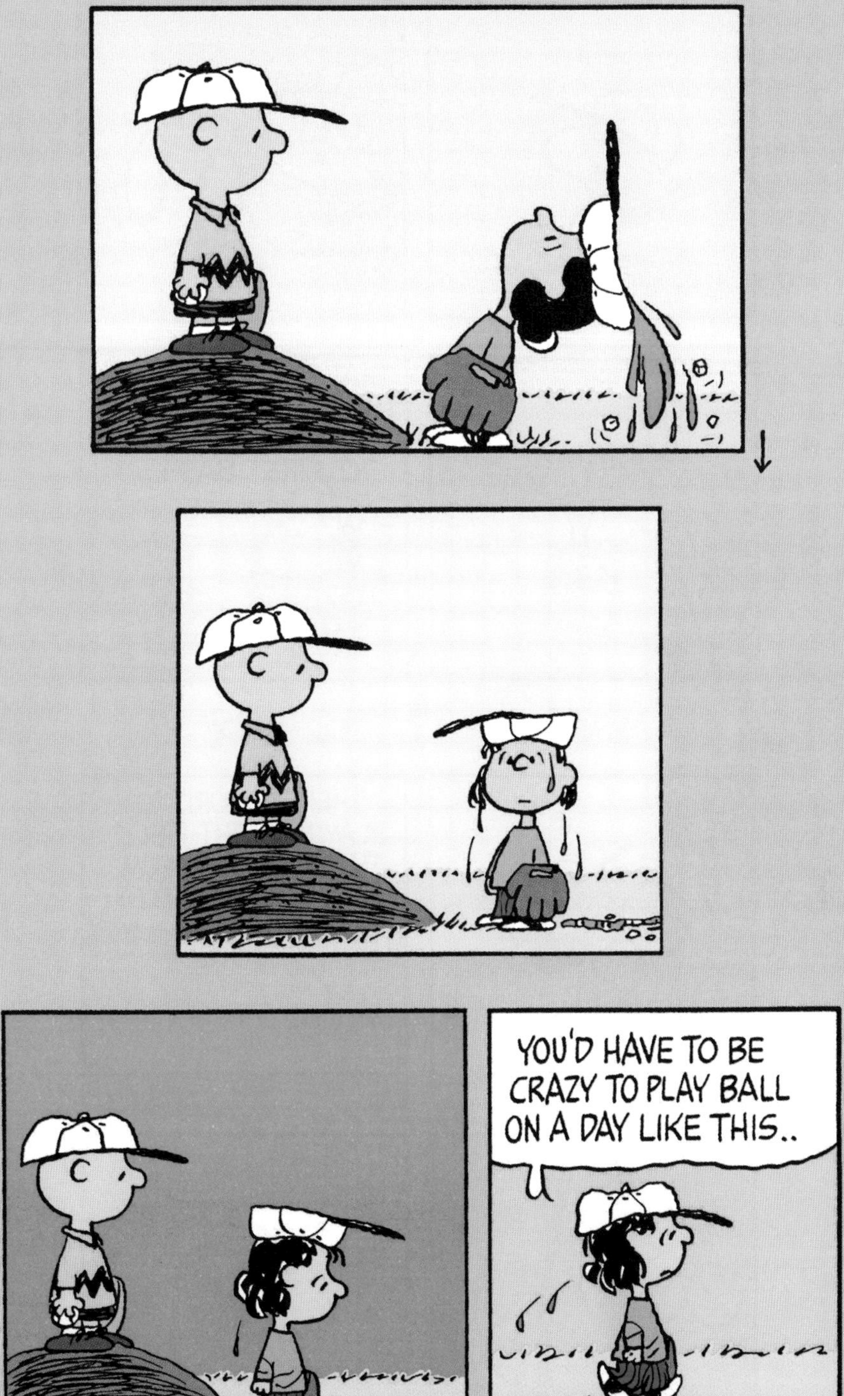
YOU'D HAVE TO BE CRAZY TO PLAY BALL ON A DAY LIKE THIS..
SCHULZ

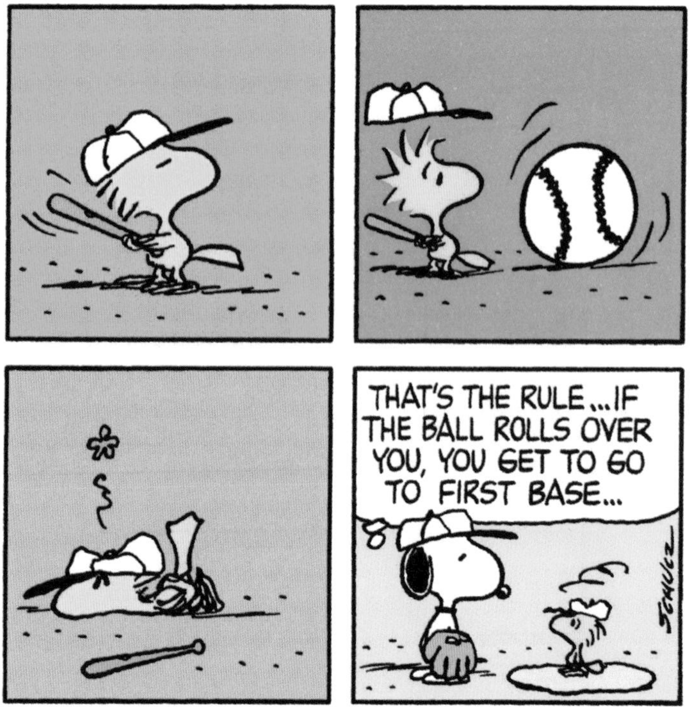
THAT'S THE RULE...IF THE BALL ROLLS OVER YOU, YOU GET TO GO TO FIRST BASE...

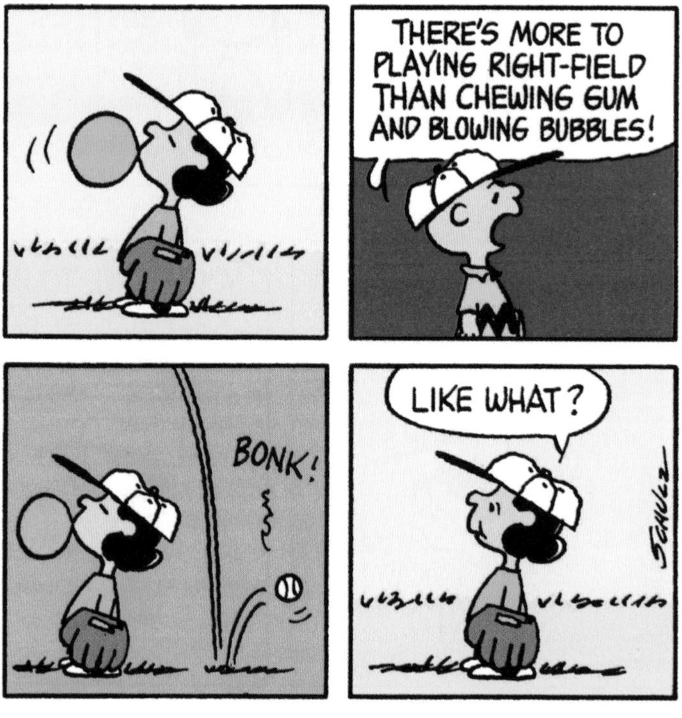
THERE'S MORE TO PLAYING RIGHT-FIELD THAN CHEWING GUM AND BLOWING BUBBLES!
BONK!
LIKE WHAT?

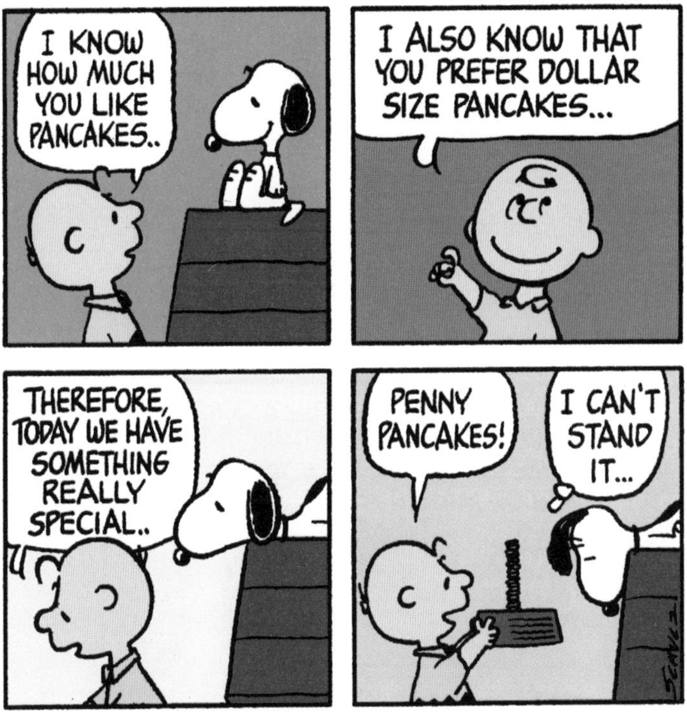
I KNOW HOW MUCH YOU LIKE PANCAKES..
I ALSO KNOW THAT YOU PREFER DOLLAR SIZE PANCAKES...
THEREFORE, TODAY WE HAVE SOMETHING REALLY SPECIAL..
PENNY PANCAKES!
I CAN'T STAND IT...
SCHULZ

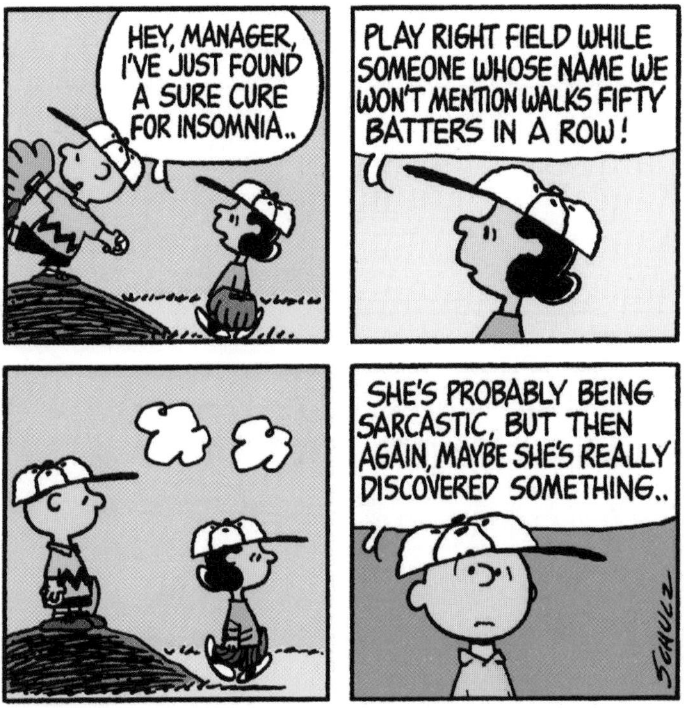
HEY, MANAGER, I'VE JUST FOUND A SURE CURE FOR INSOMNIA..
PLAY RIGHT FIELD WHILE SOMEONE WHOSE NAME WE WON'T MENTION WALKS FIFTY BATTERS IN A ROW!
SHE'S PROBABLY BEING SARCASTIC, BUT THEN AGAIN, MAYBE SHE'S REALLY DISCOVERED SOMETHING..
SCHULZ

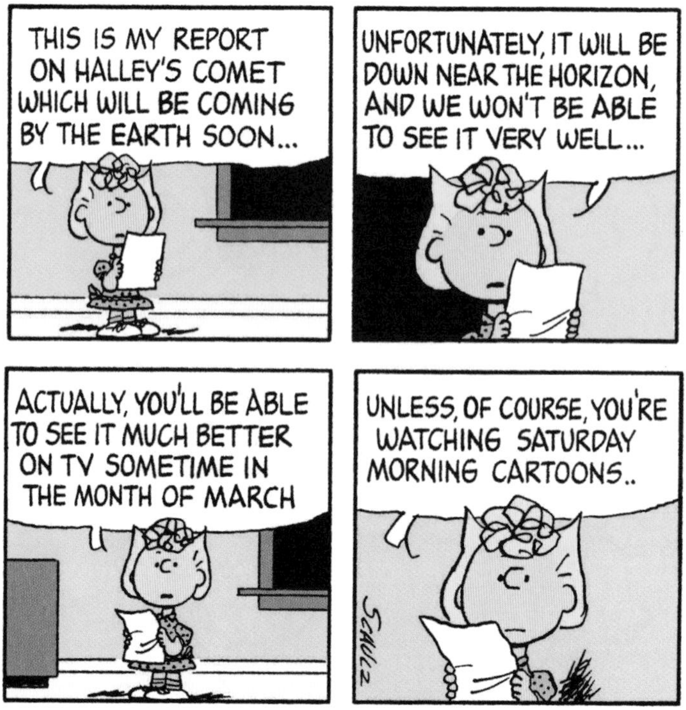
THIS IS MY REPORT ON HALLEY'S COMET WHICH WILL BE COMING BY THE EARTH SOON...
UNFORTUNATELY, IT WILL BE DOWN NEAR THE HORIZON, AND WE WON'T BE ABLE TO SEE IT VERY WELL...
ACTUALLY, YOU'LL BE ABLE TO SEE IT MUCH BETTER ON TV SOMETIME IN THE MONTH OF MARCH
UNLESS, OF COURSE, YOU'RE WATCHING SATURDAY MORNING CARTOONS..
SCHULZ

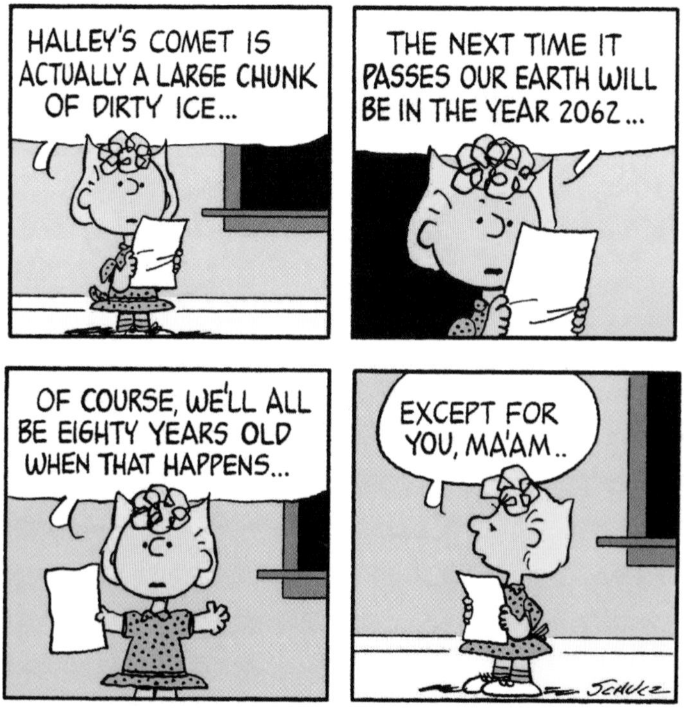
HALLEY'S COMET IS ACTUALLY A LARGE CHUNK OF DIRTY ICE...
THE NEXT TIME IT PASSES OUR EARTH WILL BE IN THE YEAR 2062...
OF COURSE, WE'LL ALL BE EIGHTY YEARS OLD WHEN THAT HAPPENS...
EXCEPT FOR YOU, MA'AM..
SCHULZ

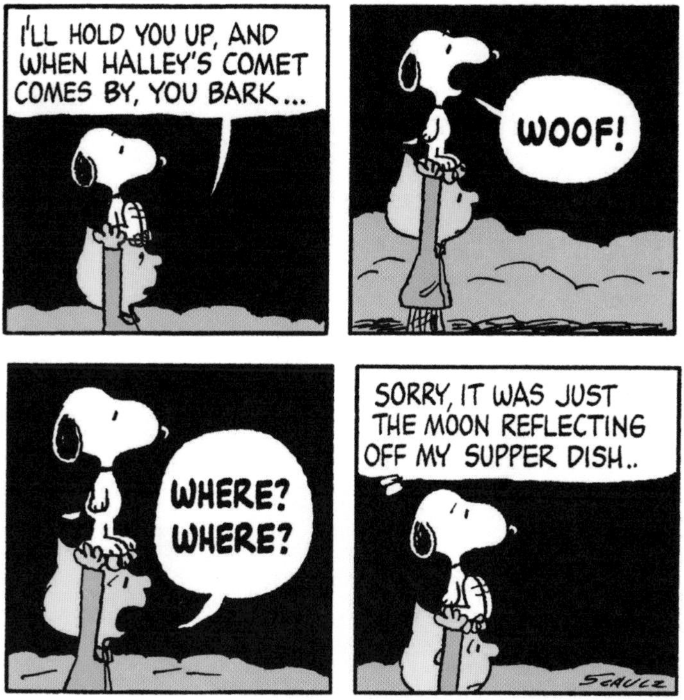
I'LL HOLD YOU UP, AND WHEN HALLEY'S COMET COMES BY, YOU BARK...
WOOF!
WHERE? WHERE?
SORRY, IT WAS JUST THE MOON REFLECTING OFF MY SUPPER DISH..
SCHULZ

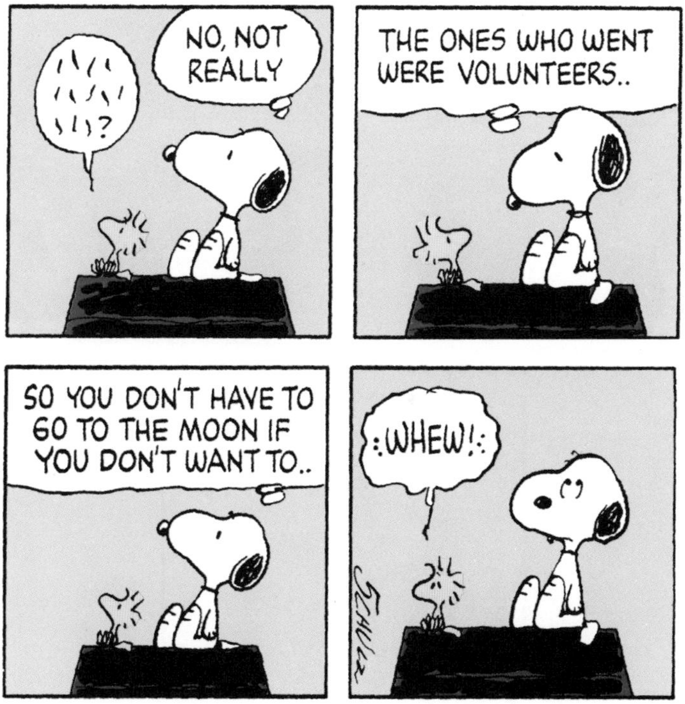
NO, NOT REALLY
THE ONES WHO WENT WERE VOLUNTEERS..
SO YOU DON'T HAVE TO GO TO THE MOON IF YOU DON'T WANT TO..
WHEW!
SCHULZ

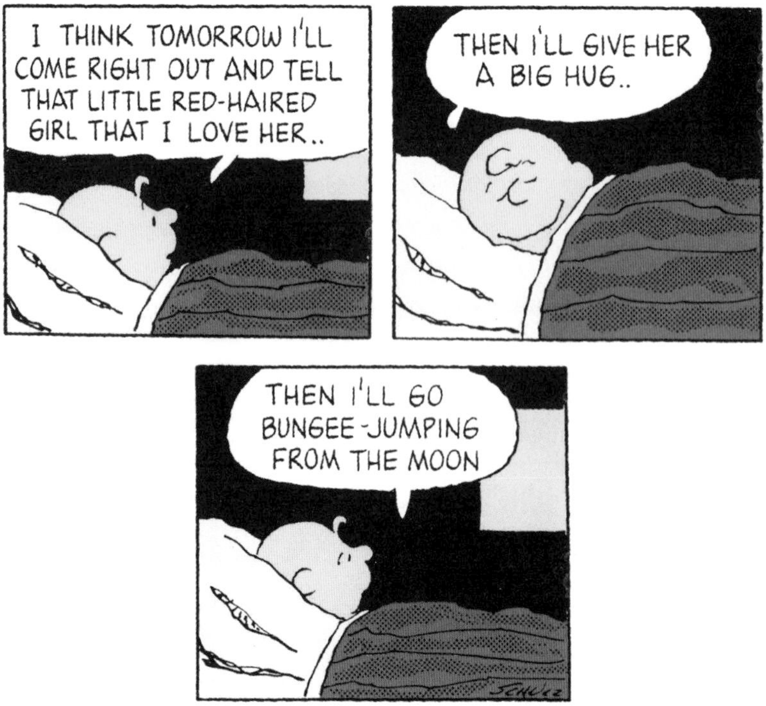
I THINK TOMORROW I'LL COME RIGHT OUT AND TELL THAT LITTLE RED-HAIRED GIRL THAT I LOVE HER..
THEN I'LL GIVE HER A BIG HUG..
THEN I'LL GO BUNGEE-JUMPING FROM THE MOON

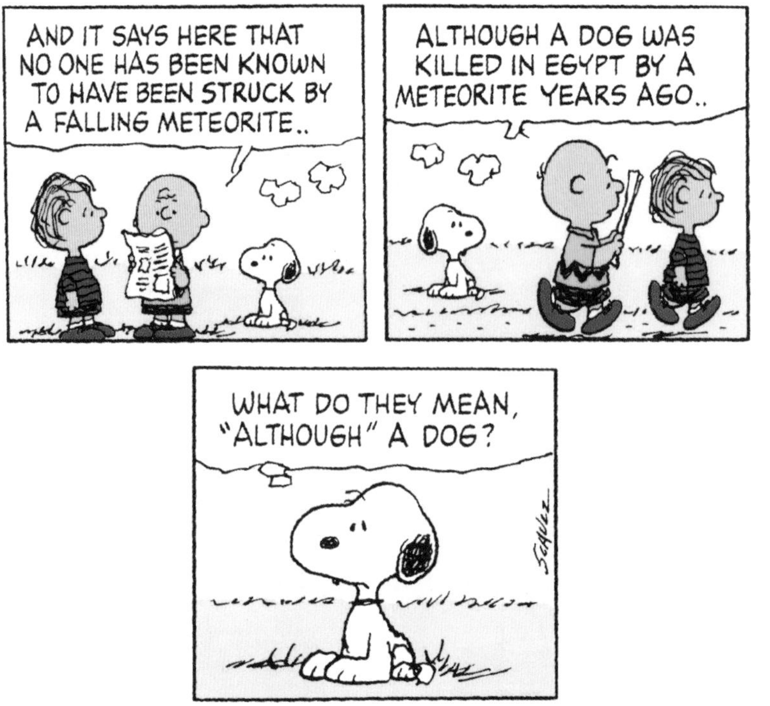
AND IT SAYS HERE THAT NO ONE HAS BEEN KNOWN TO HAVE BEEN STRUCK BY A FALLING METEORITE..
ALTHOUGH A DOG WAS KILLED IN EGYPT BY A METEORITE YEARS AGO..
WHAT DO THEY MEAN, "ALTHOUGH" A DOG?

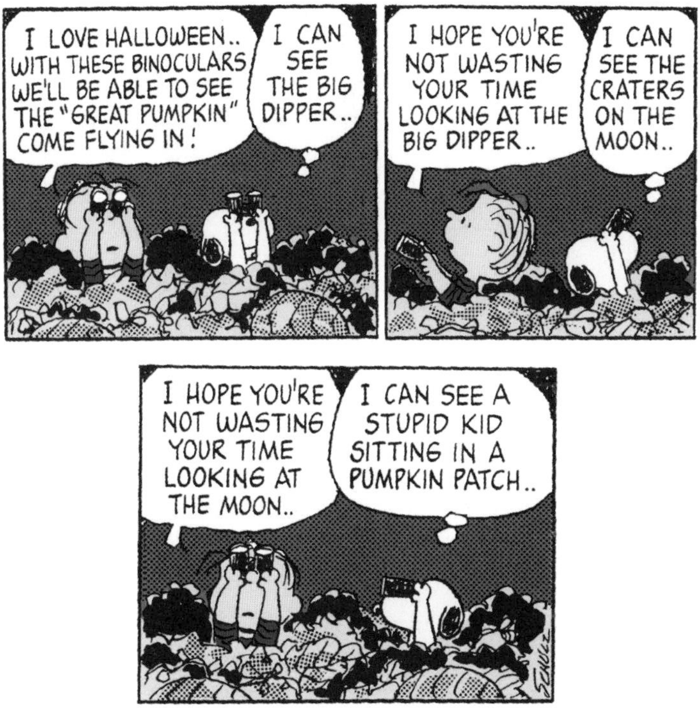
I LOVE HALLOWEEN.. WITH THESE BINOCULARS WE'LL BE ABLE TO SEE THE "GREAT PUMPKIN" COME FLYING IN!
I CAN SEE THE BIG DIPPER..
I HOPE YOU'RE NOT WASTING YOUR TIME LOOKING AT THE BIG DIPPER..
I CAN SEE THE CRATERS ON THE MOON..
I HOPE YOU'RE NOT WASTING YOUR TIME LOOKING AT THE MOON..
I CAN SEE A STUPID KID SITTING IN A PUMPKIN PATCH..

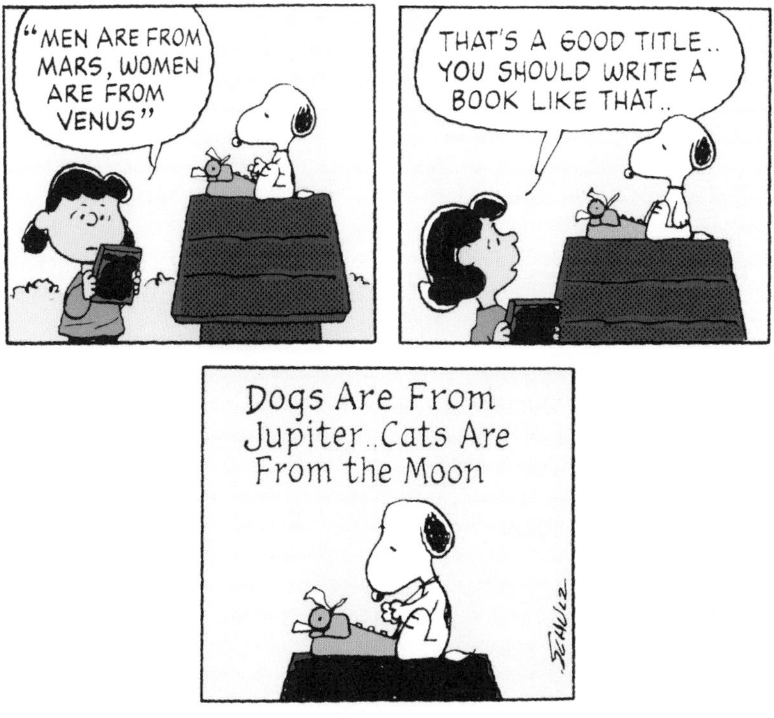
"MEN ARE FROM MARS, WOMEN ARE FROM VENUS"
THAT'S A GOOD TITLE.. YOU SHOULD WRITE A BOOK LIKE THAT..
Dogs Are From Jupiter..Cats Are From the Moon

YOU'RE GOING TO THE MOON?
BUT YOU HAVE TO WEAR ONE OF THOSE THINGS ON YOUR HEAD..
WELL, YES... SORT OF LIKE THAT..
SCHULZ

SO YOU'RE REALLY GOING TO THE MOON..
I'M SURPRISED
I HOPE YOU REALIZE THAT WHEN YOU GET THERE, YOU'RE GOING TO BE ALL ALONE..
SCHULZ

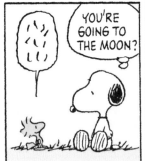

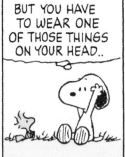

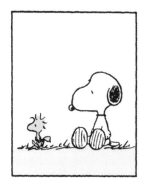

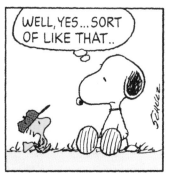

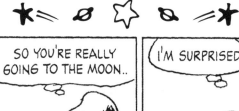

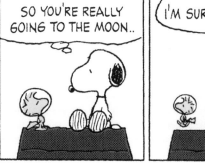

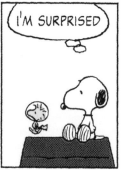

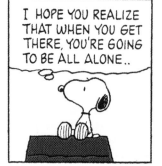

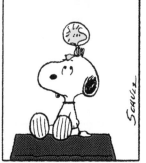

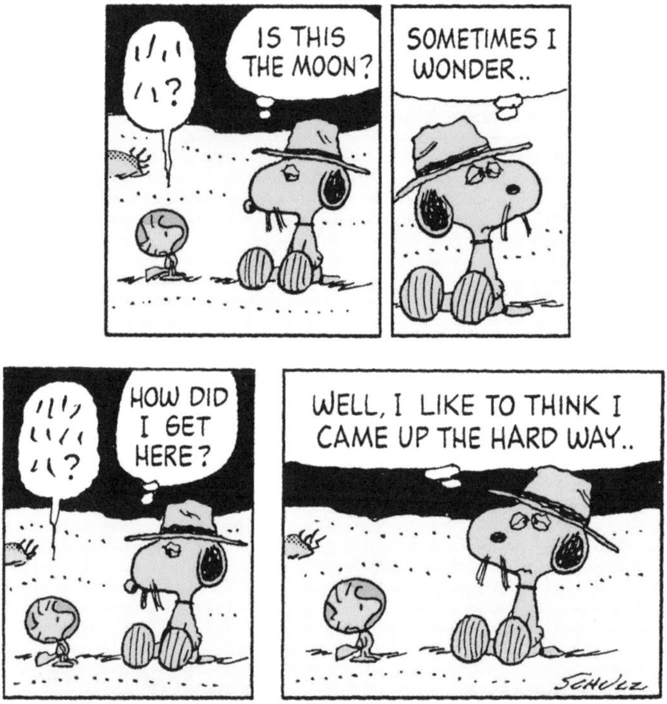
IS THIS THE MOON?
SOMETIMES I WONDER..
HOW DID I GET HERE?
WELL, I LIKE TO THINK I CAME UP THE HARD WAY..
SCHULZ

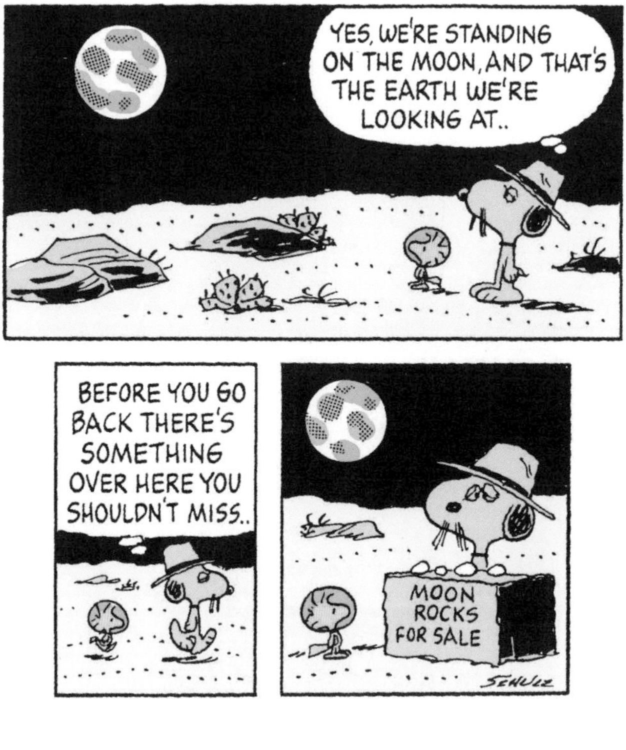
YES, WE'RE STANDING ON THE MOON, AND THAT'S THE EARTH WE'RE LOOKING AT..
BEFORE YOU GO BACK THERE'S SOMETHING OVER HERE YOU SHOULDN'T MISS..
MOON ROCKS FOR SALE
SCHULZ

YOU'RE BACK FROM THE MOON? WOW! WHAT AN ADVENTURE! TELL ME WHAT YOU SAW
A WEIRD CREATURE? LET'S SEE THE PICTURE..
THAT'S MY BROTHER SPIKE! MY FAVORITE BROTHER! GOOD OL' WONDERFUL SPIKE
HE SOLD YOU A MOON ROCK?
SCHULZ

I COULDN'T SLEEP LAST NIGHT.. I KEPT WORRYING ABOUT SCHOOL, AND ABOUT LIFE AND ABOUT EVERYTHING..
I DIDN'T SLEEP WELL, EITHER...

ALL NIGHT LONG I KEPT WORRYING THAT THE MOON WAS GOING TO FALL ON MY HEAD..
SCHULZ

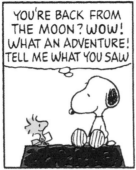

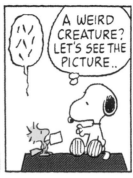

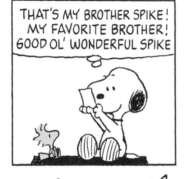

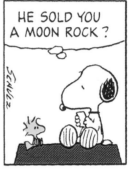

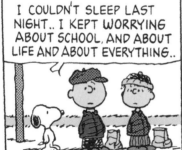

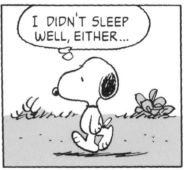

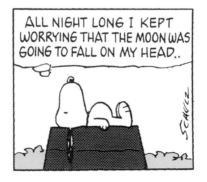

There are no cats on the moon.
EVERYBODY KNOWS THAT..
I THOUGHT IT WAS GOOD NEWS..
SCHULZ

I WONDER IF THERE ARE DOGS ON MARS..
I DOUBT IT..
I DON'T HEAR ANY BARKING..
SCHULZ

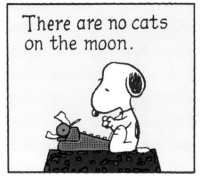

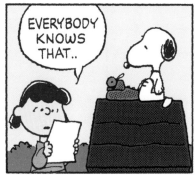

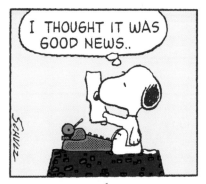

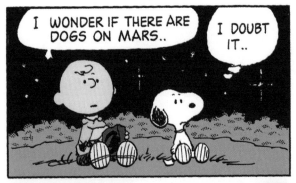

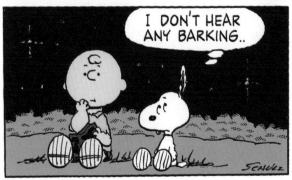

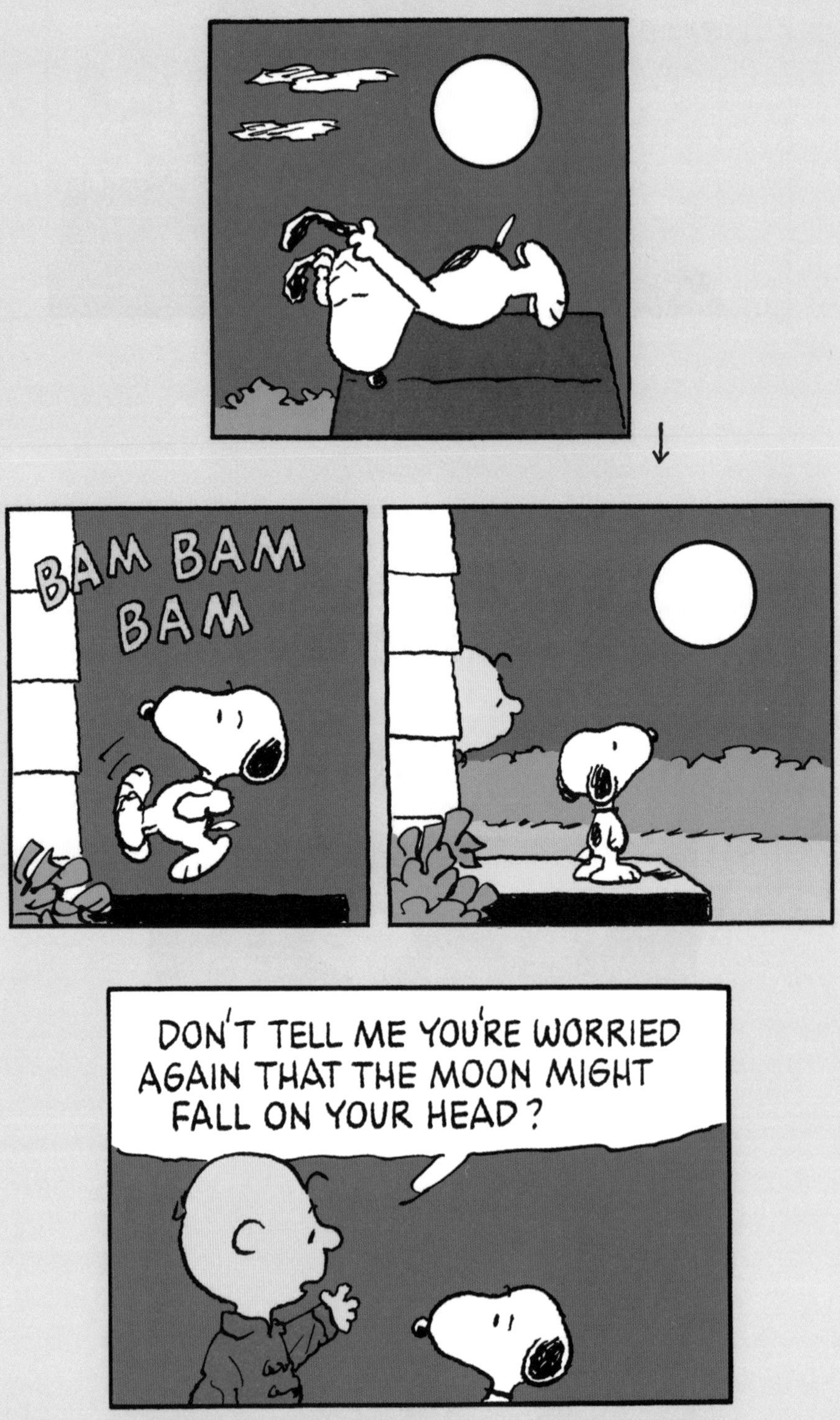
BAM BAM
BAM
DON'T TELL ME YOU'RE WORRIED AGAIN THAT THE MOON MIGHT FALL ON YOUR HEAD?

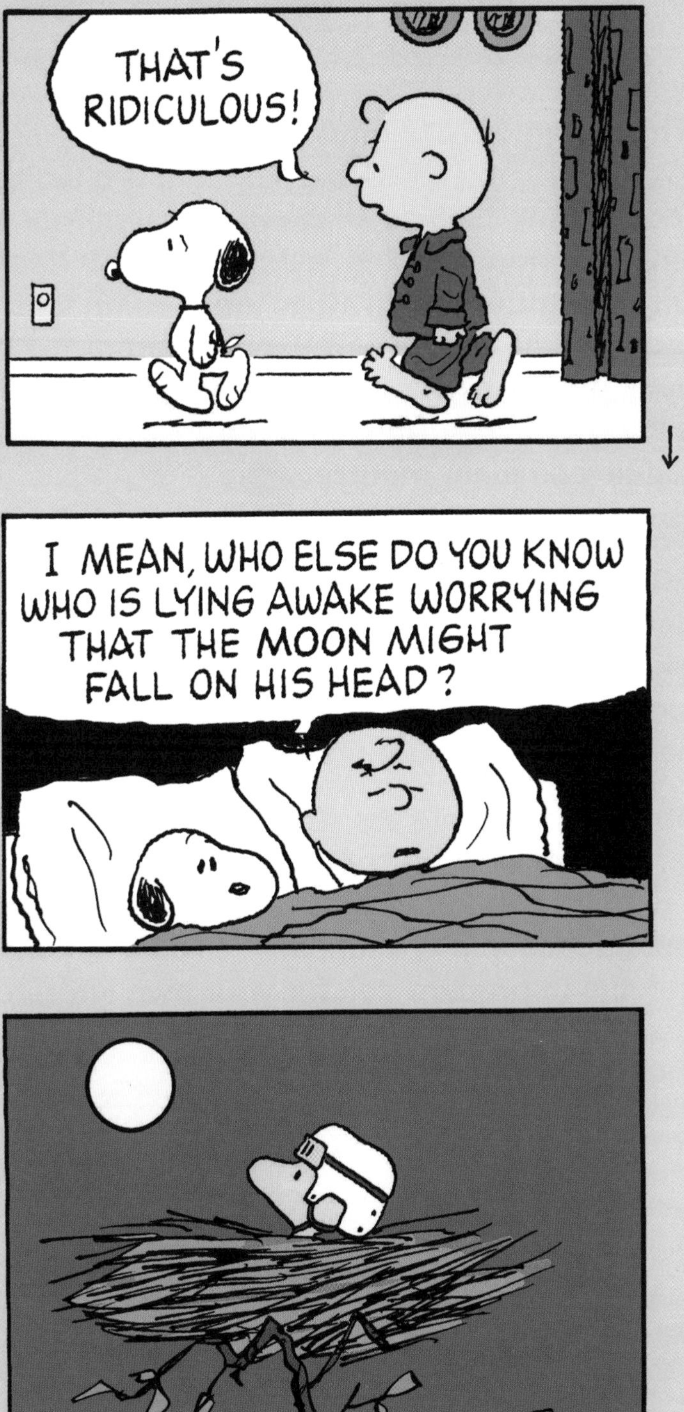
THAT'S RIDICULOUS!
I MEAN, WHO ELSE DO YOU KNOW WHO IS LYING AWAKE WORRYING THAT THE MOON MIGHT FALL ON HIS HEAD?
SCHULZ

MORE TO EXPLORE!

A special section featuring fun facts and activities!

The spring of 2019 marked the 50th anniversary of Apollo 10, the NASA mission that orbited the moon in May 1969 as a "dress rehearsal" for the Apollo 11 moon landing in July 1969. But *Peanuts* fans remember Apollo 10 as the mission that made Charlie Brown and Snoopy part of the U.S. space program, when their names were adopted as the official call signs of the Apollo 10 command module and lunar module.

The astronauts of Apollo 10 also used pictures of Charlie Brown and Snoopy to help explain the mission when they sent videos back to Earth. Original drawings of Snoopy by Charles Schulz were also hidden in the astronauts' onboard checklists by backup crew members.

To commemorate the Apollo 10 voyage and to learn more about outer space, this special More to Explore section will include some fun facts about space exploration, as well as a special exercise to prepare you for your own interstellar mission!

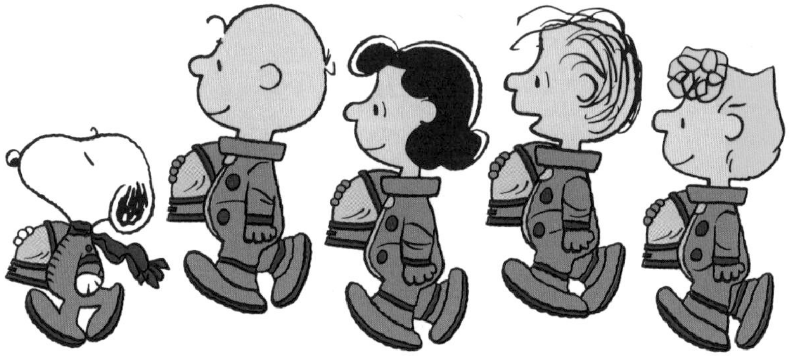

Fun Facts About Space!

Space is the huge area beyond Earth's atmosphere (the air that surrounds the earth). You can't breathe in space because there is no air, so astronauts have to take a supply of oxygen with them. Here are some more fun facts about space!

VENUS IS HOT!
Even though Venus isn't the closest planet to the sun, it has an average surface temperature of around 842 degrees Fahrenheit, making it the hottest planet in our solar system.

NOBODY KNOWS HOW MANY STARS ARE IN SPACE!
There are an estimated 200–400 billion stars in our galaxy (the Milky Way), but scientists don't know how many galaxies are in the universe.

SPACE IS COLD!
The temperature in space is nearly 460 degrees below zero, Fahrenheit.

SPACE SUITS ARE HEAVY—AND EXPENSIVE!
To protect astronauts from the extreme temperatures in space, each space suit includes 14 different layers, and the space suits worn on the Apollo missions weighed about 180 pounds each. Space suits can cost more than 10 million dollars each, with over half of that cost just for the backpack and control module.

THE FOOTPRINTS ON THE MOON WILL BE THERE FOR 100 MILLION YEARS!
Since the moon has no atmosphere, there is no wind to erode the surface and no water to wash them away.

THERE ARE MORE MOONS THAN PLANETS IN OUR SOLAR SYSTEM!
Among the eight planets in our solar system, some have many moons and others have none. Jupiter has 79 known moons, Saturn has 53 moons and several others that have not yet been confirmed, Uranus has 27 moons (some made of ice!), Neptune has 14 moons, Mars has two moons, Earth has one moon, and Venus and Mercury have zero.

THE YEARS VARY ON DIFFERENT PLANETS
Because a year is defined as the amount of time it takes for a planet to orbit once around the sun, the years on each planet are very different lengths of time. For example, a year on Mercury is 88 Earth days, while a year on Neptune is 60,190 Earth days.

Important Moments in Space Travel

OCTOBER 4, 1957—The first satellite, *Sputnik*, was launched into space by the Union of Soviet Socialist Republics (USSR).

NOVEMBER 3, 1957—Laika, a stray dog from the streets of Moscow, was launched into space aboard *Sputnik 2*, becoming the first animal launched into space.

MAY 28, 1959—Two monkeys, Able and Baker, were launched into space aboard a Jupiter missile, becoming the first living creatures to return alive from space.

APRIL 12, 1961—Yuri Gagarin of the USSR became the first person in space, orbiting the Earth in 108 minutes aboard the *Vostok 1* spacecraft. A month later, the U.S. launched Alan Shepard into space.

JULY 20, 1969—Neil Armstrong and Buzz Aldrin became the first people to set foot on the moon, as part of the Apollo 11 mission, which lasted eight days, three hours, and 18 minutes.

MAY 14, 1973—The U.S. launched its first space station, called *Skylab*. The space station was occupied for 24 weeks and eventually reentered the atmosphere and fell back to Earth in 1979.

OCTOBER 11, 1984—Kathryn Sullivan became the first American woman to walk in space.

APRIL 24, 1990—The space shuttle *Discovery* deployed the Hubble Space Telescope.

NOVEMBER 20, 1998—Construction on the International Space Station (ISS) began. The ISS opened in the year 2000 and has since hosted over 230 people from 18 different countries.

APRIL 28, 2001—Dennis Tito, a California billionaire, became the first space tourist, paying 20 million dollars for an eight-day vacation in the International Space Station.

MAY 25, 2008—NASA's *Phoenix* Mars lander arrived on Mars after a 10-month, 422-million-mile journey.

Your Mission to Mars!

Right now, NASA is making plans to send astronauts all the way to Mars! Mars is a cold, desert world and is sometimes called the Red Planet, because the rusty iron in the ground makes it appear red. Mars is smaller than Earth, so gravity there is not as strong. Astronauts on Mars will weigh about one-third of what they weigh here.

Several space missions have visited Mars, and it is the only planet where rovers have been sent. Rovers are unmanned vehicles that take pictures and measurements. Now imagine that you are part of the first manned mission to Mars, and that you have just returned from a successful mission to this alien landscape.

What were you most excited to see on Mars?

_____

_____

What did you most like about traveling through space?

_____

_____

How would you describe the surface of the planet to your friends?

_____

_____

It's not easy to answer questions about a planet you've never been to before, but part of space exploration involves researching, learning about, and planning to explore the unknown.

To learn more about Mars, space, and other NASA missions, check out nasa.gov/kidsclub.

Safe travels!

Classic *Peanuts* Space Comics

From the earliest days of *Peanuts*, space has played an important role in the comic strip. This selection of *Peanuts* comics from the 1950s demonstrates Schulz's interest in space, and reflects an entire nation's curiosity about space exploration, even an entire decade before the Apollo program.

"PEANUTS"
ALL RIGHT, MEN! ON TO MARS!!
THE BOYS CERTAINLY SEEM ENVIOUS OF YOUR NEW SPACE-SUIT, LUCY...
YOU WON'T TELL THEM, WILL YOU?
TELL THEM WHAT?
THESE ARE MY SLEEPERS!
SCHULZ

April 17, 1953

"PEANUTS"
CHARLIE BROWN, WHAT WOULD YOU DO IF THE MOON FELL RIGHT ON YOUR HEAD?
WHAT DO YOU MEAN, WHAT WOULD I DO?
JUST WHAT I SAID.. WHAT WOULD YOU DO?
I HAVEN'T GOT THE SLIGHTEST IDEA
HOW COME YOU NEVER THINK ABOUT THINGS LIKE THAT?
SCHULZ

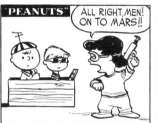

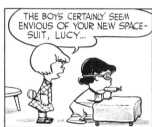

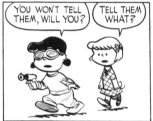

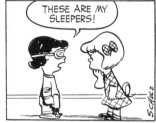

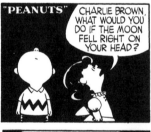

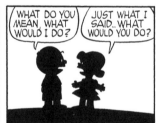

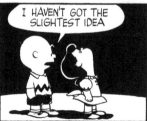

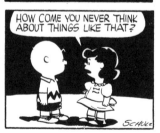

November 3, 1954

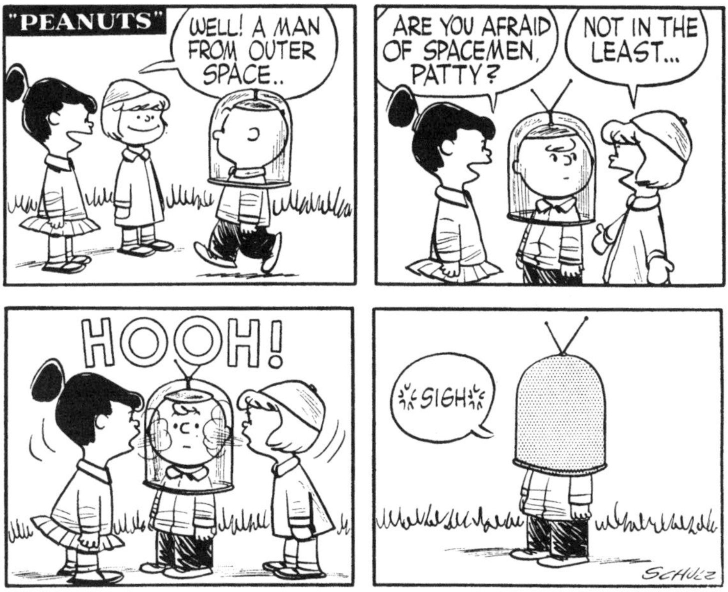
"PEANUTS"
WELL! A MAN FROM OUTER SPACE..
ARE YOU AFRAID OF SPACEMEN, PATTY?
NOT IN THE LEAST...
HOOH!
SIGH
SCHULZ

March 5, 1955

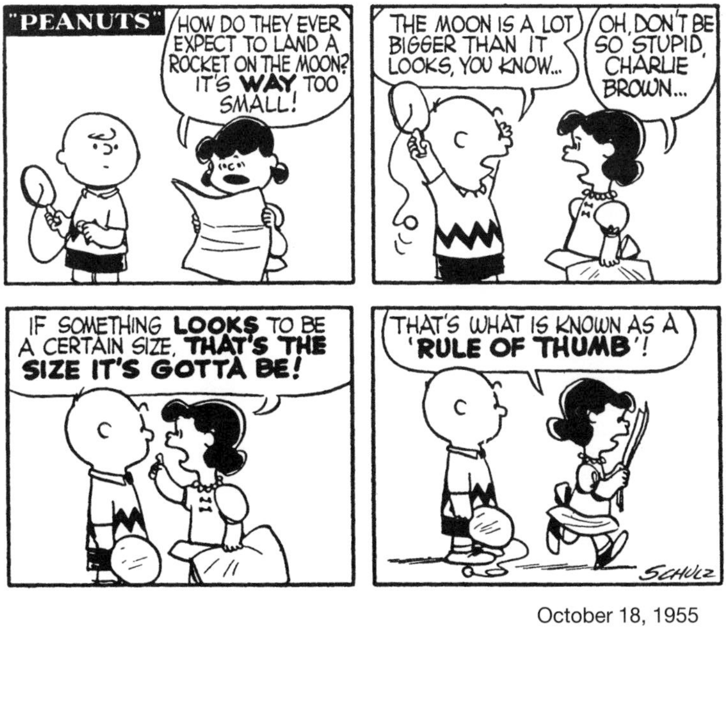
"PEANUTS"
HOW DO THEY EVER EXPECT TO LAND A ROCKET ON THE MOON? IT'S WAY TOO SMALL!
THE MOON IS A LOT BIGGER THAN IT LOOKS, YOU KNOW...
OH, DON'T BE SO STUPID, CHARLIE BROWN...
IF SOMETHING LOOKS TO BE A CERTAIN SIZE, THAT'S THE SIZE IT'S GOTTA BE!
THAT'S WHAT IS KNOWN AS A 'RULE OF THUMB'!
SCHULZ

October 18, 1955

PEANUTS
PEOPLE COME, AND PEOPLE GO, BUT THE EARTH KEEPS ON SPINNING..
"SPINNING"? WHAT DO YOU MEAN, "SPINNING"?
SPINNING THROUGH SPACE..THE EARTH KEEPS ON SPINNING THROUGH SPACE..
HAHAHAHAHA!!!...
?
OH, MY, CHARLIE BROWN! YOU MAY NOT BE THE BRIGHTEST PERSON IN THE WORLD, BUT YOU SURE HAVE SOME IMAGINATION!
good grief!
SCHULZ

May 11, 1957

PEANUTS
YOU HAVE A NICE FACE, CHARLIE BROWN..
WELL, THANK YOU, LUCY..
I ENJOY LOOKING AT YOUR FACE..
WHENEVER I LOOK AT YOUR FACE, ONE QUESTION ALWAYS COMES TO MY MIND...
WILL MAN EVER SUCCEED IN REACHING THE MOON?
SCHULZ

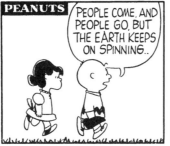

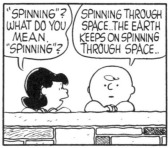

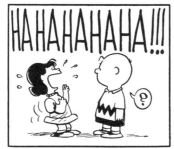

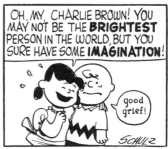

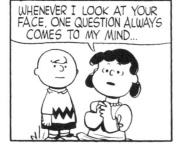

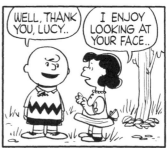

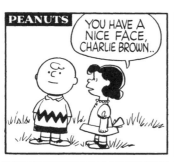

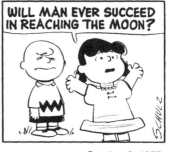

October 2, 1957

Peanuts is distributed internationally by Andrews McMeel Syndication.

Snoopy: First Beagle in Space copyright © 2020 by Peanuts Worldwide, LLC. All rights reserved. Printed in China. No part of this book may be used or reproduced in any manner whatsoever without written permission except in the case of reprints in the context of reviews.

Andrews McMeel Publishing
a division of Andrews McMeel Universal
1130 Walnut Street, Kansas City, Missouri 64106

www.andrewsmcmeel.com

www.peanuts.com

20 21 22 23 24 SDB 10 9 8 7 6 5 4 3 2 1

ISBN: 978-1-5248-5562-8

Library of Congress Control Number: 2019943822

Made by:
King Yip (Dongguan) Printing & Packaging Factory Ltd.
Address and location of manufacturer:
Daning Administrative District, Humen Town
Dongguan Guangdong, China 523930
1st Printing—12/23/19

ATTENTION: SCHOOLS AND BUSINESSES
Andrews McMeel books are available at quantity discounts with bulk purchase for educational, business, or sales promotional use. For information, please e-mail the Andrews McMeel Publishing Special Sales Department:
specialsales@amuniversal.com

Check out more *Peanuts* kids' collections from Andrews McMeel Publishing.

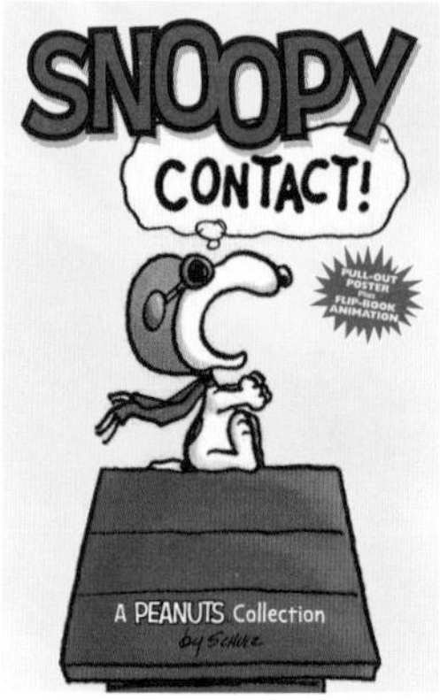
SNOOPY
CONTACT!
PULL-OUT POSTER Plus FLIP-BOOK ANIMATION
A PEANUTS Collection
by Schulz

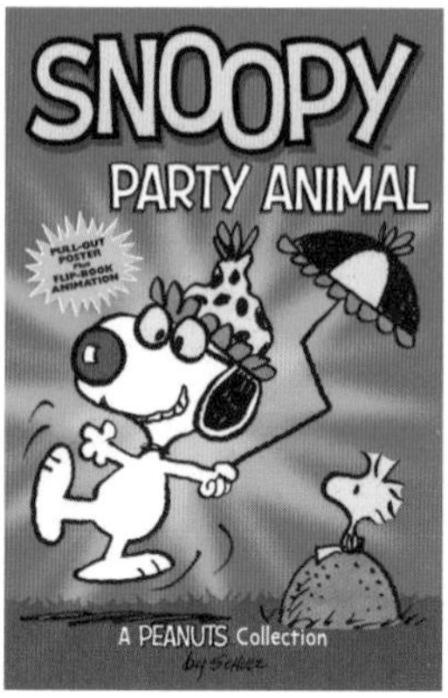
SNOOPY
PARTY ANIMAL
PULL-OUT POSTER Plus FLIP-BOOK ANIMATION
A PEANUTS Collection
by Schulz

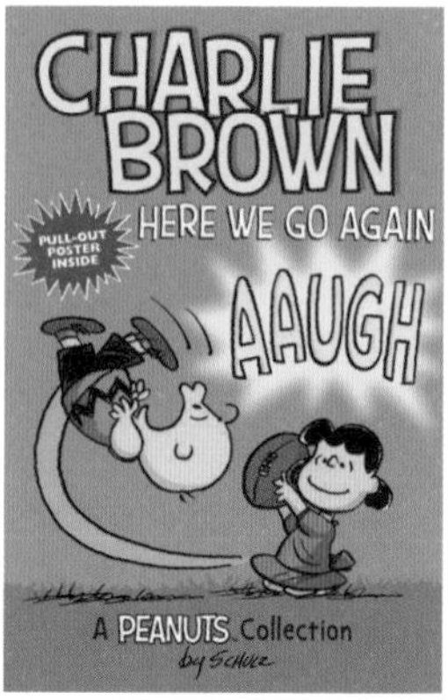
CHARLIE BROWN
HERE WE GO AGAIN
PULL-OUT POSTER INSIDE
AAUGH
A PEANUTS Collection
by Schulz

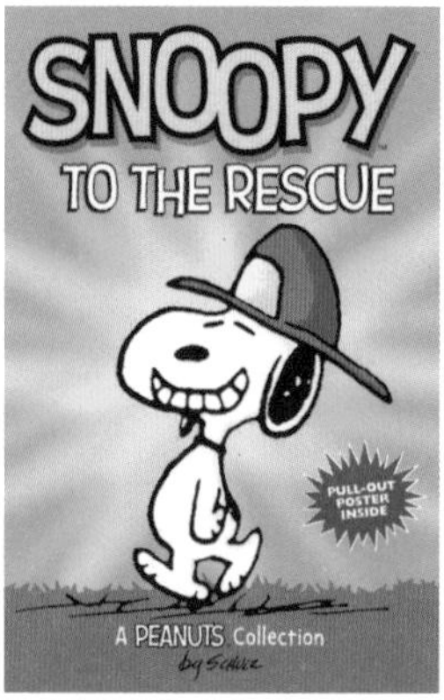
SNOOPY
TO THE RESCUE
PULL-OUT POSTER INSIDE
A PEANUTS Collection
by Schulz

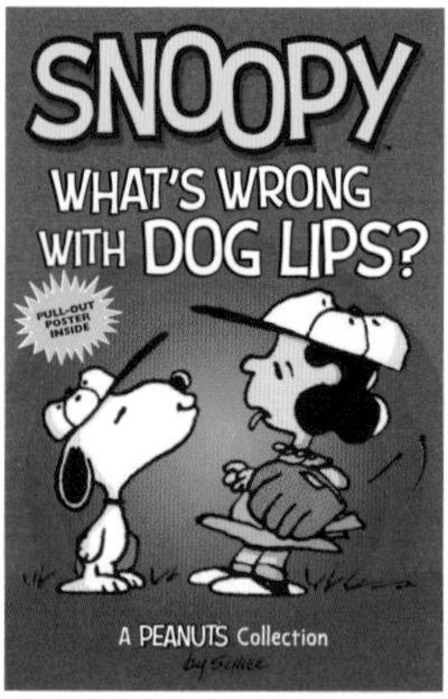
SNOOPY
WHAT'S WRONG WITH DOG LIPS?
PULL-OUT POSTER INSIDE
A PEANUTS Collection
by Schulz

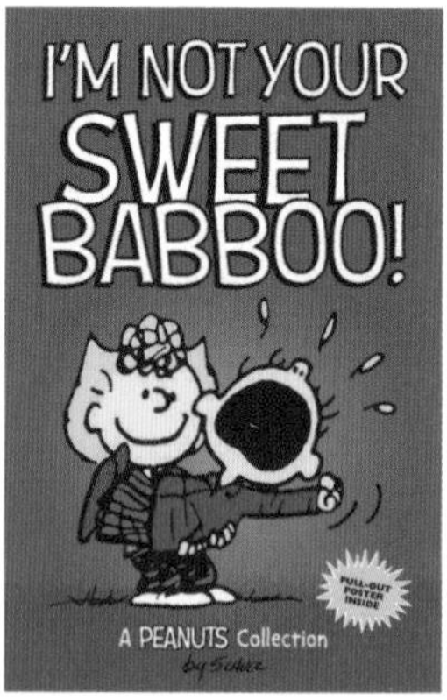
I'M NOT YOUR
SWEET BABBOO!
PULL-OUT POSTER INSIDE
A PEANUTS Collection
by Schulz

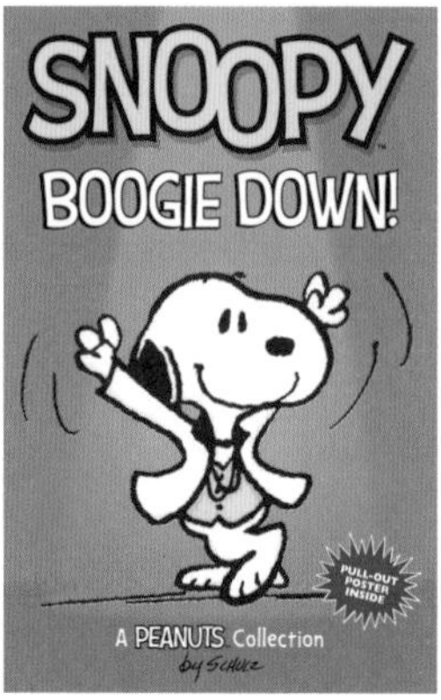
SNOOPY
BOOGIE DOWN!
PULL-OUT POSTER INSIDE
A PEANUTS Collection
by Schulz

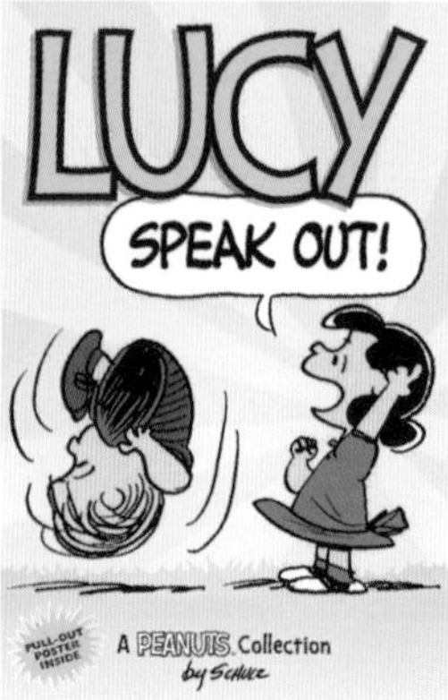
LUCY
SPEAK OUT!
PULL-OUT POSTER INSIDE
A PEANUTS Collection
by Schulz

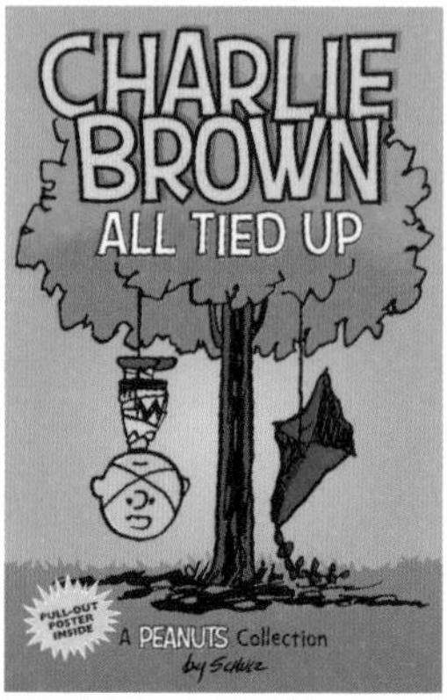
CHARLIE BROWN
ALL TIED UP
PULL-OUT POSTER INSIDE
A PEANUTS Collection
by Schulz